You are about to see a side of Ace Collins you have never seen before. In his first, and certainly not last, novel, old Ace picks you up and throws you right in the middle of an adventure on Farraday Road that you're not about to forget anytime soon. Whether it's history, nonfiction, or fiction, Ace Collins is at the top of his game. Don't miss this one!

—*Don Reid, The Statler Brothers*

More twists and turns than an Arkansas mountain highway. Riveting from start to finish.

—*Sierra Patricia Scott, TV news anchor, host of* It's ALL Good! *on KPTS-TV 8*

Farraday Road invites the reader on a transcendent journey with each character as they unravel this high-stakes murder mystery.

—*Laurie Prange, actress*

Ace Collins weaves a spellbinding work of art in his first novel, *Farraday Road*, a thriller which chills, intrigues, and leaves you craving more.

—*Emily Wierenga, journalist, author of* Save My Children

Ace Collins continues to engage our minds and hearts with mystery and humanity.

—*Dr. Rex M. Horne Jr.*

I was gripped from the first page—an un-put-downable novel.

—*Madeleine Morel, President, 2M Communications*

Farraday Road quickly leads to the point of no return. Ace Collins directs readers down a winding path fraught with intrigue and excitement taken straight from today's headlines.

—*John Hillman, author, AP sports correspondent*

Taut, inspired, and redemptive—Ace Collins' world just won't let you sleep.

—*Evan M. Fogelman,*
Sr. Intellectual Property and Entertainment Law Counsel

Farraday Road describes several fatalities, one of which is the idea that the past was a simpler time. Ace Collins is amazing.

—*David Stricklin, Butler Center for Arkansas Studies,*
Central Arkansas Library System

farraday ROAD

Other Books by Ace Collins

Turn Your Radio On:
The Stories behind Gospel Music's
All-Time Greatest Songs

The Cathedrals:
The Story of America's
Best-Loved Gospel Quartet

Stories Behind the Best-Loved
Songs of Christmas

Stories Behind the Hymns
That Inspire America

Stories Behind the Great
Traditions of Christmas

I Saw Him in Your Eyes:
Everyday People Making
Extraordinary Impact

More Stories Behind the
Best-Loved Songs of Christmas

Stories Behind the
Traditions and Songs of Easter

Stories Behind Women of
Extraordinary Faith

ACE COLLINS

Lije Evans Mysteries

ZONDERVAN.com/
AUTHORTRACKER
follow your favorite authors

We want to hear from you. Please send your comments about this book to us in care of zreview@zondervan.com. Thank you.

Farraday Road
Copyright © 2008 by Andrew Collins

This title is also available as a Zondervan ebook.
Visit www.zondervan.com/ebooks.

Requests for information should be addressed to:
Zondervan, *Grand Rapids, Michigan* 49530

Library of Congress Cataloging-in-Publication Data

Collins, Ace.
    Farraday Road / Ace Collins.
        p. cm.
     ISBN 978-0-310-27952-5
     1. Lawyers — Fiction. I. Title.
   PS3553.O47475F37 2008
   813'.54 — dc22
   2008009585

Interior design by Christine Orejuela-Winkelman

Printed in the United States of America

---

08 09 10 11 12 13 14 • 23 22 21 20 19 18 17 16 15 14 13 12 11 10 9 8 7 6 5 4 3 2 1

To Jane Davis Schaberg,
who was a bright light
in an often-dim world

A COLD JUNE SHOWER PEPPERED THE WINDSHIELD of the cruiser. As Fulton County Sheriff's Deputy Mikki Stuart drove along the narrow blacktop of a rural Arkansas highway, the slackening of the rain allowed her to relax. For hours the water had been beating against her car so hard the wipers couldn't keep up—more than eight inches of heavy rain poured out of the skies onto the hills and into the streams. Finally she didn't have to squint to see. It was the first time since noon she didn't feel as though she was fighting a losing battle against Mother Nature.

It had been a day and an evening filled with drama and tension. During the last ten hours, Stuart had rescued two teenagers swept into Little Creek as they tried to cross a low spot on Highway 289, checked out three cars that had hydroplaned on wet pavement and spun into ditches, manned a flat-bottom boat to ferry four families out of treacherous floodwaters along Spring River, and inspected most every local bridge that was susceptible to being weakened by high water. Conditions were so bad she'd had to close six of the twelve bridges.

Now, at eleven o'clock at night, she was on her way to one last bridge inspection, on Burns Creek just outside of Union. The narrow iron bridge was a relocated Depression-era structure better suited for Model-A Fords than four-wheel-drive trucks. Though it was a relic from another age and presented a certain amount of danger for those crossing in foul weather, Stuart had put off inspecting "Old Iron" simply because the rural road it served led only to Farraday Cemetery. No burials had been scheduled there, so she was certain no one would have used this unpaved county road unless the dead themselves had been washed out of their graves and were looking for higher ground.

The turn to Farraday Cemetery was hard to spot in daytime; at night it was almost impossible to find. As Stuart slowed to search for the weathered sign marking Farraday Road, she thought back to a time when the old bridge was easy to find, an era when it welcomed thousands of cars and trucks traveling Route 9 every day. Back then, in its original location spanning the meandering South Fork in Salem, the bridge had been on the most important highway in the area. As a child Stuart had traveled over Old Iron countless times, and each trip across the bridge seemed like a magical adventure. The bridge had a voice, groaning and creaking under each vehicle's weight. It had a smell too, one of river water, fish, damp grass, and dogwood trees.

And then there was the view. Because there were no real walls along its sides, anyone who cared to look out their car windows could see all the way up and down the river. They could spot Miller's Ford and Engine Bend, where, years ago, an Illinois Central train jumped the tracks and plunged into the clear waters below Nobb hill. Old-timers still spoke of that wreck as if it happened last week, and during low water, part of the rusty old locomotive could still be seen resting on the river's sandy bed.

Now as she made her way back to Old Iron, all of the memories of her youth and this bridge came to life. She remembered how the pavement that covered its roadway often cracked after ice storms. She recalled watching canoes float under it and fish jump out of the water and splash back down. She remembered the feel of the water the time she leaped off the old structure. She was seventeen then, and Elijah Evans, a senior she'd been dating, had dared her to jump. Stuart kicked off her shoes, climbed up on the center railing, and jumped. Lije followed right behind her. That sopho-moric escapade started a tradition. Soon jumping from Old Iron was a rite of passage for Salem High School seniors.

But as traffic increased on Route 9, the one-lane structure be-came a hazard, a bottleneck spawning numerous collisions and countless slowdowns. Truckers and local businessmen complained. Meetings were held. Heated debates followed. Still, everyone knew what the outcome would be: progress would win. Many of Salem's most influential citizens fought to keep the bridge, embracing it as an important historical landmark. Campaigns were launched, petitions were signed, and even the governor came to talk at a rally about saving the old structure. But fifteen years ago, the state overruled the passionate citizens and logic trumped emotion. The bridge was replaced with a state-of-the-art concrete crossing.

Old Iron was removed, but a host of citizens would not allow the vintage bridge to be discarded onto the scrap heap. The memo-ries spawned by the old bridge were simply too precious. So they raised money through raffles, donkey basketball games, and bake sales and saved the landmark, moving it fifteen miles from Salem to Farraday Road, where it replaced a low-water bridge on Burns Creek. Even though there was hardly ever a reason to go down that old road, many old-timers occasionally took Sunday drives over the span to reconnect with their past, and a new generation embraced the rarely used structure as a favorite parking spot on dates. It was a great place to watch the submarine races, they said.

As Stuart headed toward the bridge, she had no concern about the possibility of the structure collapsing. Over the past decades, every engineer who had examined Old Iron had declared that no flood could ever take it down. She knew it to be as solid as St. Peter himself. Old Iron was the unmoving rock on which they all could de-pend. Stuart was confident that long after every other bridge in the area had been torn down and replaced, Old Iron would be welcom-ing new generations of Arkansans. Still, the rain that had scoured the hills on this late June day surely would have transformed placid

Burns Creek into a torrent of muddy water overflowing its banks and covering the bridge's roadbed. If this was the case, Old Iron would have to be closed until the floodwaters receded. Except for those resting in the graveyard, no one would notice the roadblock on this ungodly wet night.

It was just past eleven when the deputy found the faded Farraday Road sign, turned her Crown Victoria squad car off Arkansas Highway 9, and directed it down the narrow muddy road leading to Old Iron. The rain had eased, almost stopped, and she switched the wipers to slow. The night was so dark it was difficult to see anything not illuminated by the car's headlamps or by an occasional burst of lightning. Slipping along at twenty miles an hour, sometimes less, her tires tossing muck up high to both sides, Stuart strained to find the ruts she needed to hold her traction.

About a half mile from the highway, just as she cautiously directed the car around a slight curve, something caught her attention. Stuart took her foot off the gas pedal. She avoided the brakes for fear of sliding and rolled to a stop in the middle of the road. She lowered the front passenger window and stared out into the blackness.

At first she thought her eyes, the night, the long hours she had worked had played a trick on her. She saw nothing but what should have been there—a mass of rain-soaked trees. The hill. She turned on her spotlight and pointed it into that area. Something out of place sprang out of the blackness to meet her. Almost hidden by a large mulberry bush was a late-model Ford Explorer. It appeared as if someone had taken the bend too quickly, lost traction on the slick surface, slid off the road, and gotten stuck axle-deep in the red clay. No different from the accidents she had dealt with earlier in the day. But something didn't feel right. Seeing no signs of life in or around the vehicle, Stuart reached to her right, flipped on her emergency lights, and pulled her radio microphone from its bracket on the dash.

"James, you out there?"

Fulton County was small and the department was more like family than coworkers, so Stuart rarely used formal radio protocol. Sheriff Wood hated her laxness and had warned her repeatedly about following procedure, but Stuart, who usually played by the book, hadn't changed. She employed the "legal" language when speaking to state troopers, but with locals she saw no reason to use anything but her native tongue, accent and all.

Stuart yanked her flashlight out from under the seat and slipped into her raincoat. A familiar voice greeted her through the radio speaker.

"Yeah, Mikki," James Simpson called back, "just pulled in to the courthouse. What do you need?"

"Got an SUV in the ditch not far from Old Iron, on the 9 side. Looks like the Explorer Lije Evans drives."

"Be no reason for him to be out that way. Hasn't been a burial out there in weeks. Must not be his. Car could've been there for some time. Probably a hunter got drunk and lost control. Anyone in it?"

"Not that I can see," Stuart said, "but I'm getting out to check. Stay close. I'll let you know what I find."

"Okay."

Stuart stepped out of the cruiser. As she sloshed through the mud, she became the consummate cop, carefully shining her flashlight all over and around the SUV, checking for signs of danger. She saw nothing even remotely threatening, but she still couldn't shake the feeling that something was off.

She jumped across the water-filled ditch and directed her beam into the Explorer's interior. A woman's purse was on the front seat, a black leather briefcase was on the floor in the back, and a half-empty Coke bottle was in a drink holder. The key was still in the ignition. The car was unlocked. She carefully opened the passenger door; nothing unusual. After closing the door, she moved forward and touched the hood.

It was still warm.

Just another wreck, she tried to convince herself as she continued her inspection. She studied the area around the vehicle and spotted footprints leading up the slope to the right of the Explorer. If this was an accident, why would they try to go *up* the hill? Standing beside the Explorer, Stuart studied the prints more closely. Maybe they needed to get on top of the rise to get cell phone service.

Stuart's years of hunting had taught her a great deal about tracking. There appeared to be at least four sets of footprints on the hill. She tracked them back toward the car. She studied the ground on both sides of the SUV. Only two people had exited the vehicle. After flashing her light around the area, she discovered the other prints originated across the ditch, on the road, about ten feet in front of the Explorer. The stride length indicated all of these folks had been in a hurry. That washed the cell-phone theory. Stuart sensed that whatever she was investigating, it wasn't just a minor accident.

Still standing beside the Explorer, she followed the jumbled footprints with her eyes as she moved her flashlight over the converging sets of tracks. It was obvious the trek up the hill had not been an easy one. There were numerous signs of slipping and falling, and Stuart noted a woman's high-heel shoe stuck in the mud. Why would someone leave a shoe? Twenty yards up the rise, her light touched on something that looked like a piece of clothing, tan. Beyond that, the signs of panicked flight became even more obvious. When this crew blazed the trail up the hill, they left broken branches and ankle-deep holes in the wet soil, as if the ghosts of the cemetery were on their tails.

Twenty feet beyond where she had spotted the clothing, her light illuminated a haunting sight. Resting awkwardly on the muddy slope was a body, half hidden by a sycamore tree.

Stuart had been operating on hunches, and her hunches had been right. This was no simple mishap. She snapped off the flashlight and listened. Every sound seemed to signal a kind of danger that, as a rural deputy sheriff, she had never had to consider. Suddenly she felt vulnerable, and her fear sharpened her senses. She could hear Burns Creek, its channel full, rushing along the base of the valley. She heard the brush of her wipers against the windshield of the cruiser. She noticed a smell that hovered in the air like smoke. Why had she not noted it before? For the first time her nostrils filled with more than just the wet trees and ground; she caught a pungent hint of gunpowder. Startled, she gasped, and then she tasted it, and the taste of gunpowder turned her stomach. She almost retched.

Instinctively, from her years of training, Stuart crouched down by the Explorer and slid the flashlight to her left hand. Then she reached down and undid the snap on her holster. She pulled her pistol from its resting place and took a deep breath. Her heart was racing too fast, beating too hard; her lungs were burning; her eyes were seeing images, ghosts maybe, that were there one moment, gone the next.

She thought of her husband, her children, both teenagers. Scott was a junior and looking forward to basketball season. Jennifer was fourteen and just beginning to flirt with boys. They were great kids, independent, self-sufficient; they could pretty much take care of themselves. But she wanted to experience their proms, homecomings, and graduations. She didn't want to die on this lonely Ozark hill.

But what if that were my kid lying up there? What if that were me?

She knew what she should do, but knowing and doing were much different matters. No one would know if she chose self-preservation over duty. What difference did it make? The person was surely dead. But another force, one she couldn't shove out of her mind, made her look again at the hill, at where the body was, maybe someone she knew.

Dear God, please help me. I can't do this. I need to do this. Please, God, help me.

With her prayer came a memory. Something about "the least of these." A Sunday school teacher had taught her that part of living out faith was to reach out to those in need. In fact, that message was why she had become a cop. Stuart sensed an unseen protection wrap around her and knew it was time to place others first, to put that old Sunday school lesson into practice. Maybe this was why she was here on Farraday Road on this stormy night. Maybe this calamity needed both her training and her faith. Maybe everything she had learned in both had made her ready for this moment. Even though she still wanted to run, she held her ground as her eyes drew a sharp, steady bead on the unmoving form halfway up the hill. Though most of the torso was cloaked in darkness, Stuart could see enough to know that the person lying face down in the mud was a woman.

Stuart straightened from her crouching position and hurried back to her radio. "James ..."

"Yes, Mikki."

"We've got a possible homicide. Get me an EMT team."

"One just left an accident a couple of miles away. They're empty. They're just beyond Union. I'll have them there in a matter of minutes."

"And get out here with backup. Something's very wrong on this hill."

"What do you mean 'backup'?"

"Send everything you've got and get it here as fast as you can. We have a crime scene with one dead."

Not waiting for a reply, Stuart tossed the mike into the seat, jumped across the water-filled ditch, and sloshed up the muddy hill, her steps staying far to the right of the trail of footprints on the hill. She was on a mission. Working her flashlight beam back and forth as she climbed, she hurried past the woman's shoe, past what looked like a coat, and continued to slog up the slope until she arrived at the body. Falling to her knees in the red Arkansas mud, she grabbed the woman's wrist and felt for a pulse. The arm was still warm. There was no pulse. Taking hold of the victim's left arm, Stuart eased the woman over onto her back.

The face was caked in mud and blood from a massive head wound. Much of the forehead had been blasted away. Stuart felt bile in her gut but forced herself to look even more closely at the fatal injury. The woman had been shot from the back as she tried to flee. She probably was dead before she hit the ground.

Reaching under her raincoat, Stuart brought a folded wad of tissues from her pants pocket and wiped away the blood and mud from around the woman's nose and eyes. The face that emerged from this quick cleanup confirmed what she had feared but tried to deny. She knew the woman. The victim was her friend.

A close friend.

"Oh Lord, why Kaitlyn Evans?" she whispered. "Kaitlyn, what happened to you?"

The roar of a truck engine drew Stuart's attention away from her dead friend. She tightened her grip on her revolver, but before she could move, emergency lights flashed through the trees; the EMTs from the fire department had arrived. She pulled back from her high-alert mode and watched the ambulance park behind her car. The vehicle had barely come to a stop when two paramedics jumped from the cab. They spotted Stuart's flashlight beam and rushed up the hill toward her.

"What happened?" EMT Thomas Griffin said as he stooped to examine the body.

"Murder. Kaitlyn Evans."

Griffin just looked at Stuart, as if frozen by some unseen force. In the few seconds of silence, Stuart heard the rain falling on the leaves of the sycamore tree, the rumble of Burns Creek, and the idling ambulance. It had been generations since the local courts had prosecuted a case of manslaughter. In this area, people rarely locked their doors. Violence was limited mostly to the football field. She couldn't fathom what she must now investigate. Kaitlyn had been brutally assaulted. Killed. Why? She was the kindest person Stuart had ever known — that the town had ever known. Stuff like this didn't happen here.

Griffin's stunned partner, twenty-five-year-old Tammy Nagal, still out of breath from her climb, finally found her voice. In a whisper, she said, "Anyone else?"

Stuart reacted as if hit by a bolt of lightning. Why hadn't she thought of that? Yes, where was Lije? Had he been with Kaitlyn? She shined her light up the hill. A quick scan of the landscape showed no signs of a struggle or footprints beyond where Kaitlyn had fallen and died. Still, she knew at least three more people had been right here; she had seen their footprints in the mud. So where were they now?

Stuart quickly replayed everything she had done and observed since arriving at the scene. She had noticed no one along the road or on the slope, yet she had smelled gunpowder on the hill and found both the SUV's hood and Kaitlyn's body warm. This shooting was recent, maybe just minutes old when she arrived. Shining her light to a point below them, she saw two sets of prints that appeared to be leaving the body in the direction of the road.

"There should be another set of tracks," Stuart said.

"What?"

"There are four sets of footprints coming up the hill," she explained, shining the light on the muddy trail leading to Kaitlyn's body. "There's only one body. Look at the tracks going back down the hill. Only two people left this spot. What happened to the other person? There has to be a third person somewhere."

She glanced back toward Nagal. Driven by a hunch, Stuart worked her way back down the hill toward her cruiser. Standing in the middle of the road in the glow of the emergency lights behind her, she bounced her flashlight beam back and forth along the ditch. A dozen feet from where she had first stopped to view the Explorer, Stuart spotted something almost hidden beside an old tree stump.

"Over here!" she cried, hurrying to the spot. She pushed

through the heavy brush and fell on her knees, landing in half a foot of muddy water. She shined her light into the face of a man she'd known since grade school.

"It's Lije Evans!" she yelled to the EMTs as they rushed toward her.

Griffin got there first. He stooped and checked for a pulse. There was none. A few seconds later, Nagal arrived and the EMTs checked for signs of life.

"He's still warm," Nagal said.

"He's not been here long," Griffin said. "Do you think we arrived soon enough to use the AED?"

"Only one way to find out," Nagal said. "Let's get him out of this water and into the wagon."

While Stuart and Nagal wrestled Evans from his muddy resting place, Griffin hurried back to the ambulance to retrieve a body board. He returned and positioned the board next to Lije, then they all rolled him onto the board and carried him to the truck. They slid him and the board onto a gurney. While Nagal worked on Lije's airway, Griffin cut open his shirt and undid the pants.

"He's been shot in the gut," Griffin said.

Nagal applied the pads for the automatic defibrillator to the man's bare chest, then made sure the AED unit was ready. "Clear!" she called and, certain no one was touching the gurney, pressed the button. Lije's body reacted to the sudden jolt of electricity, then sank back to the gurney.

Griffin searched for a pulse. "Nothing."

"We'll do it again," Nagal said.

For a second time, Lije's chest heaved upward as the powerful current raced through his body, then it fell back. Still no pulse.

"It's been too long. It's no use," Griffin said.

Nagal nodded. "You're probably right."

"Maybe the injury was simply too destructive," Griffin said as he examined the wound.

"The wound doesn't look that bad to me," Nagal said. "I think it's timing. We're too late. But the AED won't work if the heart is flat-lined. And it did work, so there's something."

"Do it again," Stuart said. "Now."

"It's no use," Griffin said. "It would take a miracle, and I'm no miracle worker."

"This man's my friend," Stuart said. "You do your job and keep trying. I'll pray for a miracle. I will not let him go without a fight."

Griffin shrugged and moved away from the gurney. Nagal again checked the pads on the bare chest.

"Clear!" she called. This time there was no urgency in her delivery or tone.

Maybe the old wives' tale is true; maybe the third time is the charm. Maybe Griffin and Nagal did work a miracle. Or perhaps Stuart's prayers got through. As the electrical charge lifted Lije Evans' body from the gurney, his mouth opened and he gasped for air. His lungs filled. Suddenly there was a heartbeat. And another, and another. Suddenly there was life.

"He's alive!" Nagal shouted, her voice echoing out of the ambulance and all up and down the hills that lined Farraday Road.

"He's ... alive," Stuart whispered, not taking her eyes from the chest that was now moving up and down. "Thank you, God."

Griffin reached for his kit. "Okay, let's keep him going, Tammy. We're going to have bleeding, we need to deal with that. And we have to get him stabilized. Let's get an IV started." Continuing to spit out orders as he worked, he looked over at the deputy. "Mikki, alert the hospital to have a trauma team set up and waiting for us. We just might be able to save him after all."

Stuart hurried to the cruiser and made the call, wondering as she waited for a response why the backup she had requested hadn't arrived yet.

Soon the EMTs turned their vehicle around and, emergency lights still flashing, drove into the rainy darkness toward Salem.

The deputy stood in the road and shined her light up the hill.

What in the world happened here? Her beam once more fell onto Kaitlyn's lifeless body. Who on God's green earth would want to kill Kaitlyn and Lije Evans? How did Lije end up at the bottom of the hill?

A bolt of lightning hit so close it made Stuart duck. The thunder exploded with such fury it shook the ground. The storm was getting worse. Night was being turned into day by flashes of lightning. While waiting for her backup, Stuart peered down the road in the direction of Burns Creek. She saw deep ruts leading down the hill toward the river. They looked fresh.

She opened the cruiser door to radio in, then, on an impulse, headed toward the bridge, just fifty yards away. She started jogging to Burns Creek, then picked up the pace. The closer she got to the stream, the harder the rain fell, the raindrops flinging mud three or four inches into the air. In all of her thirty-six years, Stuart had never experienced such a downpour. It was as if all the energy in the universe had been unleashed at once right over Burns Creek. She ducked her head and kept running. Something drove her to see Old Iron.

Darkness closed in around her. That odd sense she had had before returned. She slowed to a jog. The rain had found its way under her slicker and soaked her uniform. Finally, breathing hard, the roar of rushing water constant, Stuart stopped and aimed her beam toward the crossing at Burns Creek. Her jaw grew slack and her legs turned to jelly. She couldn't see Old Iron's girders. She couldn't see Old Iron. Chilled to the bone, Stuart stepped cautiously toward the creek. Less than twenty feet from the stream, she once more shined her light where the road ended, where the bridge should have been. The old bridge from which she and Lije Evans had once jumped was not there. Not yet fully believing what her eyes saw, Stuart moved closer to the roaring stream. It was only when the rising waters were licking her shoes and a white bolt of lightning illuminated the night that she accepted the reality that lay in front of her. The waters had torn Old Iron from its anchors. Old Iron was gone.

Cold rain pummeled the Fulton County deputy standing alone in the middle of Farraday Road. Mikki Stuart looked at the void where Old Iron had once rested securely. She felt a sense of great loss, as though nothing in her world would ever be the same again.

THE SUN HAD BEEN UP FOR THREE HOURS BY THE TIME Barton Hillman, head of the Arkansas Bureau of Investigation, arrived at the crime scene on Farraday Road. The forty-five-year-old took a last gulp of lukewarm coffee before slowly exiting his state-issued white Crown Victoria. Standing beside the car, he surveyed what lay in front of him.

The woods were alive with both local and state officers. It was hard to see the trees for the uniforms. No matter what direction he turned, Hillman saw cops. And worse, just a few feet behind the taped-off scene were a crowd of locals speculating on what had caused the nightmare on the hill. Half the county must have made the trip. What a freak show!

"Too many people," Hillman muttered as Fulton County Sheriff Calvin Wood strolled over to greet him.

"What did you say?" Wood asked, sticking out his right hand and adding, "Calvin Wood, Fulton County Sheriff."

After the handshake, Hillman sized up the man standing before him. Wood probably had not seen the inside of a gym since high school some four decades before. Though the sheriff was doing his best to look serious, it was obvious he was enjoying his brush with tragedy. Before Hillman could answer his question, Wood smiled and waved at a television crew that had come in from Springfield,

Missouri. "I've already filled them in three times," the sheriff said. "I'm doing their noon show live."

Shaking his head, Hillman leaned down, placed his face directly in front of the sheriff's, and said, "Too many people. The scene's been so compromised I don't know how my team's going to figure anything out."

Wood glanced over his shoulder. "We had a lot of rain, a man in need of urgent medical care, and a missing officer. My people didn't have time to gingerly tiptoe around in the dark. There were lives at stake. Besides, our top concern was and remains Deputy Stuart. So you can understand our rush."

Hillman didn't raise his voice but spoke a bit slower when he said, "Yeah, I know about all that, and I truly sympathize, but now I want your folks out of here. This is my crime scene, and if we have any hope of tracking down your deputy and finding out who did this, I need to have this location completely secure. I assume you have filled my lead investigator in on all that you know?"

Wood's tone showed his disgust. "She's been told, but there's not much we could give—"

"Figured as much," Hillman muttered. "Now round up your guys and let them get some breakfast or something. Take the civilians and the news crews with you. We'll take over. Remember, Wood, my people will run the investigation from here on out. Don't butt in and don't tell the press anything without my approval. If you do, I guarantee I'll have the governor's office investigating your books before you can get back to your desk. Do I make myself clear?"

Wood nodded, started to reply, then whirled away before he said something he might regret.

"Curtis!" Hillman barked, turning toward his lead investigator up on the hill.

Looking up from the place where the body of Kaitlyn Evans had been discovered, ABI Special Agent Diana Curtis placed an evidence marker and then picked her way through the brush and down the hill toward Hillman's car.

Diana Curtis was twenty-eight, single, and driven, with a degree in forensics from the University of Arkansas and a master's in anthropology from the University of Tennessee. Sensing that her abilities might lighten his own workload, Hillman had secured her for his team three years ago. She had quickly become the engine that kept the team humming. He now had such complete faith in her judgment and powers of observation that he had let her lead two major cases in the past three months. If the victims of this new case had not included one of the governor's closest friends, she probably would have been the supervising investigator on this outing as well. But there had been no choice; the governor had demanded Hillman make the three-hour drive up from the state capital and ramrod the whole affair.

"Should have been a local job," he muttered.

Hillman removed his hat and stroked back his thinning brown hair. He lazily inventoried the scene as he waited for Curtis to reach him. Lots of ruts, scores of footprints, and rain-soaked, washed-out gullies. He also noted broken branches, a discarded coat.

"Yeah, it's a mess," Curtis said. She leaned against the hood of Hillman's car. "We've got one dead. I don't think there's any doubt she was running from her assailants when she was shot. The male victim appeared to be dead when the deputy happened upon the scene, but the EMTs got his heart pumping again. Last I heard he was in surgery in Salem, but that was a few hours ago. Gunshot wound to the abdomen. They think he'll make it, but it'll be a while before we can question him. The strange thing is the missing deputy, who just happened on the scene, probably soon after the shooting."

Hillman continued to scan the scene. "They phoned me on that. She just disappeared?"

"Her car's right over there." Curtis pointed to the Fulton County squad car parked in the center of the muddy road. "When the backup team arrived, the emergency lights were on, the door was open, but Deputy Mikki Stuart was gone. From the time the ambulance left until the backup car arrived was less than five minutes. The two vehicles met each other not two miles up the main road. Yet in that short time, Stuart vanished. More than a dozen men did an extensive search for most of the night. Sheriff Wood even brought in a tracking dog. Nothing. We've turned things upside down since we arrived, and nothing. It's like she evaporated."

Hillman didn't reply. His eyes remained focused on the efforts of his crew to uncover evidence in an area that had been trampled by a stampede of local do-gooders. The team members were working hard — after all, a woman had died — but he sensed they were finding little.

"I can see the bad news," he said, finally turning toward Curtis. "Between the weather and the locals, the scene is completely compromised. Now tell me that you've found something important in this mess."

"Nothing — no bullets, no impressions we can use, not much at all. Mrs. Evans' wound was a pass-through. No lead in her body. I called the hospital and the same is true with her husband. The bullets have to be here, but we've not found them. And with the heavy rain last night, the way the gullywashers were taking everything down the hillside and into ditches already overflowing with water, I can't guarantee we're going to find anything. More likely, the bullets are embedded in the hillside and we'll never find them. I know that's not what you wanted to hear. We do have some stuff on the site, and in time it might help us pin down a motive, but I don't see anything on this hillside that will identify a killer."

Hillman nodded. "Figured as much." He started to walk slowly down the muddy road, moving his head deliberately from side to side, taking in each carefully placed evidence marker as well as anything that seemed out of place. He made mental notes of everything he observed, stopping only when he came to the spot where Old Iron had once stood. Curtis followed along behind him.

"It was quite a storm," Hillman said.

"Had to be to take down that old bridge. I remember it well from when it was on Arkansas 9. Crossed it many times. Even drove over it once after they moved it here. I was attending the burial of a friend of my father's at the cemetery on the other side of this creek. I'd have bet no flood could take it down. Still can't believe it happened."

Hillman noted a few large logs poking out of the receding waters about thirty yards downstream. "Hard to fathom the force that can be mustered by nature." He paused. "Why do you suppose the Evanses were on this road?"

Curtis gave a thin smile. "That's one thing I can answer. Sort of. Last night they went to a charity dinner in Melbourne. At the dinner they were given an award for their work with local food-pantry programs. The event broke up about 8:30. They left and, a few miles down the road, stopped at a place called Jim's Diner. It's a locally owned joint known for its homemade desserts. It was pouring when they finished their apple pie, so, according to the manager, the couple killed some time just talking and looking out the window at the storm. When the rain let up, they rushed out to their car. Their waitress told the sheriff it was about 10:15 when they finally left. Under normal conditions, it would be about a fifteen- or twenty-minute drive to this point, but the rain probably made the trip a lot longer."

"How does that explain why they turned off the main road?" Hillman asked.

"It doesn't. When they left Jim's Diner, things shifted from a simple evening out to something menacing. Their Explorer was bumped maybe three times on the main road. Obvious white paint scrapes are on the driver's side of the SUV. We found an Explorer bumper guard and taillight pieces about a quarter of a mile from the Farraday Road turn. By the time they got to Farraday Road, they apparently didn't have a choice on where they were going.

I believe the Evanses were forced onto this road, then were pushed into the ditch where the car sits now."

Hillman continued to stare at the spot where the bridge had stood. The rapidly flowing water swirled around trash pushed down from miles upstream. Even to his trained mind, the information discovered so far amounted to very little. "Get the paint and other evidence to the lab. Get me a car make and model and put out an APB. Let's hope we find a bullet on that hillside."

With no warning, Hillman turned, setting a fast pace back up the road. Curtis stood watching her boss's retreating back, then jogged along behind, catching up with him just as he reached the victims' SUV.

Crouching down, his knees just inches above the ground, Hillman studied the vehicle. "Curtis, you said the shots on the Evanses were pass-throughs, but what about the Explorer? Were there shots fired at the SUV to force it off the main road?"

"Nothing jumps out on a quick visual. We'll have the SUV in the lab for a full workup."

Hillman shook his head and stood up. "Good. Might be they can find something that will clear up this mess. Lord, I hate cases like this. They always create a lot of press and no one believes us when we find a simple solution."

"Boss, do you think this was a hit?"

"Can't imagine why someone would put a hit out on a small-town lawyer. Makes no sense. Maybe it was mistaken identity, or possibly it was just a robbery. Still ..."

"Barton, there's one strange thing I can't explain."

"What's that?"

"Lije Evans' trench coat was ripped from his body after he was shot, causing him to roll down the hill into the ditch. The coat's side pockets were searched so forcefully that the material was torn. Then the coat was tossed. Just left at the crime scene, about twenty feet from the wife's body."

"Nothing in the pockets or on the ground around the coat?"

"No."

"Well, probably nothing more than someone looking for some cash."

Hillman figured he'd heard enough. Probably nothing more than a stoked-up, drug-induced robbery gone bad. Should be handled locally. This was no place for his team. The governor was going to owe him big time for this. "Curtis, do what you can here, get that SUV to the lab crew, and get going on that paint."

"What about looking for bullets on the hillside? That's going to take some time."

Hillman looked toward the point where the woman's body had been found. "Keep looking for a few more hours, but don't sweat it if you fail to find anything. Probably embedded in the hill or washed away by now, and I'm not going to give weeks to a crime that shouldn't have been dealt to us. I'll go to the hospital to check on Evans. Maybe he'll be awake and can clear this thing up."

With little more than a nod goodbye, Hillman eased his car away from the scene and headed toward Salem. Glancing at his watch, he silently cursed the governor as he pulled onto Arkansas 9. His only witness might be in terrible condition to be questioned, but it was the only lead he had.

3

THE LAST THING ELIJAH EVANS REMEMBERED WAS apple pie. Good apple pie—strong, sweet, cinnamony Jim's Diner apple pie. He had awakened in a hospital bed with unimaginable pain and the Reverend Nathan Adams standing nervously next to his bed, looking down at him. His physician, Dr. Herring, had been there too. It was their job to inform him that last night he had been forced off the road in the rainstorm, that he had been shot in the stomach by an unknown assailant and spent hours in surgery, and that Kaitlyn, his wife, had been shot and died instantly.

He remembered none of it. Now alone, drifting in and out of sleep, he tried to remember something—anything. He was staring off into space when a tall man wearing a suit entered the room flashing plastic-encased credentials.

"Mr. Evans. My name's Hillman, ABI. I can't begin to tell you how much I hate to have to talk with you this soon. I'm so sorry for your loss. I stopped by now to see if possibly you could shed some light on just what went down out there on the cemetery road. If time were not so important, I would put this off. I realize you're not fully awake yet. Just talked with your doctor. But I can't wait. So I'm going to ask you some questions. I hope you can forgive my intrusion."

Lije said nothing, only nodded. He had always prided himself on being strong. But he couldn't muster any strength, even to argue with the timing of this man's questions. He felt as if he were in a fight and each second another sweeping left hook dug deep into his gut, making it impossible to breathe. This must be what hell is like. Fighting for your life, taking blow after blow, waiting for the merciful knockout that never comes. "I don't know how much help I'm going to be."

"I'm sure you can give me something. Once again, let me say I am sorry for your unfathomable loss."

Lije was confused. Hillman spoke the proper warm words, but his tone was cold, hurried.

"What do you remember about the events of last night?"

"Kaitlyn ..." Lije paused. Kaitlyn. The name felt strange on his lips. He would never say her name the same way again. He would never be able to say it with the knowledge that she would be waiting for him when he got home. Kaitlyn, his wife, his *late* wife. He felt utter panic. Dead. This was impossible. This had to be a bad dream, a nightmare. She didn't have an enemy in the world. Everyone loved her.

Kaitlyn was unlike anyone he had ever met. She was beautiful in an exotic way, breathtaking; she had black hair and almond-shaped green eyes. Her father had escaped Vietnam and married a woman he met here in the States. So when people first saw Kaitlyn, they really couldn't put a finger on her family origins.

Lije met her at Ouachita Baptist University, family tradition to go there. She had a full ride in vocal performance. He'd never been around any theater types, so she both stunned and fascinated him. She was spontaneous, outgoing, and driven. She was a cheerleader too, and she never quit rooting for others. It was just a part of her nature.

Kaitlyn had taught third grade while he was in law school. Then when they moved back to Arkansas, she acted in community theater. But she often said she found a higher calling by working with charities. Lije wasn't sure he knew what a "higher calling" meant, but she believed in it. She spent more hours each week with after-school programs for children, Meals on Wheels, and such than he did working for the firm. She was a giver who believed in sharing. And because of how much he loved her, he didn't mind the time or the money she spent on others.

Everyone saw her as the perfect Christian woman. She lived to reach out to what the Bible called "the least of these." Lije went to church with her and supported what she wanted to do, but in truth her work mattered to him only because it made her happy. The world would be much better off if she were in this hospital bed and he were the one lying in the morgue.

His voice caught in his throat, but he managed to say, "We went to the awards dinner in Melbourne and stopped at Jim's Diner for pie on our way back. Whenever we were in the area, we stopped there. It was raining real hard. We watched it rain for a while from the diner window and, when it let up, we got back on the road."

The door to Lije's room opened and Dr. Herring quietly entered.

Hillman glanced at the doctor and continued to question Lije. "Know what time that was?"

"It was late. About ten, maybe ten-fifteen."

"Notice anything unusual driving back?"

Lije took a deep breath. "After that? I ... I remember a car or maybe an SUV coming up behind us. I remember it still had its bright lights on. I think I heard a tire blow out, but ..."

Lije shook his head. There was nothing but darkness after that memory. Nothing at all. "I don't know. I think I reached up to adjust my mirror, but I can't remember anything more than that. I simply can't."

"So you don't recall being forced off the highway?"

"No."

"And you have no idea how you ended up on Farraday Road?"

"No. Not a clue." Farraday Road, was that where it happened? Where Kaitlyn had been ...? He knew that old stretch of dirt like the back of his hand. Why couldn't he remember being there?

"Then, Mr. Evans, you have no idea who shot you?"

The word "shot" almost made him gasp. A bullet had ripped through him, and another bullet took the life of his Kaitlyn. Why didn't he do anything? Why didn't he protect her? Not knowing the answers was killing him in a different way.

"Once again, the answer is no, I don't remember. I ... wish I did. I really wish I could remember."

Yes, he wanted to remember; why couldn't he? But he also feared remembering. Had he been a coward? Could he have helped Kaitlyn? Shielded her? Or did he run? Surely he would have stayed there and fought to save her. Did he? Why couldn't he remember? Was it because he didn't want to see the kind of man he was when she really needed him? Maybe he didn't really want to remember. Maybe that was it. And why hadn't he cried? What did that say about him? The coldness he felt now seemed worth hanging onto. Easier to insulate himself. Easier to deny the facts than to admit how much he'd lost.

Dr. Herring said, "You probably will remember in time, Lije. Don't beat yourself up because you can't recall things now. Sometimes shock temporarily clouds our minds in order to protect us from things we can't yet emotionally handle."

Hillman said, "I've known many people who could not mentally latch on to events at first. Most recalled many details later." The investigator checked his watch and frowned. Then, his words coming faster, he said, "Maybe going at this from a different direction will help. Do you know of any reason anyone would want to murder you or your wife? Maybe an upset client?"

It was a good question, but one with no answers. His law practice wasn't much of a practice. He employed one other lawyer, Heather Jameson, a young woman who graduated from law school about five years ago. They did some deed work, wills, business issues, and other standard legal stuff, but they had never done any criminal work or even been part of a case involving a divorce or family dispute. He wasn't involved in politics or anything else that might place him in a position to make anyone angry enough to kill. He had been living on his inheritance and making enough through the firm to pay the bills and for them to travel when and where they wanted to.

But they would never travel together again. He couldn't believe it; it was impossible. But he knew it was true.

"Mr. Evans," Hillman's words broke into the dark reality in his mind, "did anyone have any reason to harm you or your wife?"

He shook his head, his eyes dry even as his heart drowned in tears.

"Were you carrying a large amount of money or valuables or legal documents with you last evening?"

"No, just some cash and my credit cards."

"Do you have any children?"

"None. We wanted kids, but it never happened. We were in the process of adopting, but—"

"And you were going the conventional route for adoption?" Hillman asked.

It took a moment for Lije to realize that Hillman thought they might have been skirting the law, trying to buy a baby on the black market, and that could have been the motive.

"If you're asking if we were doing anything illegal, the answer is no." His words were now flying from his lips. "We were going through the same agencies everyone else goes through. We also were looking overseas. We were not looking at a private adoption. Everything was out in the open. Everything we did was done in a fully accepted fashion." Finally Lije had found some strength, even if it was strength to lash out in anger toward this unfeeling lawman. He wondered what Hillman would dare to imply next. He didn't have long to wait.

Hillman paced back and forth next to the bed, his chin cupped in one hand. He stopped and looked directly at Lije. "If you and your wife had both died, who would have inherited your estate?"

Lije felt like he was now on trial. He was the one who was being grilled. He was the one who must have done something wrong, something to bring on this whole tragedy. He took a deep breath. This time he knew the answer.

"Our estate would have been left to several charities we support. There are no specific individuals named in the will. No individual stands to gain anything from our deaths."

"None on either side of the family?"

His answers seemed clear enough. Yet each follow-up question seemed like a statement of Hillman's disbelief that any part of his story was true—his loss of memory, his and Kaitlyn's record as upstanding citizens, the work he did as a lawyer. "Kaitlyn's parents died a few years ago in a car wreck. My parents have also passed away. We were both only children."

"So you're saying, in your mind, that no one had a motive to attack you?"

"That's right."

"But," Hillman said, "someone did."

"Paging Dr. Herring. Paging Dr. Herring. Room 117. Stat."

The physician, without a word, rushed from the room. Lije watched him depart, hoping—no, praying—that Hillman would follow. When he didn't budge, Lije broke the silence.

"Without my memory, will you be able to find out who did this, or does this whole thing depend on my mind coming back to life?"

"We have some clues," Hillman replied, his tone gruff. "But I'd be lying if I said this case will be an easy one. So the instant your memory of the events comes back, even if it's sketchy, I need you to call me. I'll leave my card on the bedside stand. I'll also check back in a day or two, let you know what we've found. This is probably a case of mistaken identity. You may have just been in the wrong place at the wrong time. There are a lot of green Explorers out there, and the killers could have gotten the wrong one."

Lije let that thought sink in, that his dear Kaitlyn was now dead because ... because someone got the wrong car!

"Mr. Evans, thank you for your time." And with that, Hillman walked out of the room.

Lije watched him leave. The whole scene had been surreal. Kaitlyn was the best thing not just in his life but in the whole town. She couldn't be dead. And if she was, God must be playing some kind of cruel joke on everyone who loved her.

Lije's pastor poked his head in. "Okay to come in?"

"Sure," Lije said. "Glad you're here."

Lije felt an emptiness. At least the questioning had given him something to prod his memory, something that might lead to justice for Kaitlyn.

"He thinks it might be a case of mistaken identity. I don't think he really cares if the case is solved or not," Lije said.

Pastor Adams, always the diplomat, tried to strike a positive chord. "No, it's his job to find out who did this. I'm sure he cares, but he's just kind of grim. That's probably his nature. He's probably seen too many cases and has to keep his emotions out of his work. I'm sure he wants to see justice done."

For Lije, there would be no justice. Even if they caught the killers, no sentence would make up for what he had lost. He knew that; he learned that from Kaitlyn. So he'd get no real satisfaction from the kind of justice the law dispensed. But he had to find the killers. He had to know why someone would deliberately kill a person as pure and innocent as Kaitlyn. He had to know what it was that he had done to set off this whole senseless tragedy. He had to know that her killers got their just punishment even though none of that would ever bring Kaitlyn to life again.

The loss he felt was so deep and so stark, there was no grief, no anger — just emptiness. Instead of hoping to regain his memory, he pondered the idea of how much better off he'd be if every memory of Kaitlyn were wiped from his head.

Lije decided, finally, that he would pursue his own kind of justice. He pushed his deeply wounded spirit into a dark corner. He vowed he would not rest until he had found justice—the kind Kaitlyn would want him to find.

But he had no idea where to start.

4

AFTER SUPERVISING THE LOADING OF THE GREEN
Explorer onto the car hauler, Agent Diana Curtis made her way
to the hospital in Salem. She hated hospitals—always had. Once,
when she was nine, she broke her arm. The memory was as clear
as if it had happened yesterday. A hospital was pain, all about pain,
the sharp and stabbing kind of pain. She remembered the doctor
twisting her wrist, not stopping when she screamed in pain. Hurting her and not stopping.

So each time she stepped into a hospital, she tensed up. Sure,
it was stupid, and her logical mind could cite no reason to justify
the feeling, but it was there all the same. And it was real, even if
no one believed her. To cope, she clung to a placid demeanor much
like the sterility of the hospital.

Still, chills ran up her back as she walked toward the cafeteria.
Why couldn't he have met her in the parking lot?

Hillman didn't know she hated hospitals. She couldn't reveal
that weakness—or any other. She wanted him to think she had it
all together, no weaknesses—at least none she would admit. Ever
since that first time, when she got a perfect test score in second
grade, she had tried to be perfect.

Curtis had long tried to emulate the way her boss separated himself from the players in each new case. She admired his demeanor,
his cool professionalism. She loved his calculated, unfeeling approach

to investigations. When she looked in the mirror, she wanted to see him staring back at her. She vowed that someday she would have his job, his power, his influence. Then others would try to be like her, imitating her every nuance.

To reach her goal, she studied Hillman's every move, doing whatever it took to gain his deepest trust. She always tensed up a bit when in the same room with him. After all, he *was* the Arkansas Bureau of Investigation. So on this day, when she spotted him in a far corner of the cafeteria, she froze for a moment.

She took a deep breath, cycled through the various masks only she knew were stored in her head, and selected the one that presented an aura of confidence, or at least one that she thought did. Taking another deep breath, she strolled toward her boss and blurted out a line that she immediately knew didn't measure up. "How's the food?" How she hated being stupid.

Hillman glanced up, smiled, and pushed the tray toward her. "You can have what's left."

"Don't think so," she replied. "What is it anyway?"

"Salisbury steak, at least that's what they told me. The vegetables weren't bad, though."

Before she could sit down, Hillman waved his hand toward the door. "Need for you to do something for me."

"Yeah?"

"I want you to talk to Evans."

Curtis looked away. This was not what she did. She didn't question victims. She dealt with evidence. And a man who had just lost his wife would need comfort, empathy — what Hillman probably thought was "a woman's touch." Didn't he know her better than that? "You haven't talked to him?"

"Yes, we spoke, but he seems to have amnesia. I thought maybe a woman's touch might help his memory."

There you go, she thought.

"It might spark something," Hillman said. "Unless he starts

remembering what happened, we have nothing. I'd wait around, but I'm not too optimistic."

Probably he was going to play golf, Curtis thought.

"Anyway," Hillman continued, rising from the table, "see what you can do. Call me if you get something. I'll walk you down to his room and introduce you. Spend some time with him and see if you can come up with a new angle. I want to put this thing to bed in a hurry. With the Evans name and his connections, the press is going to jump all over this case. We need an arrest, and we need it now."

HILLMAN KNOCKED ON THE DOOR OF LIJE EVANS'
hospital room, and as he pushed open the door, Curtis tried to put
on the appearance of being at ease.

Evans was gazing out the window. Slowly he turned toward
them. As his eyes met hers, Curtis's only thought was to run. She
felt lost and unsure of herself. She had no idea what to say to this
man, this stranger lying there in the hospital bed.

"Mr. Evans, this is Diana Curtis. She's a part of my team."

Curtis approached the bed feeling more like a zombie than an
experienced agent. She had no concept of how to deal with the
emotions at play here. She was too well-schooled to admit that
she would rather be anywhere else than here, to truthfully say she
couldn't comprehend and had no real interest in the man's pain.
But if not the truth, what then? She finally, almost automatically,
said, "I'm so sorry for your loss."

"Thank you," Evans replied.

"Mr. Evans has no idea why anyone would want him dead.
Though I think it's unnecessary, I promised the governor we would
help with protection. So until we get this thing pinned down and
I can move another team in from Little Rock, you and Teddy will
take turns making sure there isn't another attempt on his life."

"Understood," Curtis said as she leaned against the wall.
Great—the bodyguard. Curtis was halfway convinced that she'd

screwed up somehow and Hillman was punishing her by giving her this assignment. Nursemaid to a grieving man was about as low an assignment as she could imagine. If anyone but Hillman had dealt her this hand, she would've complained.

Catching her eye, Hillman said, "I'll call you later. Just stay here with Evans and make sure that no one gets in or out without your approval."

"Understood." And for the moment, that was about all she did understand.

"Mr. Evans," Hillman said, "Curtis will take care of you. She's my best man. If you think of anything, just let her know."

Evans nodded as the older man left them alone.

Taking a seat by the door, Curtis let the silence engulf the room. Best man her foot. The best *man* would be anywhere but here.

She might have been gifted in her craft, but at this moment it hit her that she was far less comfortable dealing with survivors than dealing with cadavers. Lije Evans scared her to death. A trip to the dentist now seemed appealing. So did silence. She prayed the silence would continue for a very long time.

But then she found herself breaking the morgue-like quiet with a simple query. "Mr. Evans, can I get you anything? Are you hungry?"

"You can call me Lije," he replied. "And no, I'm fine. I've never cared for hospital food. Even less now."

Glancing at her watch, she noted that only twelve minutes had passed since Hillman had deserted her. Evans was awake; he was looking at her. She had to say something. "Looks like the rain is gone."

"Yeah."

Curtis swallowed hard. "Guess you know I'll need to question you too?"

"Figured as much." The answer was quick, but hardly inviting.

His postscript proved even less promising. "But doubt if I can help you. It's like my mind is numb."

She had to build a bridge. She had to prove to him she was on his side. Where should she start? How about showing some empathy?

"Probably shock," Curtis said. "Tell me about why the two of you were out last night."

"It was just another charity event."

"And what about the people who were there with you?"

"Most of them were from other communities in the area, so while there was a connection due to the volunteer work Kaitlyn was involved in, it was just 'Hi, how are you?' kind of talk. Anyway, on the way home she decided we needed to stop at Jim's Diner, share a piece of apple pie. We always did that, shared rather than getting two pieces, and we talked ... over the piece of pie. We compared notes on people we'd met at the dinner. Mainly it was Kaitlyn rattling on, I just listened. I remember marveling at how beautiful she looked. Of course, she always did. Anyway ..."

Curtis remembered why she didn't interview witnesses. It was a rope, a thick one, pulling her over the edge she had always been warned about. She was beginning to care.

Evans froze, his expression shifting from an almost relaxed whimsy to one of recognition and fear. "She screamed!"

Curtis flinched. "What?"

"Kaitlyn screamed," Evans whispered, and the room again filled with morgue-like silence.

LIJE WAS DRIFTING IN AN ALMOST CATATONIC STATE.
A bloodcurdling scream was bouncing off every corner of his mind.
Like lava locked deep in a mountain, the pressure built in his head
and threatened to erupt. Covering his ears with his hands did no
good. The scream was still there, but for the moment he could not
put a body with it. Then, from out of the blackness, he saw Kaitlyn.
Even as the scream continued, she looked calm and peaceful. She
appeared just as she had fifteen years before when he had first seen
her in the university cafeteria. There was her smile. It lit up the
room. It always lit up the room. And suddenly the scream faded
and he heard her quiet giggle playing out like a melody from a
radio jingle. It was that giggle and that smile that caused him to
ask her out and that had led him to discover her dynamic spirit.
When he saw her incredible lust for life, he knew he somehow had
to convince her to fall in love with him.

Then the scream returned. He reached toward Kaitlyn, but she
seemed to be slipping backward. For some reason, even as she slid
away from him, he couldn't move. With no warning, there was
blackness, a void so intense that nothing could penetrate it except
that horrible sound. Then a flash of blinding light and he was back
in the hospital room staring into Diana Curtis's confused face.

Catching his breath, Lije said quietly, "Kaitlyn screamed."

"What else?"

Lije did not want to go back into the black hole he had just left. He didn't want to revisit the nightmare or have that scream again fill his senses, yet there was something pulling him to that awful place. And fight it as he did, it was a battle he was doomed to lose. He had to go back; he had to once more enter the madness.

Falling feet first into the darkness, he looked again for the source of the scream. At first there was nothing. Then, glancing to his right, he saw her face illuminated in the glow of the Explorer's instrument lights. They were driving somewhere. But where?

The noise of the wipers caused him to jerk his head back to the windshield. He recognized the road. Arkansas 9. Suddenly he knew where he was. No, no, he had to turn around. He had to pull off. He couldn't make this trip again.

Looking in the rearview mirror, he saw a car so close its headlights were all but hidden by the Explorer's tailgate. Then he felt the bump, followed by the grinding of car on car, and the SUV lurched forward.

"What are they doing?" Kaitlyn asked.

"I don't know," he answered.

"You don't know what?" a voice in the distance demanded.

Ignoring that strange voice, Lije fought to control the SUV. When the unknown car struck them again, he felt Kaitlyn's hand dig into his right biceps. "Make them stop!" she pleaded.

He glanced over at her face. It was etched in fear like he had never seen. She was looking to him for an answer he couldn't provide. As he fought the wheel, he searched for words, but none came. Then suddenly he was out of the driver's seat and back in the room.

"What's going on?" Curtis demanded.

"I was there," he answered. He was shaking, bathed in sweat, and he felt like he'd been punched in the kidneys.

"You were where?"

"In the Explorer. I heard her scream. I saw her face."

"So you remember?"

"Some of it." Wiping his forehead with his left arm, he now clearly recalled details that had eluded him a few minutes before. Though he didn't look toward Curtis, he started spewing out what he had just experienced. He spoke out of fear, the fear that if he didn't tell the story now, it might just crawl back into the recesses of his mind, never to be found again. He couldn't let that happen.

"The car behind us bumped us, knocking us forward. I barely kept control. And she screamed. A few seconds later, they were beside us, and the rain was falling so hard I could barely see them. She was looking back while I was fighting to keep control of the car. I remember a burst of lightning; she must have been looking at the car because she screamed again. They were just behind us and to the side. I looked over my shoulder and saw a flash of light and heard something hit my door."

"They shot at you?" Curtis asked.

His words were now coming in quick bursts as if fired by a machine gun; his eyes were fixed as if in a trance. "They were pulling ahead, then slamming into me, and I made a turn down Farraday Road. I thought I might be able to lose them on the narrow road. But they made the cut. Mud was flying everywhere. I hit a slick spot. As we slid, mud flew up and covered the windshield. I lost control and ended up off the road and in a ditch. I knew we had to run. So we slid out on her side of the Explorer. I was urging her up the hill. My hand was on her back. We were slogging through ankle-deep mud. I had just turned around to look back down the hill when I heard another shot. It hit me. I fell to my knees. Kaitlyn stopped, reached out, and said, 'The ridge.' I didn't think I could get to my feet and get to the top of the ridge. But I knew she was right; we had to make the ridge. It was our only chance. Then there was a crack of what sounded like loud thunder and she was knocked forward to the ground. She didn't move or make any attempt to get up. I tried to get to my feet, but I must not have made it."

"Do you recall anything after that?"

Processing information at a rate almost faster than he could comprehend, Lije took a moment to come to grips with his memory. "I think I was lying face down. I must have been, because I couldn't see anything. I heard someone approaching. Their voices were muffled. I remember they grabbed my shoulders and ripped away my coat."

"Did they say anything? This is important."

He leaned back against his pillow, his mind caught in a whirl of pain and confusion. There had to be something else. The nightmare couldn't end there, but there was nothing. It was as if the next page was as blank as a clean blackboard. As if the story had ended with the most important page missing. Then he heard sounds, just sounds.

"No. They stood there for just a few seconds, and then I heard them go back down the hill. Not long afterward, I heard their car drive away. I tried to get up, to make my way to Kaitlyn, but when I stood up, I lost my balance. I remember falling backward and rolling down the hill. I think I must have ended up by the road. In the water. Water was running all around me."

"That's where Deputy Stuart found you," Curtis added.

"I don't remember anything more. Nothing. Oh, there was this odd feeling. In spite of the cold water rushing around me and over me, a warm feeling washed over me. It might sound funny, but at that moment everything was peaceful. The next thing I remember was waking up in here."

Lije paused. He tried to recover more details, something that would explain what happened. Curtis stood up and moved to the far side of the room. His eyes followed her as she pulled her phone from her pocket and tapped in a number. She spoke softly into the phone.

"Well?" Lije asked as Curtis walked back to the bed. He didn't know why, but he felt strange, not knowing what she had said, probably to Hillman, as if he was being left out of the loop.

"What you said gives us a direction," Curtis replied.

"I got that," Lije said. "But it's still not enough, is it?" The why was almost more important to him than the who. He wouldn't be able to rest until he knew if he had done something to cause this. And if his search for that answer revealed that he had, then he would curse every day that remained during his time on earth.

"It's more than we had," Curtis replied, "and maybe you'll be able to remember something else. A sound. A smell. Don't try too hard."

IT WAS MIDMORNING WHEN DIANA CURTIS ARRIVED at Fannie's Cafe. According to the menu, for two generations the native-stone building had housed a small family-run business offering home-style cooking on the northwest corner of Salem's courthouse square. It was a local favorite, and after a few bites of her pancakes, Curtis could understand why. They were the best she had ever tasted.

Barton had called at midnight with two orders—one, to continue to keep an eye on Evans after he checked out of the hospital. The man had guts, she could say that. Checking out so soon after surgery. Just a day and a half, really. He was due to leave the hospital at noon. Had told her he was going home. She figured the last thing he needed was a stranger shadowing his every move. But Hillman shot her down, said the governor wanted Evans protected by the ABI until the guilty parties were caught.

The other assignment: talk with Heather Jameson, Evans' law partner and Kaitlyn's best friend. Curtis was a crime-scene investigator; she usually farmed out the interviews with witnesses. She believed it was a lot easier to sort out the lies by reading a transcript than by sitting across from a witness. The upcoming interview might be even worse than babysitting the vic's husband.

It had been a busy morning. She had already been back to the crime scene, where she was informed no bullet fragments or any other clues of real use had been uncovered. She had reviewed her notes on the law partner. And she had checked on the search for the missing deputy. Still nothing. Hope for her survival was dimming.

The only good thing about the morning had been the pancakes and bacon. Jameson had agreed to meet for coffee at Fannie's. Thankfully, Curtis had gotten to the cafe in time to tackle her first real meal in days, alone, just the way she liked it. There was nothing like the taste of real butter and pure maple syrup in solitude to relieve the stress of an unwanted assignment.

As she ate, she kept going over the details of the case. No car appeared to have crossed Old Iron; on the other side of the bridge, the muddy road wasn't disturbed. On the highway side of Burns Creek, near where the bridge used to rest, there were signs of a vehicle pulling off the road and onto a mostly rocky area. The rain, the darkness, and some bushes would have made it difficult for anyone to see even a white car on that night. That was probably where the killers were when Deputy Stuart arrived at the scene.

Curtis sipped some coffee. Maybe they couldn't cross the bridge, which the evidence seemed to prove. They must have driven out in the few minutes between when the ambulance left and the backup arrived. And they took Deputy Stuart with them. Drowning had been all but ruled out. Curtis's team and the locals had searched all of the area downstream from the bridge and found nothing.

But there was one big hole in that theory: why would the killers shoot two people and not a third? Especially a deputy who just happened on the scene. Or did she? Had she heard something that made her investigate closer to the creek?

The background check on Stuart proved fruitless. She was as clean as a whistle, a dedicated lawman who was respected by her peers and the local citizens. There was nothing to say that Stuart was involved. For now, that was off the board.

"Then what happened to her?" Did she actually say that out loud? She had. Yet if anyone in the busy cafe heard the question, they didn't respond. They were too engrossed in their own response to the town's tragedy. The mood in the cafe was somber. The whole town was that way. It was like the whole town was in shock. This wasn't like the city, where a person died and no one seemed to notice.

After savoring the last bite of pancake, Curtis swiped her mouth with her napkin and leaned back in the wooden chair. A large white-haired woman in an apron approached her table.

"Did y'all like the fixin's?" Her voice was almost as big as her body, and while her desire to please appeared to be sincere, her smile seemed forced. Like everyone else, she probably had known Kaitlyn Evans.

"It was wonderful," Curtis replied. "I can't tell you when I've enjoyed a meal as much."

"Glad it hit the spot," the woman said, her tone now more serious. "It's on the house. I know you're looking for Kaitlyn's killers. I want you to know my place is your home kitchen as long as you're here. I loved that little girl like she was one of mine. Lije is special to me too, and to about everyone else here too, so you get whoever did this and put them away. It's only by doing that that the healing can start. And this town's hurtin' plenty right now."

"We'll do all we can," Curtis replied. Looking the woman in the eye, she added, "But you don't have to give me anything. It's my job."

"Well, I'm not figuring a bill for you, deary."

"That is very much appreciated. Thank you, but there'll be a large tip on the table."

Tears welling in her eyes, Fannie said, "If you leave anything, it'll go to one of Kaitlyn's projects. A lot of us are going to make sure her touch is felt for a long time around here." The older woman turned and shuffled sadly back to the kitchen.

"Kaitlyn Evans sure made an impact here," Curtis said quietly. Again her words were meant for no one, but this time someone did hear them.

8

"YES, SHE DID," SAID A YOUNG WOMAN APPROACHING the table. "Since I know everyone else in here, I'm assuming you are Agent Curtis."

Curtis looked up. The woman appeared barely old enough to be out of college. Well-dressed, attractive, average height. And nervous. Heather Jameson, the lawyer.

"Miss Jameson," Curtis said as she pointed to an empty chair. "Would you like something to eat?"

"No. Fannie will bring me some coffee when she gets a moment. I really haven't been very hungry since ..." Jameson didn't finish, just let the words drift off as she took a seat facing the window.

Curtis was prepared. She had an ABI file on Jameson, put together for her overnight, and some of the things in that report didn't match up with the person who was sitting across from her. Curtis had come to know that the adage "you shouldn't judge a book by its cover" definitely applied in criminal investigations. At least it did when working with evidence, so surely it applied when interviewing people.

It was Jameson who finally broke the silence. "Any leads?"

"Not much. Have you seen Lije yet? He's due to leave the hospital around noon."

"I stopped by the hospital on my way here. Lije wanted me to pick up some clothes from the house. He's sore but seems pretty strong. You know the whole town's helping him get through this. You wouldn't believe how many pies and cakes are on his table right now. All of us are worried about him. Kaitlyn was the most important person in his life."

"I think that's obvious," Curtis replied. She was determined to put an edge on this conversation and make sure the other woman sensed that her primary concern was not a mourning man but finding a woman's killer. After a calculated pause, she plunged forward. "I hope he'll take care of himself, be careful. We have a man there keeping watch on the house to make sure no one tries to finish what was started two nights ago."

"I met your agent this morning," Jameson said. "He seems like a nice man. But you need to know that keeping Lije under your control won't be easy. When he gets to feeling better, he'll resent the security, the babysitting idea. I know him well. When he wasn't with Kaitlyn, he liked to be by himself. From what I've been told, he's always been a loner. So he's not going to want you looking over his shoulder."

"Understood." Curtis smiled. How did this young woman know what Lije's habits were when he wasn't with Kaitlyn? "But that'll be my call, not his, and certainly not yours. So Lije, and you for that matter, will need to get used to seeing me and my people around." My people, that sounded good. She liked it; she could get used to it too.

"I understand and I even agree with you, but Lije might well be a challenge for you. So be warned." Jameson was picking up Curtis's tone.

It appeared to Curtis that Jameson wanted to cut short this meeting. So instead of saying anything, she simply stared at the other woman. Her look was cold and calculating, and within seconds Jameson began wilting under the pressure.

"I really don't think I can be any help to you," Jameson said. "And I have a great deal to do to help plan for the funeral ..."

Curtis repressed a grin when Jameson let her words drift off and nervously crossed her legs. She then turned her head toward the street and drummed her fingers on the table.

Curtis had this woman worried. She was beginning to understand why Barton loved this process, this one-on-one, so much. Picking people apart, making them sweat—it was actually fun. As she remained quiet and watched, the other woman seemed to shrink before her eyes.

According to the ABI report, Jameson had come to town three years before. Lije hired her, and Kaitlyn adopted her like a sister. The two women went to church and the gym together and even played on the same softball team. They made frequent shopping trips to Little Rock. They were like family. It would seem that this closeness, combined with her excellent work at Evans' law practice, made her the last person anyone would suspect of being involved in a serious crime. But the woman the town knew and the woman revealed in the file resting on the table were very different indeed. It was the hidden Jameson that Curtis relished unveiling, and there was no better time to start than now.

"Miss Jameson, I understand you partied hard in college."

The question caught Jameson by surprise. "Yes, but I don't see—"

With a gesture, Curtis interrupted her. She opened the file and leafed through some pages. She wanted to let Jameson squirm a bit longer before dropping a series of bombs on her.

"You almost died one night from an overdose. During your junior year, you were caught forging checks to pay for your habit. Opted out of jail time by entering a rehab program. Then you came back to college, seemed to get your life together, and were accepted into law school. Does that pretty much sum up your college life? I can toss out some affairs, a bit of cheating, and a few other things, but why bother?"

"I wasn't Snow White," Jameson said.

Curtis didn't reply. She read through an email message she had printed out that morning. One of her investigators, Art Skymanski, had looked into Jameson's family and discovered her father was an alcoholic. In the last few years, the booze had affected his focus and pretty much ruined his life. He even lost his business. His wife, Jameson's mother, had grown so distraught she committed suicide about five months ago. "Your mother's death must have hit you hard."

"It wasn't easy. Don't think I could've gotten through it without Kaitlyn. ... Am I being charged with something?"

"Should you be?" Curtis sat back and gauged the woman's reaction. She was not shocked when the words came quickly and with great force. Denial was often the first line of defense.

"No. No way. The Evanses were like family to me, and I'd rather die than have anything happen to Kaitlyn."

Ignoring the protest, Curtis plunged on. "Your father is up to his gills in debt. He's close to losing his home. I can't begin to imagine what it'd be like for me if I saw my dad in that situation. I'd do just about anything to save him."

Jameson appeared both angry and hurt but kept her voice down. She knew everyone in the cafe, so she probably wasn't ready to be openly hostile. Though you had to be impressed that the woman kept punching back and remained in the fight.

"If you're implying that I might have been involved, then you're way off base. If I needed any kind of help, I could've asked Lije and Kaitlyn directly. They would've jumped right in."

"I would agree with you," Curtis replied, "if it was just your father who needed help."

"What's your point?"

Everyone in the cafe heard her this time—exactly what Curtis wanted. Taking a deep breath, the agent, lowering her voice a bit, aired out her theory. "I think it's possible that the pressures of your father's problems, combined with your mother's suicide, awoke some old demons. It'd be very understandable if you collapsed under the weight and got reinvolved with drugs. It says here that cocaine was your drug of choice, and that's not cheap."

Jameson didn't pause to consider the accusation. "Unless you have proof, you appear to be out on a limb. I'm clean and have been for years."

Curtis nodded, then continued calmly, "Your bank account is overdrawn by more than a thousand dollars. You're behind on your car payments. In the past three months, you have somehow gone through more than twenty-five thousand in savings." Pointing, she added, "You obviously need money and need it badly."

Jameson was now close to cracking. Curtis recognized the signs. Even if the financial meltdown wasn't caused by drugs, when word got out, imagine what this would do to her pristine image in this small town. It would kill her law career before it really had a chance to get started. She was in deep trouble, and she probably was just beginning to realize how everything Curtis had laid out must look.

Jameson looked down at her hands and the napkin her fingers were shredding. When she looked up, her eyes were filled with tears. "I know the pain that comes with causing a death. I still have problems living with that. My ... I could never ... I just could never."

Curtis absorbed her words; they sounded sincere. They seemed as honest as any she had heard in a long time. But what was she referring to? What death? Her mother's suicide? If Curtis had learned anything in all of her investigations, it was that people can get a warped sense of blame, of responsibility. The other thing she had learned was that everybody lies. The file in front of her spoke volumes.

"Heather, I don't have any more questions now. But I'm asking you to stay in town, where you can be reached," Curtis said and closed the file.

Head down, Jameson cried silently for a moment, then she

looked up at Curtis, put on a brave smile, and got up and left. Curtis watched as she got into a well-used car and drove away.

The agent jotted down a few notes in the file and sat there, just thinking. Then she dug out a ten-dollar bill, placed it on the table, and got up to go.

She stepped outside and took in the scene for a moment, this time as a tourist, not as an investigator. From the century-old two-story courthouse to the sidewalks that sat four feet above the streets, Salem looked like something out of a Norman Rockwell painting. It was the America of the past, a living postcard of a day when people didn't lock their doors and paid for everything with cash. Yet there were cracks in the veneer; many of the beautiful stone and brick buildings that lined the square were empty, the businesses they had housed replaced by discount chains and new stores out on the highway. The whole country was changing that way. Progress. She wished she could've seen the town in its hey-day, when the buildings were filled, business was bustling, and the sidewalks were crowded.

"It was a nice town until two nights ago," Fannie announced from the door of the cafe.

Curtis turned back.

"You know," Fannie said, "I remember as a kid getting cherry Cokes over in the stone building on the left side of the square. Humphrey's Drug. They had real cherry Cokes. You ever tasted a real one, mixed by hand? I doubt if I'll ever taste anything that good again."

Curtis looked at the place where the drugstore had once oper-ated. On the outside, the building looked sound. A Coca-Cola sign still hung in the window, neon letters spelling Rexall still topped the awning, and store hours were still posted on the door. Driving by, one might think the store was open. But from where she stood, she could see through the dusty glass that there was nothing in-side but a memory. The building was simply a shell, a relic from another age.

"It was an innocent time then," Fannie added. She pulled her apron up to her eye and wiped a tear. "They'll bury that innocence this week with Kaitlyn."

Curtis nodded. What she kept trying to understand was how one woman could mean so much to so many different people. Maybe it was because this was such a small town and everyone knew everyone. Whatever the reason, the agent had never experienced anything like it.

Of course, this case had presented her with a lot of firsts.

"Thanks for the wonderful breakfast," Curtis said.

The woman nodded. "You're wrong, you know."

"About what?"

Forcing a smile, Fannie corrected the agent. "Not what. Who. Heather didn't have nothing to do with what happened. I warn you, if you spend your days chasing down that trail, the one that matters will go cold."

Curtis didn't reply. She tossed off a quick wave and made her way to her car. Leaning against it, she again took in the scene, but this time she didn't see the cracks in the architecture or the lack of shoppers. All that was an out-of-focus blur as she stood there and thought about the case. Her gut told her to go after Jameson. There was something that young woman wasn't telling her.

9

LIJE EVANS STARED OUT THE WINDOW AT THE TOWN that lay below. It was midnight, and for the first time since he had been released from the hospital, he was essentially alone. Sure, there was an ABI agent somewhere on the grounds, assigned to make sure no one got a second chance at killing him, but the friends who had gathered in his hilltop log home had finally departed, so the agent could let his guard down a little.

Turning from the window, Lije collapsed into an overstuffed antique leather chair and took a deep breath, surprised that physically he felt as good as he did. Except for a bit of soreness in his abdomen, there were no lingering signs of his having experienced near-death just two days before.

But that didn't help his wounded spirit. There was a huge hole in his life, one that would never again be filled. That hole was bottomless, filled with cold darkness.

Men in his family had never shown deep emotion. He had no memory of tears from his father or his grandfather, no memory of anger or of love. His parents had never shown any sort of affection for each other in front of him when he was a child. So maybe that explained why no tears had poured from his eyes and why he fought them every time they threatened. Even as he had spoken with others about Kaitlyn, his voice had rarely wavered. It was unusually strong, his words cracking like baseballs off a wooden bat.

But now, alone in his study, surrounded by mementos of a life that was no more, he no longer had to keep up the false front. Everywhere he turned, in each corner and on every wall, there were memories of Kaitlyn. All those good times—together—now gone forever.

For hours he sat there, unmoving, lost in myriad thoughts, trying to shuffle through the questions and come up with answers. Yet there were no answers. There was no logic. No cause and effect. He had never had a major dispute with anyone. He had stayed away from controversy. He had never even publicly supported a political candidate. He had never been a joiner. And he realized that he had never been much of anything. Nothing he could name or list. If anyone could go through life standing for nothing, he was the one; he had made fence-sitting into an art. He had no enemies, and not a single person held anything against him. He had been generous with those who worked for him. Even the bond between him and the man who mowed his lawn was solid. There was simply no reason for anyone to be gunning for him. He was certain of that.

And who would shoot Kaitlyn? She was about as close to a saint as anyone could be. She was loved and respected by everyone he knew. She brought smiles everywhere she went. People stood in line to hug her. Children hovered around her like moths around a porch light. She was pure, sincere, beautiful, giving, and generous. If love could be banked, her vault would be overflowing. So why? There was simply no way anyone could have a vendetta against her. Yet somewhere in his life—or her life—there had to be at least one misstep that led to the tragedy at Farraday Road. And it must have been a big one. He had to figure out what it was.

The hours dragged by, each a lifetime. Two o'clock became three, and three became four, and sometime after that, tired of the darkness, he switched on a table lamp, reached to his right, and picked up a framed portrait of the only love he had really ever known. He still couldn't begin to fathom her incredible beauty. The silky dark hair, the green eyes, and that incredible smile—wherever she went, they set her apart from everyone else in the room.

Could someone have hated her because of her heritage? Her Asian ancestry? Could there be a racial motive behind all of this?

Laying the photo in his lap, he thought back over his years in Salem. Yes, there had been some who had questioned their marriage at first. Many did not cotton to the idea of his marrying outside of his race. Yet when they had come to know Kaitlyn, when they had met her spirit, the shape of her eyes no longer mattered, at least not on the surface. But what about simmering underneath the surface? What if there was someone out there who had grown to resent her? Or maybe there was someone who hated her because she was an outsider, an Asian who married into the Evans family's large bank account. What if this whole tragedy was about race? After all, lots of people had died because of racial hatreds. Could this have been a hate crime? Kaitlyn dying for hate—how ironic would that be?

With no money taken, ruling out robbery as a motive, and nothing in his background that offered any reason for murder, might someone have seen them that night, maybe even at Jim's Diner, and been consumed by rage at seeing a happily married couple who happened to have different racial heritages? He remembered some of the comments he had overheard when they were first married. That was so long ago, he had all but forgotten the racial hatred that had spawned the words back then. But now, maybe ... He didn't want to consider that, but for the moment it was about the only thing that made any kind of sense. The thought sparked fury in his soul. As if by a hangman's noose, he was strangling in the horrible belief that she was dead because she was different and that he should be dead because he dared to love someone who didn't look like his own kind.

10

THERE WAS SIMPLY NO WAY THE FIRST BAPTIST CHURCH could hold all those who showed up for the Kaitlyn Evans funeral. Hundreds were hovering outside the doors as Diana Curtis flashed her badge and was escorted into the building. Walking past three old-timers, she heard one say, "Biggest funeral in the history of the county, no doubt." News crews were everywhere, catching the mourners, even wrangling interviews with a few publicity-happy visitors. She had read in the local paper that Lije had requested memorials be given to different charities rather than be spent on floral displays, yet it appeared that no one had paid any attention. Every florist within forty miles must have sold out of flowers. For one afternoon even the cleanup of the immense damage caused by the flooding was taking a back seat to this one event. How Kaitlyn Evans must have been loved!

As Curtis walked into the sanctuary, it seemed those already in the pews did not want to miss the entrance of the next important person and kept looking back toward the door. The eyes that stared at her belonged to every age and demographic sector. The governor and his wife sat in row three beside a man she had seen on a garbage truck the day before. Looked like all the area state representatives were already seated, as were a senator and several members of the state supreme court. This was the place where everyone who was anyone had to be. The murder and the long-standing importance of the Evans family in the area and Kaitlyn's immeasurable resume of good works made this much more than a memorial service; it was the event of a lifetime.

Or should that be deathtime? Not a pleasant word, *death-time*. Probably didn't exist, but maybe it should be added to the dictionary.

The organ music announced the beginning of the service. Curtis clung to her professional demeanor with less success than usual. She might have been tough and proud of it, but she simply couldn't help getting emotionally involved in the drama unfolding in front of her. The masses of flowers and the sincere verbal and musical tributes focused the spotlight for a brief time on the ideals of Kaitlyn Evans. As the pastor spoke, recounting the victim's character and deeds, those around the agent could no longer keep from crying. When Lije rose to share a few of his special memories and to read Kaitlyn's favorite scripture, First Corinthians chapter thirteen, his eyes were among the few that remained dry. The crowd rose to sing "Sweet, Sweet Spirit," and Curtis noticed that Heather Jameson remained seated, sobbing so hard she had to fight just to grab a breath. Even after the song ended, Jameson continued wiping her eyes with a tissue. This Kaitlyn, Curtis decided, had been something very special. Yet how could anyone really be that good?

It took almost two hours for the funeral and burial. Curtis took in each moment as both a curiosity and a chance to study the faces in the crowd. One of them might well be the killer.

The grief created by this final farewell seemed impenetrable; not even faith could dent it. Curtis couldn't fathom the gloom that surrounded her like a dark cloud, and even the preacher seemed unsure and unsteady despite speaking words of comfort and peace and heaven as home.

Silently, the crowd made its way from the graveside back to their vehicles. It was as if a mute button had silenced everything in town.

Curtis had ridden to the cemetery with the local newspaper editor. They hadn't spoken about the case; in fact they hadn't spoken at all. He had just offered, and because she didn't know her way around, she had accepted. She was set to ride back with him, but as she took a final look at the departing throng, Heather Jameson approached.

"Do you want a ride back to the church?"

Curtis nodded and followed Jameson back to her beat-up old Toyota. It was hard to believe Jameson still owed money on the car and was behind in her payments to the bank. Curtis slid in and buckled her seatbelt and waited to see what Jameson's plan was for this car ride. She hoped to exploit a moment of vulnerability, gain some more understanding of Jameson's relationship with her boss, Lije Evans.

But that moment never came. They rode in silence back to the church, and Jameson dropped Curtis off at her car without a word.

BARTON HILLMAN HAD JUST FINISHED HIS PHONE
conversation with Diana Curtis when one of his lab techs walked
through his office door.

"Mr. Hillman?" the techie asked, his voice wavering.

"Yeah, what is it?"

The lab tech held out a report. Hillman took it and glanced at
the top page.

"The Evans car?"

"Yes, the Explorer and the coat."

"Anything I need to know?"

"The white paint was from a GM vehicle. The car, truck, or
SUV could have been manufactured anytime in the past decade. So
we put out an APB on a white General Motors vehicle with damage on the passenger side."

"Well, that narrows it down to several thousand cars in Arkansas and Missouri alone."

"We had more luck with the bullet."

"What bullet?" Hillman barked.

"We found a slug in the driver's side door. It wasn't obvious
because that area was caked with mud."

"And?"

"It came from a .32."

"Hardly unusual."

"True, but it's a match for a previous homicide."

"Oh?" This was not the news he wanted to hear. It muddied the waters. He wanted this case to be clean, neat, and short. If this turned out to be complicated, the investigation could drag on for months. "Well, now we seem to be getting somewhere. We might just wrap up two cases at once here."

"Maybe not, chief. The other murder happened a couple of years ago. A man's already been tried and convicted. He's in prison. The same gun was used to murder a Stone County man, Micah Dean."

"That sounds familiar," Hillman said, feigning ignorance. He knew the case well. He looked away and pretended to go page by page though a mental file of cases. Just enough time for the techie to be awed by his recall. "I remember now. We did some lab work for the local sheriff on that one, but we weren't involved in the investigation. As I recall, Dean was shot over a piece of river property. A real estate man who was deep in debt was nailed for the crime. He still maintains he didn't do it. I met him on death row last year. He seemed as crazy as a loon to me. He fired his lawyers and is fast-tracking his execution. A strange tactic for an innocent man. Especially when it was an open-and-shut case."

"His name is Jonathon Jennings," the tech said. "You probably know the gun in the case was never found."

Was that sarcasm? Hillman wondered. "Yeah, it's all coming back now. I read a newspaper story on the trial where he claimed he didn't even own a gun. Never had. The jury didn't buy it. He probably ditched it somewhere after he shot Dean. I think his court-appointed attorney even made that statement after the verdict."

"If he did toss the gun, then someone found it," the techie said. He paused a moment before continuing, "Sir, what are the odds of two murders being committed with the same gun and the two shooters and the victims having no connection to each other?"

"Long," Hillman replied. "So long that I wouldn't want to try to compute it. Anything else?"

"Nothing on or in the coat that offers us any direction. The deputy's still missing—no trace of her—and the search has been expanded statewide and into Missouri. In fact, about all we have is the bullet."

Hillman nodded. He knew that if the deputy hadn't been found by now, she likely was dead. He didn't dwell on it; it was simply part of being a cop.

"Sir, with the bullet matching an earlier case and that man on death row, do you think there's a chance he is telling the truth? And he's innocent?"

The director shrugged. "Not my call. He was convicted by a jury of his peers and he has now chosen to get to the death chamber as quickly as possible. So it seems that everyone got it right on that case." Hillman paused, studied the report briefly, and without looking up said, "Who found the bullet?"

"I did, sir."

"Anyone else know about it?"

"No, sir. I did all the work on it."

Tossing the report on his desk, the director walked over to the lab tech, put his hand on his shoulder, and smiled. "This is good work, son—the kind of thing that gets you promoted around here. Now, to keep things in the proper context on the case and protect the evidence, I need for you to do a couple of things for me."

"Yes, sir."

"First, gather all the information you have on the bullet—photos, lab reports, everything. Box it up and bring it all back to me."

The techie nodded.

"Then take the rest of the day off. You've earned it. Have some fun. But until I give the word, this is between you and me. I need to check something out on this. It's urgent. Am I making myself clear?"

"Yes, sir."

After the lab tech left, Hillman hoped the tech was grateful for the time off and intimidated by his authority. His linking the bullet in the Explorer with the gun from two years ago was good work but now created a puzzle, an unknown. And Hillman didn't like unknowns. That gun might just confuse the issue and give a defense attorney a wedge to keep the guilty party out of prison.

But Hillman's real concern was the gun's use in that previous case. What if Jennings was innocent after all? Police never did find the gun. Just the bullet. At the time, Hillman had been concerned that the prosecutor was working with weak evidence. With the same gun now used in another shooting, that previous conviction could be overturned. And that just wouldn't do. That case was prosecuted by Stone County District Attorney Martin Gooch—Hillman's brother-in-law and possibly the next governor of the state.

THE HOUSE WAS BUILT OF LOG AND NATIVE STONE, two stories high, and sat on top of Shell Hill overlooking Salem. It had been built in 1910 by Lije Evans' great-grandfather Grover Evans. Grover's son, John, had made a small fortune in East Coast real estate in the 1930s and, after living on Park Avenue, returned to Salem upon his father's death. At that time most thought of him as a city slicker, so they were shocked when he stayed in town, built a law practice, and doubled the size of the family home.

Like his father, John's son Thomas pursued a career in New York, making his own modest fortune and surprising everyone by returning to the Ozarks as a bachelor. He married and the union produced one son, Lije. The youngest member of the Evans legacy was still in high school when his father passed away and had just finished his undergrad work when his mother suffered a fatal stroke. The old place sat vacant for several years until he returned to reopen his grandfather's law practice and move his wife, Kaitlyn, into the family home.

While Lije remodeled and updated the old law offices on the first floor of what was once the Salem Hotel, Kaitlyn resurrected the old home place. With her touch, the once dark walls gave way to open rooms filled with light. Hitting antique malls and garage sales, she added period pieces as well as fun items, such as a nickel Coke machine, a jukebox, and a soda fountain. Rather than the solitary and somewhat mysterious retreat it had been, the house became, according to *Southern Living* magazine, a relaxed, inviting home that hosted everything from church socials to charity bazaars. Those who cozied up next to the native-stone fireplace that dominated the two-story great room claimed this had to be the warmest spot in the country.

The home had always been a refuge to Lije, especially in the days after his father's passing, but now it seemed like a prison. If he could choose anywhere to be at this moment, it would be anywhere else. High above the town on the hill, the family home had always been on display. The site had been chosen by his great-grandfather. That was the nature of the family. They didn't do anything in a small way. So tonight, besides the guests who were wandering around the old place, there were scores in town below, looking up at the hill, wondering what he was doing and how he was coping. He could feel their eyes and almost hear their thoughts, as if he were haunted by ghosts.

The doorbell rang again and Lije answered it.

"Miss Curtis ... it's so good of you to come."

He knew it was the right thing to say, the proper words for this occasion, but he didn't want anyone in his home, especially not an ABI agent assigned to follow him around for "protection." He was sure the vibes he was sending clearly said he just wanted to pull a Garbo, but she was missing the signal.

"It's a beautiful home," Curtis said as Lije ushered her through the foyer and into the great room.

"That would be Kaitlyn's touch," he explained. "Before she came here, it was always dark and cold. My family didn't actually live here, we hid here."

Even as he spoke, he realized the irony of his words. Hiding was what he wanted to do now. He wanted to close out the world and keep it out. He would even love to return the home to its dark days. Yet he couldn't, at least not at the moment. So he forged ahead with hollow words to describe what the home had been under Kaitlyn's influence.

"Until fifteen years ago, few in this area had ever seen the inside of this house. It might be hard to believe, but this place once seemed an imposing fortress sitting over the town, a place that generated stories of ghosts and goblins. After Kaitlyn and I arrived, we put the lights back on and the welcome mat out. Seems like everyone in town has been here several times. Kaitlyn opened things up. She saw the potential in everyone and in everything, including this ancient wooden palace."

This was a tour he didn't want to give, but he continued nonetheless. "And she didn't waste any of her gifts or her time. I guess for that I can be grateful." He paused, staring at a photograph of Kaitlyn that sat on the mantel atop the six-foot-wide fireplace. Suddenly, not wanting to remember or speak of Kaitlyn, he skirted the few remaining guests and led his uninvited guest into a sitting area at the back of the house. When he spoke, his voice contained none of the warmth it had just a few moments before.

"I KNOW YOU'RE HERE TO GUARD ME," LIJE TOLD
Curtis. "Still, I think I'll be safe in my own home. So I believe
you're wasting your time. And mine too. It's pretty easy to see
anyone approach as they come up the hill. Besides, all thirty acres
up here are mine. I own Shell Hill."

Curtis smiled. "I won't get in your way. I know you still have
some guests here. You do what you need to do with them, and I'll
kind of look around. And I agree, my job would seem to be pretty
easy up here on top of the world. I'm sure I can all but disappear."

Lije decided she sounded sincere. It seemed she didn't want
to be here any more than he did. He almost felt a moment of ca-
maraderie with her. "All right, but I wouldn't be a good host if I
didn't show you a few more things." Maybe being with someone
who didn't know Kaitlyn was better than being around those who
couldn't wait to bring up another anecdote or memory.

"Let me take you over to what we called 'the road show.'" Leading her to a far wall, he pointed out scores of photos, most of them
taken on their many trips. In each of the snapshots, their happiness didn't just show, it exploded from inside the frames. From the
snow-capped Rockies to the beaches of Hawaii to the streets of
Boston, Lije and Kaitlyn knew how to have fun while sharing the
wonders of the world with each other.

"You look very happy in all these photos," Curtis said, then looked down as if embarrassed.

"It was easy," he said. "There was real life wherever she was."

He gave the agent a few minutes to glance through the vacation shots before directing her to the den. "Here you can really see Kaitlyn's talent as a decorator. She could take anything and make it look like a piece of art." He pointed to a display case with a small college pennant, an old washboard, a Vietnamese sketch, a dish of what looked like pink pearls, and a framed grade-school report card. As he worked his way through the room, he directed Curtis to other small mementos: buttons off a military uniform, portraits taken a century before, an oriental fan, a brightly colored scarf, and a wooden baseball bat. As she studied the dozens of seemingly unrelated but carefully displayed keepsakes, Lije said, "She put all these things together as a creative history of our two families. She felt that by looking at each of these unique items, any person could write a fairly complete biography of both of the individuals who called this place home."

Curtis seemed oblivious to time as she slowly went from wall to wall, table to table, and, finally, room to room. When he felt a need, Lije told her the story behind a certain item. But usually he just observed her. There was something about the woman's enjoying Kaitlyn's touch that brought him a temporary sense of peace. She got it. She at least knew intellectually why his wife had been so special. She was carefully examining a gold pocket watch when Lije felt a little warmth sneak into his soul. The timepiece reminded him of one of his wife's favorite jokes. He leaned over the agent's shoulder and said, "That was my grandfather's watch, not to be confused with his clock, which is next to the door in the foyer."

Curtis smiled and put the timepiece back on the shelf. "All of this stuff is from your family?"

"And hers. It was a part of our past. Until I met Kaitlyn, I never really thought much about this sort of thing. My family keepsakes were stored in the attic. Though she was born in the States and never even visited her father's home country of Vietnam, I still feel there was a part of her that was very Asian. She seemed to revere not only her ancestors but mine too. She constantly pulled things out of trunks or closets, cleaned them up, and found a special way to make them a part of our daily lives. So ninety percent of the things you see in this home are part of the story of either the Evans or the Do clans. There's even a scrapbook on the desk in the corner of the great room where she wrote what each item is, where it came from, and why it's important. She used to tell me, 'Everything we touch shapes our lives and defines who we are.' I'd laugh when she said that, calling her Confucius. Then she'd remind me that the great philosopher was actually Chinese. It was our joke."

Curtis nodded.

"Enough about me and my past. Do you want something to eat?"

"No, not now."

"As you can imagine, I was given enough food to feed an army. Before they left, some of the women from church somehow found a way to stuff it all into the fridge. I can avoid the grocery store for weeks. I really hate shopping anyway."

Actually, he had once enjoyed it. There was a time when he and Kaitlyn had good-naturedly fought over food choices. But now those times were past and being in those familiar aisles would just pull into sharper focus the loneliness he'd feel for the rest of his life.

As Lije considered this facet of his loss, Curtis slowly looked around the den, then casually strolled through the foyer and into the great room. "Are we alone?" The agent seemed surprised.

He glanced around the room. "Yep, I guess so. You must have scared everyone off." It was a forced joke, he knew, and it brought no laughter, not even a slight grin. But there was a good chance it was true. "It's seven-thirty. They'd been here for hours, and I guess they had pretty much run out of good memories to rehash.

If your coming actually did drive them off, thanks." This time he was sincere.

Curtis nodded a reply, then started to work her way through the home, checking the locks on the doors. As she undertook her security detail, Lije said, "You can check them if you want, but they're all locked. Your partner did that already. I'm sure you know the sheriff has a man stationed at the bottom of the hill, and my lane is the only way up here. But I'm sure you know that. And to answer the question you're probably about to ask, I'm tired, still a bit sore from the wound, but hardly sleepy." He was rattling on now, knew it, and didn't care. Following her from room to room, he added, "In fact, I really don't want to go to bed tonight. Not here anyway. What sleep I got last night was in a chair in my study. Might choose that route again tonight."

Curtis didn't reply. She spent the next few minutes closing the blinds that covered the home's oversized windows.

Her silence upset him. He was talking and she didn't seem to be listening. So much for thinking she had a warm spot buried under that icy glare. "You're going to miss a great sunset," he said as the last shade came down.

"Maybe, but I'll feel much more secure if no one can see in."

Just to the left of the final window were two photos. They had been placed in a double 1930s-era frame. The first shot was printed in black and white and showed the law office of John Evans in downtown Salem. Out in front of the entrance sat an unusual antique car. It had huge pipes exiting from under the hood and entering the front fenders. There didn't appear to be any headlights and the squared-off hood resembled a coffin. The rest of the body seemed more like a classic art-deco sculpture than something that came off a Detroit assembly line.

The second photo was shot in the same location, but captured the scene in color. The building had been updated, new streetlights now lined the square, and a green bench sat under the law office's large front window. Sitting in the very same spot was the car. It was the only thing that appeared the same.

"Is the car in these photos the same? There must be seventy years' difference between the photos."

Lije removed one photo from the wall and studied both the antique shot and the newer one. What a car! How he loved it. Now *there* was a tie to a past he treasured even at this horrible moment. After rehanging the photo, he said, "That's a 1936 Cord Westchester 810 Sedan. My grandfather saw the new Cords at the New York Auto Show and fell in love with them. In the summer of that year, he made a trip to the Auburn-Cord-Duesenberg company headquarters in Auburn, Indiana. He talked to the officials, test-drove one of the latest models, and placed an order. He asked for a red sedan. Since they didn't have that color in their 1936 line, he took one of the executives over to a Packard showroom and showed him a red he liked. The man told him that if he paid them an extra seventy-five dollars, they would build the car for him and paint it Packard red. He was thrilled, wrote them a check, and gave them instructions for shipping it.

"He was about to leave when he noticed a car parked at the back of the building that had stainless-steel side pipes. A company engineer informed him that Cord was going to use those exhausts on supercharged models that would be a part of the next year's line. Grandpa walked back into the building, sat down with the president, pulled out his checkbook again, and convinced the company to upgrade his car a few months early.

"Six weeks later, the car was delivered by rail to Mammoth Spring. Grandpa picked it up and drove it the twenty miles home. I later found out he hit a hundred miles per hour on one of the few straight stretches on Arkansas 9. And this was before it was paved! The Cord was passed down to my father and my father passed it down to me."

Curtis seemed amazed as she again looked at the photos. It was the first time Lije had seen her act unlike an ABI agent. At the moment, she seemed almost human.

"So you still own this car?"

"At times, when I have it worked on, I think it actually owns me. But yes, it's mine and is parked in the barn."

The car was his escape. It had always been there for him, even before Kaitlyn. "Would you like to see it?"

Without hesitating, Curtis said, "Of course."

CURTIS FOLLOWED LIJE THROUGH THE HOUSE, INTO the garage, out a back door, and across the yard. About forty yards from the home, nestled in a grove of walnut trees, sat what Lije called "the barn." He had designed it to match his home. Constructed of native stone, with a green metal roof and matching shutters, it looked more like an upscale house than a dwelling built for farm animals. She was impressed.

"I could live here," she said.

"It doesn't look as good on the inside," he said, typing in a numerical code on a keypad by the large garage-style entrance. A moment later, the door began to roll up. When the mechanical opener cut off, the two strolled into a building filled with antique farm equipment, a vintage road grader, a woodworking shop, and an incredible red car.

As Lije stood to one side, Curtis slowly circled the vehicle. From its hand-tooled dash, lined with more instruments than most people had ever seen, to bumpers that appeared to be constructed of styled chrome towel racks, the car was an art deco masterpiece. Everything from the podlike front fenders to the small double rear window seemed to have been as carefully conceived as a Da Vinci painting.

"What did you say this was?"

"A Cord."

"It looks like a 1930s Batmobile. Why have I never heard of it until now?"

He was aware that he was distracting himself from his grief over Kaitlyn's death, but he didn't care. It was a welcome distraction. "The company went out of the car business in 1937. The cars were simply too expensive to survive the Depression. And they were probably too radical too. This car had front-wheel drive when all other cars were driven by their back wheels. It had hideaway headlights, a transmission where you preselected the gears, and a stance that was so low it couldn't really navigate some of the horrible roads of the era. The dash setup seemed to be designed for an airplane, which is what actually inspired the configuration and look. As you could guess, it was meant for high-powered executives and movie stars, and at that time, there weren't enough of them around to keep the assembly lines moving."

As he spoke, the investigator walked from one side of the car to the other.

"You drive it?" Curtis asked.

"About once a week. Not good to let them sit. Kaitlyn and I used to take the Cord to church and then out to eat when the weather was pretty. We even drove it to the big Labor Day Auburn-Cord-Duesenberg reunion in Indiana a couple of times."

Shaking her head, Curtis smiled, her eyes glued to the car. "It's remarkable."

The sun was just starting to set as they walked out of the barn. As the automatic door rolled downward, Lije stopped and took in the full beauty of the Ozarks. From where they were standing, he could see for miles in three directions. From the city below to the rolling hills in the background, the scene was simply picture-postcard perfection.

Strange that nature went on with its beautiful displays even when life itself was immersed in ugliness and decay.

"I don't guess you'd ever want to live anywhere else," she said.

Turning from the view, he motioned for her to follow him

toward the house. "Actually, there is a piece of property about twenty miles from here that I always wanted to buy." And what a piece of land it was. It had to be the prize of the region, the most incredible spot in all of the Ozarks.

"It's on Spring River," he continued, shortening his stride so she could more easily keep up. "I used to canoe down that stream and I never passed Swope's Ridge without wondering what the view looks like from up there. It was our dream to purchase that place someday, build a new home, and then Kaitlyn wanted to turn this place into a meeting center and camp for some of her charities. We thought it would be like living two dreams at once."

"Swope's Ridge must be something if you'd give up this place for it."

Lije turned to her, but never got the chance to respond.

Two shots rang out. The first struck a tree branch just inches over Lije's head, sending leaves floating to the ground. The second bullet hit a boulder to their left, ricocheting past them before burrowing into the Arkansas clay.

"Hit the ground," Curtis yelled, shoving Lije down as she dove headfirst to the turf with him.

"Can you tell where it came from?" he whispered.

Her answer was typically clinical. "If you think of the hill as a clock, look for the hour of three. But don't raise your head too high or they'll blow it off."

He followed her instructions and locked on to the grove of trees that offered the shooter almost complete cover. Straining against the darkening shadows of dusk, he tried to spot a human form. He saw nothing.

"Are they still there?" he asked.

"Not if they're as smart as I think they are," Curtis said. Rolling over, she pulled out her cell phone and tapped in a number.

"Teddy, it's Diana. We've had another attempt. This time it was a sniper with a rifle. We're pinned down and I can't leave my mark. Get up here ASAP."

Lije clung helplessly to the grass and pressed the side of his face to the ground. For the second time shots rang out and he offered no help. As he hugged the turf, he wondered if he had responded the same way on Farraday Road. Had he lain there just as scared that night? Was the final image Kaitlyn had of him one of an impotent coward, and was that why he was alive right now?

Curtis pulled out her gun.

"Teddy'll be here in two or three minutes. There's not enough cover between us and the trees for the gunman to approach, and the angle of the hill makes it impossible for him to get us while we're on the ground. We'll be safe until backup gets here. Just keep hugging the grass."

She had been right to close the shades, Lije thought. "I'm starting to get mad. I'm tired of being used for target practice."

"Can't blame you. I'm not thrilled about this either."

If she was scared, she didn't show it. "It's my fault," he whispered. It was a reality that he had to admit. That he was the target all along.

"What?" Curtis hissed.

"I must have done something to put myself in danger, but I have no clue what it is."

She didn't respond, which only confirmed his fear. Kaitlyn was dead. With the shooters still after him, this was all about him. And he was to blame. But what had he done?

Not seeing a gunman or hearing more shots almost made things worse. The silence brought new fear. Each second seemed like an hour. Was someone sneaking toward them? And the darkness, creeping closer with each tick of the clock, created its own insecurities. It was only the sound of a siren followed by bright blue emergency lights that allowed him to finally breathe easier.

"Can we get up now?" he asked.

"Not yet," Curtis said. "We've got to wait until Teddy checks that clump of trees." Hitting redial on her phone, she set up the search pattern with Teddy, then waited.

"Got it," Curtis said as she snapped her phone closed. She looked over at Lije. "There was no one in the trees. But I'm not taking any more chances. I'm putting out a warrant for my main suspect's arrest."

"I DIDN'T DO IT! NOT ANY OF IT!" HEATHER JAMESON cried as she was paraded out of her apartment. "Lije, you have to believe me!"

Lije nodded, assuring her that he did believe in her, even if there was nothing to go on but faith. He stood and watched as the crying woman was marched toward the squad car. Just before she was forced into the back seat, Heather turned to look back toward him. "In my desk, the third drawer down on the right, there's a box. In it is something that Kaitlyn was saving for your anniversary present."

Lije nodded and smiled, but said nothing. He opened his cell phone.

"What are you doing?" Curtis said.

"Calling a friend who's the best defense lawyer I know. This is not just hard to believe, it's impossible to fathom. And I don't believe it. Heather's going to need a top-flight criminal mind at her table. After all, she's battling the fabled ABI and its up-and-coming star, Special Agent Diana Curtis."

"Before you make that call, you need to have some of the evidence we have against her. There's a lot more than you know about. It's not just about finding her in the vicinity of your home tonight. She had guns in her apartment. That's not unusual, but they had been fired recently. Her car was warm."

He turned to face her. "You know the evidence, and that's all well and good; I respect you. But I know Heather Jameson, and I know she would have had no part in any of this."

"You don't know about her drug problem."

"We knew about it. She told us about her past when I interviewed her."

"She's up to her ears in debt."

"Kaitlyn informed me of that a few weeks ago. She found out by accident. Neither of us let on to Heather that we knew. But we would have bailed her out before she lost everything."

"Then I'm guessing you know why she has spent so much money in the last few months."

He looked at Curtis. "Tell me what you know."

"We figure she fell off the wagon. Probably pushed by her mother's suicide."

"You're wrong. Dig a little deeper and you'll find a logical reason for her problems. I'll bet you it won't be drugs either. And, by the way, just in case I'm right and you're wrong, you might want to keep your eyes open. Someone is still trying to kill me, and it's not Heather."

THE LARGE OUTER ROOM OF THE EVANS LAW OFFICE
was furnished with well-maintained antiques. Most of the wood
in the desk, tables, chairs, and shelves was tiger oak. On the walls
were paintings of scenes from the area as well as an imposing
three-by-four-foot portrait of Lije's grandfather. John and Lije
shared the same dark hair, gray eyes, and firm jaw.

Lije went through the swinging gate in the railing that separated the entry from the working part of the firm. Curtis was
about to follow him when she glanced back over her shoulder.

"Come on, Diana. Heather's office is down the hall and to the
left."

"You go ahead. I'm going to lock the front door and close the
blinds. Anyone in the area could see us."

"And get off a good shot." He hoped his mocking tone wasn't
too subtle to be missed. She wasn't as sure about Heather as she
claimed to be, and they both knew it.

Lije made his way into the young lawyer's office, flipped on the
desk lamp, and slid open the drawer. Sitting on top, right where
Heather said it would be, was a small, slate-blue metal box with a
combination lock. He placed it on top of the desk.

"That's it?" Curtis asked as she entered the room.

Turning the box so the numbers faced him, he studied it. For
several minutes, he didn't move. All the while he felt Curtis staring

at him. Finally, when her patience ran out, she asked, "Are you try-ing to guess the combination?"

"Nope," he replied softly. "I'm sure I know it. It'll be Kaitlyn's birthday."

He hesitated because he was afraid. Did he really want to see what was inside? If this was meant to be an anniversary gift, then it was meant to be something they would share. Kaitlyn was dili-gent in always finding the perfect surprise, so this would have to be very special. The better the gift, the more it was probably going to hurt. He wasn't ready for that pain. He wasn't sure if he would ever be ready for that kind of pain.

Laying the box back on its base, he moved past Curtis and into the hall. "I'm going into my office, catch up on the news online, and check my email." Did he really need to explain himself to her? Of course not. So why did he?

For a few minutes Lije tried to read the top stories of the day and run through his work-related email. He even spent a couple of minutes searching for car parts on auction. Yet all the time, the box was begging him to come back, pleading with him to spin the lock. Even though he tried to put it out of his mind, make it disap-pear, it wouldn't leave him alone. Minute by minute, its call grew stronger. Finally, it was screaming at him.

He got up from his desk, folded his arms, and closed his eyes. A part of him was curious, but that side of his brain was having problems competing with the side that held an overriding fear. He leaned against the wall and tried to guess what the box might hold, but the fear was scoring the most points. Fear was mak-ing a good argument too. With Kaitlyn gone, what difference did the gift make? There would be no anniversaries to celebrate any-way. Didn't that fact trump the need for gifts? Didn't that trump curiosity?

The only sounds were the ticking of an antique wall clock in the front room, the hum of fluorescent lights, and his own breath-ing. He looked back across the hallway, into Heather's office, and saw that Curtis hadn't moved. She had taken a seat in front of Heather's desk and seemed content to wait for Lije to return and break the silence. He wondered how long she would wait. Would she break before he did?

Just when he was about to cave in to his fear, he decided he needed answers. He needed answers so he could move on.

Still there were doubts. Did he really want to move on? What was the point? Because he knew that when he took that step forward, it would be a step taken without his wife.

In silence he waited another twenty minutes.

"I used to tease Kaitlyn by not opening her presents when she gave them to me. I'd set them aside and find something else to do. It could be a bit of work, or checking my email, or watching a television show, or maybe taking out the trash. I'd just find anything to keep me busy, because it would drive her crazy having to wait for me to open her gift. A couple of times she grew so frustrated she would grab the boxes and open them for me. Then just hand me the presents."

"You were mean," Curtis said.

He nodded. "Now, here I am putting off opening this box, not as part of a game but because I know it will be the last present. This is her final surprise. After I see what's inside, then the joy of wondering what her special gifts are will be finished forever."

The thought chilled him. It sucked the air from his lungs and the blood from his brain. It was that reality he was still unwilling to face, the unspoken truth he was avoiding. He had to talk about it. He needed to explain how he felt. And Curtis was the only one here to listen.

"Diana, until this moment I've done a really good job of running from the fact that Kaitlyn died. I think I was the only person who didn't cry at her funeral. The reason ... I was too much of a coward. I've been using the same tactics I used with her gifts to not acknowledge her death. I've found menial things to keep my focus off the one thing I can't face—that I'm never going to see her again. When I open this box, I'll be admitting that she's dead."

He didn't expect her to comment. She didn't. And then he was disappointed. Did she not care or just not know what to say? He might as well have been alone. In fact, he wished he was alone.

Grabbing the box with his left hand, he spun the four small dials. Once he had them positioned, he returned the box to the desk and turned his chair toward his guest. "You're the CSI. Any guesses?"

"No."

"That's disappointing. I figured with all your training you'd at least have a hunch."

"No hunches." She lobbed the question back at him. "How about you? Do you have any ideas?"

Lije turned his gaze back to the box and shook his head. He made no move to open the lid.

Curtis waited a couple of minutes before announcing, "It's time."

"Forgive me if I sound bitter here," he said, "but not everything's about the case. This might just be personal."

He ran two fingers along the edge of the box. Then he looked up. "Something hit me as I stood alone in the hallway. Diana, sometime in the near future, when the ABI puts a closed stamp on what happened here, you'll walk away. Your life won't be that greatly influenced by this case because, for you, there will be hundreds of others. But for me, the rest of my life has been dramatically altered. And, if you're right, and Heather is the one behind this, then my faith will be altered too. Faith in people. Even my faith in God."

She offered no words of comfort. He wondered if she was trying to understand what he was feeling or just curious about what Kaitlyn had found to surprise him.

Lije sighed. "Like you said, it's time."

Dread consumed him as he placed his trembling hand on the box, his thumb resting at the front edge of the lid. A sharp pain ripped through his gut at the point where the bullet had exited his body. He looked down to see if the stitches had ripped open, but there was no blood on his white shirt and he felt no flowing warmth against his body.

He would have simply respun the numbers that controlled the lock, put this box back in the drawer, and let it sit for months if not for one thing. He felt there was a chance—probably a very slight one—that what was under the lid would help him make some sense of what had happened. Clinging to that thought, he pulled open the lid and forced himself to look inside.

On top of a stack of folded papers was a ring holding several keys. The metal was dark and the keys, except for one, appeared to be decades old. Unfolding the documents, he read through the first page and then scanned the next one. After leafing through them all, he put the papers back on Heather's desk and fixed his gaze on the key ring.

Curtis seemed to feel the need to respect his silence, but finally her curiosity got the better of her. "Lije?"

"Kaitlyn bought Swope's Ridge, the old German's house, and all 359 acres."

"That's the property you wanted to build a home on?"

"Sure is, the most beautiful site on Spring River."

Kaitlyn was going to surprise him with the chance to finally see what the world looks like from on top of the hill. Swope's Ridge. She had really outdone herself this time. Her last gift was a real winner. Yet it was the one, more than all the others, that was meant to be shared by two. Now it was nothing more than a scenic hand of solitare.

"How could she make such a huge purchase without your knowing? I mean, this must have cost …"

"Over a million dollars," Lije said. "And she paid for it in cash."

"I assume that you'd have had to know if that much money was being withdrawn from your account."

"I'd have known if it was out of the joint account. But about a dozen years ago, when her father died, he left her several hundred thousand dollars. We didn't need the money, so I suggested she invest it. After giving away about twenty percent to some of her causes, she opted to buy stock in Apple Computer. Let's just say that Steve Jobs and his company were very good to her. I knew she'd sold some of the stock a while back, but I have no idea how she could have bought Swope's Ridge."

"She just keeps surprising you."

Lije didn't hear Diana's comment. He'd tried to buy the place for years, but the original owner wouldn't sell it to him. How did Kaitlyn get him to change his mind?

Lije put the paperwork back into the box, closed the lid, spun the dials, and slid the metal case back into the desk drawer. He slipped the keys into his pants pocket and turned out the desk lamp. "Let's go."

They walked out the front door of the office and got into the Cord.

"It seems to me," Curtis said, "that you were less surprised by the gift and more surprised by the fact that Kaitlyn could actually buy the property."

He pulled up to the street and slid the car into first. "Yeah, the German immigrant who bought the property right after World War II was very reclusive. To my knowledge he had no family and, based on what those around that area told me, no friends. He didn't farm, raise livestock, or hold a job. Yet he lived pretty well. I was told he always had plenty of money for the modest things he needed. Of course, who knows about such talk — might have been rumors. Yet he had this incredible property and, from what I understand, rarely left his home. It was like he was hiding from the world rather than enjoying it. So, needless to say, he wouldn't even hear an offer, though I understand plenty of folks tried to talk to him."

"So Kaitlyn charmed him?"

Lije preselected second gear and mashed on the clutch before answering. "No, he died about five years ago."

"Who did she buy it from?"

Bathed in the glow of the ancient car's green dash lights, Lije thought back to the papers he had just scanned. He had glanced at the name. A few minutes later, as he pulled the car into the barn, he finally admitted, "For the life of me I can't recall the name of the previous owner. I'm usually really good with both names and numbers. I can look it up tomorrow."

Curtis shrugged. "Let me know who owned it."

About halfway along the path back to the house, Lije stopped and glanced back toward the clump of trees that earlier had sheltered the shooter. Pointing to the spot, he asked, "The rifleman was right down there?"

"The riflewoman."

For some reason, the old television show *The Rifleman*, which he had watched as a kid in reruns, jumped into his mind. And then he had the name. The first name of the sheriff on the show was Micah. "That's it," he shot back.

"That's what?"

"The name of the previous owner of Swope's Ridge. Kaitlyn bought the property from the estate of Micah Dean."

"Does that name sound familiar to you? I feel like I've heard it somewhere."

Lije made his way to his study and did an internet search for Micah Dean. The results led him to the archives of the *Arkansas Democrat-Gazette*.

"Micah Dean was murdered a couple of years ago. Shot by a man named Jonathon Jennings. He was found guilty and got the death penalty."

"Yeah," Curtis said as she walked into the study from the kitchen. "That's it. We didn't do any actual location work on that case, but we did process evidence. I think the motive was over some real estate. Could that have been ..."

Turning his attention back to the monitor, Lije read through several more paragraphs: "'The disagreement began when Dean would not listen to a financial offer presented by real-estate agent Jennings. The offer, made by the agent on behalf of a supposed out-of-state party whom Jennings could not produce at the trial, was for several hundred acres of land on the Spring River. The property is best known by the name of the lumberman who initially settled the land back in the mid-1800s, Oval Swope.'"

"Swope's Ridge," he whispered.

THE MATRON ORDERED HEATHER JAMESON TO STRIP. Silently, with the stranger's eyes taking in her every move, she did what she was told. She had never been so humiliated and never felt so hopeless.

"Turn around," the woman ordered as she slipped on a latex glove. After Heather had slowly done a three-sixty, the matron said, "Now bend over and spread your legs." It simply couldn't get any worse, but it did.

She was left to stand naked for a while before being issued an orange jumpsuit. Then the same unyielding eyes that had watched her undress studied her just as carefully as she put on the uniform of an accused. Finally, convinced she wasn't hiding anything anywhere on or in her body, the guard left her alone in the eight-by-eight cell.

The blame had started when she was just a kid, and she realized she had no control over it. Her dad was a drunk, coming home every night to tell her that his drinking was her fault. Her mother's death—her fault. That even she knew was her fault. She had told her mother that her dad would change if only her mother would stick it out, stay in the marriage. But her real reason for not wanting her mother to leave was that she didn't want to be from a broken home. Her dad could change; she knew it. But he didn't change, and her mother ended her life with a bottle of pills.

In college she had a clean-cut boyfriend who had his act together until she convinced him to start doing drugs. He saved her one night from an overdose, and she cleaned up her act. She showed up too late one night to save him, and he died. Because of her.

She told her little brother to join the army to escape life at home. He was one week from returning home from Iraq when the officer showed up at their house to deliver the news of his death. Because of her.

And now Kaitlyn, murdered.

Was that her fault too? If only she hadn't ...

The cell contained a sparsely outfitted bed, a metal sink, and a commode. There wasn't even a mirror. But that seemed like a gift. She couldn't bear to look at herself. This jail cell was her present and her future. This was the way it would be from now on.

Death suddenly seemed like a welcome friend. Life had the sting. Her best friend dead. Her family ... she couldn't think of that. In over her head in debt. And now she was accused of killing a woman she admired more than any other she had ever known. Sitting there, alone, she continued to warm to the idea of taking an early leave from a cold and cruel world.

Pressing her knees to her chest, she pulled her arms around her legs and began to gently rock back and forth on her bunk. After a while she felt her lips form a strange smile. Was she taking the first step toward madness? The thought of falling into the snake pit somehow brought her a sense of security. Crazy! She could blame it all on being crazy. But what if she really was crazy? What if she was so crazy she had done it and blacked out? What if? No, no, no, that wasn't right. She wasn't crazy. Or was she?

Minutes passed like hours and hours like days and at dawn her face was still wrapped in a look of mental confusion. She was going mad, and it was a trip she wanted to make. She wanted to go so mad that she forgot everything — her father, her brother, her mother, her boyfriend, Kaitlyn.

The journey to oblivion was interrupted when she heard footsteps outside her cell door. She glanced up and heard a key inserted into her door lock. The door opened and a tall man with kind brown eyes walked into the cell. He seemed like a tired old dog that needed a pat on the head. He did look tired, but he wasn't old.

"I'm Kent McGee."

She knew who he was. He and Lije were friends. But could she trust him? Rather than answer, she just nodded. He looked like a young Mark Harmon. She liked Mark Harmon. Loved him on *NCIS*, Tuesday nights. He was nice. Maybe McGee was all right. He had made a name for himself. But why had he come to see her?

A few days before, she would have tried to get a date with McGee. She would have turned on the charm and given herself permission to flirt. But that was the old Heather. This was the new crazy Heather. So he could've been Brad Pitt and it wouldn't have mattered. Nothing mattered now.

She stayed on the bunk, her arms still wrapped around her legs.

"Miss Jameson, Elijah Evans called me and asked me to represent you. He believes you're innocent and wants to make sure we get this cleared up as soon as possible. I am here to help you."

LIJE WOKE TO THE SOUND OF THE PHONE RINGING.
It was already past nine. He rolled out of bed, not believing he
had actually slept, much less slept this late. The pills Dr. Herring
had prescribed and that Curtis had forced him to take had really
knocked him out. It was the first real rest he'd had in days.

But he still felt horrid.

"Lije here," he said.

"It's Kent. I've spent some time with Heather Jameson and she
won't talk to me. I've tried to explain that I need to have certain
information and she just clams up. I know she's a lawyer and I
know she knows better, but as scared as she is, she's not going to
help me help her. It's like working with someone with mob connections. To them death's not as scary as dealing with the dark human
forces of this world. I think she's given up. I think she wants to be
found guilty. Or crazy."

Lije was confused. This sounded nothing like the Heather he
knew. "That's not like Heather. What's the sticking point? Where's
the roadblock?"

"Where the money went. You told me she's in big financial
trouble. She simply will not tell me anything about it. She claims
she can't. I think she's protecting someone. But if she's not going
to help me, then I'm not going to be able to help her. By the way,

the drug test came back clean. She says she's been clean for a long time."

Trying to overcome his grogginess, Lije attempted to put together a plan. Heather had to wise up, but maybe she had to be with someone she trusted. It might be that he was the only person who was close enough to her to have a chance at getting the truth. "Where are you now?"

"I checked into the Creekway Motel when I got here," McGee answered. "Not much in the way of luxury, but I did get a good night's sleep."

"Well, check out now. We'll move you into my guest house. There's lots of room. And you can use my office to work."

"Listen Lije, sounds great, but I want to keep you out of the middle of what's going on. A media circus has come to town and you don't need to be one of the performers. I've seen this show before and it's always ugly. Hordes of news crews camping out, TV and cable networks, *Court TV*, newspapers, magazines. I've even heard that *Entertainment Tonight* is coming. What I need is an office with a couple of desks, nothing fancy."

"You're probably right. I'll arrange an office for you. But why the national attention?"

"Your case is big news. It's been the number-one story on TV and in the print media in this region. It's now gone national. And why not? Murder of a beautiful woman in a small town, wife of the local rich guy, who also is gunned down. Another attempt on his life. A lawyer who works for him is arrested. Lije, I've been in this business long enough to know that this is the perfect story for the press."

"I know. I've watched it myself too many times," Lije said.

"I figure the shows will start by implying a sordid love triangle. Think of the worst thing you can imagine, then go further. Not only is Heather going to be dragged through the mud, so are you, my friend. You don't need to be seen with the chief suspect's lawyer.

Not good for you and not good for her. We have to keep you as far away from me as possible. We can't even be seen talking."

Stunned, Lije stood up and carried the cordless phone to the far side of the master bedroom. Peeking between the blinds, he saw that it was a beautiful, cloud-free day. No reporters were camped outside.

"Listen Kent, from your experience, how long before the real media circus comes to town? I don't see anyone outside now. How long before it's more than just the area and state media?"

"Probably a few days. The ABI doesn't want the lid to blow off until they're sure they have a bulletproof case. And, for the moment, they seem to have local authorities under control."

It was time to shuffle the facts. What did he have? What did he know? If he placed his cards on the table, he might come up with a plan that would help clear Heather. He knew she was innocent. Which meant the real killers were still out there. Heather had no connection to Farraday Road, at least none that he knew. But the ABI was acting as if the case was all but over. Heather supposedly near the house last night; Heather and her debts.

And then there was Swope's Ridge. One man had already died because of it. Was that the connection?

Those were the cards, and this was not a hand he wanted to hold. To begin to understand how to play, he was going to have to go to the source, the only one alive with a link.

"Okay, Kent, here's what I'll do. I'll go down and see Heather, find out what she's hiding, and give you a call. I'm sure I can convince her to talk to me. And don't try to talk me out of it. This might well be the only day I can do it without creating video footage for *Extra*."

Crossing back across the room to his dresser, he glanced in the mirror. All things considered, he looked much better than he felt. "I'll call you in an hour or so. I'll get what you need from Heather."

"Fine," McGee replied. "While you're at the jail, I'll call Hillman's office, try to get the full details of the crime, then I've got some research to do. Listen, if you don't get Heather to open up, I'm afraid all my courtroom theatrics won't do much good. And whatever you do, avoid the media."

"I'll call you when I know something." He tossed the phone onto his bed. It was time to go to work.

Lije was drinking a Coke for breakfast when Curtis entered the kitchen.

"Are you still babysitting me?"

"Yes, for the time being."

"Then I guess the only way you're going to do your job is by sticking with me. I'm going to visit Heather and then visit Dean's widow in Mountain View, which is south and west of here."

Before she could reply, Curtis's phone rang. She listened for a few moments, asked, "Are you sure?" and then hung up.

"What's up?"

"Somebody just brought a coat back to the diner. Seems a local businessman picked it up by mistake the night you were there. Said it looked a lot like his. So the one in Melbourne could be yours. There wasn't anything in the pockets, but I still need to pick it up so the lab can go over it. And I need you to confirm it is yours."

"I'll go with you." Kaitlyn had bought the coat for him in New York. It was made by the Westchester Clothing Company. She thought it was a perfect match for the Cord. He always figured that when she bought it she had been motivated by the romantic image of Humphrey Bogart in the old films she loved so much. She always insisted he wear it when they went out on a foggy or rainy night. When this was all over, when the lab was finished, he wanted that coat back.

"There's one more thing," Curtis said. "With Jameson in jail, the state isn't going to foot the bill for protection anymore. So I'll be leaving."

Lije wasn't going to argue with the hand fate had tossed his way, even if it placed him in greater danger. "Do you want me to take my own car then?"

"No, not for the trip to the jail," the agent replied. "I'll take you down there and to Melbourne. But after you look at the coat and I bring you back, you're on your own."

"Tell you what. I'll take the Cord. Once I get to Melbourne, I don't want to have to come back home and then drive all the way to Melbourne again to get to Mountain View."

LIJE WAS ALONE IN THE CLASSIC CORD AS HE DROVE
down Shell Hill. After stopping off at his office to pick up the
metal box containing the papers for the land deal, he drove to the
jail. He parked the Cord and saw Curtis standing by her Victoria.
He nodded in her direction, but headed toward the front door of
the building. He wasn't shocked when she jumped into action. It
was as if she were racing him for a prize. Lije grabbed the door
handle a second before Curtis.

"I win," he said. "No, it's your turn to listen. This is private.
There's information I need. Heather's not going to tell me anything unless we're alone. So you're not coming any farther than
the front desk. Understand?"

Curtis didn't like it and he could see she thought about arguing.
"Fine. Just don't keep me waiting too long."

After being processed, Lije was led into the visitor's room. It
was stark, cold, and smelled of Lysol. It seemed more like a morgue
than an area set aside for meetings. For two minutes he shared the
room with only the odor. Then the matron, a heavyset woman he
had known for years, ushered Heather in.

Heather was handcuffed and shackled, dressed in an orange
jumpsuit. It was obvious she hadn't slept. Looking at her dishev-
eled hair and frightened expression, he couldn't believe this was

the same woman he had worked with for three years. The zombies in old horror films looked better than she did.

"Heather, how are you doing?"

The matron guided her into a chair across the table from him.

"I'm okay, I guess."

"Could you leave us alone?" Lije asked the matron.

"Sheriff Wood doesn't want this woman hurting anybody else, so he ordered me to stay with y'all."

"She's chained," Lije pointed out. "She weighs about a hundred and ten pounds, and she's across a four-foot table from me. I'm fine. Watch through the window if you like, but we need to be alone when I talk to her."

"But you ain't her lawyer," the woman argued. "I met him this morning."

Lije stood and walked toward her. "Gladys," he whispered as he put his right arm around her shoulder, "I've known you a long time. You know me well enough to realize I wouldn't be here if I thought for an instant Heather was behind any of those things they're saying she did."

The woman leaned closer. "Lije, you mean you really don't think she did it? Really?"

"I don't think she had a thing to do with any of it, but for me to set the record straight, I must have a few minutes alone with her. Go tell the sheriff what I just told you, and then the two of you can watch through the window over there. If anything happens, just rush in. Okay?"

She nodded, took another look at Heather, and walked out the door. He waited for her to appear at the window before moving back to the table and taking a seat. "Okay, Heather, how are you really doing?"

She fell apart. "I really didn't do any of this! I had no part in it! But I realize I've dug a deep hole and jumped in. How did I get into this mess?"

Leaning forward, Lije said, "McGee can get you out of that hole and show everyone connected with this case that they're wrong about you, but you have to help him. The motive they're tying this to appears to be your urgent need for money. I'm told you've gone through more than twenty-five thousand and you're even behind on your car payments. The DA will combine the money with your past drug addiction and your family situation. They know about your guns. There's enough circumstantial evidence to make Mc-Gee's job very difficult. So I have to know what you were doing with the money."

Moving her chair closer to the table, she whispered, "I can't tell McGee and I can't tell you."

"Why?"

"Because …" The word seemed to freeze on her tongue. Her eyes darted back and forth before she mouthed, "Because they'll kill him if I do."

Lije leaned back in his chair, tented his fingers in front of his face and studied Heather. The confident and outgoing lawyer was gone. The woman sitting across the table looked as if she was being strangled by a silent and invisible foe. Something had complete power over her. But what was it and when had it begun?

"They'll kill who?" he asked.

She just shook her head.

Putting his hands on the table, he said, "At least tell me when this started."

She hesitated, looking over at the matron through the glass. "About three months ago."

He knew her well, had seen her almost every day for the past three years, but he could not think of anything that had occurred then that would've so altered her life and judgment. But as he thought about it, there *had* been a subtle personality change. She had tried to mask it, but she had seemed more on edge and much more emotional than normal. She had made silly mistakes on contracts, gotten angry over seemingly insignificant comments from clients, and had been late to several meetings. Until this moment they had all seemed insignificant and he had written them off. What had triggered that erratic behavior?

"Heather, this is between you and me for the moment. I trust you enough to know that you didn't kill Kaitlyn. Now you have to trust me."

"But ..."

"If I find that what you tell me is so sensitive that it might cause someone else to die, then I won't pass it on to McGee. But you have to tell me ... now."

The terrified woman looked down at the table. He watched her for just a moment and then said, "Heather, snap out of it. What's going on?"

"It's ... about my brother." Her voice was barely above a whisper.

"Jim?"

"Yes. If I tell you what's going on, they'll kill him."

"Who?"

"The terrorists."

"Heather, Jim was killed in Iraq over a year ago. I was at his funeral."

"WE ALL THOUGHT JIM DIED IN IRAQ," HEATHER whispered, "but he's alive!"

Lije stared open-mouthed at her. He couldn't believe what she had just said. "How do you know? How did you find out?"

"Three months ago the assistant director at the funeral home in Springfield called me. He said the army opened the grave and reexamined the body. It wasn't Jim in the coffin. It was another member of his unit. DNA proved it. We had been told that Jim's body couldn't be identified because of the IED blast, so they had used his personal effects and dog tags to ID the body, or what was left of it. They made a mistake."

"Didn't the army call and tell you?"

"No, they just told the funeral home to rebury the casket. My dad and I were never notified."

"What about the other family?"

"I checked. I got the name from the funeral home. Also the town where they lived. They had a funeral for their son a few weeks later."

"So where is Jim now? Why did the funeral home call you?"

She sighed. "I'm getting to that. The man at the funeral home—his name is Paul Meyers—told me that the casket was empty. He said he would not have known that except my mother had asked him to put a Bible in with Jim before he was buried.

He'd forgotten, so before they put the casket back in the ground, he opened the lid, and that's when he discovered there was no body inside."

"This all sounds pretty unbelievable. Is Meyers your only source for this?"

Now that her secret was out, Heather seemed more like herself. "Yes. Meyers told me he confronted the colonel who was in charge of the exhumation. The colonel told Meyers that Jim was considered missing in action, but to make it easier on us, since they still believed he had been killed, he was still being listed as killed in action."

Lije nodded. "Sounds to me like someone is covering their tail. Go ahead, let me hear the rest of it."

"So the colonel told Meyers to forget the exhumation ever happened. Meyers told me it bothered him so much that he couldn't sleep and that's why he called me. He said he'd done some checking and found someone who could help me. He said that person would call me in a few days."

"And did someone call?" Lije asked. His skepticism had kicked in and he wondered why Heather had not recognized what he believed was a carefully orchestrated scam targeting grieving military families.

"Yes. A few days later I got a call from a man in Memphis. He asked to meet with me. He said Jim was alive. I took the next day off from work and drove to Memphis. We talked for about an hour in the corner of a motel restaurant. His name was Charles Sutton. He said he had spent thirty years working for the CIA. He showed me some identification. He explained that when he retired, he started using his contacts to quietly rescue people who were being held captive in Third World nations. He produced a blurry photo of Jim and said he was being held in Iraq by one of the radical groups aligned with Al-Qaeda."

"And you believed him," Lije said.

"I was horrified. Sutton said that every horror I could think of was being used on my brother. He said his sources indicated Jim probably couldn't last another six months. To me, this was worse than his being dead. He was alone and forgotten. He had no way to get out."

"I'm guessing," Lije said, "that Sutton told you he had the connections to get Jim out of Iraq and back home."

"Yes, he even gave me a list of names of people he had helped to free. I recognized two Italians and a man from New Zealand from photos I had seen in *Newsweek*."

"Heather, how much did he tell you it was going to cost?"

After brushing at her tears with the back of her hand, she said, "He assured me he had a solid retirement plan and wanted nothing for himself, but it would take at least fifty thousand dollars to buy Jim's freedom and pay his way back to the States. He also told me that if the story got out in the news, Jim and several other Americans being secretly held in Iraq would be executed. He showed me video on his computer of a beheading. It was horrible. I couldn't let Jim die like that."

"When was the last time you heard from Sutton?"

"About a week ago."

"How much have you already paid him?"

"Thirty thousand dollars."

"And how much more do you have to pay him to buy Jim's freedom?"

"I have to FedEx twenty thousand dollars to his office by the end of the month. The address is in my desk. And it has to be in cash. The terrorists want American money."

Drumming his fingers on the table, Lije considered his options. His first impulse was to roll his eyes at Heather; she'd been taken in by a scam that anyone should have seen through. Yet if the story the funeral director had told her was true, then he could see how she would fall for the pitch. With no real family other than an alcoholic father, she had tossed reason out the window and embraced the impossible story. No use yelling at her now; she could beat herself up later.

"Lije? Is it all a lie?"

Reality had set in.

"I don't know about the part concerning your brother's body—that much might be true. But you can be sure that Sutton took you for a ride. Now that I know what's going on, we'll get this thing fixed. Don't worry."

Getting up from the table, Lije waved at Gladys. He watched her come in, help Heather from her chair, and escort her from the room. He considered his next move. McGee could pull the strings needed to find out quickly if Jim's body was in the grave. That would be easy. Armed with this information, McGee surely had the contacts to find, dress down, and then expose Charles Sutton.

He picked up his personal items at the front desk and walked back out into the sunny parking lot. Curtis was waiting for him just outside the front door like a loyal puppy.

"Well, did you get the information you needed to free her and make me look like a fool?"

"Nope. But I'm just getting started."

ARKANSAS 9 WOUND ITS WAY THROUGH THE OZARK foothills like a gray ribbon batted about by a kitten. In places it almost met itself coming and going. As with most things in the northern Arkansas Ozarks, the shoulderless asphalt had changed little in fifty years. The scenery along the highway was so tranquil it was hard to believe that a murder had taken place just off this stretch of road. But as Lije motored the Cord past Farraday Road, which was now closed, the peace of the morning was shattered by haunting images sucking the air from his lungs and the strength from his resolve. To bury memories he could neither accept nor change, Lije spent most of the thirty-minute drive down Arkansas 9 to Melbourne talking with Kent McGee on his cell phone, updating him on his conversation with Heather. He was only a couple of miles from Jim's Diner when he finally snapped shut his phone and followed Curtis's Crown Victoria into the parking lot.

He switched off the motor and eased back into the soft fawn-leather seat. He let his mind drift a moment. Then he saw Curtis was waiting for him. He sighed and got out of the Cord and closed the door. Then he leaned forward and rested his arms on the roof of the car and waited for her to join him.

"Diana, I want you to consider this." Though it hardly seemed the wise thing to do, Lije told Curtis what Heather had told him.

"She's clearly guilty," Curtis assured him. "This explains the motive."

Lije shook his head. "This Sutton obviously is preying on families who've lost loved ones in the war. I'm sure he's done his homework, knows who Heather is and who she works for. So when she was having problems coming up with the cash, he might well have seen an opportunity to soak her for even more money. Probably figured Heather would get some business insurance payoff if he could get my wife and me out of the way. Then, instead of picking up another twenty grand, he could probably stretch things out and collect a whole lot more."

The look on her face indicated Curtis might be considering what he was suggesting. Still, when she didn't respond, he doubted he'd gotten her to change her mind.

"Has anyone found out anything about Mikki Stuart?" he asked.

"No, the trail's gone cold."

"The fact that you have Heather but can't find Mikki is kind of strange. Do you really think that Heather, in her state of mind, had the ability to find and hire a hit man and arrange for the investigating officer to disappear? I don't. I think pulling off something like this had to involve some planning and brains."

He was trying to push Curtis into a corner, but she wasn't falling into his trap. "I don't care what you think about her state of mind," she said, "Jameson's a smart girl. She was desperate. You just told me she believed time was ticking down for her brother."

"Diana ..." He said the name as if they were friends, which he was now sure they weren't. "If she *was* as smart as you *say* she is, then she would've seen through Sutton's con." Lije knew he was the last line of defense for Heather, so he refused to give an inch. "You want to make this case fit, but if you look closely at every facet, you'll see there's no solid evidence."

"Do you want to go in with me to get the coat or not?"

Lije leaned back against the rear driver's side door. The last

thing he wanted to do was go inside the last place he and Kaitlyn
had visited before her death. "No. If you aren't going to be gone
long, I'll stay here."

"I'll make it fast."

As he waited, Lije studied the small building of native stone,
which was common for the area. He knew from what his parents
had told him that the building had always been a restaurant since
its construction in the 1920s. In the three decades he had been
stopping here, very little had changed. Even the tables were the
same ones he had sat at with his parents. Yet he would never again
be able to look at the third window on the left side and not remember the last minutes he spent with Kaitlyn. It was almost as if he
could see her sitting there now, looking out into that fatal night's
dark rain. He remembered her calm. He had wanted to rush out to
the car and drive through the downpour, but she convinced him
it was smarter just to wait it out. "What's the hurry?" she had
asked.

Then she had smiled. "We have our whole lives ahead of us,
you know."

"WHAT ARE YOU LOOKING AT, LIJE?"

"Nothing." He was not ready to admit he had been staring at a memory that looked more real than Curtis did. "Did you get the coat?"

"It's in the bag," she said, holding up a paper sack. "I need you to identify it."

In truth, he wasn't interested. Seeing that image in the window had weakened his resolve for freeing Heather Jameson. Yet the coat somehow played into the case, so he nodded.

"You're going to have to put on gloves."

Curtis opened the rear door of her car and retrieved two pairs of latex gloves from her kit. She put on her gloves, handed the other pair to Lije, then pulled out the coat from the bag.

"I looked at it in the office of the diner. I didn't see anything of note except for cleaner's marks written inside the left pocket."

Holding it at arm's length, Lije studied the coat for a few seconds, glancing at the label. He opened the pockets and looked at the numbers written on the inside of the left one — 2765-17.

"It's not mine. My coat, as I told you earlier, was made by the Westchester Clothing Company. The label says this one came from Holland Clothing. Looks like someone else got mine that night. There were several on the rack when we came in. The one I thought was mine was the only one hanging there when we left."

"Well," Curtis said, "another dead end. We'll let the lab guys go over it and see what they find."

Curtis slipped the coat back into the bag. Lije smiled. Kent would be able to use this against the prosecution. He'd point out that the way the coat Lije was wearing that night was ripped off him meant the killers were after the coat or something in it. With more than two coats in the mix, it would cast doubt on the case against Heather.

Curtis stepped away and started talking on her cell phone in a hushed tone. She didn't look happy, and Lije was sure that if she was talking to the ABI director, they were both upset by this new turn in the case.

As he got back into the Cord, he looked again at the third window of the diner, hoping ... and then he saw her ... Kaitlyn looking out as if there were again rain falling. He sat very still, not moving, not wanting to lose sight of that beautiful face that would forever be at a distance.

LIJE WALKED UP ON THE FRONT PORCH OF THE DEAN
residence, a modest farmhouse about three miles west of Mountain
View. His 1936 Cord had taken a beating on the poorly maintained
dirt road leading in. Anyone driving by would think the red car
was brownish gray. It seemed he had managed to find the bottom
of every pothole as he wound through the mud and puddles.

Though the home and outbuildings needed major repair, the
tree-covered property was beautiful, peaceful. The small frame
home sat on a hill beside a huge oak. Large pines stood off to the
right and a small creek had cut a channel at the slope's base. With
some work, this out-of-the-way farm could become a gem.

But he had a job to do. And it was time to focus on the mission.
He walked purposefully to the front door. Just before ringing the
bell, he glanced over his shoulder. For the first time he wished
Curtis were with him. She'd probably be much better at uncovering evidence than he was going to be. Yet this was now his baby
and he had to rock it for all it was worth. Raising his hand, he
rapped on the wooden door. Would it bring him luck?

A heavyset, middle-aged woman opened the door, a diet drink
in her left hand and a cigarette dangling from her mouth. "What
do you want?"

Lije had met pit bulls with a friendlier bark.

"Mrs. Dean? I'm Lije Evans. I called you this morning."

"Yeah, I'm Mable Dean." Her gruff reply was followed by a se-ries of muffled coughs. Pulling the cigarette from her mouth, the woman wheezed a bit, cleared her throat, and glanced back toward the door. "You said you're from Salem?"

"Yes, that's right."

She waved her hand, leaving a trail of smoke as she did. "You said you wanted to ask about my husband and that cursed piece of land."

"If it wouldn't be too much trouble," Lije replied.

"I'll be happy to tell you what I know. Ain't got nothin' else to do. You can come on inside or we can talk here on the porch. Got some comfortable chairs around the corner on the south side."

Lije shifted his eyes to his left. He didn't relish breathing in smoke. "It's a pretty day. Let's take advantage of it."

"Fine with me," Mabel replied. "You go around and get com-fortable. I'm going to grab a pack of smokes and my lighter."

As his hostess disappeared into her home, Lije worked his way to the place Mabel had pointed out. He chased two cats and a mon-grel dog off an iron lawn chair and sat down.

To his right were three old cars partly concealed by tall weeds in the back yard. Beyond the cars was a jumbled pile of weathered boards that once might have been a barn. He was staring at the pile of wood when Mabel Dean returned.

"Yep, the old barn finally fell down in that storm. Of course, it was leaning pretty good for years. Micah didn't care much about fixing anything while he was alive, and since he's been gone, noth-ing has been done. I'm just not healthy enough." She waved at the wood. "That's the place where he died. Killed inside that old build-ing." Then, as if the thought of her husband's death meant little to her, she pointed to another part of the yard. "Guess I need to sell those old cars, but then where would I keep the chickens?"

Just then a yellow hen half flew and half jumped out of a broken rear window of a dark blue Chevy.

"I see what you mean," Lije said.

The bird scratched on the trunk of the car for a moment before hopping off into the weeds.

Lije turned back toward Mabel. "Mrs. Dean, I didn't come here to waste your valuable time, so I'll just get to the point of the visit."

"Cut to the chase, as Daddy used to say." Mabel laughed, pushing a strand of chestnut hair from her face. "But sweetie, I've got lots of time." Then she looked at Lije and winked. "And though it may not look like it, I'm a pretty rich woman."

"I'm sure you are," he replied, ignoring her flirting. "Anyway, I came over to ask you about—"

"Swope's Ridge," the woman said, taking a long draw on her unfiltered smoke.

"That's it," he answered.

"I was never so happy in all my life to get rid of that place. I absolutely loathed it."

"And why's that?"

Tossing her cigarette down on the porch and snuffing it out with her tennis shoe, Dean took a seat in one of the vacant chairs, pulled a pack from her pocket, and lit a fresh Camel. She savored a few puffs before looking back at her guest.

"Micah was obsessed with that place. We were married for more than thirty years, and for most of that time, it was all he talked about. Other men had hobbies, took vacations, watched TV, but not him. No, he just looked at maps of that place. The few times he did talk to me, it was about that cursed property. Really, Swope's Ridge was his mistress."

After taking another long draw on the cigarette, she said, "For the first twenty-five years or so, the German who owned it wouldn't let Micah on the land. I remember one night, about a decade ago, he took a canoe down the river and snuck onto the property. He thought he could explore the place after dark. Ah, the German was watching. They say he was always watching. Took a shotgun and pumped Micah full of rock salt. I was picking it out of him for days." She grinned. "I thought it was kind of funny."

She paused, laughed a bit, and took another puff. "You know, up until the German died, Micah had a good job working down at the water department. He was the supervisor. But then everything changed."

As Mabel turned her attention back to her cigarette, Lije waited impatiently for the story to continue. It would be a considerable wait. Mabel finished her smoke and lit another before she picked up her tale. While he waited, he considered her late husband's obsession with a piece of wooded riverfront property. Other than the view, what could be there worth dying for?

"When the German died," Mable continued, "Micah took all the money he had been saving and tried to buy Swope's Ridge. The lawyer handling the estate told him the German had left all his property and personal belongings to his great niece, who lived back in the Old Country. I hoped that'd be the end of it, but it wasn't. A few weeks later, the lawyer called, said the woman wanted to sell. The old fool accepted the asking price. Didn't even make a counter offer. Imagine, more than a half million bucks just flying out of the bank like a wild bird headed north for the summer."

"A half million?" Lije asked. He was shocked Micah Dean had been able to save that much cash.

"Yep, half a mill." Taking another drag on the cigarette, Dean smiled. "You're probably wondering where he got that kind of money. Well, I'll tell you, he never spent a cent on anything. He saved every dime he made. About twenty or so years ago, he was left a piece of nice property down toward Conway. It'd been his father's. My, there was a beautiful home on that place. I wanted to move there, but Micah sold it. When I started setting up a howl, he gave me a thousand and told me to spend it. I did, bought some new clothes, but that was all I got. You know, I don't even have any kids because he claimed we couldn't afford them. Kind of lonely now."

She suddenly seemed melancholy, as if remembering a sad moment. But it didn't capture her mind for long. Soon she was again weaving her tale.

"Should have left him. Should have never married him to begin with. You know, you might not guess it by looking at me now, but I was pretty once. Had my share of guys too."

"I can believe that," Lije said. By her smile, he sensed he had her momentarily charmed. "Why did Micah want Swope's Ridge? I'm guessing it wasn't so that he could move there."

"Heck no." The woman laughed. "I never even saw the place. I'm not sure he was ever even in the German's house. If he was, it was only once. For Micah, it was all about that darned old family legend." She tossed the spent cigarette onto the dirt and pulled out a replacement.

"Legend?" Lije asked, his voice showing both curiosity and confusion.

"You familiar with the property, Mr. ... I'm sorry, I've forgotten your last name."

"Evans. It's Lije Evans."

She stopped, as if trying to recall something, then took another long draw on the cigarette. "Your wife's the pretty thing who bought that place from me. She had kind of an Asian look about her."

Lije felt a jab of pain. It was all he could do not to show the grief that was suddenly rushing over him. "That was her."

"I heard she was killed a few days ago." Mabel's tone hadn't changed, as if death meant little to her.

He nodded.

"I'm so sorry. I tried to warn her."

WARN HER? WHAT DID SHE MEAN? LIJE LEANED
forward, suddenly alert. "Why did you warn her?"

Taking a nervous puff on the smoke, Mabel shivered as if overcome by a chill. She got up from her chair and walked to the edge
of the porch. With her back to Lije, she looked off toward a large
elm tree. "I need to get this place fixed up. Got peeling paint everywhere, and look at the yard."

He got up and walked over to her. "What do you mean, you
warned her?"

Mabel tossed the cigarette out onto a patch of dirt and went
back to sit in her chair. "I had to have the money. I'd spent what
was left in the account. I would've sold the place even sooner than
I did, but Micah's will was really messed up. It took almost two
years for me to get my name on it, all legal, so I could even put
that property up for sale. I didn't advertise or nothing. The lawyer
who handled the will and everything, the same one who worked
for the German, put me in touch with your wife. We settled it in
twenty minutes right here on this porch. But afterward I felt guilty
for doing it, so I tried to get out of the deal. I called her back the
next day. I told her the property was cursed, had been for more
than a century, but she didn't believe me. Didn't even ask me about
the curse. So the deal went through. When I heard she had been

killed, it cut through me like a knife. I remember thinking the old Cherokee claimed another soul."

None of this made any sense. Lije wondered how an old Indian curse could still affect people today. Following the woman's ramblings was confusing. It was as if she was speaking in a riddle. "You knew there was a curse on the land. Then I take it you didn't want Micah to buy the property?"

"Of course not" — she almost spit as she spoke — "but he wouldn't listen to me any more than your wife would. That property just sucks you in. It's — what do those scientists call it? — a black hole. It's a damn black hole."

Nothing he knew about the place fit with what he was hearing. "Why is it cursed?"

"It's no secret, the old-timers all know. Old Swope killed an Indian in a dispute over who owned the place. That's when the medicine man put a curse on the land. Swope was sick from that day on, and a few years later he fell into the river and drowned. The next owner died in the Civil War. It kept happening. If you look back at the history of the place, most folks who've owned Swope's Ridge have died violently. Even Micah. The German was the one exception. He died of old age, but he was completely alone and folks said he always looked like he was haunted. They said he saw things. He claimed there were ghosts after him."

Lije couldn't figure out why Micah, who knew about the curse, would be so obsessed with owning the land. Or didn't he believe in the curse? "Why did your husband want the place?"

"That's probably my fault." She sighed. She started coughing and Lije didn't think she'd ever stop. But she did, finally. "I took him to my family reunion," she said. "Down at the park in Batesville. Wasn't long after we got married. My great-grandfather was there. The old man must have been close to a hundred then. He lived to be one hundred and four. He got to telling old stories, like he always did, including one about Swope's Ridge. It was that story that started Micah's compulsion for the place."

"Must have been some story," Lije said.

"Oh, it was. It sure was. I remember my great-grandfather's grandfather was the focus of his stories that day. Can you follow that? I know it must sound confusing."

"Two generations back from your great-grandfather."

"That's right. Seems that Joshua Lucas—no, his name was Justin Lucas—was fishing on the river one afternoon when a group of riders forded at a spot just above where he was sitting on the bank. It was either 1875 or '76, and although he was a farm boy, no more than sixteen years old, and had never seen any of the men before, he recognized two from wanted posters that hung at the sheriff's office in Hardy. You'll be surprised. He saw none other than Jesse and Frank James.

"To the people in the hills, right after the Civil War, the James brothers were folk heroes. My great-great-great-grandfather was thrilled to meet them. Evidently they liked him too. Told him they were on the run from a railroad posse. A few hours before, they had robbed a train between Hardy and Mammoth Spring. Stole two chests filled with gold coins, but the load was slowing them down. They asked Lucas if he knew of a safe place to stash the loot. That way they figured they could get away, then come back and pick the stuff up when things cooled down. Justin knew the woods well, having hunted all up and down the river, so he mounted his horse and led them to Swope's Ridge. On one of the hills, way above the stream, supposedly not far from Horseshoe Falls, he took them to a cave. Told them he had discovered it and was the only white man who knew about it. The gang stashed the loot, gave Justin a gold coin from one of the chests, and rode off. A few hours later, when the Pinkerton men the railroad had hired to catch the James brothers forded the river, Justin was fishing. He told them nothing, and the posse moved on.

"I need another smoke." Mabel picked up the pack and swiftly hit the bottom, causing a single cigarette to slide forward.

"It probably would've ended right there if Micah hadn't asked what happened to the two chests filled with coins." She lit the cigarette and inhaled. "You know, I'd heard the old story many times as a kid, but this time was different. When my great-grand-father finished his story, he pulled out a double-eagle gold coin and showed it to all of us. You should have seen Micah's face."

Mabel brought the cigarette back to her lips. Lije expected her to pick up her tale after she took another draw, but she didn't. Instead she leaned back in her chair and closed her eyes.

"What did happen to the chests?" Lije asked.

The woman smiled the kind of smile that revealed more pain than joy and looked off in the distance. "Less than a year after the incident, Justin married my great-great-great-grandmother. He told her the story and gave her the coin. They moved into a small home in Hardy. A few months after the wedding, Justin fell off a horse and was killed. He died so unexpectedly, he never told anyone the location of the cave. My great-great-grandfather was born six months later, and though he spent his life looking for the gold, he never found it.

"The James brothers' gang had been all but decimated in a failed bank robbery in Northfield, Minnesota, a few months after they crossed Spring River. Most locals believe they never returned to pick up the loot."

Lije considered her story. "Frank and Jesse James weren't captured at Northfield. In fact, Jesse lived another five, six years, and Frank lived a lot longer. So why wouldn't they have come back for the loot?"

"I was told," Mabel explained, "that the law was watching them closely for the rest of their lives. So they never had a chance to come back to Spring River and Swope's Ridge. Who knows? Maybe they did. But when Micah heard that tale, he thought he had won the lottery. He was convinced he could find the loot and become rich beyond his wildest dreams. From that day on, he lived for that gold."

"Mrs. Dean, I understand the man who was convicted of shooting your husband was also trying to obtain Swope's Ridge."

Mabel nodded.

"Did he want it for the gold too?" Lije asked.

"Naw, Jennings was a real estate agent who had clients back in Cleveland or Chicago. I've forgotten what city, but they wanted it. He claimed they had lots of money and wanted to build a vacation lodge or something. They offered Micah twice what he had in it. I tried to point out to him that that much money was more than the gold coins were probably worth, but he wouldn't even consider it. Jennings, they said later, was in need of the sale just to keep his head above water. I guess that's why he threatened Micah right here on this porch three times and again in the old barn. Micah was so unnerved by Jennings that he had Moony Rivers set up a camera and videotape some of their meetings. He wanted proof in case something happened. And it did too. Jennings followed up on his threats and shot Micah out in the barn, that very barn that fell down the other night. And," she added, "when they inject Jennings in a few days, he'll be the next victim of the curse."

It was obvious she actually believed in the curse. To her it was as real as the porch on which she sat. Lije felt cursed, but he didn't believe in curses. Still, he couldn't argue that Micah had died over the lost treasure. At least that part of her story made sense.

"Did your husband have time to search Swope's Ridge before he died?"

"He owned it six months and was out there every day, rain or shine, ten to twelve hours each day. Even quit his job. Would be gone a week at a time. Even bought himself a little travel trailer. He lived only for that gold. Guess he died for it too."

"Did he find any caves?"

"I know he found one, but there was nothing in it but some bats." She paused, inhaled, then laughed. She continued to cackle until a series of coughs muffled her strangely timed fit of amusement. "Even if he'd had it forty years he wouldn't have never found anything."

"Why's that?"

"Because my great-grandfather was a storyteller. He told some real whoppers. Made things up to entertain anyone who would listen. All the family knew that. Only ones who bought into what he said were fools. That's what Micah was, a fool … after fool's gold. I knew it, told him so, but he wouldn't listen to me. Sad, isn't it? He was looking for something that never existed. Spent a half million bucks on a fable. Who would believe there were chests of gold in the Ozarks? Only Micah."

"So," Lije said, "you believe in the curse but not the treasure?"

"That's right." She sighed. "I feel sorry for you, sir. You lost your wife, and I'm sure you lost a lot more than I did when Micah died." Reaching into her pocket, she retrieved a shiny round object. She studied it for a moment, then stretched her hand out toward Lije.

"This is the gold piece my great-grandfather used to lure my husband into wasting the rest of his life. When I sold your wife Swope's Ridge, I should've given this to her too. But for some reason, even knowing that it drove my husband to his death, I kept it. Now, I want no part of it."

He took the coin and examined it. Though it had been minted in 1872, it was unworn and appeared brand new. "Are you sure you want me to have this?"

She spoke quietly, "I honestly don't know if I want you to have it, but I know for sure I don't want it. Now, do you have any more questions?"

Lije studied the gold piece a moment and then stood. "I want to thank you for your time, Mrs. Dean. I've learned a bit of what I need to know. But if I have some more questions, can I call you?"

"No problem, sweetie. And if you come back in a few months, I'll have this place all fixed up. It'll be a nice place then."

"I'm sure it will be," he replied.

He slipped the coin into his pocket and walked off the porch to the car. He opened the door and looked back at the house. Mabel

Dean was still sitting in her chair. An orange cat leaped into her lap. Her head back, she took another long draw of smoke into her lungs.

Lije started the Cord and steered back into the road's deep ruts.

HE PROBABLY SHOULD HAVE BEEN A ROCKY OR A Hunter, but his mother's maiden name was Ivy, and that's what ended up on his birth certificate: Ivy Beals. Made him tough as a kid. Tougher as a middle linebacker. And toughest as a private investigator.

But this hit was going to be easy. Four hours after the call, Beals had found Charles Sutton, in Memphis. The guy had lamely covered his tracks with stupid moves and amateur tricks. He never changed his appearance, he used predictable aliases (Chuck Simpson, Charles Saffron, always with the C. S.), and his credit card? Billed to his home address.

Worst of all, he ate lunch at the same place every day. Was this guy for real?

Beals punched 1144 South Childress Lane and Memphis into his GPS navigational system and followed the arrows. Simple.

Childress Lane looked just like a lot of other streets in the river city. It was lined with three-bedroom tract homes, set on small flat lots, all built in the 1970s. About the only thing distinguishing one from the next was the color of trim or the shade of brick. The trees were tall, and the yards, though half were littered with toys, were well kept. This was the last spot he expected to find a seedy kidnap-and-ransom scam artist. When crime pays well enough to afford a suburban paradise, then it's time to go to jail.

Sutton lived alone. His car was gone, so Beals had nothing to do but wait. Half of his job was waiting. He unscrewed the cap of a Dr. Pepper. It was going to be a long afternoon.

And it was a long afternoon. Right before sunset, Sutton pulled into his driveway in a large blue Cadillac.

Definitely time to go to jail.

There were still a few children out playing in their yards, so Beals took his time. The fewer folks who saw him, the better. He waited for Sutton to go inside, get comfortable, and settle into his routine. When dusk turned to night, Beals checked his nine millimeter, dropped it into his shoulder holster, and got out of the car.

Three rings, no answer. He knocked and noticed the curtains in the picture window move. He knocked again. How rude. Beals hated rudeness. Figured he might just have to be rude back. He brandished his weapon, lowered his shoulder, and crushed the door like it was an opposing team's running back.

Was he kidding? He loved this.

He dropped to one knee, gun pointed into the living room. Out of the corner of his eye, he caught Sutton bolting toward the kitchen. When Beals first started work as a P.I., he might have yelled "Stop!" or "Wait!" or "I just want to talk!" Now he just got up, strode into the kitchen, and dove at his fleeing prey. The tile floor must have really hurt, but Beals didn't feel it. Sutton sure did.

Beals holstered his gun, flipped on a light, and threw Sutton into a chair.

"Charles Sutton," Beals said into Sutton's clammy face. "Or should I say Charlie Smith, Chuck Simpson, Clint Schmidt, or Chance Spencer? What is it about the C. S. initials? If you were any kind of real con man, you would know that the pattern makes it much easier to track you down."

"What do you want?" Sutton asked, his attempt to sound defiant failing so miserably that Beals had to look the other way to keep from laughing. When he turned back, he watched Sutton shrink with fear, as if Dorothy had tossed a pitcher of water on him.

"What do I want? I *want* to kill you, but I would hate to explain that mess to the cops. So I may have to settle for just beating you within an inch of your life and leaving you to bleed on your kitchen floor. You get to clean up the mess."

"I don't understand," Sutton sputtered. "I ain't done nothin'. And if you're here to rob me, if you want money, I don't have any. But take anything I've got, just don't hurt me and I won't call the police. I promise you that."

Beals grinned while pulling a chair around so it was directly in front of the man he had so terrified. This was so easy. He turned it so that the chair's back faced Sutton, then straddled the seat and sat down, leaning his arms and his chin on the chair back.

"I believe you. Let me assure you of something I wouldn't do. I wouldn't call the cops if I had been bilking innocent families out of hundreds of thousands of dollars. Just wouldn't do it. So I don't think you would call the cops either. In this one area, and only this one, I'll take you at your word."

Sutton cocked his head sideways, as if that position would help him think. "I still don't know what you're talking about."

Beals smirked. This guy was really playing it dumb. Or maybe he was that stupid. It didn't matter. He was cracking faster than an egg at Denny's.

"Listen punk, the Rhoadses, the Hendersons, the Youngbloods, and the Perezes have all forked over more than fifty grand each so that you could get their supposedly kidnapped relatives out of the hands of terrorists. You have tooled them along for months, squeezing harder while you pushed their hopes higher and higher. Yet during all this time, you've made no overseas calls. In fact, the only research you've done is newspaper searches of men and women who are missing in action. And you've also done a bit of work conning people into believing that the army or the marines misidentified their loved one's remains. That they buried a stranger. That's when you tell them that their son or daughter or brother or sister is still alive. And you promise them you can get them back home. All it will take for a ticket back to the living is a bit of cash."

"My information's correct," Sutton argued, "and you can't prove it isn't. I am helping these people. It's the government that's lying to them."

Beals wanted to knock the man across the room, but knew it would not help him get what he needed. So he resisted the urge. For the moment.

"I can tell you one thing, you have a few solid contacts in the grave units of the military and you have a flair for making up stories that play on the hearts of grieving souls. But you don't know much about truth."

Sutton's eyes darted to the back door.

"Don't even try it," Beals warned. "If you do, I might think the effort of chasing you was simply too great and just shoot you instead. Probably should have done that to begin with. With as many people as you've conned, the suspects would be so numerous the cops would never pin it on anyone. I have no connection to you. No one even knows I'm here.

"You know, the more I think about this, the more I'm finding this to be a waste of my time." Beals pulled the gun from inside his coat.

"You wouldn't."

"Don't bet on it. I'm not in a good humor tonight. Missed supper while waiting for you to get home and I bruised my shoulder inviting myself into your lovely abode. Now, why don't you improve my mood?"

"How?"

Beals watched the man sweat. At this rate there wasn't going to be much fluid left in the guy's greasy body.

"By giving solid, truthful answers."

"But none of it was illegal," Sutton argued. "They *might* be alive. In fact, I know some of them are. I was simply providing a service."

Beals stood up and slapped Sutton so hard with the back of his left hand that he almost knocked him out of his chair. Plopping back down, Beals stared intently at the red welt coming up on the man's left cheek. Then he spoke in a very calm tone.

"Now, before I realize how much I enjoyed that, I'm going to cut to the chase and you had better be ready to run with me. My name is Ivy Beals. I'm a private investigator working for an attorney. He has a client whom you took for thirty grand. I'm here to get that money for her."

Tears slid down Sutton's stinging face. "Who are you talking about?"

"Heather Jameson."

Beals watched Sutton's expression grow more hopeful. He was not surprised when the man started to spin the conversation in a new direction to work a con. "Her brother's really missing. I know for sure that he's not dead. My sources are good on that case. I can provide you with real information. This isn't a scam! This was money well spent."

"Yep," Beals agreed, "we had the casket exhumed today. It's empty. Like you said. But that doesn't mean her brother's alive, and it certainly doesn't mean you had information on the case or were actually doing anything to find him. Suffice to point out, I'm not leaving without the money she gave you."

"I already spent it," Sutton said.

It was a con job so easy to spot a grade-school kid wouldn't have swallowed it. "Don't think so." Beals pulled his left hand back as if to strike Sutton, but before he could follow through, Sutton hurriedly put forth a deal.

"I've got a little left. I can give you ten thousand, but no more, at least not right now. I'm a gambler and I don't do it very well. So I'm pretty much broke."

The detective ran his hand slowly across the top of his bald head. Acting as if he were considering the offer, he returned his gun to its holster and smiled. "If you can only give me ten grand, then I guess I'll have to take something you do have as collateral."

"That's great!" Sutton said, the color returning to his face. "I have some jewelry and you can have my car. How does that sound? Okay?"

"Ah … doesn't sound good to me." He got up from the chair and strolled to the kitchen cabinets. He opened three drawers before finding what he needed — a nice twelve-inch butcher knife.

"What's that for?" Sutton's voice cracked.

Beals pulled the well-worn wooden kitchen table against the man's side. Sutton squirmed like a rat in a cage watching a cat trying to spring the door.

"You've been bleeding these families, thousands of dollars at a time. I think it's time you bleed some too. It will give you some idea as to the pain you have caused them. Now, you promised to give me some collateral. I'm the banker here. I'm not interested in your jewelry and I have a car, so I think I'll take something more personal as a marker for the rest of the cash."

"What?"

"A few fingers. Maybe an ear. Do you have children?"

"If I did would you want me to give you them as well?"

"No, I have kids of my own." Beals laughed, then suddenly took the knife, drew it over his head, and slammed it into the table with such force the noise echoed off the walls. The knife stuck there, its blade buried at least an inch into the wood, and wobbled for several seconds. Beals studied Sutton for a moment then leaned down until his eyes were just two inches from his face. "I just wondered if you ever wanted to have any children. Like maybe in the future?"

A look of panic crossed Sutton's face. Beals laughed. He let the man sweat for a moment before retrieving the knife. "Relax, Charlie, I'll keep everything I cut off and give the stuff back to you when you give me the rest of the money. After all, once the note is paid in full, I won't need the collateral."

Sutton broke. "I've got cash hidden here at the house. If you'll let me up, I'll get it for you."

Beals was almost sorry it was over. He had a few more ideas that he knew would take at least a decade off the man's life. It was ten years this skunk needed to give up too.

"Lead the way, Charlie."

Sutton headed back to a room that seemed to serve as an office. Beals watched as he opened the closet door and pulled a shoe box from a shelf. He set the box to one side and reached back, moved a loose piece of sheet rock, and fished out a plastic file box.

Before he could open it, Beals stepped closer. "Put it on the bed where I can see it."

Sutton did as he was told. He flipped the box's two latches and opened the lid. He was about to reach inside when Beals stopped him. "Move over to that chair against the wall and sit down."

Beals looked inside the box. There must have been more than two hundred thousand right there, within easy reach. He glanced over at his host. "I could make a lot of house payments with this stash," he said wryly.

He counted out thirty thousand dollars. Stuffing the cash into his inside coat pocket, he glanced back at Sutton. "Been a pleasure doing business with you, Charlie."

"You aren't going to take the rest of it?"

"Didn't come for that. Just came for Heather Jameson's part of your con. I guess you get to keep the rest, at least for the time being."

Beals slipped his gun back into his holster, took a final look at that disgusting leech of a human being, and slipped out of the house and walked down the front sidewalk to his vehicle. Once inside, he punched a few numbers on his cell phone and waited.

"I got what I needed. He keeps his loot in a plastic file box in his office closet. It's hidden behind some old board in the wall. My guess is he'll be hightailing it out of town in the next hour or so."

Smiling, Beals punched in another number.

"I got the thirty grand and I alerted the FBI. They'll be moving in on him in a few minutes. I'll drop the cash by your office in the morning."

Beals took one more look at the quaint neighborhood, now lit by a few streetlights. He shifted into drive. A surprise party was on its way to the Childress Lane home of Charles Sutton, and he didn't want to be there when it arrived.

IT WAS JUST BEFORE EIGHT IN THE MORNING. LIJE got up and showered. He slipped on a pair of jeans and a white polo shirt and walked into the kitchen. After pulling a Coke from the fridge and retrieving a muffin and a plate from the cabinet, he sat down at the breakfast bar and studied the pond. Several ducks and two geese were gliding across the water. For a second, he yearned to be one of them. To have no cares, no grief, and not to be concerned with an unfathomable mystery.

His bullet wound didn't hurt anymore, but there was still pain everywhere around him. Everything that once was good—the memories, the all-but-forgotten bits of happiness—now caused only pain. Scenes from the past, memories of wonderful times, flooded his mind. But it was torture. Kaitlyn was everywhere. He could not make a turn without seeing her. He struggled to come to grips with the reality of his loneliness, his aloneness, and finally opted to embrace a simple plan of escape. To keep from drowning in the knowledge of all that he had lost, he decided to work, at something. He would find a purpose, a focus. Work would be his balm.

He entered his study and booted up his Mac, watched as it automatically connected to the internet. Scanning a cable news site, he saw that the story had now broken big time. The national media had arrived in Salem. A media camp was set up outside the county jail. Now he really was in prison. The world had come to his sleepy Arkansas hamlet.

The headline read, "Law Partner Arrested in Double Murder." He read the story, obviously slanted to convict Heather Jameson long before she faced a jury. They couldn't even get the headline right. She was all but hung. It would take a Perry Mason moment to keep her off death row. He scanned other accounts and realized the urgency in finding the real motive for the murder and attempted murder on Farraday Road and for the shots fired at him outside his home. Could he provide that motive? Investigation of murder was completely out of his range of experience.

Taking a final swig of his soft drink, he got up from his desk and wandered back into the kitchen. He placed his plate in the dishwasher and a wave of despair rushed over him. He glanced at the bottle of sleeping pills Dr. Herring had prescribed. A couple of them could allow him to escape for a while. Mindless slumber was incredibly appealing. The rest of the bottle could ... No, he couldn't escape, not now; he had Heather to think about. Perhaps that was a good thing. Perhaps it was a way for him to focus on the living and not on how much he had lost. What he needed to do was uncover the real reason for all this deadly madness.

He looked out at the pond. He even wished Curtis and her combative personality were back. He needed fresh ideas. He needed a new perspective. He needed some real help. Someone with experience. As much as he didn't want to admit this, he couldn't do what he wanted to do all by himself.

He walked back to his study and, after looking up a number, made a call.

"Robert Cathcart," the voice said.

"Dr. Cathcart. My name is Lije Evans. I live in Salem and need to tap into your vast knowledge of local history. I know this is short notice, but could I drive over and take a few minutes of your time today? Maybe as much as an hour?"

Until now, he had never been so socially inept. His request was too quick. This wasn't how business was done. There should have been small talk, a bit of explanation, and then the request for a visit.

"What's this about?" Cathcart's voice crackled as he spoke. If he had been put off by Lije's abrupt manner, he didn't show it.

"It concerns a train robbery the James brothers committed on the old Hardy train line. I need all the information I can get on it."

This time Cathcart's speech was slower and seemed more calculated. "I'll see what I can find, but—"

Lije didn't let him finish. "I'll be there within the hour."

THOUGH LIJE HAD NEVER MET HIM, HE HAD KNOWN
of Dr. Robert Cathcart for years. A retired history professor, he
was also a train nut who had a vast library of materials in his
home. Those materials gave a complete picture of railroading in
the area from the day the first track was laid in Mammoth Spring,
Arkansas, until now. Supposedly, if he didn't know an answer on
railroading off the top of his head, he could find it in his trove of
papers.

Lije hurried out to the barn and fired up his Cord. The Lycoming
engine roared to life, and he felt a little life return to him.

So lost was he in thoughts of century-old train robberies, he
forgot about the media circus. The crowd at the bottom of the hill
shocked him. There were RVs, tents, and satellite dishes everywhere.
It looked like a scene outside the White House. He couldn't
turn around. And he couldn't drive through. His car rolled to a
stop at the point where his lane intersected the highway, and he
was engulfed by a sea of humanity.

"Mr. Evans," a young woman screamed as she stuck a microphone
in his face, "how does it feel to have one of your employees
arrested for the murder of your wife?"

Before he could respond, a middle-aged man shoved his microphone
in. "Are you in favor of the death penalty?"

Scores of other questions followed, all shouted over each other.

Still cameras clicked and video rolled. Lije looked for a way to exit through the throng. There was none. He was trapped. Curtis could have flashed her badge and gotten him right through. On his own, what could he do but give them what they wanted?

He turned off the engine and stepped out. He raised a hand in an attempt to silence the crowd. "I'm not in any shape to answer your questions," he began, "but I don't mind making a statement."

As scores of men and women jockeyed for position, leading with microphones and cameras, he sought the words he needed to explain his position. "First of all, I believe that Heather Jameson is innocent. I think the ABI and local officials have arrested the wrong person. I stand behind her as her employer and friend and will do whatever I can to make sure her case is presented in such a way that proves her innocence."

Three voices shouted out the same question: "Then who did it?"

Lije shrugged. "I don't know. But I'll find out."

"Mr. Evans," a tall black woman in the back of the group called out, "if you believe that Jameson was not responsible, then you also must realize there's someone still out there who wants you dead."

Lije nodded. "I'd think that likely, and if they are successful, then I guess it'll clear my friend. Now, I have an appointment I must keep. Could you please let me through?"

Lije slid back into the Cord, started the motor, and edged forward. The reporters, apparently satisfied with what he'd given them, parted for the car to ease onto the highway. He glanced into the mirror to see them looking at him. They were doing their jobs, but their perspective too often was skewed. They wanted something uncomplicated and quick, a sound bite, a headline. Were any of them willing to do what it would take to uncover the real story?

Was he willing to do whatever it takes to find the killer? To unravel the mystery?

"CURTIS," BARTON HILLMAN BARKED INTO HIS DESK phone. "My office, now!"

Diana Curtis knew the tone well and dropped everything she was doing in the lab to rush downstairs to the director's office. She didn't bother knocking, just barged right in.

"We've got a problem."

"Which case?" she asked.

Hillman got up from his desk and moved to a corner window. He pointed toward the state capitol building. "Not really with a case. We have that under control. It's the governor."

"The governor?" This sounded like politics to her. And politics never solved a case.

"Yeah. Did you catch Lije Evans' impromptu press conference that just ran on all the cable channels?"

"No, I've been in the lab."

Hillman waved his hand toward the TV. "Evans told the national media that we had it wrong. That Jameson is not behind the murder of his wife."

"Well, doesn't surprise me. He finds it hard to believe that anyone that close to him could betray him."

"That's not the issue. Doesn't make any difference that we know we have it right. The governor's a close friend of Evans. What Evans said put huge doubts into his head. The governor just called here demanding that I assign someone to protect Evans. Because you know Evans better than the rest of us, that person is you."

Curtis shook her head. This was not what she wanted. There were cases that needed her attention and she was due a few weeks off. She just wanted to catch up and get out of town. The last thing she needed was to be a babysitter to a man who had no reason to have one. She knew that talking Hillman out of the assignment would be next to impossible, but she wouldn't accept the job without at least showing some fight.

"Listen, Barton, send a junior agent. This is a waste of my time. I have no business being a bodyguard, Evans doesn't want one, and the case is solved."

"I promised the governor I'd send you. You're the one he asked for. Seems you made a good impression at our banquet last month."

Banquet? More like a royal waste of time. Held to award various medals for valor in the service of the state. She'd been forced to go to that too. Luck had placed her at the table by the governor and his wife. For reasons she didn't understand, by the end of the meal they seemed ready to adopt her. They were even pushing her to meet their single son, who was about her age. The whole night had been a nightmare. She was just happy to get away without their suggesting names for her future offspring.

"Of all the dumb luck. Just call and tell him I'm jammed up."

Hillman ignored the request. "Take some case files, a few books, your laptop, and a lot of coffee. It'll be the easiest assignment you'll get in a while. I'll make sure there's someone else up there to give you relief."

"No way out?"

"Nope."

"When do I leave?"

"After the meeting this afternoon. I'd suggest being prepared to spend a week. When that much time passes without any kind of attack on Evans, then I'll be able to convince the gov to let us bring you home."

"Fine."

"Don't forget, I'm going to be out of town this afternoon and we're hosting that official from Germany—Schmidt. You need to be the one to show him around the facility. I simply don't trust the tech geeks with anything other than evidence, and our field agents would probably take him out to a bar and create some kind of international incident."

"Why don't you stick around?" Curtis suggested. "Practice your German."

"I would if I could. Language is no issue anyway. Schmidt speaks English better than either one of us."

"Fine," Curtis grumbled, "and while I'm at it, I'll clean the building too." The last was said on her way out.

After his unexpected meeting with the press, Lije drove in silence, his eyes locked on the curvy road. It was a beautiful day, but he didn't notice. He barely noted the tiny village of Glencoe. He was lost in thought. And lost in so many other ways. Only the ringing of his cell phone caused him to see the city limit sign for Agnos.

Glancing at the number, he flipped open the phone.

"Kent, what've you got?"

"Well, a few things," McGee replied. "Thanks to you, Heather is talking to me, and that's helped me dig up some information. It took some wrangling, but once I got near the top of Army Intelligence, I found a person who would confirm Jim Jameson is now unofficially considered missing in action rather than listed as dead."

"So, does that help Heather?" Lije asked.

"Probably not. I figure you need to know the rest of it. One of the men in Jim's unit claimed he recently saw Jim in an Iraqi hospital working as an orderly. It's unconfirmed information, so I'm skeptical. But there does seem to be some validity to the report that Heather's brother was seen outside the green zone in Baghdad not long after he was supposedly killed. Heather told me this morning that the last few emails he sent home before he was said to have died indicated he was at the breaking point.

"Anyway, the current Army theory is that the IED that killed his buddy pushed him over the edge. He might have just dropped his dog tags and his identification and taken off, hoping the badly mangled soldier would be identified as him. Or, even more likely, he just went completely bonkers and raced off into the night. I'm leaning toward the latter. I don't think in his state of mind he planned anything."

"If he's alive, that's good news," Lije said. "What did you find out about the coat the ABI thought was mine?"

"As you surmised, the ABI's not doing much with it. Hillman has pretty much shut down anything that doesn't focus on Heather. Ivy Beals, one of my men, did a bit of investigating. He found out the coat you saw at Jim's Diner was sold through a chain of about forty men's stores located in Ohio and Pennsylvania. And, before you ask, Ivy's working on finding what cleaners mark laundry with numbers like you saw, but, as you can guess, there are a lot of cleaners in those two states."

"I'm sure," Lije replied, "but who's to say the cleaners are in those two states? My coat came from a New York City store and it has never been cleaned anywhere but here in Fulton County, Arkansas. To pin it down even more, only at Statler Brothers Laundry in Salem."

"Yeah, I thought of the fact that the coat's owner might live someplace else rather than where the coat was sold, but we're going to hope that's not true."

"So you're at a dead end." How Lije hated to consider that fact, much less voice it.

"For the moment anyway."

"Well, keep me informed," Lije said. "I want Heather out of jail and that media circus out of town."

Building a defense was usually a slow, long, and expensive proposition. The expense often killed the chances of those who had court-appointed lawyers. At least Lije had the money to fund Heather's defense. What about all the others who had nothing?

He hadn't considered that before, even as a lawyer. Without his bankroll, Heather would be one of those who had no chance. A sobering thought.

LIJE KNOCKED ON THE DOOR OF A ONE-STORY SANDSTONE home that seemed to stretch forever along the top of a pine-covered hillside. It was obvious the builder spared no expense when he constructed the place. Magnificent did not come close to describing the eclectic mix of style and substance. In the past, Lije had seen the home only from the river below. Now, as he noted the intricacies of the unique design, he gained a new appreciation for the craftsmanship that went into the construction. The fact that the porch sported polished stone floors and the house had leaded-glass doors, stained-glass windows, and brass exterior light fixtures hinted at something very special behind the entry. It looked so much like a rustic depot, he half expected to hear a train pulling up at any time. Who had the creativity to have this place built?

With a high-pitched creaking, the door opened and a small man, standing barely five and a half feet, his dark eyes set off by wavy snow white hair, bowed his head in greeting.

"You would be Lije Evans?"

"I am," Lije replied, sticking out his hand. "I know this home's older than you are, so I have to ask, who had the imagination to build it?"

"An interesting question, and the answer would be a very wealthy Chicago businessman who used it as a summer retreat during the Depression. As is obvious, he loved trains as much as I do."

"Very impressive."

"Wait until you see the inside."

"I've heard a great deal about you, Dr. Cathcart. It is nice to finally meet you."

"Mr. Evans, I would be remiss if I did not first share with you something that lies heavy on my heart. I met your late wife on three different occasions. She was a remarkable woman. I cannot begin to comprehend your loss. She was strong, driven, and yet caring and loving. Her beauty was simply breathtaking. I was at the funeral, and the service, as beautiful as it was, did not begin to cover the majesty that was Kaitlyn."

"Thank you, sir," Lije replied. "I was unaware that you two had met. But I'm glad you did and even happier that she had a profound effect on you. In fact, her death is what brings me to your door today."

"I'm at a loss as to what I can do," Cathcart replied. "But if I can be of some aid, it will be my honor to help. Now, come into my home. I have some tea prepared, both hot and iced. We can sit in the study and you can explain why you think this poor student of history can shed light on the events of a modern world."

Cathcart's home was the stuff of local legend. Lije had wanted to visit it for years. He and Kaitlyn had once been invited to a charity event for an after-school program that was held in the house, but it had conflicted with a previous engagement at their own home. He had wanted to cancel his own party just to attend the one in Hardy, but Kaitlyn wouldn't let him.

Now, as he followed his host through the massive structure, what filled his eyes was almost too much to comprehend. In every one of the large rooms they passed, from the stone floor to the top of the vaulted, two-story-high ceilings, were railroad paintings, memorabilia, and scores of electric trains. Old signal lanterns hung from the ceiling's thick hand-hewn log beams. Crossing signs were nailed to walls. Sidecars served as end tables. Ticket windows were room dividers. And a twenty-foot-long mahogany table dominated what appeared to be a library. There had to be more than a thousand different items in the foyer, hallway, and the first four rooms they passed. When they finally crossed into the study, Lije saw that sticking through a back wall was a full-sized diner car, circa 1930s. It rested on rails that had been built into the floor. It looked as though it had just come out of the factory.

Cathcart must have noted the awestruck look on his guest's face. "Yes, it's real. I also have a caboose in my bedroom. The car you're looking at is from one of the famed Zephyr trains. They were the railroad's first attempt at streamlining. I always thought they looked like cousins of the rocket ships seen in the old Buck Rogers movies. Would you like to sit in the dining car to talk? If you walk to the end that's on the outside of the house, there's a beautiful view of the river."

"That'd be fine," Lije replied, suddenly feeling more like a little boy than a grown man.

"Then get on board. I hope you'll pardon my mild pun. And I'll bring the refreshments. What would you like, iced or hot?"

"I'll take iced tea, sweet if you have it."

"This is the South. Of course it's sweet," Cathcart answered.

Climbing onto the platform, Lije opened the door. From the velvet curtains to the bone china and heavy silverware, it was just as if he had stepped back into the glamour age of railroading. Even the magazines sitting on the bar were relics from the Depression era. There was Jean Harlow on the cover of *Time*, FDR on *Life*, and Clark Gable smiling from *Liberty*. As if the memorabilia inside the old relic were not overwhelming enough, seeing Spring River from the bluff was breathtaking. Two hundred feet below, the stream sparkled in the sun as its water splashed over rocks following a course it had mapped out thousands of years before John Smith landed at Jamestown. The natural glory of this scene would be hard to beat anywhere between the Smokey Mountains and the

Rockies. Tears found their way into his eyes as he was struck by how much Kaitlyn would have loved this.

"Here we go," Cathcart announced as he brought a silver tray holding the drinks onto the train. "I hope this will meet with your approval. An old bachelor like myself usually doesn't take much pride in cooking."

Cathcart sat opposite his guest. "Mr. Evans, when you called, you said that you had a question about train robberies on the old Hardy to Mammoth line. You specified one involving Jesse and Frank James. My guess was this would have taken place from just after the Civil War to sometime in the mid- to late 1870s. Is that right?"

"I don't know the year. A woman in Mountain View claimed the loot was hidden in a cave on Swope's Ridge. The information had been passed down in her family for generations."

The educator rubbed his brow, his expression reflecting a hint of disappointment. "I know the location of the Ridge. Yet I found it strange I recalled nothing of a train robbery on the line. Still, as I have studied so many papers and done so much research in my sixty years of life, I thought I could be mistaken. I've committed much of my collection of records and newspaper clippings to computer files, so I did some digging. Sadly, in all of my materials, there's not a single mention of a train robbery by the James Gang or the James-Younger Gang or anyone else. If Jesse had robbed another train in southern Missouri or even eastern Oklahoma, he would not have carried heavy chests on horseback very far. So I think this is nothing more than, as the hill folks call it, 'a big windy.'"

Lije had been convinced that the story was real even though Mabel Dean had warned him that her great-grandfather's story was nothing but a fable. Was this the end of the trail? If it was, then Kaitlyn, Micah Dean, and probably Mikki Stuart were all killed for nothing. Nothing but fool's gold.

Cathcart took another sip of tea. "I'm sorry I couldn't give you better news. But there's nothing there. If there had been a robbery, it would've been covered in the newspapers and recorded in the railroad logs. In fact, during the late 1800s, only one mystery was ever connected to that old rail line, and Jesse James had been shot and buried before those events transpired."

Lije stood up and forced a smile. "I'm sorry to have taken so much of your time. I do appreciate seeing your place."

"I too am sorry," Cathcart said, "but I'll keep digging. When it comes to legends, there's usually some truth in them. Maybe I can find something that'll open a door for you."

33

EVEN IF THE LEGEND WASN'T TRUE, THOSE WHO believed it had pursued it and possibly been killed for it. Lije had one more stop to make before he returned home.

The outer office of James R. Cook's law firm was crammed with second- or third-hand furniture pressed into service by someone who had no instinct for decorating. It was the business equivalent of a male college student's apartment. It appeared that no one was home. Lije waited awkwardly for a few moments, then yelled, "Anybody here?"

"I'm in the back office."

He headed down the twenty-foot hall and found himself at the door of the modest office Cook called his business home. A large, middle-aged man, Cook was dressed casually in blue knit slacks, a pullover short-sleeve shirt, and black eel cowboy boots. Above his lip was an unruly mustache, badly in need of a trim. His hair, dyed black, was thinning in spots, and he made full use of what little hair he did have in a comb-over.

"What can I do for you?" Cook asked, pointing Lije to a wooden chair.

"My name's Lije Evans, and as I mentioned on the phone, I need some information on a piece of property. I've been told that you handled the last two sales of Swope's Ridge."

Cook leaned back in his chair and placed his hands behind

his neck. "Your information is right, Mr. Evans. I did the work five years ago and assisted again about a month ago."

"What can you tell me about the German who originally owned the property?"

When asked about the German, Cook's professional side seemed to kick in. He acted as if he was about to clam up. The last thing Lije needed was a man with lockjaw. The only card that might open up the game was the last resort for many lawyers: the truth.

"My wife, Kaitlyn, bought the property off Mabel Dean. As you probably know, Kaitlyn was killed a few days ago, and I feel the reason for her murder might be tied to the land purchase. I need to get as much information as I can to at least be satisfied whether this is the case. I feel sure that you know more than anyone else in regard to the property itself."

"Evans. I should have made the connection when you called. But there are so many Evanses in this area. My grandmother was an Evans." Cook paused for a moment. He looked as if he was searching for words. When he spoke, his voice was much softer. "Your wife was a very beautiful woman. I'm sorry for your loss."

It appeared the door was opening. Now it was time to push his way through and pray that there was something of value on the other side. "Thank you. I hope you understand why I need the information."

"Let me be honest, Mr. Evans, I don't know of anything that will help you, but here is an overview of the information I do have. His name was John Schleter, and he was a German. I represented him the last few years of his life. I can tell you he was very tight-lipped. He rarely spoke of himself or his past. I do know he was a German soldier in World War II. He did tell me a little bit about that. He claimed he was a truck driver and never fired a gun during his four years in uniform. I have no reason to believe that wasn't true. My grandfather had the same role for us in that war."

"Any idea what brought him to Swope's Ridge after the war?"

"Not really. I know he had no connection to the area, but after World War II, a lot of land could be bought around here for back taxes. That was the case with Swope's Ridge. So he picked it up. It was pretty cheap. I do know he bought an old school bus about the same time he purchased the property. He lived in the bus while he built his house. The bus is still up there behind the house, but it's been pretty much covered over by new growth."

"Did he have any friends?"

"Not really. He did attend the Lutheran church over in Chero-kee Village some. Even gave the money for the addition they built a few years back. But he didn't talk much and left right after each service. Mainly he just stayed in that strange house."

"Strange?"

"Well, I was only there once. He was pretty sick toward the end, and I took him some papers he needed to sign. The house looked like something out of a Bavarian forest. It was dark and drab with a steep roof. It had thick brick walls, almost like a fortress. He even had metal shutters that he could close to cover all the windows. He had more locks on the front door than a maximum-security prison. On that visit, he told me that everything in the home, as well as the building materials, had been imported from Germany. It had all been shipped over in large crates after the war. Then he built the house, every bit of it, by himself."

"You mean nothing came from America?"

Cook quickly rethought. "I guess nails, mortar, and basic items like that. But even the doors and windows were from the Old Country."

"That must've cost a pretty penny." Why, Lije thought, would someone spend so much to bring in materials that could be easily and cheaply purchased locally?

"Well, he never seemed to lack for pennies," Cook said. "He never worked, raised nothing on his land. Yet he had no problem buying food and other items he needed for the house. Always paid his taxes and utilities. He only kept a small amount in the bank, and that amount always remained about the same. If he took some out, it was soon replaced. He never waited to pay bills either. I'd give him my invoice in person and get the payment. He'd just write me a check and hand it to me."

"Did anyone visit Schleter?"

"As far as I know, and I have asked a lot of the old-timers, the only people who ever approached that home were men like Micah Dean who either wanted to buy the place or at least get to hunt on it. Each of them was pretty rudely turned away."

Yeah, having your backside filled with rock salt might make a person feel a bit unwanted, Evans thought. Why was the German so protective of Swope's Ridge? "What did he do with the property? Did he fish? Hunt?"

"He was as pale as a ghost, so I'm guessing he spent most of his time in the house. I know he was never outside when folks drove down the old logging road that runs by the property or when they passed by on the river. He never bought a television and didn't even have a phone. He did have an old radio, but when I was there, it wasn't on. One day I asked him what he liked best about the place. His answer — 'the solitude.' I inquired about what the land away from the house looked like, and he shook his head. By the way he reacted, I'm not sure he ever walked the property. He was a peculiar one."

Lije agreed. Anyone who didn't marvel at the scenery on the ridge had to be peculiar. But why stay there and spend so much to build a fortress if no one ever visited? "I understand that he left the estate to a niece in Germany."

"Actually, it was his brother's daughter's daughter. So it would have been a great-niece. She didn't want to have anything to do with it. Wasn't the least bit interested in her uncle or in America. Just asked me to sell it as quickly as possible and get her the money. I knew Micah was interested, so I called him. I set the price at the appraised value and that was it. I later found out I moved too fast. If the great-niece had been more patient, I could have gotten twice what Micah paid."

"Really?" Now he finally had discovered something that hinted at a motive. Someone besides the German and Dean who felt there was something of value on that property.

"Yes, two men from Cleveland called and made an offer just two weeks later. They vaguely explained to me they were going to develop the land somehow. They really didn't say anything more specific about their plans. When I informed them that Micah Dean had bought it, they asked me how to get in touch with him. I gave them his number, but I understand that when they called, he wouldn't even give them the time of day. I think that's when they turned to Jonathon Jennings. He was trying to establish his own real-estate company at the time. That's when everything went really bad. I always thought that Johnny was a good guy, but he must have snapped." Cook added, "They're going to execute him next week."

"The two men from Cleveland, did they call you back?"

Cook nodded. "Yes, a few weeks after the trial ended. They again asked if the property was for sale, but I told them it wasn't. Then they asked if they could lease Swope's Ridge for a year. I couldn't arrange that either. Dean's will was out of date and it took his wife a long time just to get the property put in her name. Then she had to pay some taxes before she could sell it. So nothing could be done with it then. Earlier this year when she finally got control of it, she contacted me, asking if I knew of anyone who wanted the place. I immediately called the old number for the men from Cleveland. The number was no longer in service. That's when your wife contacted me. The timing was right. Mabel Dean wanted to sell, and the rest is history."

"Do you still have the old number for the men from Cleveland?" Lije asked.

"Yeah. It's here in my address book."

"Could I have that number?"

"Won't do you much good; it's out of date."

As Cook scribbled the number, Lije posed a final question, "What were the men's names?"

"I know this is going to sound crazy, but even though both of them called me from time to time, only one ever left me a name. You're gonna laugh, but he said he was Robert Smith."

Lije did not laugh. Nothing about this was funny. He stood and reached across the desk to shake the other man's hand. "Thanks. I appreciate the information." He stuck the number in his pants pocket.

"Hope I've been some help to you," Cook replied.

"I think you have."

LIJE HURRIED FROM COOK'S LAW OFFICE AND WALKED back to the car. The story Cook told did not ring true. Two elements were not logical.

First, the men wanted to buy Swope's Ridge to develop it. When they couldn't buy it, they tried to lease it for only a year. Why would anyone lease something they wanted to develop? A building project made sense only if they had title to the property.

And who would buy in to such a development once it was completed? While Swope's Ridge was beautiful and had a host of wonderful building locations, it was too remote. The property was not on a main highway. The incredibly high offer the men made for just the land would have pushed the price for each parcel way up. Only the wealthy could afford such a place and this area had few wealthy people. Plus there were already too many places like that on Spring River. Lije was certain the men were not planning a major development on the property.

So that meant they were convinced there was something else there that was very valuable. Perhaps there really was truth in the story about the Jesse James treasure.

Back in his car, Lije decided to start with a background check on Schleter. But how would he dig up information that went back almost a century? Did he go to D.C.? Or to Berlin?

He drove slowly, his eyes glued to the curving road, and considered the other strange tidbit dropped by Cook. To many it would have seemed insignificant, but for the moment it was the focus of his thoughts. The men who tried to buy Swope's Ridge were from the same area as the trench coat found at the diner.

His cell phone rang.

"Lije here."

It was Diana Curtis.

"What? You mean you're coming back to babysit me again? I don't care who ordered it, I ..." Lije paused. He'd been looking for a way to get past the media and to interview key people. She had the channels to find out information he needed. All he had to do was convince her to use those channels.

"Can't argue with the governor," he said. "But listen, I need to make a trip to Little Rock. Why don't I meet you there? Maybe we could ride back together once I finish my business in town. I'm going to head back to Salem in a few minutes, pick up my Prius, and will call you when I'm finished with my work."

Lije hung up, tapped in a few numbers, and waited.

"Kent, Lije here. I need a favor."

KENT MCGEE HAD MORE CONTACTS THAN ANYONE LIJE had ever known. In and out of the courtroom, he was always pulling rabbits out of a hat. The legal magic was as much about his being well connected as it was about his talent. Yet to have arranged on short notice a visit to the Varner death-row facility in Grady had to be his best stunt yet. Best of all, McGee had promised that the press and the ABI would learn nothing of the trip. Lije was one of the few people ever thrilled to be on his way to the death house.

He arrived in Grady just after five. He met with Warden Jeff Charles at a local highway rest stop and was given the rules for the clandestine meeting with condemned killer Jonathon Jennings. The warden had arranged for Lije to meet with Jennings in a large and open room. This was unusual, but the warden believed the prisoner would be more likely to respond in such an environment. Lije would have up to an hour to obtain the information he needed. Except for a handshake, there was to be no contact between the two men. And since Jennings was thought to be no threat to anyone, he would not be shackled. A guard would be watching through two-way glass, and if at any time the prisoner did make any kind of threatening move, security would quickly move to address the situation.

After agreeing to the terms, Lije was ushered to a plain white

cargo van, and he and the warden were driven to the Varner facility. The only conversation during the ten-minute drive was a
warning from the warden.

"Mr. Evans, Jennings is anything but stable. He's not violent, but his mind is deteriorating at an alarming rate. The other
inmates call him the screamer. If Kent were not one of my best
friends, I wouldn't allow you to visit. But he swears you might be
able to help clear an innocent woman with knowledge Jennings
might have. I hope so, but I doubt it. His brain is pretty mushy and
his memory is hardly reliable."

Those words made Lije wonder if he had come all this way and
would learn nothing. But they weren't enough to dissuade him
from moving forward. Jennings had to know something that was
not in the news stories. To have murdered someone over the land,
he had to know what made Swope's Ridge such a prize. If he didn't,
then who did?

Lije was processed by guards. He was searched for weapons,
drugs, and other prohibited items — he even had to give up his
comb — then was escorted into a large white room. In the middle
of the room, the staff had placed two plastic chairs. Lije was directed to one of them; the other sat four feet away.

Under stark fluorescent lights, he waited. The room felt op-
pressive, yet he couldn't determine why. There was no antiseptic
odor. In fact, there was no smell at all. The air didn't move. It was
like being in a vacuum or a tomb. A sense of hopelessness and
death pressed in from every side. No wonder Jennings was going
mad. Who wouldn't?

Lije was beginning to develop his own version of a panic attack when Jennings entered the room. He was short, pale, and
unnaturally thin. His pale green eyes seemed to involuntarily and
constantly jump from side to side. His face was so thin it appeared
as if his bones might cut through the skin at any moment.

A guard walked with Jennings to the empty chair, had him sit
down, then bent over and released the handcuffs. Jennings kept his

head low until after the guard had left the room. Then he slowly lifted his eyes to study his guest.

"Mr. Jennings," Lije began gently, "I'm Lije Evans."

"I know," came the response. "I used to see you on the streets of Salem from time to time." He paused a moment, seemingly lost in a memory. "The warden told me you needed to meet with me, but I don't understand why."

"It's about Swope's Ridge."

The mention of the property sent Jennings' eyes back toward the floor. It was obvious this was the last thing he wanted to discuss. Even four hours and one hundred and sixty miles away, the property still had a grip on him.

Lije continued, "My wife bought the property from Micah Dean's widow. My wife's now dead, shot by someone, and I don't know who or why. I think it has something to do with the Ridge."

Jennings' head jerked up and he stared at Lije. "I'm sorry." The words were sincere. He was sorry.

"And I'm sorry about what's about to happen to you," Lije replied.

Jennings' voice was suddenly stronger. "I didn't kill him, you know. I threatened him that night, but I didn't kill him."

He sounded truthful. Of course, most of those who claimed their innocence sounded sincere. But why would he lie now? He had nothing to gain.

"If you're innocent, then why haven't you made any appeals? Why are you walking to your death without a fight?"

"No one told you?"

"No."

"When I'm closed in, I can't breathe. I can't even move. I scream, I cry, and I pray to die just to escape the pressure pressing down on every part of my body. In here, sitting in that tiny cell ... Unless they knock me out with meds, I scream and cry all day, every day. Been like that week after week, month after month. If I can't be free, then I can't wait until dying releases me from this hell on earth." His eyes filled with terror.

Lije nodded. "But if you're innocent ..."

Jennings vigorously shook his head. "It's not about innocence anymore. Next Wednesday the nightmares will stop. I haven't felt any peace in two years."

MAYBE THERE WERE THINGS WORSE THAN DEATH. LIJE couldn't begin to fathom what the man's last twenty-four months must have been like, but he found it easy to understand why he'd want the horror to end.

"Would you answer a few questions, Mr. Jennings? I think your answers might help me figure out who killed my wife. And if not who, maybe at least why she was murdered."

"I'll try to help," Jennings whispered. "If you find that person, you'll probably find the one who shot Micah Dean. I'd like to think that someday my name could be cleared."

Hearing those words, delivered in such a genuine manner, Lije believed him. "What was so important about Swope's Ridge?"

"Mr. Evans, for years I've tried to figure that out and, honestly, I don't know. Robert Smith told me his boss wanted to develop the land, but he never spelled out what that meant. When Micah Dean refused to deal with me, I offered Smith several other pieces of property that would've been far better than the Ridge for any kind of development. Smith insisted that his boss had to have Swope's Ridge and the price didn't matter. So I kept going back to Dean with new offers. Dean wouldn't listen to any of them."

"Who was Smith's boss?"

"I have no idea. Smith wouldn't tell me, and I asked, a couple times. He did provide proof that the man had the money to make the deal."

"Nothing he said gave you a clue who was behind this venture?"

"No." Jennings paused, then after bringing a finger to his lips, contradicted himself. "Well, there might have been one. That last visit, his cell phone rang and he went outside for privacy. I moved over to the door to try to catch a bit of the conversation. Smith wasn't talking in English. He was talking in German."

"Could you make out any of the words?" Lije asked.

"No. Just recognized that it was German."

"Did Smith ever mention anything about the legend Dean was chasing?"

"You mean the Jesse James gold stash?"

"Yeah."

"I don't think that was even on Smith's radar. Not with what they were willing to pay for the Ridge. The gold wouldn't have been worth that much. I figured the property had great value for some other reason, but nothing connected to legends. The money this guy was offering told me he knew what made the property extremely valuable and had a firm idea how to realize that value."

Lije leaned back. Sounded plausible. But nothing Jennings had said seemed to provide a motive for Kaitlyn's death. What could be so valuable? The mystery had to be on Swope's Ridge. Lije decided he and Curtis would be taking a field trip. She would hate that. "Do you think they killed Dean?"

"I've always assumed it was Smith or the guy who was always with him. I saw Smith the day before. When I talked with him, it was obvious there was pressure on him to deliver, and Dean was the roadblock. When I left my last meeting with Dean, he was alive and standing in his barn. I called Smith and told him it was no go. Less than an hour later, Dean was discovered dead. In the barn. Not long after that, one of my shirts was found in my home with Dean's blood on it. But I hadn't been home yet. I left Dean's place and returned to my office. So the only thing I can guess is that Smith set me up, figured he could buy the land from Dean's widow."

Lije nodded. "No way to prove your alibi?"

"None. Just my word. I've thought about the Ridge a lot. Micah was passionate about that land. He may have first wanted it because he thought it would make him rich. But as I talked with him, I learned something. I learned why he wouldn't sell. His goal had changed. He no longer cared about the money from the treasure. Instead, he was obsessed with finding the gold to justify his compulsion. He wanted everyone to know he hadn't been a fool. Wanted everyone to know the truth about the Ridge. And he died before the truth was known. I'll die next, in just a few days now, with my own obsession nipping at my heels. I just want to clear my name. Neither of us deserved to pay for that land with our lives. Whatever it is out there simply can't be that important."

Lije felt a strong sense of urgency to uncover the mystery on Swope's Ridge, not only to find Kaitlyn's killer but now to help save Jennings. "I read your file on the way over. The warden bent some rules and allowed me to see it. Seems those prosecuting the case didn't believe Smith actually existed. They said you made him up."

"No one ever saw him besides me. I can see their point."

"A lawyer in Hardy talked to him on the phone," Lije said.

"How do you know that?" Jennings asked, leaning forward.

"I talked to him. His name's James Cook."

"Yeah, but I bet Cook never saw him. I understand the ABI spent some time looking for Smith. Or they told my lawyer they did. They supposedly found nothing."

"What about the guy who was with him?"

"He never spoke to me face to face, and I was never told his name. If you've seen my file, then you've seen the sketches that were done from my descriptions. Those were circulated, but no hits."

"And where was Smith from?"

"He told me Cleveland."

"What about the cell number you called?"

"Well, my lawyer was pretty worthless, but he did make a point there. The phone was purchased under a false name, and the bills were paid via money order. Some kind of pay-as-you-go service. As soon as Dean died, the phone disappeared."

Lije nodded. His time was almost up and there seemed to be no more roads to travel. He wasn't any closer to finding an answer. It looked like all this had been a wasted trip, a wild goose chase.

"Mr. Jennings, I appreciate what you've told me today. I know you didn't have to meet me, and I thank you so much for doing it anyway. Is there anything you need? Can I get you anything at all?"

Jennings shook his head. "I only want the hours to move more quickly. Going back to the cell will be like being tossed into hell again. The good thing about next Wednesday is that hell will no longer be my address." He started to get up, then stopped.

"Mr. Evans, I'm a man of faith. I believe that I've been saved. I know that Christ knows I am innocent. I'm sure that at the next Judgment Day, I'll be given a much lighter sentence. So if I can just survive until the state brings me that peace, I'll be fine. I sincerely hope I helped you some."

Lije took the man's hand, shook it, and then embraced Jennings, to both men's surprise. The guard quickly entered and pulled Jennings away.

Lije stood silently as Jennings was handcuffed and led out of the room. The final image he had of Jennings—shackled, shuffling down the hall, his head bent forward—cut to the bone.

37

DIANA CURTIS HAD JUST GIVEN HER FAREWELL TO the visiting Deutschlander. She glanced around at the empty cups and dessert plates that littered Barton Hillman's office. This is where Barton had wanted Schmidt to finish his tour. Send him off in style, he told her. But now she had to clean the place up.

Curtis was convinced that giving tours to diplomats was a waste of time. Yet it had to beat her next assignment. How she yearned to get back to the lab and commune with the dead. Bodies didn't grieve, talk back, or ask stupid questions.

"Miss Curtis," Lije Evans announced as he stepped into Hillman's office.

"Just in time to help me pick up this mess." Why not put him to work?

"I had no idea cleanup was a part of your duties. You should be very handy around my house this week." He grinned at her.

"I'm planning on catching up on my reports, not cleaning your house. After all, since the person who tried to kill you is in jail, there's little security I need to do. Hope you didn't mind my sending you on a tour of the lab while you were waiting for me."

"No problem. In fact, the lab was very impressive. I still have no clue what most of those machines do. It looks far more advanced than the equipment I see on TV."

"That's why we have techs run that stuff," Curtis replied. "Barton doesn't know any more about most of it than you do. It's hard to keep up with the advances, but I'll admit this, all that lab equipment makes my job a whole lot easier."

Curtis walked over to Hillman's oak desk to pick up plates and cups. She wondered how many square feet the desk actually covered. She had often joked that, moved to the roof, it could serve as a helicopter pad. She had even tried to estimate how many trees died to construct it.

A knock at the door interrupted her thoughts. She tossed the cups and plates into the trash can and went to open the door. A lab tech was waiting outside, a file in his hand.

"Is the boss here?" he asked.

"No, he's out of town for a couple of days. He left me in charge, so what do you need?"

The man struggled for a few seconds, looking for words that he seemed unable to find. "Guess I better wait until he comes back."

The tech seemed concerned. Why? Curtis grabbed his arm, led him to an overstuffed leather chair, and pushed him down. As the temporary chief in Hillman's absence, she needed to find out the reason for his visible distress. She couldn't let something important slip by. She couldn't be negligent.

"Does the file you're holding contain information on a current case?" she asked the tech, looking down at him.

He nodded. "In a way."

"What way?" she demanded.

"I gave a report to the director the other day."

"And?"

"He ... thanked me for my good work and then ... took the file and ... all my evidence. I wasn't to tell anyone, like I never did the work. He said he had to check on something ... that he'd keep it safe until it was needed."

That was quick. He spilled his guts quite easily. Now what would Barton find so important he would hide it even from her? She did almost all his reports for him. She kept track of the paper trail and oversaw all the lab testing. In many cases she ran the whole show. So why would he suddenly want to keep something from her?

This was not like Barton. Was it just an oversight? They had both been so busy he probably just failed to apprise her of this new evidence. He hadn't trusted the tech to tell anyone because maybe the information needed to be explained or maybe it involved a person whose name was too well known. Barton must have had a good reason not to want those who were at a lower level inside the ABI to know. But surely that didn't include her. After all, as Barton always said, she was his right-hand man. In his absence, she needed to know. This was one of her cases.

"You know my relationship with the boss," she said, putting a hand on the man's shoulder. "You know he tells me everything. So I already know about what you were asked to hide. And if this applies to that, I need to hear this so I can alert Barton when he checks in with me. If I don't get the information, then you and I will both pay dearly. And we don't want that, do we?"

The man shook his head.

"So what've you got?"

Stalling no more, the lab tech divulged the results of his work. "You know about the bullet we found in the door of the Explorer?"

Not allowing her ignorance to show, Curtis nodded. "Yes. You have something new for that report?"

"It's weird, but I guess I do. And really, I wouldn't have it if it wasn't for your new orders. So I guess I can tell you."

"Which orders?" Curtis asked.

"You asked me to go through some of the backlog of old cases and put them to rest. While I was working on those, I came across a gun and bullet from a suicide that happened two years ago."

The back cases, of course. She had given him the job to keep him occupied. She figured it would tie him up for weeks; at least, that's what she'd hoped. Old cases were the KP duty of the ABI.

Nothing in them of value. So how could he have found something worth sharing with Hillman? "And this ties in how?"

"That's the interesting thing. The Stone County Sheriff's Department sent the gun and bullet from the suicide to the ABI as a matter of routine. Nothing more. Just the usual ballistics to find out if there are any matches with other crimes. Nothing to do with their case, which was a suicide. We test these but never connect them to anything — until this time.

"First, the bullet and the gun didn't match. The .32 found at the suicide scene two years ago was not the same gun that fired the shot. The man couldn't have killed himself. It was murder.

"I ran the two-year-old bullet from the suicide case against current cases. Including the bullet from the Explorer. They were both fired by the same gun. The .32" — the techie stopped and opened the file to study his notes — "that killed Moony Rivers in Stone County two years ago was involved in the Evans murder in Fulton County last week. And as you know from what the boss told you, that same gun was used in that other case, the Dean case, two years ago. Three murders with the same gun!"

Three murders?

Diana Curtis smiled at the tech, took the file from him, and guided him to the door. "Fine work. Great job. I'll get all this to the director immediately."

The tech stood hesitantly outside the office as Diana, still smiling, closed the door.

She spread the file out on Barton's desk and studied the reports. "Incredible."

Lije was looking over her shoulder.

"The gun that fired on you on Farraday Road was used to kill this man in Mountain View, Moony Rivers, just two days after it was used to shoot Micah Dean."

"Why didn't you tell me about the connection to Dean?" Lije asked, angry at not being told of the link before.

"Because I didn't know."

"But you told the tech that Hillman had filled you in."

Her eyes never left the papers. "I lied."

"Then that same gun killed Kaitlyn? But you never found the bullet. So there's no way to prove it. This knocks a big hole in the case against Heather. And it might be just what's needed to get Jennings off death row and out of prison. He just might be innocent. What happened?"

Curtis didn't answer. She walked over to the window and stared blankly at the scene before her. She could not believe that Barton Hillman, director of the ABI, would withhold evidence. Any evidence. But this was crucial evidence. He must have a valid reason, but what was it? She couldn't even begin to guess. Yet even in her confused state, one fact did ring true. She now had to take her role as bodyguard very seriously. There was someone out there with a gun who was looking for a chance to finish a job that started two years before. Maybe he was working with Jameson or maybe ...

"Swope's Ridge," she whispered.

"What?" Lije asked.

"The answer has to be on Swope's Ridge. We need to go there. Let's get packed and head to your place. I'm thinking you and I are suddenly on the same team."

"When I tell you what I found out the last couple of days, you'll know we are."

"What did you find out? No, don't tell me now. I'll take you up on your offer to ride with you. We can talk on the way. We have a couple cars still up in Fulton County. I'll use one of them once we get to your place."

She now had a sense of purpose and direction, but she also felt a hint of disillusionment. She didn't bother finishing the cleanup in Hillman's office.

THE NEXT DAY CURTIS AND LIJE ARRIVED IN AN agency car at the overgrown lane that led to Swope's Ridge. Their trip had taken them through deeply wooded hills and valleys along Route 289 before they had turned onto a logging road that evidently hadn't been graded in years. The recent heavy rains had deposited rocks and a few tree limbs onto the road's washboard surface. These new obstacles, combined with the mixture of soft sand and hard bedrock, bounced the passengers in the agency's Crown Victoria like popcorn in a microwave bag. They could travel no more than fifteen miles an hour. They cautiously crossed two low-water creek bridges, wondering each time if they'd make it across.

"Should have checked a National Guard tank out of the armory for this junket," Curtis said.

Lije grinned. "Yep, but it's sure a good road test of the Ford. I'm impressed."

Swope's Ridge had long been Lije's Promised Land. For much of his adult life he had dreamed about going through the gate. He and Kaitlyn had spent hours planning what they would do when they finally were able to buy the property. He felt exhilarated and disappointed all at once. Kaitlyn would never be with him. To distract himself, he told Curtis about his conversation with Kent McGee the day before.

McGee had called with more information on the old German, Schleter. It was true that he was a truck driver during World War II. At least part of the time he was driving tanker trucks, and because Allied planes always went after those, it was a pretty dangerous job. He never advanced past the rank of private, and he evidently never saw combat unless it was during the last few days of the war when everyone was pressed into defending Berlin. He never married, never had children. He had filled out all the proper paperwork to come to the United States in 1946. He never returned to Germany.

He didn't come over on a passenger ship, but instead worked his way over as a seaman on a cargo boat. He paid to have a large amount of stuff brought from Germany on that ship. Maybe it was the materials he used to build his house, but records were sketchy, so who knew? He kept his nose clean, became a citizen, paid his taxes, and never got so much as a parking ticket.

The source of his money remained a mystery. He was the son of a day laborer. His parents never owned a car, much less the small apartment where they lived, so he didn't inherit a penny. There was no record of his ever earning a fortune.

When they arrived at the gate to the property, Lije got out and, using the keys he had found in the box in Jameson's desk, set about unlocking the last obstacle between them and the ridge. He ran through the set twice. None of the keys fit, even though the small brass one had been clearly marked as the gate key. He studied the gate and realized the lock and chain looked brand new.

Curtis got out and popped the trunk of the car. From the side pocket of her field kit she pulled a set of lock-picking tools. With Lije following behind her, she examined the lock and went to work. Within a minute, the lock's arm snapped open.

She headed back to the car. "Lije, swing the gate open. After I drive through, close it again and lock it."

"What?"

"You heard me."

"But why use a lock we don't have a key for?"

Curtis smiled. "Because someone obviously cut the old lock and chain off the gate to get in, then replaced them so they could come back. When we leave, I don't want it to be obvious that we've been here."

"Setting a trap?"

"Don't know if we need one, but if we do, then no reason to announce our presence. At least not yet."

The Crown Victoria worked its way through the nearly overgrown path with very little trouble. Curtis parked in knee-high grass along the back of the house and looked at Lije. "Did you notice the other tracks?"

"Even an amateur couldn't miss them. Besides, I grew up in the woods. I can read a trail. Whoever has been up here has used the old road several times. The grass is pushed down pretty good. Looks to me like a four-wheel-drive pickup."

Curtis looked impressed. "You're probably right." She studied the area around the back door. "They came this way, but they didn't stop at the house. Note the truck tracks head down into that draw, and there are no recent impressions made from walking in this area. After we survey the house, we can follow the truck trail on foot. I'm going to treat this as we would any other crime scene. I want gloves on, I want us to take our time, and I want you to stay out of my way. Put some gloves on, but follow me. If you see something you want to examine, don't! Use your voice and call me over. Okay, let's get started."

Lije snapped on a pair of latex gloves and trailed Curtis around the outside of the house. He quickly grew bored and looked out over the ridge, at Spring River in the valley below. It was his dream to own this view, and now that he did, it was even better than he had imagined. The morning sun was pushing above the ridge and dancing on the ripples in the swift water of the river. The sounds of the river's joyous melody as it tumbled over rocks and boulders could be clearly heard from where he stood. As far as he could see, there was unspoiled beauty, almost unchanged since the moment a divine breath had brought it to life. He was so drawn in by nature's composition that he lost all track of time.

Curtis walked up to him. "Lije, you ready to go inside?"

"Sure."

At the front door, Lije tried the keys on the ring, found the right key, and started to open the door.

Curtis stopped him. "Don't go in yet. It's like I thought when we drove up. I don't think the house has been visited in some time, probably months. But I can't be sure, so we have to be careful. At one time someone forced open a window on the other side, but it doesn't appear that whoever has driven by this place recently and headed down that trail has shown any real interest in the house. First we need to get the flashlights."

Lije walked behind Curtis to the car, took the flashlight she handed him, and then accompanied her back to the house. Curtis entered the house, and Lije followed, breathing in a large dose of stale air as he crossed the threshold. The house smelled of mold and old furniture. As his eyes grew accustomed to the dim light filtering through the small windows, and as his own flashlight beam floated through the dusty interior of a large open living area, a realization began to settle in. With its steel-shuttered windows, dark walls, and meager furnishings, the German had confined himself to a voluntary house arrest. Schleter's life appeared to have more in common with the death-row existence of Jonathon Jennings than with the life of a normal person. Why would anyone choose to live this way? It boggled his mind. Schleter moved thousands of miles, made no friends, and holed up in a man-made cave. His was the ultimate game of solitaire. What was the payoff?

"Someone's gone through everything," Curtis said after peering into a few closets and the kitchen and studying the contents of a large bookshelf in the living room.

Lije scanned the stacks of papers, books, and pots and pans. "Maybe this was just the way he lived."

As she walked into an adjoining bedroom, Curtis explained her reasoning, raising her voice so Lije could hear her. "Dust. Examine the dust that has accumulated in the years since Schleter died — such as on the kitchen table — then compare it to the dust on the books spread out in every direction. Big difference. You can see that a person or persons were here moving things around within the last few months."

Lije leaned over and studied one of the books on a ladder-back chair just to his left. The cover was only slightly dusty while the dust on the seat cushion was almost a quarter-inch thick. Obviously this CSI stuff was not as hard as it looked on TV.

Curtis continued the lesson from the bedroom. "There's something else about the scene that reveals the way this place was ransacked. What's in front of us tells us that these were not thieves looking for something to steal. Whoever entered this house was searching for some kind of information, perhaps written on a piece of paper. The books were thoroughly thumbed through, probably picked up by the spine and shaken, with their pages down, in hopes that something would fall out. The visitors went through this home, room by room, and they weren't in any hurry. It's apparent one of them sat in that large chair in the corner, where he probably went through a book, then set it to the side of the chair and went through another one. They weren't worried about being caught."

Curtis appeared in the doorway and added another observation. "The shoe prints indicate two men, about average height and weight, dressed casually."

"How could you tell that?" Lije asked. "I mean the casual part."

"Well," Diana explained, "it's just an educated guess, but they were wearing Nike cross-trainers — the shoe tread gives that away. So you have to figure they wouldn't have been in dress clothes with the tennis shoes. And, based on a few markers from their stride and step patterns, both searchers were men.

"Now notice the walls," Curtis continued. "Even the pictures have been taken down. It's readily apparent they pulled the backs off to see if anything was hidden behind the prints. They went through everything in here with a fine-tooth comb. And they covered their tracks pretty well too. I have not seen anything in the way of a fingerprint."

"So they wore gloves?" Lije asked.

"The places where I've found hand impressions, such as on this desktop, it's obvious their hands were covered. I'm sure there *are* a few prints around, but with the dust coating them, I'd guess they belong to Schleter."

Lije attemped to stand in a manner that created the illusion he was looking for something specific, but he sensed Curtis saw through his ruse and chose not to make fun of him. Finding nothing crime-related to point out, he straightened up and glanced at his watch. "It's ten-thirty."

Curtis moved over to an easy chair, swept away the dust with her gloved hand, and sat down. "We can guess that two men were looking for something rather small, something that could be hidden in a book. Looks like they searched through the entire house. I'm surmising they didn't find the object of their search. Or, if they did find it, it was in the last place they looked and they would not have to look further. Since someone has been on the property in the last few days and did not come back into the house, they probably decided to expand their search to another part of the property. That leads me to believe they're still looking for that something, whatever it is."

Lije listened intently. It all sounded logical. But there was something she hadn't addressed. As weird as this place was, there was one thing that really stood out. It was time to take a step of faith and see if what he had noticed was important. "The place is built like a bomb shelter. The outside walls are thick enough to take mortar fire."

"Schleter was an eccentric and probably paranoid. He constructed a fortress to ease his fears and make himself feel secure."

"That was my first thought when we walked in," Lije said. "But then I noticed that the inside walls are just as thick."

Curtis looked at the wall between the kitchen and living room. It was at least two feet wide. The wall between the bedroom and the living room was made in exactly the same fashion.

"Would I be stupid to think there might be a hollow place between the walls?" Lije asked.

Curtis hurried back to the bedroom and pulled a hammer from a drawer she had gone through. She went to the nearest interior wall and started tapping. Lije listened as she continued the exercise all the way through the house. When she returned, she said, "They're as solid as the outside walls."

"What about the attic?"

"There's a crawl space in the bedroom that allows entry to it," Curtis said. "It's a large open area, but the only thing stored up there is a trunk. The guys who got here before us opened it and dumped the stuff on the attic floor. All I saw were some German military uniforms, a couple of ancient family photo books, and some personal letters postmarked 1944 and back. Nothing that caused any alarms to go off."

Curtis and Lije poked around some more, exploring the house. The building not only was in a time warp but was a home that reflected another country. The books were all in German, the prints in the frames were scenes from Germany, the furniture and the dinnerware all looked as though they were purchased in Europe and shipped here. Nothing, other than some canned goods in the cabinets and a few items in the laundry and bathrooms, appeared to have their origins in this country or even to have been purchased in this decade. Yet even as antiques, nothing appeared to have any real value.

Curtis led the way out of the house, and Lije locked the door. They walked back to the car. Curtis dropped off most of the gear in the trunk and picked up two handguns. She handed Lije one of the weapons (in case he was right, she said, and someone was still after him). She picked up a backpack that she said contained peanut butter crackers and bottled water, then led the way as they set off down the hill, following the recent tire tracks in the foot-tall grass.

THEY MOVED DOWN A SLIGHT INCLINE AND FOUND themselves headed up a fairly steep hill. "Lije, what do you know about this land?"

"Well, as you can see, it's pretty much untouched by man. This whole area is like that. If you were to go deep enough in the woods, you might find some signs of stills that were used to produce moonshine, but not much else. Except for a handful of hunters, few modern men or women have ever seen what we are seeing now."

Curtis stopped and glanced skyward. Sitting atop a hundred-foot oak tree was an eagle. It stared at them, studying their moves, its head slowly bobbing from one side to the other.

"That's a golden eagle," Lije said. "There are a few bald eagles that have recently come back into the area, but the golden is much more common."

As if bored by the humans' actions, the eagle took off, spreading its wings and riding a breeze that took it above the tree line. Banking to the left, it headed toward the stream, gliding down toward the water.

As they continued their climb up the ridge, Lije noted several places where the truck that had chosen this same path had lost traction and slid to the right, then the left. It was clear the vehicle had gotten stuck in a soft spot near the top of the hill.

"Bet they got muddy trying to push their way out of this mess," Curtis said. "Must have been a day or two after the huge rain."

Her words sliced through Lije like a knife. The huge rain had almost left his memory. Was that good or bad? Had he been hiding from the memory? What kind of memory had driven the German to hide inside his fortress of solitude?

They kept climbing. Curtis pulled out her cell phone. No service. No reason for towers out here. No one ever came out here. They stopped for water and crackers. Lije mentioned the two caves he'd noted in the property description.

Within a few miles, they found a place where the vehicle had been parked. They were in a small meadow, maybe fifty by thirty feet across. Lije judged them to be about a quarter of a mile from the river, about a hundred feet higher. He could hear the swiftly flowing water, but the thick forest made it impossible to see. On the north side of the meadow was a long sharp cliff. The other three sides were dense with trees and bushes. Curtis bent down to try to find some evidence of footprints.

Lije walked toward the edge of the cliff. Ducking under a low-hanging elm branch, he worked his way along a pathway that ran beside the cliff for fifty yards, then, as the sharp edge of the cliff ended, the trail made a soft right up a steep grass-covered hill. Working his way upward at about a thirty-degree angle for another twenty feet, he felt a sudden rush of cool air. Partially hidden by the leaves of a dogwood tree was an eight-foot-high, four-foot-wide opening in the hillside.

Should he go get Curtis? He kept climbing and soon was standing at the entrance. The cool air coming from inside the cavern made it feel as if an air conditioner had been left on. It was a welcome relief from the heat and humidity. He took the flashlight from his pocket. He'd get Curtis only if he found something interesting. For now, it was his land and his cave. He turned the flashlight on and followed the beam inside.

The cave was at least twenty feet high and probably thirty feet wide. About twenty feet past the entrance, the cavern made a sharp left. So there was at least one more chamber. Stopping to adjust his eyes to the darkness, Lije shined the light off each of the walls and across the floor. He spotted only bat droppings and dirt. Then the flashlight beam picked up a sharp edge. Footprints. Definitely footprints. And they looked recent.

He considered going back for Curtis, but moved on. Shining his light ahead, he hugged the rock wall, leaning out only to see if his beam could pick up anything. At first he saw zilch, just another chamber, this one perhaps twenty by fifteen and no more than ten feet high. He continued to flash his beam off the walls, the ceiling, the floor. Something at the back of the cave caught his eye. Something sticking out from behind a four-foot-high sandstone boulder. Keeping his light aimed at the object, Lije slowly put one foot in front of the other. When he was less than ten feet from the wall, he finally recognized what he had caught in his beam—two black boots.

He froze. His heart pounding, he moved closer. The boots had not been tossed behind the rock. The boots were attached to a body, and it was a body he knew well.

"Mikki."

Lying on the ground, her hands and feet bound, a blindfold tied over her eyes, was his old high school classmate, the very first girl he had kissed and the girl he had taken to the junior prom. Falling to his knees, he reached down and felt her face. She was warm. Grabbing her hand, he put his fingers on her wrist.

"She's alive!"

MIKKI STUART WAS ALIVE BUT UNCONSCIOUS. LIJE untied her hands and legs. She had to be dehydrated, and there appeared to be a gunshot wound in her back, but since Lije knew so little about medicine, that was only a guess. Unable to rouse her, he removed her blindfold, patted her head, and spoke in reassuring tones.

"If you can hear me, I want you to know that I'll be back. You just hang on. I'm going to get help."

After checking Stuart's pulse a final time, he got up and raced from the cave. As he retraced his steps, stumbling along the uneven path, he screamed, "Diana!" Twice he fell, but quickly he was up and moving along the trail. Heart pounding, he pushed aside branches and stepped over rocks. Ignoring the pain in his side from his own healing wound, he was consumed by one thought—get help. Curtis was the only one who might be able to save Mikki. He wasn't going to lose another person close to him.

"What's wrong?" Curtis demanded as she raced toward the clearing.

"I found Mikki Stuart. She's alive!"

Curtis pulled out her cell phone. Still no signal. "Where is she?"

He whirled, pushing past tree branches and headed back along the trail to the opening in the hill. He led the way through the cave until they finally reached the deputy.

Curtis made a quick but thorough examination. "She's been shot. She's alive, but I'm not sure how much longer she has. Her breathing is shallow and her pulse is weak. She's probably been without food and water for a week, and she's covered with insect bites. We need a medical team here now."

Curtis looked back at Stuart, placed her hand on the woman's forehead. "She's burning up. Lije, you know the area better than I do. If I run back and get the car, how long will it take us to get to the nearest hospital?"

"From here ... an hour, maybe more."

Shaking her head, she leaned back down and rechecked the woman's pulse. "The car won't make it down the trail anyway. It's not four-wheel drive. You any good at climbing?"

"I did my share when I was younger."

"Can you find a quick way up the bluff and call for a medical copter? It could land in that meadow."

"I can try."

"You've got your cell?"

"Yeah."

Curtis reached into her pocket and retrieved her phone. "Here's mine. Better take them both. One might work even if the other doesn't. Don't take any risks, but get up there as fast as you can."

Rushing from the cave, Lije quickly made his way through the woods and back to the meadow. In the clearing, he looked upward. The highest point in the area was some three hundred feet above, but without a rope, he wasn't going to be able to scale the cliff. He'd have to run along the base to the point where the slope was more gradual, climb up that section, and then make his way back to the high point.

Except ... standing on top of a hundred-foot rise just a short distance to his right was a walnut tree that had to be at least a hundred and thirty feet tall and probably was older than the United

States. It could be the quickest way of getting help. He had climbed a bunch of trees as a kid. Like riding a bike, surely it was something you never forgot. Right?

Pushing to the east, he worked his way through thickets and over boulders, barely able to see the sky above his head. Thorns tore his pants and scratched his legs and arms. The forest's uneven surface caused him to stumble and fall more times than he could count. Progress was slow.

After excruciating work, sweat soaking his clothes and his legs aching from scrapes and bruises, he broke out of the underbrush and walked through a wild blueberry patch into a clearing. There, just ten yards in front of him, was the walnut tree.

This had better work. It was his only chance. It was Mikki's only chance. Surely it was tall enough. But what if it wasn't?

Lije swung up on the lowest branch and started to climb, moving from branch to branch like a fireman climbing a ladder. The only interruptions in his ascent were when he stopped to check for a cell phone signal. At the halfway point there was nothing. No signal at the hundred-foot mark either. The gamble looked like it was not going to pay off.

Pushing up, he continued to check at each limb. Nothing, and he was running out of tree. Now within ten feet of the top, at a point where the wind was causing the trunk and branches to lazily sway from side to side, he wrapped his arms around the trunk and glanced at his phone. Finally, it was there, faint, but it was a signal! Locking his legs around the tree, he quickly punched in the number. Though the transmission was almost completely engulfed by static, a few seconds later the operator picked up.

Hold, baby, hold! The connection was so weak. But he didn't lose it.

"Emergency services, I'm on Swope's Ridge, a woman badly injured. … S-W-O-P-E-S Ridge! … Yes, that's right, we need help! We found Deputy Stuart!"

He listened for a moment, trying to make out the crackling

words, "Yes! Swope's Ridge on Spring River. Lock on to my GPS. There's a clearing not far from here, at the end of an old logging trail. The helicopter can land there."

She couldn't understand. She couldn't hear him. His voice was breaking up. He had to try again. Moving a few feet higher, he repeated his instructions. This time he was yelling. Shouting. He kept repeating his words and finally she got it. Help was on the way.

Snapping his phone shut, he slipped it back into his pocket and took a deep breath. It had worked! Thank God it had worked.

41

LIJE HUNG ONTO THE SWAYING TREE UNTIL FINALLY his heart rate returned to near normal. He looked out over the land—his land—and was amazed at the incredible view offered by his lofty perch. He was on top of the world. Or at least near the top of Fulton County, and that felt like the top of the world. The ridge was almost at eye level. To his left he could make out the cave and the meadow. He could even see that Curtis had managed to move Stuart to the clearing and was waiting there for help. He prayed Mikki was all right. She just had to be. She was tough; she'd make it.

He looked back toward the river. The sun was almost directly overhead. A rotting post oak was leaning out over the water as if waiting for the next big storm to tear it from its foundation. Two fishermen were floating down the stream in a flat-bottom johnboat. One was trying to reel in a trout. Lije watched the man work the rod and reel, then saw something glinting on the bank, reflecting the sun's rays. Looked like metal, at least a yard long. Focusing on the object, he wondered what it could be. It was too small to be a boat pushed on the bank. He moved to get a better view and it was gone. As if it had been moved.

He needed to alert Curtis that help was on the way, so he began his long descent. Once on the ground, he patted the tree, took a final look at his perch, and began hiking through the woods.

On his way back, he heard the helicopter fly in and land. He arrived at the meadow just as the medevac crew was loading Mikki onto the copter.

"Good job, Lije," Curtis said. "The flyboys think she has a chance to pull through. They got some fluids in her before they loaded her up."

Lije watched as the copter lifted off. Mikki was a good person. She didn't deserve this. Then again, no one deserved what had happened—not Dean, not Jennings, and surely not Kaitlyn. And the other man, the suicide, what was his name?

Laying her hand on Lije's shoulder, Curtis said, "You saved her life."

"She saved mine a week ago."

How had Mikki survived in the cave for that long? Anyone else would have given up and died. She was always tough—state champ in cross-country in high school. And she was still going the distance.

Curtis and Lije walked back toward the trail. Curtis said, "I got on the medics' radio and ordered an ABI team to come up here and look at the cave. Doubt if we'll get anything that'll help us solve this thing, so we have to pretty much hope Stuart can tell us what happened. I need to stay here with the team. Hope you don't mind hanging around for a while."

Lije turned his gaze from the sky to the river. "Don't mind at all."

THE TREK DOWN THE HILL TO THE RIVER WASN'T AS easy as Lije had expected. While Curtis waited for the arrival of more ABI agents to investigate the cave—and probably survey the whole ridge—Lije made his way down to the river. It was a solid forty minutes before he finally broke out of the woods onto the grassy bottomland. He paused there, resting, and took a long drink of bottled water.

The river was much cooler and much louder than Lije had remembered it in his many trips downstream by canoe. The water rushing over the rapids made it difficult to hear anything else.

Spring River was fed by Mammoth Spring, one of the largest, if not the largest, springs in the world. More than nine million gallons of water poured out of the ground each hour. Even at its headwaters the river was more than seventy-five feet wide. The water temperature never varied; it was always fifty-eight degrees—winter, spring, summer, and fall. The cold water acted as a natural air conditioner for the bottomland. At night, fog would drift off the water and swallow almost everything on both sides of the river.

In the first ten miles of the river's run through these hills, it fell in waterfalls or rapids more than twenty times. Some of the falls were six to ten feet in height; most were no more than a foot or two, like the series of rapids he was standing beside. But any of them could flip a canoe as easily as he could pick up a rock and toss it in the water.

He walked over to the bank's edge and looked upstream. About five hundred yards away, the water splashed over a series of rocks that formed a horseshoe-shaped falls. Looked like someone had lost an ice chest that was caught in the rapids. Probably lost their lunch. The falls looked harmless, but there was a whirlpool waiting below the spot most people picked to shoot the rapids. That bit of water had humbled him several times. Someday it was going to drag someone down and not let go. Even the placid places in this stream could be killers.

Lije leaned over to look down into the water. It was so clear that if your eyes were good enough, you could read the date on a penny at a depth of ten feet. Or so he'd been told.

There weren't many places in the country where a person could still see this kind of unspoiled nature. Kaitlyn would say, "Anyone who experiences the majesty and the power of this river has to believe in God." She had enjoyed capsizing the canoe and watching Lije's shock at the cold water. When he was with her, a day on Spring River always erased any doubts he might have about a supreme being. Yet now, even with so much splendor all around him, he wasn't so sure.

Kaitlyn was dead.

Lije turned from the water and began the short trek up the bank and back into the bottomland. He thought what he had seen from up in the tree was somewhere over there. He studied the ground to his left and to the right. What should've been right in front of him wasn't there. Things looked a lot different at ground level. The angle of the sun was different too.

He studied the ridge, found the walnut tree, and turned back toward the water. Initially he saw nothing familiar. It looked so different now. But then he saw it, the rotting post oak tree leaning over the edge of the stream on the other side of the river next to the Frisco Line track.

Turning back toward the ridge, he walked a few feet to his left. This seemed to be the right place; it was in line with the walnut tree and the dead post oak. Curtis might use CSI techniques to find things, but Lije opted to use the time-tested rural method: walk the area until you stumble into something. He turned and took three steps forward. On his fourth, his toe caught on something hard, and he fell forward. He landed on his hands just as his knees hit the rocky soil. It was at least the fifth time that day that his knees had tested the solidness of rock.

Wincing, he pushed himself up and brushed off his jeans. He took a step back to see what had caused his fall, and there it was. Sometimes the old ways of doing things were the best ways.

Lije thought he'd tripped over a rock, but the object was metal, a little rusty. It looked like iron or steel. He began brushing away the dirt. The rains must have washed away the ground and exposed this for the first time in decades. He pushed away more dirt and realized what he had seen from up in the tree.

It was a railroad track rail. But the Frisco Line was on the other side of the river.

Lije pulled out a pocket knife and carefully went to work, pushing away the clay and pebbles from the object. After ten minutes on his knees, he had cleared a square foot of ground to a depth of almost four inches. He bent down to more closely examine the object. It was hard to believe what he was seeing.

Dr. Cathcart was going to want to know about this.

Lije was sure now that the rail hadn't been washed up here or just dropped here as trash; it had been set in place. Some rusty spikes and even remnants of the wood ties were still in place. Could this railroad track be what everyone was looking for? And if it was, why was it here? There was no place for it to go.

He followed the rail, uncovering more as he walked toward the river. The track didn't end until it was five feet from where the bank sloped down to meet the water's normal level. He walked down the bank to the water's edge and looked up at the place where the track was buried. On the shore where dirt and grass had been washed away by the recent high water, he saw stacked rocks at least a foot wide and two feet high. Probably a stone wall had been constructed there. It almost looked like part of a bridge support wall.

Lije should have gone back for Curtis, or at least for a shovel. But he wanted to find out how far the tracks went. He walked back up to the tracks, dropped to his knees, and kept digging with his knife. After fifteen minutes, he had uncovered only a few more inches of track. He'd convinced himself he needed help.

As he started to stand up, he made one last swipe of his knife into the hard clay. The knife freed something. It looked like a stone encrusted with clay. Then he noticed the intricate design of a cross.

He picked it up, got to his feet, and walked back down to the river. Dipping his find into the water, he rinsed off the dirt and wiped it clean with his shirttail. He had found a gold ring, a man's ring, with a cross—not the typical Christian cross, but a squarer, more intricate design—made of red stones. He wasn't sure, but they looked like rubies.

THE NEXT MORNING, LIJE HAD A CONTACT AT THE courthouse bring him copies of everything in the public records about Swope's Ridge. He and Curtis were going over the copies at the kitchen table. Older records showed three caves and three springs; newer records showed only two caves. The springs might well have dried up over the years. There were no details on where the caves were.

Curtis got a phone call; the ABI was finished with the examination of Swope's Ridge. Agents had found a second cave and evidence that someone had recently searched every corner of the cave and even done some digging. Still, no evidence that could tie anyone to the kidnapping of Deputy Stuart.

"Stuart's awake," Curtis said. "She's going to make it. Hillman said she didn't see who attacked her. Just that she had gone down by the creek and had just discovered Old Iron had been swept away. Someone must have come up behind her. Her neck's bruised and she's got a lump on the head. She remembers waking up in a moving vehicle. Her head was covered. Must have blacked out again. She didn't know she had been shot."

Lord, he had been hoping that she would have at least seen a face. Heard something.

"Diana, did they go down to the river?"

"You mean the team? No."

"So they don't know about the railroad tracks?" He had told her about the tracks on their way back to Salem.

"I didn't see how they tied in to the case, so I didn't give Barton that information."

Lije tried not to smile. He liked knowing something Hillman didn't. "Thanks. Did Hillman tell you about the bullet information?"

Curtis avoided his eyes. "No, he hasn't told me anything. But I'm sure the lab tech told him that he gave us the file."

"I need to go back to Mountain View today, so I'm guessing you'll be going with me."

She was almost robotic as she turned and began walking toward the door. "I'm ready."

"I meant after I finish my peanut butter and syrup sandwich."

"Is that what that is?"

"Old family recipe. Our breakfast of champions."

Curtis shook her head. "Go ahead and finish. Then we'll hit the road. How in the world are you so thin?"

As he ate, she walked out onto the back patio, now shaded by a large maple tree. He watched through the window as she placed her hands on the deck railing and leaned forward. After he had savored the last few bites of his breakfast, he joined her.

"I can understand why your grandfather bought this hill and built his home up here. I can't believe someplace this tranquil is actually in the city limits."

"I've lived here almost my whole life, and I never get tired of it. Must admit, I've wasted a few days doing little more than looking out at this view."

He turned to look at her. "I finished my breakfast."

THE SKY BEGAN TO CLOUD OVER AND THE SUN PLAYED hide and seek as the white Crown Victoria pulled through the horde of reporters and media satellite trucks and headed out of Salem. Curtis had cleared a path by flashing her ABI credentials.

"Looks like rain," Curtis said.

Lije nodded. As they rolled down Arkansas 9 at just under a mile a minute, his mind was not on the road but rather firmly locked onto the image of an old friend. He hadn't thought of it until he heard about Mikki Stuart's memory of that night. "Diana, where did Old Iron end up?"

"Actually, the sheriff's department found it a hundred or so yards downstream. They tell me it's in pretty good shape too. They're trying to figure out how to get a crane in there and extract it. From what I hear, that's going to be a tricky operation."

"Have you seen it?"

"No. Why?"

"I'd like to take a look at it. We're almost there. This may sound stupid, but that old bridge was always there, kind of like an old friend. I still can't fathom any flood being able to knock it down. Guess I just want to see it to believe it."

"Well, your timing's good," Curtis said. She tapped her turn signal and made a left. As she drove down the old road, Lije's eyes were drawn to the hillside where he and Kaitlyn had tried to elude their attackers. The crime scene tape had been removed and nature had already started to reclaim the area.

His memory was no problem now. He could clearly remember the struggle, Kaitlyn's screams, her last words, and the cold pain he felt when the bullet tore into his back. A sense of loss flooded his soul and a voice deep inside begged him to cry, to let loose a torrent of tears, to allow himself to grieve. Instead, he forced his eyes back to the road and looked ahead to the place where the bridge had once securely crossed the now docile creek.

After easing the car to a stop, Curtis stepped out into the humid air. Lije followed her to the creek bank. It was all he could do to keep from running down the bank as if the hounds of hell were nipping at his heels.

"They told me it was down this way. I can see where they've been walking," Curtis said.

They silently trudged along the creek, following the path the sheriff's deputies and county road crew had blazed. They rounded a sharp bend and, like a ghost from another age, Old Iron appeared. It was resting upside down, with one end on the creek bottom and the other rising above the sloping bank.

As they approached the bridge, Curtis slipped into investigator mode. "Pretty much how I would have expected it to rest. Imagine the force of the water needed not only to tear it from its piers but then to carry it this far! Pretty amazing! I don't know of a machine in the county that could have accomplished that."

Lije didn't reply. Instead he worked his way to the top of the bank and examined the end of the bridge that was most exposed. There it was, the place where he had carved his initials on his tenth birthday. Seized by a childlike urge, he climbed onto the bracing and up to what had once been the bridge's roadbed. Though the metal framing was still solid, the wooden plank floor was all but ripped away. It was like seeing a friend mangled in a car wreck. He sat down on the base of the bridge and dangled his legs off the edge toward the creek.

This was the bridge where he and Mikki had played as kids. It was the place where they had shared their first kiss. It was the structure that had served as their diving board into the river and the last thing they'd drive over as they left town heading to Thayer for a movie. For hundreds like them, the bridge had been their anchor.

Finding his voice, he said, "When are they going to let folks visit Mikki?"

Curtis looked up from the bank. "Not for a few days. She's still in ICU. With the meds they have her on, she's not really aware of much anyway. Maybe when she gets off them she'll remember more."

"Sure hope so," he replied. "Thankful she didn't give her life for this madness." Lije thought of Mikki's kids and her husband, how glad they'd be to have her back. How lucky they all were that she was still alive.

Shaking the horrors of the near past from his head, he glanced back toward the spot where the bridge had been bolted to the concrete supports. Though he was hardly a mechanical engineer, what he saw surprised him.

"I wouldn't have thought it would have snapped like that," he said as he slid toward the end. "Did the ABI look at the bridge?"

"Probably not," Curtis said. "No reason to. It was just an accident or an act of God. Why, what do you see?"

"Look for yourself."

Using the rails as if she were a grade-school student on the monkey bars, Curtis scrambled up beside him and looked at the spot where Lije was pointing. She then quickly crawled across the rail to the other side of the bridge. Reaching into her pocket, she retrieved her phone and tapped in one of her most frequently used numbers.

"Eddie, is your crew still in Fulton County? . . . Good, because our initial crime scene just got larger. The bridge — the one they call Old Iron — I'm sitting on it right now, and it didn't just get pushed off the supports by the floodwaters. ... Right. There are obvious charge marks on the metal. Someone blew this thing off its anchors. I have to get on down to Mountain View, but you and the guys need to take a closer look at this and at the bridge's original location."

She paused, then said, "Sounds good. Keep me posted. I've got Lije Evans with me. We'll wait for you here."

Lije caught her eye. "Did I hear you right?"

"Yep, you did see something strange. This thing was blown off its moorings. I would guess it was a professional job. This wasn't just a prank. Someone who knew what they were doing took out that bridge for a reason."

Curtis continued to examine the barely visible scorch marks on the iron. After looking at one, then scooting back to the other, she nodded. "There's only one reason I can think of."

45

LIJE WAS GLAD CURTIS HAD A THEORY. HE SURE DIDN'T.

"Lije, you said someone forced you off the highway."

He turned until his eyes met hers. What was she saying? What did he have to do with the bridge? "Yes, they forced me off the highway. Best I can remember, they had stayed behind me until just before we got to Farraday Road. Then they pulled up alongside and started ramming us. I had no choice but to turn." ·

"That makes sense. And it fits my theory. Why did you stop on the side of the road and get out?"

"I lost control, slipped in the mud, and skidded over to the right shoulder. Ended up across the ditch. My original plan was to outrun them over the bridge and try to lose them on the other side of the old cemetery. I thought I was going to make it too. They had dropped back quite a long way behind me. I thought they were having trouble getting traction on the muddy road."

Moving along the upside-down structure's few remaining boards, Curtis plopped down beside him. "And that's exactly what they wanted you to do. It was supposed to look like an accident. I think they blew the bridge earlier in the day or that evening, followed you from the diner, probably even followed you from the charity event, and then forced you to take Farraday Road. With the bridge out, they were going to chase you into the flooded creek. It would've all looked like an accident. Your skid forced them to take a different tactic."

"We were supposed to drown? The shooting was not in the plan?"

"And no one would've ever investigated that accident. As far as hits go, this was about as well planned as I've seen. They knew your schedule. They understood the problems the weather was creating. And they knew how to cover their tracks and make it look like a horrible accident. It was really ingenious. But the weather played a trick on them. Caused you to get stuck. At that point they panicked. They had no choice. They had to get rid of you some other way. Probably figured they'd get away with it too until they saw the deputy's car coming down the road."

"But why?" Lije asked.

"Don't know that ... yet. I'm working on it. My guess is that they had gone toward the creek to turn around and, when they saw Stuart's car approach, they pulled off the road and stayed hidden. Then, when the ambulance left, they waited for Stuart to leave. Just her bad luck that she ran down to check on the bridge. Probably afraid she'd seen their car, they came up behind her, knocked her out, stuffed her in their vehicle, and hightailed it out of there. The backup patrol car couldn't have missed them by more than a minute or two. Their only real mistake was not killing Stuart. Can't figure out why they left her in the cave. Still, when they came back into town, they heard you were alive. That's when they took the shots at us by your house."

Lije shuddered in disbelief. Why would he and Kaitlyn be targets? Why would anyone go to all that trouble? What had they done? What did they have? And then he knew ... Swope's Ridge. But who was behind all this?

"You may not like it Lije, but this new element with the bridge just slipped the noose tighter around Jameson's neck."

"How?"

"She knew your schedule. She could easily set up the people to follow you. She knew that you would come home from the charity event via Arkansas 9. She knew you always stopped at Jim's Diner. She knew about Farraday Road and the bridge. That you'd cross over into the cemetery. Someone had to be aware of all of those details to create such a perfect plan."

"I still don't believe it," Lije said.

"I think Swope's Ridge is little more than a diversion to take our focus off the real plan. Jameson doesn't care about the property. She probably thought of the cave because Kaitlyn and she went there and found it as they toured the place, figured it was a good way to get rid of Stuart. The body'd never be found. Jameson had access to the keys, so it was easy to get in. But I'll bet money she didn't know about the Jesse James legend."

"But the house was turned inside out," Lije pointed out. "The caves have been thoroughly searched recently. Someone was looking for something, and it had to have something to do with why Micah Dean and Kaitlyn were killed." There had to be something on Swope's Ridge that triggered everything. Surely she could see that. It was clear.

"But who was doing the looking on the ridge?" Curtis asked. "Has it crossed your mind that we may have two different groups here? Jameson admitted during her jail interview with Hillman that she visited Swope's Ridge with your wife on two occasions. She could've told the men she hired, the ones who shot you and your wife and kidnapped Stuart, about the caves on the property, told them to dump the body in one of them. Shot Stuart, left her for dead. The folks who ransacked the house might have been someone else entirely. They could've finished their search weeks or even months ago."

Lije mulled over the theory. Two groups, unrelated. Made no sense. Swope's Ridge had to be connected to Kaitlyn's murder. It was the only way things made sense to him.

"Small town crime is usually open and shut," Curtis said. "Murders in rural areas are often the easiest to solve and have the least intrigue. The guilty party is almost always a relative or a close friend. I think your lawyer is there in the middle of it. She was like family. She fits the usual pattern of rural murders."

Lije stared back down at the creek. The experts seemed to be gathering more and more evidence against a woman he knew was innocent. It now appeared he was Heather's worst enemy. The more he did to try to give Heather hope, the stronger the case against her seemed to grow, as far as Curtis and the ABI were concerned. And what if they were right? If Heather was behind all of this, he didn't know what he'd do.

THE SIGN READ, "WELCOME TO MOUNTAIN VIEW, HOME of the Arkansas Folk Festival."

"What's that?" Curtis asked as she drove into the city.

"A sign," Lije replied.

She glared at him. "You know what I mean."

"The Arkansas Folk Festival is a music festival. This is a hopping little town. Everyone plays an instrument, and they often gather to have bluegrass jam sessions. They actually make handmade fiddles, guitars, and banjos here."

"Sounds like fun."

They pulled into a parking spot and got out of the vehicle. They stepped up onto the sidewalk and headed toward the police station. Curtis looked over at the man she'd been assigned to protect. This was not proper procedure, reopening a case like this. It bothered her. But not enough to stop. Like Lije, she needed to find out something. Had her boss compromised the truth? What was he trying to hide? Had she become an unknowing party to his agenda? And if he had done it this time, had he done it on other cases?

She followed Lije into the quaint small-town police station. He introduced himself to the receptionist and they were promptly ushered into the chief's office. Curtis allowed all of this to happen even though she knew they were in way over their heads.

"Chief Hall?" Lije said.

A wiry man not more than five-foot-eight greeted the two with a warm smile and firm handshakes. "I know you. You're Diana Curtis from the ABI. Pleasure to have you here. I met you once at the ABI offices. And I know you, Lije Evans. I knew your father very well. A wonderful man. Of course, Mr. Evans, I can't begin to tell you how sorry I am about your wife. I understand it was your partner was responsible. That makes it doubly tragic. Come on in, sit down."

The chief continued, nonstop. "In fact, the *National Enquirer* has a cover story on the woman this week. I never read those things, but I picked one up last night at the Town and Country grocery. I also saw a piece about her and the problems that led her to commit this crime on one of the major cable news networks last night."

Why didn't Lije cut him off? Curtis wondered. This kind of talk was going to dig deep and just might set him off. Even if it was the truth, he didn't need to hear it, not now, not yet. Yet Hall's mouth just kept moving.

"You know, we in small Arkansas towns constantly fight for publicity and then someone from outside the area moves in and places us in the spotlight for all the wrong reasons. Mr. Evans, this coverage must make things doubly difficult on you. Once again, my heartfelt condolences. Why in the world would she do this? She must be a real animal."

Lije said nothing. His only movement was a casual glance at the cover of the *Intruder* resting on the chief's desk.

"Miss Curtis," the chief began, his brown eyes afire with excitement.

"Please, call me Diana."

"And you call me Luke. I insist on it." He took his place behind the desk and leaned back in his chair. "Can you tell me what brings the ABI here?"

She glanced over at Lije, feeling nervous. He seemed to want her to take the lead. Though she knew what he was after, she wasn't ready to reveal information that *would* throw this case wide open.

She had broken a host of rules just by coming here. Now she'd have to fake her way through an off-the-books visit while making it look official. The hole she was already standing in was going to get much deeper.

With no real exit, she made like a professional, smiled, and tried to act as casual as possible. "Chief Hall — excuse me, I mean Luke — I'm also working on the case in Salem, so I need to do this as quickly as possible. If I decide there's something here, then we'll send in a full CSI team. Anyway, this is going to take you back a couple of years. I need a little background on a Mr. Michael Rivers."

"Wow, that does take me back. Hadn't thought about him in a while. This important?"

"I don't know. It might have relevance to a cold case. If it does pan out, then you'd look like a big hero in Little Rock." Appeal to his ego. Nice job, Curtis.

"Well for starters, everyone around here just knew him as Moony. He was in his late thirties, kind of strange, I guess disabled in some ways. I mean physically he was fine, but" — Hall pointed to his forehead — "upstairs he was a bit off center, if you know what I mean."

"Would you say he was retarded?" she asked.

"In some ways, I guess," Hall admitted, "but in other ways he was a genius. He could do anything with computers, cameras, clocks. You should see the photographs he took. They were like something out of *National Geographic*. He took pictures of everyone and everything around here. And the decade before he died he got into video. Had several cameras and he shot everything that happened."

"So everyone knew he was good," she said.

"Sure did. If your kid had a great basketball game, Moony caught it and then went back to his house and edited it. He would even put it on a DVD and give it to you. He did that for folks who sang specials in church or were in local car shows and just about everything else. He even filmed a lot of the local musicians and made DVDs that they sold at shows. And if there were two things going on at once, he would set up what he called a slave camera. He'd video one event while he was at another. You want some coffee or something?"

"No, we don't have much time," Curtis said. She smiled.

"Anyway, while Moony wasn't very good at reading and writing, he was amazing in a few things that the rest of us didn't know much about. And he was always so happy. Never saw him without a smile. That's why it was such a shock when he killed himself."

Hall's brown eyes took on a far-off look. "I have a DVD of my daughter's graduation. She spoke that night. Moony caught it all and it looked so professional. Jessica died a few weeks later in a car accident. You have no idea what that DVD has meant to my wife and me over the years."

Dean used Moony to videotape his conversations with Jennings, Curtis remembered. Was it something he caught with his camera that got him killed? Where were the tapes now? "Chief, why did you think Moony committed suicide?"

"Well, no one had seen him in a couple of days. Let me see, this would have been two years ago. I guess I should've noticed earlier, but I was all tied up with the Micah Dean case. Anyway, when he didn't come around, we got concerned. I knocked on his door, and when I didn't get an answer, I forced the lock. He was sitting in his chair in the living room, a gun in his hand and a bullet in his head. There was a note printed out—guess he had written it on his computer—and it gave his reasons. I've got the note here somewhere." The chief rolled his chair over to a filing cabinet, opened a drawer, and leafed through the folders. "Here it is." He glanced at it and handed the note to Curtis.

She read it and handed it to Lije. He studied the words they both knew were penned by someone else: "I am just too sad to go on. My life is meaningless. I am very lonely and I want to be with my mother."

Curtis looked back at Hall. "What did you think when you read the note?"

"Well, Diana, I thought, what a waste. What more could I think? The whole town felt the same way. If we'd known he was that lonely, we would've done something. We all felt guilty about it."

Lije glanced over at Curtis, but she gave him a look that told him she wanted him to keep quiet. Off the record or not, she was intent on taking the questions according to the game plan she had witnessed Hillman use countless times. She was going to push, but she was going to make sure Hall didn't realize he was being pushed.

"So I take it he had no enemies?"

"None."

"What about the site where he died?"

"His little mobile home. It hasn't been touched since I found him, other than cleaning up the blood. His closest kin is in New York and they still haven't come to claim the estate, what little there is. The town's just sort of left well enough alone. Don't think anybody's even been in the place lately."

"Can you show it to us?" she asked.

"Sure. Got the keys right here in the folder. Appears it'll be your case now," the chief said, getting up from his desk.

CURTIS DONNED HER GLOVES AND BEGAN EXAMINING
the modest four-room trailer that had been home to Moony Rivers.
The musty smell that engulfed them after the police chief unlocked
the door had made it clear that no one had been inside for a long
time. By habit she flipped a light switch and was surprised the
power was still on.

"I thought the REA would have cut that off," Hall said. "Maybe
because there was nothing using power, they just didn't notice.
Guess the meter reader thought it was off too or he'd have had
them cut the power. I'll have to alert the office."

After looking around, Curtis asked, "Was he always this
messy?"

"Yeah. He usually just stacked stuff in places, but he knew
where everything was."

"Did he keep copies of the DVDs he gave to other people? Like
the video you got?"

"Oh, yeah, he did that in case someone lost their copy or their
DVD got scratched. A lot of us ended up asking him for a second
or third copy to give to relatives."

Curtis studied the living room. It was what she didn't see that
bothered her. No matter where she looked, there didn't seem to be
any tapes or DVDs. "Do you know where he kept the copies?"

"Sure," the chief replied, "I watched him pull them out of the filing cabinets over there. He kept them in order by date. Had them in sleeves in notebooks. So if you knew the date something happened, he could find his copy of it just like that. He then took it over to the DVD burner and made you a copy."

Curtis moved to the far wall. Beside the computer desk were two four-drawer file cabinets. Starting at the one closest to the desk, she opened the top drawer. Empty. One by one she looked in the other seven. They were all empty. Glancing back at Lije and Hall, she said, "I want the two of you to put on some gloves and see if we can find any DVDs or videotapes. There's nothing in these file drawers. No DVDs. No notebooks."

The three worked for an hour. After every cushion had been squeezed, every drawer opened, and every closet checked, they met back in the tiny living room. It was Hall who stated the obvious. "Someone's taken every video and DVD in this place."

"They got even more," Lije said. "I fired up his computer. No files. It's been wiped clean. And I didn't find a single external hard drive."

Curtis nodded. She now had a motive for murder. Someone wanted to make sure that something Moony filmed was never seen again.

"Chief, are you sure no locals came in and took his stuff? Part of the investigation?"

"There was no evidence taken from here but the gun and the bullet. Sent those to the ABI long ago. I've got the only set of keys, and you can see that no one broke in."

She sat down at the desk and went back through the drawers. Nothing seemed out of the ordinary. She found a few coins, some baseball cards, and several hundred dollars in bills. It wasn't a robbery gone bad.

Barton knew something about this case that he was hiding. One call might give her the answer, but making that call was not possible.

Turning back to the chief, she said, "Did Rivers have much money in his savings or checking accounts?"

"Are you kidding?" The chief laughed. "He didn't even have a bank account. He lived on Social Security, his late mother's pension, and what he could make mowing a few lawns. But I guess that was enough to get by. Some folks gave him money to buy computer and video equipment and everyone gave him clothes and groceries, so he didn't need much money to live."

After taking a final look around the room, Curtis pulled off her gloves. "Did you find any guns other than the one you sent to our lab for testing?"

"Naw. We didn't even know he had that one. He was never a violent man."

She got up from the desk. "You said he didn't have a bank account."

"Didn't trust them," Hall explained.

"I found only a few hundred dollars here," she pointed out. "So when he cashed his checks, where did he put his cash?"

The chief shrugged, "I honestly don't know, but you might talk to the folks at the lumberyard."

"Why the lumberyard?"

"Moony's father worked at Hunter Lumber for many years. The old man was almost as strange as his son. He kept his valuables, the few he had, in the company safe. Maybe Moony did the same thing. Listen, I hate to rush you, but I need to get back to the office. I have a staff meeting in a few minutes, but you could go over and talk to Bob Hunter. I know he'd be happy to help you."

They returned to the station, said their goodbyes, and walked over to their car. Hall raced back out of the police station and hollered in their direction.

"Diana, be sure and give my regards to your boss."

She was shocked by the request. "You know Barton?"

"Sure, he's been a great help down here. His contacts have gotten us a lot of state and federal money. Some big projects. We owe him."

"Really?" Lije chimed in. "Why does Hillman show such favor to Mountain View?"

Hall laughed. "I figured you knew our district attorney is his brother-in-law. So give him our best!"

Martin Gooch. Hillman's brother-in-law. Gooch prosecuted Jonathon Jennings in Dean's murder. He had gotten a lot of state press for the way he had handled the case. That spotlight had made him the darling of the "law and order, crime and tough punishment" set. In fact, the Jennings case was the springboard that Gooch used to launch his current run for governor.

Curtis waved. "Sure, chief. Oh, and if you will, don't tell anyone, including the D.A. or even my boss about our meeting. Barton told me to keep this thing quiet. If you mention it to him, he'll come down hard on me. Might even hold it against you too!"

"I understand." He waved as he stepped back into the station.

Sliding into the car, Curtis glanced over at Lije.

"So what do you think?" Lije asked.

"I think I'm glad Barton doesn't know we're here. But I also figure he'll find out soon. If he's trying to cover something for Gooch, we'd better move quickly. Let's get to the lumberyard."

CURTIS DROVE THE FEW BLOCKS THAT MADE UP THE
city's main drag. Her mind raced to connect what they knew—what
Mabel Dean had told Lije, what the lab had reported on the death
of Moony Rivers, and what she had seen at Moony's home. She
now had serious doubts about the case against Jameson. Still, she
wasn't ready to let Lije know about her taking a step onto the
conspiracy bandwagon. Not yet. There had to be another reason.
Maybe at Hunter Lumber she'd find the answer.

Robert Hunter, a heavyset, jolly-looking man, appeared to be
in his late thirties. He met them on the showroom floor. After the
introductions, the third-generation owner led the two back to his
private office. Curtis took a seat, placing her CSI kit beside her
chair, while Lije walked over to look at a series of black-and-white
photos hanging on the far wall.

"I had those matted and framed a few years back," Hunter explained. "As you can see from the ones taken the first few years of
operation, this place hasn't changed much. We've been fortunate.
We're far enough away from a city of any size that we've not had to
compete with the big chains like Lowes and Home Depot."

He looked at Curtis. "Now what kind of questions would someone from the ABI have for me? I hope I didn't accidentally do
something that'll send me to the big house."

Curtis accommodated him with a laugh. "No, you're fine. I'm here on an old case. This shouldn't take long at all. I don't want to waste your time. I understand you knew Moony Rivers pretty well."

"Better than pretty well. We were almost raised together. His father worked for my father and we practically grew up in the lumberyard. I guess he kind of looked at me like I was a brother. In fact, I was the one who convinced Luke Hall to kick in the door and check on him. What he found still chills me to the bone. I just can't believe, even now, that he would take his own life. For the past two years, I have sat in church and worried that suicide is unforgivable. Hard for me to think of a man like that making one irrational mistake and ending up in hell."

Lije moved over to an empty chair beside Curtis. "Mr. Hunter, I don't know much about theology, but the more I do my job, the more obvious it seems that there are forces of good and evil on this earth. From what I've heard about your friend, his heart was evidently filled with goodness. That goodness had to come from somewhere other than hell."

Hunter shook his head. "Thank you. I'm sure you're right, but I've never had such doubts as I do now. Something like this shakes you. I could've accepted an accident, maybe even murder. But suicide? That really unsettled my world. Just didn't fit his personality. Or maybe I didn't know him very well. The other thing that eats at me. I feel like I let him down. Maybe I should've checked on him more often."

"Mr. Hunter," Curtis said, trying to bring the meeting back on track, "Chief Hall said Moony didn't like banks."

Hunter nodded. "Not to keep money in, anyway. He didn't mind them cashing his checks, but what he didn't keep he always brought over here. See that antique safe in the corner? It was manufactured by the Meilink Safe Company in the early 1900s."

Curtis glanced at the black iron safe. With its brass handle and combination lock, it would have made a perfect prop for a movie set in the days of stagecoaches and outlaws, but it looked out of place in today's world.

"You still use it?"

"Actually, no. It's here for decoration. Too heavy to move anywhere else. About the only time I opened it was when Moony wanted to store his stuff. Then I would spin the wheel and leave the room while he put whatever he felt was valuable in an old shoe box he kept on the bottom shelf."

"Are his belongings still in there?" Curtis asked.

"Haven't opened it since he died. Figured it was best to just leave the box in the safe until his family claims his things."

Curtis walked over to the old safe. She studied it carefully. A thick layer of dust covered the top of the old unit. She couldn't believe she had gotten lucky for a second time in one day. No one runs into virgin evidence this old. She turned to face her host. "Are you sure you haven't opened it in two years?"

"No reason to. All I keep in it are some historical documents and photographs. Keep them in the safe just in case of a fire. Have had no reason to look at them."

Curtis picked up her kit from the floor, unlatched the top, and retrieved a spray bottle. As the two men watched, she spent several minutes going over the front, sides, and top of the safe. "Not a single print. At some point since the last time it was opened, the front of this thing has been thoroughly cleaned."

"That's strange," Hunter said. "I mean, that's impossible. I promise it has been years since I dusted anything in here except my desk. If you don't believe me, take a look at the book shelves."

"I'm not saying *you* cleaned it," Curtis said, "just pointing out that someone did. Can you open it for me?"

Hunter went over to the safe. After a few spins of the dial, he flipped the handle and pulled on the heavy iron door. It slowly swung open to reveal a few stacks of photos, some yellowed papers, and a pocket watch. There was no shoe box on the bottom shelf.

"Well, I'll say!" Hunter exclaimed as he reached down toward the empty shelf.

"Don't touch anything," Curtis warned.

"It was right there. I walked back in just as he was putting the box back, then he closed the door. It was the day he died. No one knows the combination but me. I was in here when he closed it, I swear!"

"Mr. Hunter," Curtis said, "without touching anything, can you tell if anything else is missing?"

He quickly scanned the rest of the items. "No, looks like it's all here. The only thing gone is the box."

"Do you have any idea what was in the box?"

"I never looked, but I know he had a few old baseball cards, some cash. Knowing how little he got from Social Security, it couldn't have been much. And some family photographs. Other than that, only Moony knew. He never told me what he put in and I never asked."

Curtis found what she assumed were only two sets of prints. The ones belonging to the owner and the other set belonging to Moony.

"Mr. Hunter, I'm going to close the safe. I'd like for you not to touch it. I may send a team down from the lab to go over it in greater detail. I also don't want you to tell anyone what we've just discovered here. Not even your wife, the chief of police, or the district attorney. In other words, we haven't been here. Do you understand?"

"No problem," he replied. "So someone broke in just to steal the things that Moony thought were valuable?"

Curtis nodded. "That's the way it looks. Thank you for your help."

"I still can't believe he would kill himself," Hunter mumbled as they made their way out of the lumberyard.

Back in the car, Curtis drove out of Mountain View so absorbed by what she had unearthed there that she was oblivious to the fact she had a passenger.

LIJE RODE IN SILENCE. HE WAS TRYING TO PIECE together some kind of connection between three dramatically different crimes. Nothing he came up with fit a pattern. Even as he flipped the pieces in every direction, nothing seemed to fit.

"You hungry?" Curtis asked as they rolled into Melbourne.

"Been that way for three hours or more."

"I don't want anything fancy, just a burger or something, but I do want to get out of the car. What do you suggest?"

"Well, the diner would be the place most folks would pick," Lije offered, "but I don't have any ambition to go in there yet. We could go to the downtown cafe, but there's one place that's closer. The bowling alley has a pretty good snack bar."

"The bowling alley?"

"Yeah, Melbourne Lanes. Take a right at the next stop sign. It's only a block down the road. Shouldn't be the least bit crowded on a Tuesday afternoon."

Melbourne Lanes was a typical small-town bowling alley — a dozen lanes with a tiny snack bar on the left of the entrance and a game room to the right. Except for a few lockers on a back wall and the ball racks that separated the lanes from the business section, there was nothing else. When Lije and Curtis entered, four senior citizens were using one of the middle lanes. A man was sitting at the counter eating a ham sandwich.

Lije led the way to the counter and sat on a padded green stool. Curtis picked the red-topped one on his right. They had barely landed when the owner sprinted out from the tiny kitchen to greet them.

"What'll it be, folks?"

Curtis looked at the menu on the back wall, but Lije was ready. "I'll take the burger basket, plain and dry on the burger, and give me a Coke."

The owner appeared a bit put off with the choice. "You don't want anything on the burger? No mustard or mayo? Or maybe a pickle?"

"Nope, just the meat and bread."

"Sounds dull to me." He turned to Curtis. "And for you?"

Curtis shrugged. "Same, but I want everything on the burger."

"Much better choice. It'll be up in a few minutes." With that he rushed back to the kitchen.

"Want to bowl a game?" Lije asked as he turned his stool around toward the lanes.

"I'm not any good," Curtis admitted.

"Who said I was?" Lije grinned. "Just thought you might welcome a chance to get your mind on something else."

Curtis didn't answer. Instead, without even excusing herself, she got up and headed toward the restrooms. With nothing else to do, Lije watched the two couples on the lane. They weren't any good, but they sure did look as if they were having fun. They laughed whether their rolls brought a strike or a gutter ball. Kaitlyn had liked to bowl and she wasn't any good either.

They should have bowled more. There were a lot of things they should have done more. Suddenly the fun that had seemed so infectious faded, replaced by hopelessness. He had been too busy, left too much undone. Way too much had been lost.

The man at the counter got up and temporarily obstructed Lije's view of the game. "Excuse me," the man said as he passed.

"No problem," Lije replied.

"You know, you look familiar. You from around here?"

"Salem. Lije Evans."

"Collins. I'm from out of state. Up here doing some fishing. Hope you don't mind me saying this, I mean it's none of my business, but you seeem to be kind of down."

"Tough times," Lije said. He glanced up at the man. "You know ... you look familiar too. ... I know, you were at a car show in Texas last year. You had a—"

"Thirty-four Auburn."

"That's it. Great car."

"I remember you too. You had an incredible Cord. Your wife was there too, right? I could never get a woman to come to a car show with me."

"I was blessed," Lije said.

"Did you lose the car?"

"No, I still have it. My wife died."

The stranger shook his head. "Tragic. She was so young. Now I understand your sadness. What happened?"

This time Lije whispered, "She was murdered."

"No. Any idea who did it?"

"Don't know the who or the why."

Collins patted Lije on the shoulder. "Sorry. You'll catch a break soon. ... Hey, if you ever need to talk ... about anything, cars or anything else, let me give you my number." He pulled a receipt out of his pocket, bent over the bar, and scribbled down his number. As he handed it to Lije, he added, "Good luck, man."

LIJE TOOK THE PHONE NUMBER FROM COLLINS, forced a smile, and nodded.

Collins tossed some cash down on the counter and walked out.

Just then the owner brought out two baskets filled to overflowing with crinkle-cut fries and bun-encased meat patties. "Here you go. Can I get you anything else?"

"Not right now," Lije replied.

"How 'bout some mustard for the burger?"

"Nope."

"Well, if you change your mind, I'll be over organizing the shoes. It's league night tonight. Starts at seven."

Lije nodded and watched as the man seemed to bounce toward an area behind the cash register. How could someone that old have that much energy? Picking up the burger, he turned his attention to his hunger. And he was hungry. It was the first time he had really been hungry since the night Kaitlyn died. The burger even tasted good. It was the first time he had actually enjoyed food since the apple pie.

"Well, I see you waited for me," Curtis said.

"He who hesitates is lost. Hey, by the way, I thought you were supposed to protect me. You left me all by myself."

"I'm beginning to believe that your days of hiding are over. I think the ABI will soon free you to your own devices."

"No offense, but I'm looking forward to that day."

"No offense taken, and so am I."

They ate in silence. The burgers were good, even better than those at the 63 Drive Inn, which he rated the best in the world.

He was finishing his last few fries when the bowlers completed their final game. He watched them as they put on their street shoes and walked away from the lane.

"Must be regulars," he noted.

"What makes you say that?" Curtis asked.

"They have their own shoes, balls, and bags." The two couples wandered to the far wall and fiddled with the combinations on two lockers. After opening them, they slid their equipment in and closed the doors. "Yep, they're regulars all right."

"You ready to go?"

"Sure," Lije replied. "This one's on me." He got up, took a last sip of his drink, and headed toward the cash register.

The owner turned his attention from the shoes to Lije. "Can I get you all anything else?"

"No," Lije said, handing the man a twenty. "What you brought us was great."

The owner glanced at the bill and then the ticket. "Thanks. Don't get many folks who come in here just for the food. Most eat between games. That'll be ten-oh-seven, out of a twenty."

As the owner retrieved the change, Lije turned and glanced toward the mint green lockers. They appeared to be much newer than anything else in the building.

"Here's your change," the owner announced.

Reaching for the money, Lije nodded his head toward the wall behind him. "Do many folks rent lockers? I notice those two couples have their own."

"More than you'd probably expect," the owner said. "The rent's cheap, especially if you pay a year or more at a time, and the regulars don't like taking their gear home. After all, this is the only place most of them ever bowl. Would you like to rent one? I've got several vacant right now."

The sales pitch. "No, not really."

"They're real nice. Let me show one to you. I had them installed just three years ago. They're practically new. You'll be surprised how deep they are." He quickly walked over to the far wall and adjusted the numbers on the four dials of the first unit. "This one's mine."

Not wanting to seem rude, Lije followed and looked inside. "Very nice."

"Like I said, put these in about three years ago. You know, some folks use them like the lockers at bus depots. You could open at least a dozen and not find a single thing that had to do with bowling. They're fireproof. Cheaper than a safe-deposit box. Put your hand on them. Give a strong rap. They're solid."

"Lije, we need to hit the road, now," Curtis said.

"Guess you're right," he answered.

And somewhere in Lije's brain, a connection was made. Melbourne. Numbers. The coat.

Turning back to the man, he said, "You know, when I was a kid they had combination locks down at the post office. I used to try to see if I could spin the dial and open one."

Curtis marched over to his side. "That would be a federal crime. Now let's get moving."

"Never got one open. Still, might be fun to try it one more time."

Walking down a few lockers, Lije knocked on three or four units before zeroing in on number seventeen. He was enjoying the show.

"Two. Always liked two. It was on my uniform when I played Little League baseball down at Preacher Roe Park." He dialed the number two on the first wheel of the lock. "Seven. A lucky number, right?" He spun the second dial to seven.

As he continued to play his little game, the bowling alley owner and Curtis looked on as if he had gone crazy. Even though it was obvious neither appreciated his performance, he added exaggerated moves to display even more showmanship.

"In the third slot on this four-wheel device, I'm going to pick … the start of summer, June. That would be six. Finally, because I have no other numbers on the tip of my tongue, I'll go with the days in a normal work week. Another seven."

"Five," Curtis corrected him.

"Ah, yes." He laughed. "Just checking to see if you were being observant."

After spinning the final dial to five, he glanced at his audience. While their eyes remained glued on him, he sensed the spotlight would soon be turned off, unless, of course, he could come up with a thrilling finale.

He was sure he had one. "*Voila*, the door opens."

With a flourish, Lije pulled the locker door open.

Curtis and the owner stood staring, mouths open.

Bowing, Lije added, "Well, that never worked before."

Sitting in the locker was a battered shoe box.

"How did you do that?" the owner demanded.

"I knew the combination. Who rents this locker?"

The man shook his head. "I can't tell you," he said, slamming the locker shut. "There's a privacy agreement that goes with each rental."

"Diana, show him your badge?"

Curtis reached into her pocket and presented her credentials. The owner looked at the card, then at her face, and hurried back to the other side of his cash register. He pulled a book from a shelf and placed it on the counter. He quickly thumbed through a few pages. After spotting the right one, he ran his right index finger down the page to guide his eyes. He stopped at number seventeen. "R. Smith. He didn't leave a phone number or an address. And though I'd never seen him before, I remember him well. He's the only person I know who bought a lifetime lease. That's five hundred dollars. And he paid in cash. I wasn't going to argue with that."

"When did he rent it?" Lije asked.

The man didn't have to look back at the book. "Just over two years ago."

Lije glanced over at Curtis as he held up his hands in a gesture that indicated *well*.

"Okay," she replied, "I get the name. But how did you know the combination and the locker number?"

"The coat."

"Which coat?"

"When you picked up the coat at the diner, the one you thought was mine, it had what you assumed was a cleaning number written inside one of the pockets. That number was 2765-17. Do you have the sketches of the two men Jennings claimed he met? Perhaps they're on your laptop?"

"Yeah."

"Why don't you get your computer from the car and see if—" Lije looked back at the owner. "I didn't catch your name."

"It's Joe Martin."

"See if Mr. Martin recognizes the two men. Also, you might want to bring in your kit. Since the only thing in that locker is a shoe box, I'm betting it belonged to Moony Rivers."

Retrieving the needed items from the car, Curtis booted up the computer and located the images. As soon as the first one came up on the screen, Joe Martin almost yelled, "Yeah, that looks like the one who did all the talking. I think he's a bit fleshier than that picture, though." She clicked on the second image. As it filled the screen, Martin nodded his head. "That's the other one. What did they do?"

"We're not sure," Curtis said, "but the contents of that locker might be very important."

Rubbing his hands together, Lije smiled. "Let's take a look."

"Can't just yet," Curtis replied. "I called Hillman while I was getting my laptop from the car. A warrant's on the way. I want to make sure we do this in such a way that no sharp attorney can make the case we didn't follow procedure."

Lije was incredulous. "You called Hillman?"

"I had to." Curtis sounded apologetic. "In matters of finding new evidence for a case, I have to follow a chain. He is the link on the chain that I must report to."

"How long will it take for him to get here with the warrant?"

"Not more than half an hour," she replied.

"And how long will it take him to erase all the information needed to get Heather out of jail?"

Curtis ignored the remark and turned to the bowling alley manager. "Mr. Martin, what do you have in the way of desserts?"

"I've got some Yarnell's Angel Food Ice Cream."

"Sounds great. You want some Lije?"

"Yeah, double scoop," Lije said bitterly. "And I'll eat mine at the bench in front of the locker."

Curtis nodded. "Guess I will too."

"Do you mind if I join you?" Martin asked.

"As long as you don't touch anything," Curtis said.

The only thing Lije could think was that the truth was so close and they had called in the only man who seemed to have nothing to gain and everything to lose from the truth.

52

"Good to see you, Barton," Curtis said as the ABI director walked through the double doors of the bowling alley. "I was beginning to wonder if you had taken the long way around to get here."

"The judge was busy," the director explained. "It took me a bit longer than usual to get the warrant. It was just lucky I had to be in Batesville. It was an easy drive over."

Though trying to act normal, Curtis was seething, her anger boiling like a summer storm. Why was he holding out on her? Now would be the perfect time to fill her in, but nothing. She hoped he would pull her to one side to talk, but no, he just handed her the warrant. That was it. She took the paper from his hand, briefly showed it to Joe Martin, then donned her latex gloves and went to work.

She felt betrayed, and for the first time since she joined the ABI, she was having problems focusing on case work. She opened the locker and carefully examined the inside walls before even glancing at the box.

"No prints in the locker, but that's not surprising. They've wiped everything they've touched so far."

Martin, who was watching her work, said, "I remember Mr. Smith wore leather gloves. He also had a rag that he used to wipe out the locker. His friend said he was a germ freak."

"More like an identity freak," she noted. "Barton, you think this connects to anything else we're working on?"

"Doubt it."

Was he *that* dishonest? She'd lobbed him an easy one. How she wanted to blurt it out, slam him with what she knew, but she didn't. She couldn't. It'd be like running a knife through her hero. There's got to be a reason. There just has to be!

She looked inside the locker. "Lije, you were right. The only thing in here is a shoe box."

After pulling the well-worn Nike container from the locker, she set it on a countertop she had already treated and covered in preparation for the examination. Lifting up the lid with a gloved finger, she peeked in. "A few very old baseball cards, some family photos, and under them, a bit of cash, but not much. I'd guess just a few hundred." She carefully pulled the items out, cataloging and shooting photos of each before extracting several twenties and two one hundred dollar bills. "The only other thing is an unmarked DVD. It's in a plastic case."

She looked over to the ABI lab tech, who had just arrived. Theodore Mitchell, six-foot and 280 pounds, was the agency's top video geek. "Bear, have you got your laptop with you?"

Mitchell nodded and patted his briefcase.

"Good. I've got a DVD you need to pop in and take a look at."

Mitchell quickly moved over to a table, pulled a Mac Pro out of a hardshell case, popped it open, and waited for it to boot up. As it did, he hooked up a portable external hard drive through the firewire port. When his desktop appeared, he started up a video program he had designed and was now being used by law enforcement departments all over the world.

"Has the disc been dusted for prints?" he asked.

"None there," Curtis replied, "but still pick it up with gloves."

Mitchell grabbed a pair from his case, snapped them on, and retrieved the DVD. He started to slip it into the computer, then stopped. "Diana, would you all give me a few minutes to study this thing by myself?"

She nodded. Lab techs liked to work on their own, then make a presentation. When Bear felt it was showtime, he'd call them over. To Lije she said, "Let's give him some room. It won't take him long."

Lije nodded, but rather than following her, he moved to the counter and took a seat. She wasn't surprised. When she called her boss in, Lije must have felt betrayed. But she had no choice. She had to deal with protocol. Rules were rules and they had to be followed. Still, having Lije now distrust her created a pain she hadn't bargained for. Lord, she hated getting emotionally involved. Though she had to admit this was the most complicated case she had ever worked on.

Curtis walked over to Hillman. "Let me catch you up on what's going on."

She explained what they'd found in Mountain View, at the trailer and at the lumber yard. Throughout her point-by-point recap, she dropped numerous opportunities for the director to provide her with the information on the bullet, but he remained mute on the subject. He wasn't going to cave.

"Interesting," Hillman said, "but where do you suppose Evans got the idea to go to Mountain View? How did he know about Moony Rivers? And why did you agree to it? You should've cleared it with me first."

She shrugged. "This area's all interconnected in one way or another. In these small towns, people are pretty much tied together." She paused, then lied. "I'm guessing it might have been something he heard from Micah Dean's widow. It might be tied to the Jennings case."

"A suicide is a suicide, and a small-time robbery is a small-time robbery. I don't see what this two-year-old evidence has to do with what we're working on in the Evans case. But being here when we turn up nothing will probably make me look good in the governor's eyes. He is pushing for me to follow up on anything Evans wants to do.

"This whole trip is a waste of time. Probably nothing on the DVD except some kid's birthday party or ball game."

Mitchell waved them over.

"I don't know what this is supposed to be," Mitchell said. "It's pretty simple video, shot in poor light, and looks to have been done by a home video camera. It's raw footage. No doctoring from what I can see."

"Let's see it," Curtis said.

As if her voice was the cue he needed, the lab tech pushed a button on his mouse and images began flickering on the computer screen.

"Before you ask, I've done all I could to sharpen the image, but there are limits even with my software."

Curtis studied the scenes playing out in front of her. In what looked like a barn, two men appeared to be arguing. Even though the image, as Bear had warned, was not sharp, she could easily see that the person on the right was Jonathon Jennings. He looked just like he did in the photo that accompanied the internet story Lije had pulled up a few nights before. His body language showed he was more than a little agitated. Though the image was blurry, it was still sharp enough to present a facial expression indicating his blood was nearing the boiling point.

Moony had been hired by Dean to secretly tape some of his meetings with Jennings. Obviously this was one of them. Had Moony caught the actual murder? Was that the shocking development? Is that why he was killed? Curtis wanted Bear to hit the fast-forward button. But that was not his style. He would want them to see every bit of what had been captured on the DVD.

"Okay," Lije cut in, "I know Jennings. He's on the right. Is the man on the left Micah Dean?"

"I don't know," Curtis said, "but note the time and date codes on the bottom right of the screen. According to the story we pulled up from the *Democrat-Gazette*, this video is from the night Dean was murdered."

HILLMAN'S INTEREST EVER SINCE HE HAD ARRIVED
had been peripheral. Now he could not take his eyes from the
screen. His gaze was suddenly transfixed by what Bear was spinning on the screen.

The images showed the two men coming closer together, separated by only a yard, their body language indicating both were
caught up in deep rage. Curtis fully expected to see Jennings pull
a gun and shoot Dean. But at the moment the anger had grown to
where that should have happened, a woman entered the barn.

"That must be Dean's wife," the tech explained as he paused the
DVD. "You'll note that she says something to her husband, then
leaves. As she exits, watch Jennings."

As she headed out the door, the real-estate agent shouted something while shaking his fist at Micah Dean. The agent continued
his rant for what the time code showed were two more minutes
before turning and rushing from the barn. A few seconds later,
Dean followed him.

The tech again paused the video. As he did, Hillman offered
an observation. "As you can see, the tape confirms the testimony
of both Jennings and Mrs. Dean. The men could have come back,
and that's when the murder took place. We don't know the exact
time of the shooting. Besides, there's no proof the time coding on

the video is accurate. By the way, how was it that we didn't have this surveillance video during the trial?"

"I guess no one knew about it," Mitchell replied. "I just emailed the lab and had someone check the evidence log. There was nothing listed. You have to remember, the ABI did not participate in the crime scene investigation. That was all taken care of locally. And it was probably a rush job of looking at the scene. All we did was the lab work."

"That's right," Hillman said. "Mrs. Dean told investigators at the time that her husband always met with people in his workshop, which obviously is what he called this old barn. She said he wouldn't talk business in front of her because she wanted him to sell Swope's Ridge and fix up their home property. That's why he didn't want her to meet anyone interested in buying the land. As I recall, a few locals told me that he couldn't deal with her badgering."

"You worked the case on the ground?" Curtis asked. "I didn't know we had any real contact with anyone. I thought all we did was the lab work."

On the surface it appeared her remarks had not affected him. Hillman seemed unflustered, but there was a light sheen of sweat on his brow. When he answered her question, there was an uncharacteristic crack in his voice.

"Didn't work it. I was in town on a fishing trip a few days after it happened. Had some friends give me their read."

She wanted to ask who the friends were, but Mitchell jumped in with, "When I went through this the first time, I figured the person shooting the video must have stopped after everyone left the barn. But the video kept running. After a gap of almost a minute, I found more." Mitchell could no longer contain his grin.

Anxiously, Curtis watched as Bear again clicked his mouse and everyone leaned in closer, so close that Hillman and Lije lightly bumped heads. Neither apologized or even acknowledged their quick meeting of the minds.

The video showed Dean reentering the barn. The cameraman had moved. The video was blurrier and was shot from farther away. At first Dean was alone, working on what appeared to be a metal detector. Then, with no warning, three men walked into the barn. It was obvious from his expression that Dean was surprised by their arrival.

At first the exchanges between Dean and his guests appeared to be civil. The man in the middle appeared to be the spokesman. He would talk to Dean, Dean would answer, and the man would then turn to the man to his left and say something. The third man, standing over on the right, said nothing.

The man on the left — his back always to the camera — started displaying more arm movements. Though he continued to speak only to the spokesman, it was clear the man's anger was directed at Dean. Then Dean shouted two words and picked up a shovel and pointed the blade at the visitors. That's when the spokesman pulled out a handgun. My Lord, Curtis thought, they *were* watching a murder.

Mitchell froze the image on the screen. "You can get a pretty clear look at one of the men here. The man in the middle, the spokesman. I can blow it up and clean it up a little. Still, it's a bit fuzzy. He pushed a button and the face was pushed to a full frame.

Curtis studied the grainy image. "Hold it right there," she ordered, reaching to her right and grabbing her own laptop. After waking it up, she pulled up the image of the man Jennings knew as Robert Smith. "I think we have a match."

Mitchell nodded.

Lije smiled.

Hillman shrugged. "Looks pretty close."

She glanced back at the tech. "Bear, any idea what was being said?" Another skill useful to a video tech with the ABI.

"Because of the poor quality, no. I do think Smith was translating for the other man, based on the pattern of conversation."

"So," Curtis said, "we figure the man who has his back to the camera, the only one we can't really see, might well be a foreigner."

She almost blurted out that Jennings had heard Smith speak in German, but caught herself. That information came from death row, from Lije. She had not learned it from a case file. Knowing it was unwise to reveal that Lije had been to Varner, she decided to play it close to the vest. "If you're right, Bear, I think this video confirms that the man on the left was speaking another language and that Smith is bilingual. Wish we knew what language. What else is on the tape?"

"Wait a second," Hillman barked. "What about the guy we haven't seen? Bear, you've watched the whole thing. Do we ever get a look at his face? This could be important. We need to get this back to the lab now and use your equipment there."

"Boss, we never see his face, and I would be using the same computer and the same program there. I know the quality isn't great, and I wish we could see the guy's face, but this is as good as it gets."

When Hillman didn't offer another protest, the lab tech clicked the mouse and the images on the screen again sprang to life. Initially it appeared that Smith was now ordering Dean to drop the shovel. Instead, Dean raised it higher. The man with his back to the camera then pulled what looked like a bundle of cash out of his pocket and tossed it on the table in front of Dean. Micah glanced at it, shook his head. He brought the shovel blade down, scooped up the cash with it, and flung it back toward the man. This action seemed to so enrage the man that he lost his composure. He took three quick steps over to Smith, grabbed the gun from his hand, and aimed it at Dean. It didn't take a lip reader to see that Dean screamed, "No!" Even in the muddy images, they saw the man assumed to be a foreigner fire the gun at least twice. Dean dropped the shovel, fell to his knees, looked back up at his assailant, then crumpled to the floor. None of the visitors moved.

Finally, Smith—looking stunned—took the gun from the foreigner and pushed him toward the door. The third man picked up
the money and followed.

The video continued to roll, then the screen went black.

54

"ANYTHING ELSE ON THE DVD?" CURTIS ASKED.

"No," Mitchell replied.

This changed a lot of things and made the hidden bullet information even more important. Obviously Jennings was telling the truth. He was innocent.

Yet Hillman didn't budge. Even when he looked at Curtis, he said nothing. He even appeared much more relaxed than he had been while watching the DVD. What was going on in his head? It appeared she wasn't going to find out—not now, perhaps not ever. At least there was still time to correct a mistake.

"The state will be executing the wrong man in less than seven hours," she said.

"It would appear," Hillman replied.

"You need to call the governor."

The director considered her words before turning to Mitchell. "Bear, give me the DVD."

The disc popped out of the laptop and into the tech's gloved fingers. After slipping it back into its plastic case, he handed it to Hillman, who dropped the evidence into his suit coat pocket.

"Will this play in any DVD player?" Hillman asked.

"Should," Mitchell assured him as he packed his gear back in his briefcase.

"Okay, I've got my car here. I can be back in Little Rock in two hours. The governor is out of state, but the attorney general will be at a dinner tonight. He'll want to see this before he takes any action. Once he views what we just saw, we can stop the execution. We still have time. In a day or so, Jennings will be a free man. Thanks to each of you, justice will have been served and an innocent man will have been saved."

Hillman smiled, looked at each of them, then added, "Curtis, take the rest of the material with you back to Salem. You can ship the box to the lab tomorrow, but go over the material again before you do. And again, thanks to each of you. Now, I've an important errand to run. Bear, will you be in the lab?"

"Should be there by the time you get to the dinner," he said.

After the two men walked out, Lije took a seat at the table. Curtis figured he'd probably never seen anything like what they had just watched. "So one of those men in the video killed Moony Rivers?" Lije asked.

"That's what I'm guessing," Curtis said. "They probably saw him rush away from the barn. He must have eluded them that night. They finally found him. I'm guessing they scared Moony and he either told them where the DVD was or went to get it for them. They then arranged his suicide and, just to be safe, took all his DVDs and tapes."

Lije leaned back in his chair, closed his eyes, and tented his fingers together in front of his face, apparently lost in thought. Curtis eased into the seat beside him. He opened his eyes and looked at her. "Why did they keep the shoe box and the DVD? Why not pitch them? Destroy them? After all, this was evidence that could be used against all of them."

On the surface, there would seem to no longer be a need for the men to keep the DVD. But Curtis had enough experience in the thinking of criminals to at least present a sound theory. "In business, mistakes made by CEOs are often filed away by those working under them. The underling then has some bargaining power for positioning in the company. Crime works in much the same way. Smith didn't shoot Dean. The killer was the foreign man who appeared to be Smith's boss. When Smith and the other man got hold of the DVD, I'm guessing they opted to keep it because it convicted not them but the man at the top."

"It was their safety net," Lije said.

"That video may also have meant a bigger cut of whatever their boss was after."

Her theory was logical, it was solid, and it sounded right when she said it. But was there more? Was there something else in Moony's box that she had missed? "Well, I've got a shoe box full of stuff that seems to have nothing to do with the case, but I still need to take a closer look at it. So what do you say we get back to your house?"

"Sounds good to me," Lije said as he got up from his chair. "Hey, isn't that one of your briefcases?"

Curtis looked beyond him. "Bear's good, but he's often absent-minded. That's his. We can take it with us. I'll give him a call later and tell him. He'll at least buy me a meal for not informing Hillman."

"Insurance, like the DVD?"

She grinned. "Exactly!"

IT WAS JUST PAST SEVEN, THE ROAD WAS ALL BUT empty, and this new twist in the case had given Lije a feeling of excitement. Jennings was innocent and would not be executed. His name would be cleared. But Lije didn't know what all of this meant for Heather Jameson. There was no real connection. The DVD was two years old. Worse, it seemed to Lije that Hillman's response to the video had removed any doubt Curtis may have had that he wasn't on the up and up.

Thus, the trip to Mountain View, while it saved Jennings, had brought Lije no closer to freeing Heather or finding out who killed Kaitlyn. Nor had he learned anything about what was actually up there on Swope's Ridge. He struggled with the convoluted elements and realized that he was all alone. The bond between Hillman and Curtis was once again strong. He could no longer trust the woman driving the car.

"Just when you think it can't get any stranger, it does," Curtis said, sighing.

He looked over at her. She seemed relaxed. Instead of being happy for her regained faith, he was angry. He wanted to shake her, force her to see Hillman as he was. Yet what could he say? Maybe the director wasn't cutting corners or hiding anything. There was no real proof. Maybe Kaitlyn's death had so skewed his thinking and vision that he was the one whose judgment was screwy. Maybe the murders of Dean and Moony weren't connected to his case. Still, he knew he was right about Heather. He also felt sure something on the ridge was behind everything that was going on. But what? He and Curtis had been there. They had searched the place. Except for the railroad tracks, nothing. And that piece of track was probably never noticed by the German, so it too was a dead end.

Curtis suddenly straightened up and firmly grabbed the wheel with both hands. "That guy's crazy!" she yelled.

"What guy?"

"Behind us!"

Craning his neck to see out the back window, he saw a four-wheel-drive GM truck speeding toward them. What was the driver doing? It was as if the truck was going to run right over them.

Curtis floored the accelerator and hissed, "If you know any prayers, you might want to start saying them. This car doesn't have the police package. He's gaining on us."

Lije tried to see who was in the truck, but the window was tinted black. "I can't see anything, but at this pace they'll be running right over us."

"I'm open to suggestions," she snapped.

The truck now filled the whole back window. It was a repeat performance. The bright lights, a large vehicle on his tail — it was again the night Kaitlyn was killed. It was even the same road. Someone wanted him dead, and if they continued to get enough chances, their wish would be granted.

The truck hit the back end of the car and the impact blew out the back window. Arkansas 9 took a dramatic right turn, but Curtis didn't slow down. The car was now doing ninety around a curve marked for forty-five.

About a half mile ahead was a curve so sharp that it almost met itself coming. It was marked for thirty miles an hour, and if they missed the curve, he wasn't sure they would make it. The car certainly wouldn't.

The truck rammed the rear of the ABI car again. The impact

must have pushed the car's back bumper into the gas tank. Lije smelled gasoline, then flames were licking the back seat.

"Hang on," Curtis said through clenched teeth.

She floored the gas pedal and pushed the car close to a hundred. He realized she had no intention of making the turn. Instead she kept the wheel straight, guiding the car to a spot between two thick pine trees. *She's crazy!* She was going to kill them both before the other guys had the chance.

The Victoria left the road like a rocket, flying ten feet over the ditch, scraping the limbs of the evergreens, and then soaring above the grass-covered hill. Almost fifty yards later, the flaming car hit nose-first in a patch of blueberry bushes, flipped nose to tail three times before ending its short flight upside down against a century-old elm. The fire was now curling up the backs of the front seats.

The passenger-side air bag had slapped Lije hard but cushioned the landing. As it deflated, he found himself hanging upside down, his seat belt holding him in place. He tried to unlock the restraint but couldn't. It was jammed. As the fire grew closer, he looked at Curtis. She was either knocked out or dead. He was on his own.

He grabbed the armrest and tried to yank himself out of the unyielding belt. Using every ounce of strength that he could muster, he pulled at the latch and finally felt the belt give way. He fell onto the headliner. Coughing and unable to see, he reached up and felt for the strap that held Curtis in place. Now able to use both hands, he crouched beneath her, using his shoulder to push her against the seat, providing slack in the belt. Seconds later, she dropped down against him.

The windshield had broken out on impact, so rather than try a door, he scrambled through the opening, falling into a ditch. The hood and front bumper were wedged in a tree, suspended there. Kneeling, he reached back into the vehicle and found Curtis's shoulders. Grabbing her under the arms, he yanked her through the hole. He had to move her away from the car, which could explode any second. Exhausted, Lije crawled away from the car, dragging Curtis with him. Once out in the open, he struggled to his feet, took two deep breaths, and pulled Curtis into his arms. He awkwardly jogged to put as much distance as he could between them and the burning car. He managed only twenty yards before the gas tank erupted, sending twisted metal and plastic in every direction. Plunging to the ground, he covered Curtis's body with his own. Debris fell all around them. Then all he heard was the crackle of the fire.

He rolled onto his back. After a few deep breaths, he glanced over at Curtis. He saw her chest move, heard her cough, and watched as she opened her eyes. When he was sure she was okay, he leaned over and whispered, "I was going to warn you about that curve."

She forced a smile and slowly pushed herself up to a sitting position, then looked toward the highway. "I don't see the truck."

With difficulty, he stood up and looked in the same direction. "I'm sure they thought their work was done. By the way, how are you going to explain this to your crew? I can't imagine what they're going to say when they learn you blew up this car."

Reaching into her pocket, Curtis retrieved her phone. After tapping in a number, she waited for a response. "Curtis here, we've had an incident."

Lije shook his head. That wasn't the word he'd use to describe the last few minutes. A tragedy, a catastrophe, a nightmare, but not an incident. As this latest murder attempt proved, there would be no exit until either the mystery was solved and they got the bad guys or he was dead. Over his head or not, he had to learn to swim in these deep waters.

A few days before, as he watched Kaitlyn's body being lowered into the ground, he had genuinely wanted to die. Yet now, after another close contact with the Grim Reaper, he wanted to live. He needed to live. He didn't understand why his attitude had made a one-eighty. But after this latest brush with death, he was sure that breathing was a habit he wanted to continue.

LIJE AND CURTIS HAD SOMEHOW GOTTEN OUT OF THEIR horrific car crash with only scrapes, bumps, and bruises. Even though Lije had no broken bones, his shoulders and chest hurt from the seat belt tearing into him at a hundred miles an hour. He felt every step he took as he and Curtis crossed the field toward the highway. Curtis had arranged for Jake Wilson, an ABI agent still working in Salem, to pick them up.

They had walked about forty feet when he spotted an object in the grass. "What's that?" he asked.

Curtis looked to where he was pointing. "Bear's computer case. Must've been thrown out when we hit. We'd better grab it."

"I'll get it."

Lije and Curtis were just crossing over a rusty barbwire fence when Agent Jake Wilson slid to a stop in the shallow ditch in his ABI-issued Impala. The investigator opened his door and jumped out.

"You all okay?" he shouted as he jogged over to the fence.

"We're alive," Curtis answered as she swung her right leg over the fence. Even though he was carrying the briefcase, Lije had already managed to clear the fence and was leaning against a post oak tree alongside the road, trying to catch his breath.

"I left as soon as you called me," Wilson said. "We still have a few folks in the area. I'll get guys all over that car in twenty minutes."

"Cancel that," Curtis said.

"Why?" Wilson was obviously surprised.

He wasn't the only one. If there ever was a crime scene, Lije knew he had just pulled himself from it.

After yanking her left leg over the fence and wiping blood from her forehead, Curtis said in a hoarse voice, "Get on the horn and cancel it. There'll be no investigation. At least not at this time. And what just happened didn't happen. There was no crash."

"Why?"

She looked back over her shoulder at the smoke coming from where the car had come to rest. "I don't want that car discovered and I don't want any news releases. I want no one to know it happened. From right here it just looks like a farmer burning brush. Let's keep it that way."

"I don't understand."

"Make your call!" she said as she dusted off her slacks. "And make sure the locals don't get wind of this. And don't tell Hillman either."

"You want the boss in the dark on this?"

"Yep. It never happened."

After opening the back door for Lije and watching Curtis find a place on the passenger side of the back seat, Wilson got in the Impala and turned his Chevrolet back toward Salem. Finally, when he got the car up to speed, he demanded, "Okay, now what's going on?"

Lije waited for her answer. What was Curtis thinking?

"Jake, if the scene remains uninvestigated, then whoever tried to kill us is more likely to think they succeeded. It might well be a week or more before anyone happens on the burned-out car. At the worst, we probably have a couple days. That crime scene offers no real evidence that'll help us catch whoever's trying to eliminate us. I want to play dead for a while."

Wilson shook his head. "But you're obviously alive and they'll see you."

"If they're looking for us, that's true. But with no accident report, nothing in the news, they might not even stay in the area. I think they went after us because they thought we had important evidence. If that's the case, then they'll believe their evidence, whatever it is, has been destroyed. When we get into town, we'll stay low. We'll go into the house and spend the rest of the night out of sight. But just in case someone tries to search our wreck, keep an eye on the spot. But stay hidden."

"Do you think it'll work?"

"Not for long, but maybe long enough for me to figure out why Evans is still a target."

"Anything else?" Wilson asked.

"Keep guard at the base of the hill by the house. I'll make some calls and do some digging tonight." She slid down low in the seat and pulled Lije's sleeve to make sure he did the same.

The car pulled into Salem and headed for the Evans home. Obviously Curtis was now just as much a target as Lije was.

They rode in silence for a few more miles.

"At least we saved Jennings," Curtis finally said.

57

AFTER THEY ARRIVED AT THE HOUSE, LIJE WITHOUT a word went to his bedroom, tumbled into his bed, and quickly fell into deep sleep.

It was well past midnight when he awoke. Slipping on jeans and a T-shirt, he wandered into the living room. Curtis was sitting on the leather sofa, her computer in her lap, seemingly lost in work. Seeing no reason to bother her, he walked into his study and flipped on the TV. He turned to a news channel and sat at his desk and began going through his email. He heard none of what was being reported until the anchor mentioned a familiar name. "And tonight, convicted murderer Jonathan Jennings used his last words to continue to proclaim his innocence. The forty-seven-year-old man has received worldwide publicity for resisting all attempts to delay his date with the executioner. His former lawyer stated that Jennings suffered from claustrophobia that made life on death row even worse than death. A large crowd gathered outside the prison facility to protest the execution ..."

What was this all about? What was going on?

"Did I hear right?" Curtis asked from the doorway.

"Yeah. You did. I thought your buddy Hillman was supposed to make sure that didn't happen." Lije stared at the television. "He let an innocent man die tonight."

Curtis pulled her cell phone from her pocket and began dialing.

She tried a second and then a third number. On the fourth try, she finally got someone to pick up.

"Jack. Where's the boss?... Well, find him."

Curtis punched another number angrily.

"I'm sorry to bother you, sir, this is ABI Agent Diana Curtis." She paused. "I'm sorry about the time, sir, but this is important. Have you spoken with Barton Hillman today?"

Lije didn't need an explanation from anyone. Hillman had played them. How was he going to explain *this* mess away? They had all seen the DVD. The owner of the bowling alley had seen it. Hillman was toast.

"I understand and I thank you." Curtis closed the phone. "He never checked in with the attorney general or the office. Something must have happened. Maybe someone went after him like they went after us."

Lije was not ready to cut the man any slack. He had no doubt that Hillman had deliberately hatched a plan. Something to cover up what they had all seen on the DVD that would have stopped the execution. Surely Hillman did not feel getting his brother-in-law in the governor's office was worth an innocent man's life. But who knew what he was capable of?

Curtis's cell phone rang. "What? Where? Well, get up here and get me."

"Bad news?" Lije asked, his voice dripping with sarcasm. What could possibly top what they already knew?

"Barton was in an accident. He's in a hospital in Calico Rock. Seems he missed a turn and his car rolled down a hill, struck a tree, then ended up in the White River. He barely made it out before the vehicle went under."

"Interesting timing," Lije said.

"Jake Wilson's taking us to see Barton, and then we'll check out the car."

"Don't think I want to go."

"You have no choice."

An hour later, Lije found himself staring at Hillman. A dark bruise was visible across his forehead. Hillman had obviously been shaken up pretty good. Still, the injuries elicited no sympathy from Lije. He actually began to feel sick. An innocent man was dead, and the doctors were saying that Hillman could walk out tomorrow. It was much too clean.

Lije was stunned. He said nothing. He tried hard not to show any reaction. How did Hillman know about their accident?

On the thirty-minute drive to where a wrecker had pulled Hillman's SUV from the river, Lije remained silent. He watched as Curtis and Wilson examined the vehicle. "It's not here," he heard her say. Shaking his head, he walked back to the car and waited for the trip home. Of course the DVD wasn't there. Just like Jennings, it was gone forever.

On the trip back to Salem, the two agents discussed the accident in the front seat. Lije remained mute. He was so angry he almost didn't duck to hide from the press upon arrival. Yet being dead felt right at this moment, so playing dead seemed right too. It was past five in the morning when he and Curtis finally walked back into his log home.

"He's lucky he wasn't hurt worse," she said.

He nodded and sat down on the couch. "What were you talking about not being able to find?" He knew the answer but wanted to hear her say it.

Curtis sat down in a chair opposite Lije. "Barton asked us to find his coat. Even though he knew it was too late to save Jennings, he wants to clear the man's name. He knew the DVD would be the only real way because everything else would be considered hearsay. The DVD was in his coat pocket. He asked us to see if we couldn't find his coat in the car. But it must have washed away in the river. Guess we'll never find it now."

"How interesting. Hillman is in an accident and the DVD is gone. Looks like there are just bad breaks everywhere."

"What are you implying?" Curtis asked, hostility in her tone.

"Barton was probably driving too fast trying to get to Little Rock. It was an accident. That's all it was. It's horrible that Jennings died, but that's the way life plays out sometimes."

"Maybe he did all he could," Lije said. "I'm surprised Hillman wasn't hurt worse. That trip down that rock-covered hillside must have been something. How far was it?"

"Must have been at least two hundred feet at about a sixty-degree angle."

"You and Wilson walked that hill. How many trees did the SUV hit?"

"I didn't take any real note, but he couldn't have hit anything directly until the tree his vehicle struck head-on. You saw what it did to the bumper. That impact caused the car to spin around and slide backward into the water."

"But no broken bones." It wasn't a question. Lije just wanted to emphasize that fact.

Curtis shook her head. "Only a few bruises. He was lucky. We could have easily lost him tonight."

Lije nodded. "Yeah, how do you suppose he came out so lucky? Must have been clean living."

"It's modern technology. Without the airbags, I'm sure he'd have died. Our ABI cars have them on the side as well as in front of the passengers."

"I saw that all of them had been deployed. Must have popped when the car hit that big tree. Kind of like ours did when we hit the ground out in the field."

Curtis nodded.

"Kind of funny though," he added.

"What is?"

"You're the CSI. I'm surprised you missed it. But you weren't looking for it, were you? You were thinking of this as an accident, not a staged event. You weren't looking at Hillman as anything but your boss."

"I'm not following you."

"No, you're blinded by your faith—the faith in your boss you had almost lost but somehow regained. The faith you still cling to right now in the face of overwhelming evidence to the contrary."

"You're talking in riddles."

He got up from the couch, moved over to the mantel, and picked up a picture of Kaitlyn. He studied it, then placed it back in its familiar spot. He moved to a bookcase and ran his hand across a few novels. She followed his every move. She still didn't get it. He couldn't believe she hadn't seen what even to him had been so obvious. She hadn't seen it because she wasn't looking for the mistake. If she had been, she would've immediately spotted it. And it would've been so much easier if she had.

"Diana, what was Hillman's most obvious injury?"

"The bruise he got when his forehead hit the steering wheel."

Lije smiled. "But it couldn't have happened that way."

"But you could even see the imprint of the wheel stitching in the injury. You must have seen it. He really smashed into it with some force."

"Yep, it was there, but it couldn't have happened during the crash. The airbag and shoulder belt would have kept his head from hitting the wheel."

Her look slid from confusion to disbelief. He could tell she was struggling. She didn't want to acknowledge what her training now forced her to admit.

"He staged it," she whispered.

"LIJE, ARE YOU AWAKE?" CURTIS CALLED FROM THE living room.

He felt pretty ragged as he walked to rejoin the agent who had become a fixture in his home.

For hours Lije had waited in solitude, giving Curtis time to come to grips with the information about Hillman — the staged accident, their accident, the information on the bullet. He had remained in the bedroom he had shared with Kaitlyn, killing time by looking at photo albums and recalling more innocent days. But they all just reminded him how really alone he now was. Even the attempts on his life seemed inconsequential compared with losing the love of his life. Kaitlyn had been his lover, partner, best friend, and even his mirror. He saw himself in her eyes and was always trying to improve what was reflected there. Now there was no reflection, no model, and no reason for self-improvement.

"You still sore?" Curtis asked as he joined her and poured himself a glass of sweet tea.

"More than I've been in years. What about you?"

"Everything hurts, but at least nothing's broken. Listen. I know what you believe about Hillman, that he staged his accident so he didn't have to stop the execution. I still don't know why. And I don't know how he knew about our wreck. But I don't trust him anymore."

"That's good. At least we agree on that. Listen, Diana, we know that Jennings was set up and your boss had something to do with it, at least at the end. Before they can strike again, we need to learn everything we can about the property. Swope's Ridge has to be connected in some way. It's the common link to everyone involved. The only place I know to start is with Dr. Cathcart. We need to find out what he knows about the tracks we found. So, my obviously inept bodyguard—"

"What?"

"Hey, a lot more attempts have been made on my life since you took over than ever happened before. I know we're pretending we were killed in the crash, but can we go over and see him?"

She shook her head. If that meant no, he didn't like it and would go anyway. In truth, he was just acting nice. Yet as she spoke, he realized her negative head movement was a reflection of some realization, one she seemed to want to avoid. "How many more on death row are innocent?" Curtis asked.

Lije shook his head. "Those on death row are the lucky ones."

"What do you mean by that?"

"How many innocent ones have been executed? How many are already in graves?"

She didn't answer. She headed back to the guest bedroom to pick up her stuff. "Let's go." She was out the door ahead of him and into the ABI Impala.

An hour later, halfway to the small river community of Hardy that Dr. Cathcart called home, Curtis said, "Lije, you caused me to think about what I do for a living. I've mentally reviewed all my work since I joined the ABI. I don't believe I've overlooked anything that has led to someone being falsely sent to jail. In fact, I know I've kept several innocents from being convicted."

Lije hesitated. It was still hard to be open with her, but she was starting to open up to him. "Diana, like you, I hadn't really considered these things in the past. But now, I think back to law school stories about men and women with inept counsel, and I wonder how often it happens. Jennings was innocent, but he didn't have the money to hire someone who could prove it. And worse, he was executed because a man working for the state wouldn't make one phone call. Instead that man buried the evidence that would've freed him."

"When we find the person who killed Kaitlyn, do you think he should be allowed to live?" Curtis asked.

The question took him aback. What would he do when he came face to face with the man who pulled the trigger? What would he want to have happen to that man? "At night, when I've been unable to sleep, I've thought about facing that nameless and faceless person. In those moments, I've almost always pulled the trigger and watched him fall. Yet the death of her killer never brought me satisfaction — even when I've imagined being at the execution. I finally have figured out why. Even if that person is buried in the cold dirt, it doesn't mean that Kaitlyn will be coming out of her grave. She'll still be just as dead."

"But—"

"No, Diana, let me explain something. A part of my wife is very much alive for me. I realize that whenever I think about revenge. Kaitlyn was a New Testament kind of person. Do you know what that means?"

"No," Curtis admitted, "I don't guess I do."

"It means she wasn't an eye-for-an-eye and a tooth-for-a-tooth kind of woman. She believed strongly in second chances."

He saw no reason to go any deeper. He doubted Curtis would understand. For the moment, Kaitlyn's love and forgiveness covered him like a warm blanket. She *was* a believer in second chances. It was evident in everything she did. Her father escaped from Vietnam and got a second chance in this country, a chance some people in America would rather he hadn't had. She voluntarily went to jails and talked about forgiveness with prisoners. She believed people could change. She lived by the "least of these" philosophy.

Lije thought about Jonathon Jennings. He was one of the least of these, and everyone walked away from him. If Kaitlyn had known about him, she would've walked along with him. Lije knew that if his love for Kaitlyn meant anything, he had to honor her life and honor her faith.

Curtis made the turn that led up the steep hill to Robert Cathcart's home and broke the silence. "I can understand how you feel, that no matter what, Kaitlyn is never coming back. But I want to tell you that in spite of what happened to Jennings, I want to be there when they stick the needle in the arm of the man or men who killed Kaitlyn. I don't want them on this earth. What they did makes them vermin, not human."

"Then," Lije said as they pulled up to the house, "you'd better be sure you get the right person this time. Sometimes it's hard to tell. There's a man you work for who's been fooling a lot of folks for years."

LIJE COULD TELL THAT FROM THE MOMENT THEY stepped out of the car, Curtis was impressed by what she saw. Dr. Cathcart greeted them and ushered them into the den. As she walked through the house, her eyes grew larger with each step. At one point she caught Lije's attention and mouthed, "Wow!"

After the customary greetings, the trio sat at the big table in the den. Lije was just as fascinated by his surroundings as he'd been on his earlier trip. The place was unlike anything he had ever seen.

"I have taken the liberty of pouring three glasses of sweet tea," Dr. Cathcart said. "I hope that's acceptable."

"Perfect," Curtis replied.

"I love having your company," Cathcart said to Lije, "and especially the company of this beautiful young woman, but I know this is not a social call. So what brings you to my home?"

There was no reason to waste time, so Lije went straight to the point. "Dr. Cathcart, Diana and I found a rail bed on the opposite side of Spring River from where the Frisco Line now runs. Any idea why that would be there?"

If the professor was stunned by the discovery, he didn't show it. He nodded, got up, walked over to a file cabinet, and retrieved what appeared to be a very old map. He returned, carefully unfolded the linen-rich pages, and looked at his two guests.

"Can the two of you show me approximately where you found the train tracks?"

Curtis leaned over, slid the map across the table, studied the river for a moment, pointed to a spot, and looked at Lije for confirmation. Getting up and going round to the far side of the table, Cathcart looked over Curtis's shoulder.

"This makes a certain degree of sense to me," the professor announced as he walked across the room to a bookshelf. He pulled out an oversized book that resembled a court docket, returned to his seat, and opened the volume. "After your first visit, I decided to dig deeper into some old railroad company logs I have. I found that in the late 1860s, during the first years of the line's existence, there was a bridge built across the river to Swope's Ridge. The bridge connected to the main line through a switch, and a spur line ran over the bridge to the other side of the river."

"Why?" Curtis asked. "There was no one there, no town or passengers, no reason to drop off freight."

Content for the moment just to be an observer, Lije waited for the answer to the reason for this bridge to nowhere. After all, only the government did that sort of thing.

"Yes," the professor agreed, "there were just a few locals and certainly not the number of passengers to justify the expense. But the man who bought the land from Swope's estate was on the railroad's board of directors. He pressured the company to build the wooden bridge leading to his land so that he could sell logs to the line. A train would drop off an empty or near empty tender car on the spur and pick up one that had been filled by the men who worked for Mr.—let me see, I have his name here somewhere—Jefferson. Though it was hardly economical, after all there were woods everywhere around here, all of it much easier to obtain than by using this method, this practice continued for several years. This scheme ended when Jefferson drowned in the river on a fishing expedition. My notes show that within months of his death, the spur rail was taken up and only the bridge remained.

According to news accounts back then, the bridge was washed away in the June 1891 flood."

"No," Lije cut in, producing a few photographs that Curtis had taken down at the riverbank, "you can clearly see the track's still there."

Cathcart picked up the pictures and examined them. After pushing them back across the table, he began to lightly drum his fingers, momentarily lost in thought.

"What you're showing me has nothing to do with Jefferson's logging venture. In the late 1800s, rails were at a premium. Many other lines had more money to buy them than did the local ones here in Arkansas. This line was a marginal moneymaker at best. So when a spur was discontinued in this part of the country, the rails were removed and reused. Besides, the track they built for the firewood project ran along the bank and looped. That way the train didn't have to back across the river to pick up the filled tender car. What you're showing me is just a line that went across the river and stopped. No loop."

"More precisely," Curtis added, "it ran to a bluff and stopped."

An exasperated look on his face, Cathcart said, "Which is one of the stupidest things I've ever seen in all my years of studying railroads. Facts are facts. This is not the same line as the one built to retrieve firewood. This is something very different. I have no record of it being built or any idea why it would have been built. It makes no sense at all. This line is a complete mystery."

Lije leaned back in his chair, tented his fingers together in front of his face, and considered the new information. Why was it there? What reason was there for this track being built in such an unlikely location? And if Cathcart didn't know about it, then who did? "It couldn't have been built later?" Lije asked. "Like in the 1940s?"

"No," the professor said. "I'd definitely know about that, as would a lot of other folks around here." He paused. "What's this?"

He pointed to Lije's hand. "Can I inquire about your ring? May I ask where you bought it?"

The ring, the one he had dug up by the track. As an afterthought he had slipped it on his pinky right before they left the house, then promptly forgot about it. "Actually, I found it down on the riverbank when I was examining the track. Have you seen anything like it before?"

Dr. Cathcart bent forward. He took hold of Lije's wrist and brought his hand closer to the table lamp. As he did, the jewels seemed to come to life. They shone like cat eyes caught in headlights.

"It appears to be very old," Cathcart said. "In fact, I would guess it was made well before any Europeans came to the New World. Would you mind removing it so I can look at it more closely?"

Lije slipped the ring from his finger and handed it to him. If Cathcart was right, then this wasn't something a fisherman had dropped.

"Yes," Cathcart said, "I can clearly see this is high-quality gold. The ring was made by an artist. These are real rubies. High-grade stones."

"Professor," Curtis said, "are you an expert on jewelry as well as trains?"

"Oh, heavens no," he answered, waving at her, "but I do know something about the symbol on this ring. You see how the inlaid jewels form a rather unique cross?"

"Yes, but it's not like any cross I've ever seen. Is this some kind of religious symbol?"

Cathcart placed the ring on the table and left the room. He returned a few moments later with a small book. After skimming through a few pages, he turned to a color photograph showing a similar ring.

"This ring is in a museum in France," he explained as he tapped on the page. "It was worn by one of the first members of the famed Knights Templar."

"I've heard that name," Curtis said. "Didn't they lead some of the initial Crusades into the Holy Land?"

"Over nine hundred years ago," Cathcart said. "In the 1300s, they were disbanded. Many were burned at the stake. That's far too simple of an explanation, but by that time they had become so powerful they were a threat to the church and to European monarchies. The allure of the Crusades had faded. The Arab armies had become powerful enough to offer great resistance to the Christian invaders. With the death toll mounting, most felt it was best to keep the young men at home and out of harm's way.

"When they fell out of favor, the remaining members of the Knights Templar fled north. Some stayed in the upper reaches of the British Isles. They found a welcome home in Scotland. It was rumored that a few even went as far as Scandinavia, becoming powerful Viking warriors. As they were renowned for their seamanship, there might be some truth in that. Legend has it that the Knights took with them untold riches, as well as several biblical relics, including the preserved head of John the Baptist, the ark of the covenant, and even the cup from the Last Supper. There have been a lot of movies and books that centered on their exploits. I find it strange that what appears to be an original Knights Templar ring should end up buried on the banks of Spring River."

Lije retrieved the ring. "Doctor, I think the word that best fits this entire case is not strange, but bizarre."

"So much of history is forgotten and so much is lost. You have found a wonderful artifact, Mr. Evans, but none of us will ever know the real story behind its coming to Swope's Ridge. When you visited me the other day, do you remember I spoke of a real railroad mystery?... No? I'm not surprised you've forgotten. You were lost in grief and shock that day. Well, I believe this might well be the time to tell you that story."

ANOTHER MYSTERY? LIJE SMILED. HE DIDN'T REMEMBER and didn't much care. What could it possibly have to do with the more urgent mystery that was going to get him killed if he didn't find the answer to it soon?

But the hint of a historic unsolved mystery seemed to fascinate Curtis. She smiled at Dr. Cathcart and said, "Another mystery?"

"Yes, it's one of my passions. I'd love to share the story with you. Sitting here all alone in my retirement, not getting many guests, I'd almost forgotten how nice it is to talk with people face to face."

He stood up. "I tell this story much better in my library. I have a display there that will bring the events into sharper focus. Please join me."

Cathcart signaled for them to follow, leading them past the front of the dining car, then through a sitting room, and finally into his library. This was the smallest room they had seen, yet it was still impressive. Every one of the room's walls was lined from the floor to the crown of the twenty-foot-high ceiling with books, many looking as if they were more than a hundred years old. This was not a room for show; it was stocked as if for a purpose. Each book must have earned a spot on the shelves.

A large dark table sat in the middle of the room. The huge piece was surrounded by matching chairs. In the center of the table sat an ancient green-shaded brass lamp. But the real focus was an intricate scale model of what appeared to be a nineteenth-century train.

"Well, I see what caught your eye," Cathcart began. "This is a replica of a train that left Hardy on June 7, 1891. You can see that Ole 74 was a normal locomotive of the era, followed by the tender loaded with wood, a postal service car where a mailman sorted mail for delivery down the line, a standard boxcar carrying the typical load of its day, two more rather unique cars, and a caboose. Those two green cars are what make this train interesting. Why don't the two of you take a look at them as I talk."

Cathcart waited for his guests to move closer to the exhibit. "The car closest to the caboose was a private club car. That club car and the green boxcar were owned by a gentleman from Canada. Records show the man's name was Godfrey Payens, though that might well have been an alias. Payens used the club car as his home on wheels. Think of it as a nineteenth-century RV. It probably had an office area, a sleeping section, and even a small kitchen and dining area. To this day no one knows what was in the boxcar that was coupled to his private club car. My studies indicate it was always securely locked and never inspected. Try getting away with that today."

Curtis leaned in closer to examine the scale model of the club car. "Where was he headed?"

The professor smiled. "Best to try to answer that by explaining where he was coming from. Though records are sketchy, I think Payens was about forty years old. To have two private cars, he had to have been a man of means. But the strangest part in all of this is that I can find no record of his existence until he purchased the cars in January of '91 in Canada. He bought these two cars from the Canadian Railroad. With cash. A few days later, in the dead of winter, he began a long odyssey that led him to Hardy."

"Why Hardy?" Lije asked. Why would anyone coming from a

great distance make this obscure area a destination? And why these two very different foreigners, the German and the Canadian?

"Why indeed. In fact, why would he have gone to any of the places he went?" Cathcart sat down and leaned back in one of the leather-backed wooden chairs. The professor's face almost glowed. He was enjoying the drama of revealing his tale bit by bit for his guests.

"Payens avoided all the major railroad lines of that time. He stuck to small lines, contracting with them to take him from one point to another. That took him on a rather bizarre route through the Northeast and into Tennessee. It often took him several weeks to make distances he could have made in a day or two had he used one of the bigger railroad companies. When he arrived in Hardy, he had been traveling for almost five full months."

"Maybe he just wanted to see the country," Curtis suggested.

"I don't think so," Cathcart said. "His route suggests he was headed generally west, but nothing indicates why he was employing the unpredictable method he was using. No record of where or when he planned to stop riding the rails. I believe he had a purpose but felt a need not to allow anyone to know what that purpose really was. He was avoiding detection. It was almost like he was running from someone or something."

The host's right hand reached down just below the tabletop and slid open a drawer from which he retrieved what appeared to be an old document. He carefully unfolded the yellowed paper, placed it on the table, and pushed it toward his guests.

"If you will look at the map, you'll note the original rail line between Hardy and Mammoth Spring. As it still does today, it pretty much followed the river. There are no spurs or places where the line connected with any other rails. You left Hardy and you ended up sixteen miles upriver in Mammoth Spring.

"When Payens and the train pulled out of Hardy, the area was experiencing the worst storm it had faced since the Civil War. Spring River was well up over its banks."

Lije had seen the river like that three times. He could clearly picture the scene being laid out through Cathcart's words.

"This was no normal flood. On that day the river was in an ugly mood as rain continued to pour from the skies. Ole 74 had just pulled its cars across the bridge outside of Hardy when the wooden structure gave way. It's doubtful anyone on the train realized that they could no longer turn back. What the engineer, fireman, postman, brakeman, conductor, and Mr. Payens also didn't know was that the telegraph line had gone dead just as they left the station. Hence, no one in Mammoth Spring was aware that the train was on its way. Because most of the area roads were washed out and water levels stayed above flood stage for almost a week, Hardy was pretty much cut off from the rest of the world for seven full days. It was another full week, making almost two weeks, before the telegraph lines were finally repaired and the railroad discovered that the train never arrived in Mammoth Spring. As you can imagine, on a normal day that would've been big news and featured in all the regional papers. But with half the area having to rebuild after massive flooding, unless you were a family member of a victim, this was just another problem, and a minor one at that. You see, railroad accidents were very common. So beyond Hardy, it went almost unnoticed.

"Over the course of the following week, search parties were sent out along the rail line. They expected to find a place where a landslide had washed out the tracks. They figured they'd discover the train in the river. It was a logical theory. It had happened at least five times on that stretch of track. But this time the track had survived the floods with no damage. You can imagine the shock when the search parties found no sign of the train on the track or in the river. It had simply vanished."

"Maybe," Curtis said, "the train made it through Mammoth Spring and no one noticed it due to the heavy rain."

"They looked at that theory, but it didn't hold much water either. None of the men ever showed up. Except for Payens, these were local men who had families. They were stable individuals, not the type who would just run away from their homes and everything they loved. Besides, the train would have needed to stop at the Mammoth Spring station to get more wood."

The room was quiet, the only sound coming from an old depot clock ticking in its place on a wall in the entry. It seemed the trio was searching separately for answers that simply didn't exist. Only when the old timepiece chimed the six o'clock hour was the silence broken.

Pushing his chair back from the table, Lije walked over to the open French doors between the library and the foyer. Kaitlyn would've loved this mystery. She would've probably come up with a reasonable theory on what happened to the train. Yet he was drawing a blank. Turning, he asked, "Professor, what do you think happened?"

"Ah, Mr. Evans, you've just done what every good student always wants to do. You have cornered the teacher. You have found yourself confronted with a puzzle that you believe must have a simple solution, but you think the facts in the matter are obscuring your ability to find the answer. So you admit defeat and hope the instructor will share with you the one element in this story you have overlooked."

Returning to the table, Lije again studied the train model and then the map. "What am I missing?"

Cathcart drummed his fingers on the wood for a few moments before shaking his head. "I first found out about this story when I was ten years old. It began my real interest in trains, which led to my spending my inheritance to buy this house and much of the contents. I've puzzled over the events of that long ago June day for many, many years. Several times I've even walked the complete distance on the tracks, hoping I'd suddenly see something that no one back then saw. As time went by and technology gave us new tools, I examined satellite imagery and performed information searches on everyone connected with that train. And after examining every scrap of evidence I've been able to find, my conclusions are anything but logical."

Curtis searched the older man's face. She found no hints in his expression. "As an investigator I know there's an explanation for everything. By looking at all the evidence, most crimes can be solved. Yet I'll admit that even with our modern tools, there remain cold cases today. Still, it's hard to believe that something that large could vanish with no signs at all. After all, David Copperfield hadn't been born yet."

"Which brings me to another question," Cathcart said. "Mr. Evans, Miss Curtis, do you believe in magic? I'm not talking about the kind of magic you feel when you fall in love; I'm speaking of real magic, the kind where a man can make something appear out of nothing."

They both remained silent.

"I don't believe in magic," the professor continued. "I didn't even buy into it as a boy. I knew any of the stunts I saw on stage were tricks. Yet if I were to write a book on this mystery, my final chapter would state that Ole 74 and all of the cars it was pulling, as well as all the people on those cars, simply vanished into thin air. I can give you no other answer for what happened on that rainy June day. And, might I add, you have no idea how much admitting that frustrates me."

Lije again leaned back and brought his fingers together in front of his eyes. "Dr. Cathcart, did you ever find out anything else about Payens or what was in the locked boxcar?"

"No, I didn't. Godfrey Payens was a man who appeared out of nowhere only to return to that same place. What secrets he held disappeared with him. Maybe he's the one soul who proved that you can take it with you."

"Interesting thought," Lije replied, "but not very satisfying."

"There's one more thing," Cathcart said. Lowering his voice as if he were afraid someone would overhear his words, he added, "The disappearance of that train might just tie in to that ring you're wearing."

Lije was now completely drawn in to the mystery of the train. He looked down at the ring on his finger. How was the ring tied to this? He could see no connection.

"When I saw your ring, my heart skipped a beat," Cathcart said. He paused. He started to fold the old map, then stopped. Cathcart seemed almost afraid to speak. And when he finally did, his words were barely audible. "Two of the founding fathers of the Knights Templar were Godfrey de Saint-Omer and Hugues de Payens."

Lije needed no help connecting the names to the professor's greatest passion. And now he saw how it might tie in with the murders.

"The Canadian's name was Godfrey Payens," Lije said, as if to confirm the name.

"I doubt it means anything," Cathcart said, "and I really believe what we are looking at is just a coincidence, but I'd love to think there is a connection."

Curtis said, "The ring might be the Canadian's?"

Cathcart nodded. "Could very well be that we are looking at

Payens' ring. Rumor has it the Knights Templar continued to exist underground for centuries. Some think they still exist in secret societies. Maybe the man on the mystery train was one of them. How I'd love to believe the ring is connected to Ole 74."

"I'm going to Swope's Ridge tomorrow," Lije said.

Cathcart nodded. "And I need to be with you."

"Why?" Curtis asked.

"When you uncover those tracks, recognizing how they are laid might well help us determine their purpose. Plus, I can show you where the switch was on the far side of the river. With that knowledge, we just might be able to learn a great deal more than any of us know right now."

"Okay," Curtis replied. "Lije, how well do you know the river?"

"Grew up on it. I know every bend and whirlpool. Why do you ask?"

"I don't want to climb down and then back up the ridge. I was thinking it'd be better to float down to the area, looking more like fishermen than a CSI team. Once we get to the property, we could quietly go ashore, hide the boats, and try to keep what we're doing a secret from prying eyes. If I remember correctly, it's almost impossible to see the riverbank from high on the ridge."

She was right. Going by canoe would not only attract very little attention but also be the quickest route to the buried rail line.

"Okay, Diana," Lije said, "we go by water. We need to get there early. We can put in to the river at dawn. We can drive down to Fox Landing. There's a public access point there. It's only about two miles above Swope's Ridge. But we can't come back up the river to that point. We're going to need a second vehicle parked below the property so that we can paddle downstream to it."

Curtis nodded. "Do you have a place in mind?"

"A private camp, Many Islands, and it has parking for fishermen. To keep the cover you suggest, it might even be good to buy some bait from them."

"What about fishing equipment?" she asked.

"I've got plenty," Lije replied. "We can bring enough of my stuff to make it look real. Besides, while you all are digging, I just might want to try to catch a few brown trout."

Laughing, Curtis said, "You mean you're not going to dig?"

"I would, but I feel a need to leave that to the professionals. Besides, all that work will probably lead to lots of hunger. I can supply the food."

Cathcart leaned in, a smile on his face. "I suggest we bring along some snacks just in case the fish aren't biting."

"Professor, you read my mind," Curtis said, then turned serious. "This may be dangerous. At least three people have died because of something on Swope's Ridge. Whatever's hiding there brings out a murderous spirit in those chasing it. I don't have any idea what we'll find, if anything, but I don't want to be party to any more deaths. We need to be careful."

Cathcart nodded, and Lije added, "You might have to worry about watching our backs, but I have to worry about getting the canoes downriver without dumping any of us or the equipment in the cold water. Just in case, make sure you have everything securely wrapped in some type of waterproof material and a float attached to the stuff. That river can be tricky. We'll see you in the morning, professor."

IT WAS JUST PAST SEVEN WHEN DR. CATHCART, Kent McGee, Curtis, and Lije pulled their canoes up on the bank of Swope's Ridge and started unloading their gear. Lije had decided he needed one more person who was solid with a paddle and knew the river. Three in one canoe was too risky. So he had called McGee and invited him as soon as they left Cathcart's.

The morning was perfect and promised a clear, warm, sunny day. Lije couldn't have asked for better. Even though their trip had begun in dim morning light, they had managed to make it through the series of rapids after Fox Landing without spilling either canoe. That alone made this day one for the books.

The quartet dragged the two aluminum canoes about fifty feet to a clump of trees where they couldn't be seen from the river or the ridge. After organizing their gear, Curtis and Cathcart began digging next to the exposed rails.

"This is fascinating," Cathcart announced. "Look at this section. The people who built this did a quick job."

Looking over Cathcart's shoulder, Lije asked, "What do you mean?"

"Well, they drove only about a quarter of the spikes they would've needed for any kind of heavy use. This set of rails was meant as a temporary line, nothing more."

Lije kneeled down to take a closer look. As he did, McGee

offered his take. "Are you sure this wasn't caused by decades of exposure to the elements? Time can change the way things look. A lot of the cross ties have rotted away. The spikes could have been carried away too."

Glancing up at him, Cathcart said, "I understand your point, but I'm sure this shows a pattern. They drove just enough spikes to hold the rails in place for a few passes at a very slow speed. This was never meant to last long. It looks just like some of the quick rerouting jobs early railroad companies did when they were fixing a short section of bad track."

Lije posed the next question. "If they were using a handcar or pulling small railroad cars with mules or horses, would this type of job hold up for a while?"

"Who would do that?" Cathcart asked.

"I'm thinking moonshiners. They could have the still partway up the ridge, and if they had a big operation, it'd be better to use boats than cars or trucks. The track could have taken the brew down to the boats."

"You have a point." But it was obvious Cathcart didn't want this to be about home brew.

Still, to Lije, a moonshine operation just made more sense than anything else. He walked down toward the river and began digging at a point where the bank sloped sharply down to the water.

McGee joined him. "Lije, you really think it's just part of a forgotten still operation?"

Lije nodded. He used his shirtsleeve to wipe the sweat from his brow, then continued to work his spade in an attempt to expose more of the old bridge supports. Then he stopped. "Does anything here look strange to you?"

McGee slid down the bank to get a better look at the top of the stonework. Lije pulled a rag from his pocket and brushed away more dirt. Not satisfied with the cleaning, he walked down to the river, dipped the cloth in the water, and returned to scrub the surface.

After finishing, he studied his handiwork. "McGee, go get Diana. She's got to see this."

McGee walked up to where Curtis was working and the two returned to the river's edge. Brushing her hands against her pants, Curtis bent down to see what Lije had uncovered. "Interesting. Do you suppose there's anything left of the bridge support on the other side of the river?"

"I wouldn't have a clue," Lije replied. "But was I right? Is there something strange here?"

"Maybe. We need to see what the other side looks like. Lije, can you paddle me over? And let's take some equipment with us so we can act like we're fishing if anyone comes down the stream. Kent, can you keep one eye on Lije while you work? He'll signal you if he sees anyone coming, and then you can let the professor know so the two of you can either hide or look like sportsmen."

"Got it," McGee replied.

For the next hour, Lije tried his luck with a hook while Curtis explored. Only once did he have to signal everyone to stop what they were doing and appear as if they were fishing. During this interruption, Cathcart and McGee looked like real anglers. Curtis tried one cast, got her hook caught in a tree, and broke the line attempting to pull it free. As she struggled, Lije reeled in a brown trout. He smiled; she grumbled. Finally, when the tourists floated out of sight, she tossed the rod into her canoe and went back to work. Lije knew that even over the noise of the river, she could hear his laughter.

His luck with the line and the beauty of the sun's rays bouncing off the rapids upstream normally would have captured all his attention. It had been a couple of years since he'd experienced this kind of fishing. But because of the circumstances, he spent far more time looking across the stream at McGee and Cathcart than he did casting. And even though he had no real interest in the endeavor, he kept up the pretense of fishing, reeling in more trout, until Curtis was ready for him to paddle her back across the stream.

McGee was ready to catch the canoe when they drifted over to the bank. Curtis and Lije got out, and together he and McGee lifted the canoe out of the water and placed it on dry ground. After Curtis removed her kit, they carried the canoe back to its hiding place in the trees.

"Find anything?" McGee asked Curtis.

"Not sure. I need to check something with Dr. Cathcart." After the three joined Cathcart at the dig site, Curtis said, "Professor, do you know if in that 1891 flood, when the bridge for the spur to the ridge was washed away, was it all in one piece when it got to Hardy?"

"Well, I wasn't there, but the news stories at the time indicate it was pretty much intact."

"Then that would point to sabotage rather than the floodwaters. Most wooden structures I've seen destroyed by high water are pulled apart, a section at a time. In fact, most usually have long stretches remaining, especially along the bank, after the floodwaters recede."

"But why would someone destroy the railroad bridge?"

Curtis smiled. "And why would someone build a rail line on this side of the river that served no purpose and ended against a bluff? There doesn't seem to be any logic here at all."

Lije stepped away from the exposed rails and walked back to the river. The river was hypnotic, always moving and morphing into a new breathtaking view of nature. He picked up a stick and, sitting on his haunches, poked at pebbles in the water, turning them over to watch the river fill the hole left in the sand with more sand. The diversion was just what he needed to recharge his batteries and produce a semblance of hope. He was just about to rejoin the others at the dig site when he saw it.

A hundred yards upstream an unnatural orange object was floating down the middle of the river. Its movement seemed erratic, as if something other than the current was determining its course. It was too small to be a boat and too large to be litter tossed out by a careless fisherman. As the object drew closer, Lije realized it was a life jacket and a woman's head was sticking through it. She was struggling, fighting the current, grabbing for anything.

The woman would be battered to pieces in the rapids!

63

"CURTIS! MCGEE! GET DOWN HERE!" LIJE YELLED. Not waiting for them to answer, he ran into the cold water. The river's fifty-eight degrees took his breath away. For a second as the water got deeper, he floundered. Then, after forcing air into his lungs, his feet found secure footing on the stream's slippery floor. Balancing against the strong current, he worked his way out toward the middle of the channel, half wading, half swimming against the current, and always trying to stay as close as he could to the shallower water in the stream. But he was not making enough progress. He was moving much too slowly. He had to pick it up or he would never get to her in time. She'd be carried past him and into the rapids.

Holding onto moss-covered boulders, Lije slowly brought one foot in front of the other, fighting a current so strong that he felt he was barely moving. That demanding flow twice knocked him into the water, and he floated downstream a few feet before latching onto another partially exposed boulder. Spitting the river from his mouth, he braced himself, shook his wet hair out of his eyes, and looked upstream. The woman, her arms flailing, was now only about a hundred feet from him.

Like a defensive back trying to run down a wide receiver, he took a pursuit angle, moving upstream, scrambling from one boulder to another, slowly closing the distance. Just as he stepped onto a rock where the deep pools ended and the rapids started, the woman spun in a series of small circles. She was now just a few feet away, but as quickly as she was moving, it might as well have been a mile.

With time running out, Lije pushed off from a large flat stone, trying desperately to latch onto the orange life preserver. Finding the canvas with the fingers of his right hand, he slung his left arm around the woman's body, all the while desperately trying to turn back and catch his right hand on one of the exposed boulders. She fought his every move, hitting and scratching as she tried to break free. He was impressed with her strength. But the river was taking its toll on both of them. With his chest almost bursting, now submerged in the cold stream, swallowing more water than he normally drank in a week, he continued to pull the woman toward the riverbank. She finally was simply too worn out to struggle. Perhaps sensing the end had come, the woman went limp. The jacket slipped up over her head and was sliding up her arms. With only seconds before he lost his own ability to act or react, Lije wrapped his arms around the woman's upper body and pushed off from one of the boulders with his left foot.

Gasping for air, they rolled together between a series of smaller boulders and were tossed under the surface. Lije continued to push and kick toward the riverbank. The current slowed and Lije slipped his arm under the woman's neck.

McGee waded out to meet him. "Lije, you all right?"

"Yeah, I think so, but don't know about her. Grab her."

Freed from having to pull two people to safety, he stood up, waded slowly to the bank, and sat down in the grass. He looked back at the river that had fought his every move. It no longer looked peaceful and inviting.

She was small, maybe only five feet tall. She had blonde hair and light blue eyes. Judging from her pale skin, Lije guessed she didn't get outside much. Her fingers were thin. Her arms, exposed in her sleeveless shirt, were well defined. Her shorts revealed muscular legs, like those of a runner. Her hair was cut in what appeared to be a stylish shoulder-length but no-nonsense manner, easy to care for or fix. She looked to be in her early thirties. She was surprisingly calm, considering she had almost drowned.

"Are you okay?" Lije asked.

She sat up, resting her arms on her knees, and coughed a few more times before answering, "Yes. I'm a little wet though."

Curtis took a seat on the bank beside their drop-in guest. "What happened?"

Looking straight ahead, staring at the river, still shivering from the cold, she said, "There was a group of us going down the river. We had rented three canoes and were putting in a little ways upstream. I was in the first canoe, already sitting down, when someone else showed up. I think there were two men, but I don't know, it could have been more. They ordered everyone back on shore, and as I stood up, I fell back in the canoe and it started to float off the bank. By the time I got my balance and got seated, I was already a ways downstream. I had no paddle, so I couldn't control anything, just had to ride it out, and I was going backwards. I somehow made it through the first rapids, but I was dumped out on the second one. I floated in the current for a while, then someone tried to drown me."

"I believe the operative word would be 'save,'" Lije said.

Even as he approached, the woman's gaze remained fixed on the river. "It felt more like a mugging."

"Sorry, but it was hard to get to you. For a few moments I thought we were both going to die." She still didn't look his way. It was as if the liquid monster that had come so close to stealing her life still had her under its spell. She simply couldn't take her eyes off the water.

"I'm Lije. The distinguished gentleman on your left is Dr. Cathcart, the pretty woman is Diana, and the man behind you is Kent."

She nodded. "I'm Janie Davies. Like the group I was with, I'm from Little Rock."

"Miss Davies," Curtis said, "why did the men order you back to the riverbank?"

"They seemed to want the canoes," Davies said. "I don't know why, but they were gruff and rude. I doubt if they were Boy Scouts."

McGee chimed in, "Did you get a look at them?"

"No. I hope you don't think this is rude, but you all sound like policemen."

"Actually," Curtis said, "I'm an agent from the Arkansas Bureau of Investigation. So you're right, I'm a cop, and these two are lawyers."

Davies laughed. "At least I had the good sense to be rescued by the authorities and will have representation when I figure out who to sue."

Lije stretched and looked around in an attempt to get his bearings. The river had taken them about a hundred yards beyond where the tracks ended at the ridge. And then something else caught his eye. "Diana, I need for you to come over here."

The agent left Janie and walked over to Lije's side. There were two canoes coming toward them with only one man in each. "Could those be the men who hijacked Janie's group?"

"Lije," Curtis spoke quietly, "let's get her on her feet and see if she can ID them."

"She won't be able to," Lije replied.

"Why not?"

"She's blind."

"How did I miss that?"

Lije's own eyes never left the canoes, now about a hundred yards upstream. "She never made any eye contact with us or focused on anything else. When we asked her a question, she tilted her head in the direction of our voices, to hear us, not see us. If she'd seen me, she probably wouldn't have fought me off. She probably thought I was one of the men."

"If you're so good at observation, what do you make of those guys?"

"We've got trouble in River City."

Curtis started handing out orders. "Lije, you and McGee get Cathcart and the woman and work your way back up the bank to where the kits are. Secure what you can, then find someplace to hide. These guys haven't spotted us yet, but my gut tells me they're not the kind who want to swap fish stories."

Now close enough to make out some of their features, Lije said, "Looks like the sketches of Smith and his partner."

"My gun's with my kit."

"Go get it. I'll get the others out of sight."

As the agent set off in a careful jog up the bank, keeping as close to the ground as possible, Lije returned to where Cathcart, McGee, and Janie were standing.

"Miss Davies, I think the two men who hijacked your canoes are about a hundred yards upstream. We need to get away from this open bottomland and work our way to some cover. Are you rested enough to run?"

"I can keep up."

Nodding, he grabbed her right hand with his left. "Hang on, try to keep your head down, and I'll warn you if you need to duck or hit the ground. You two guys ready?"

Cathcart answered, "I'm right with you, son."

McGee nodded.

Crouching, the four of them moved at a slow pace across the grass-covered flatland, up the gradually sloping hill, and toward the ridge. Ahead, about fifty yards beyond the crest, Curtis had grabbed the kit and the backpack filled with food. For a second, as all the parties closed in on their meeting point, it seemed they had escaped detection. Then, from somewhere near the bank, a shot rang out, followed by two more. The first flew just over Lije's shoulder, ricocheting off one of the boulders that lined the bottom of the ridge. The next two whizzed just in front of and just behind his head. Tucking his shoulder and rolling forward, he dragged the woman to the ground, partially covering her body with his.

"Hey, I thought you were going to warn me before you did something radical," Janie said in a hoarse whisper.

65

LIJE SPOTTED SOME ROCKS THAT COULD SERVE AS cover. "We need to move about twenty-five feet. Crawl forward and try to keep your heads down."

At they began the slow trek up the slope, another round of gunfire broke out. This time it was answered by shots from Curtis, firing as she retreated toward them.

"Y'all okay?" she asked as she took up a position behind two rocks that were at least seven feet tall and six feet wide.

"We're fine ... for the moment," Lije said.

Curtis peered around the boulder and looked upstream. "They're now off the river. One is positioned pretty close to the river. The other's moving around us. I think he's headed for higher ground. It'll take him only a few minutes to get to a position where we'll be sitting ducks."

Curtis scanned the area, looking for other shelter. She had more bad news. "I have only one clip and have already fired about half of those rounds. So I'll have to save the rest for when they get above us and start shooting again. Odds are I'm not going to see anyone to shoot at."

"Well," Cathcart said, grinning, "it could be worse."

"How's that?" McGee asked.

"It could be raining."

Just then bullets smashed against the hillside above the rocks, causing dust to sprinkle down on them.

"It is raining," McGee said. "It's raining lead."

Curtis answered the volley, firing two rounds toward the river. The agent's reply didn't discourage the shooter. He peppered the boulders with another half dozen bursts.

"An automatic," Curtis noted.

A shot bounced off the top of the boulder. Curtis stood, turned to her left, and fired two quick replies in the direction of the hill. Sinking back to her knees, she said, "He's getting close to where he can really see us. Anyone got any ideas?"

As if trying to push his way into the grassy soil, Lije fell back against the ground. The professor instinctively did the same. Janie was stretched out face down. She tilted her head and held her left hand slightly aloft, letting it hover just inches off the ground. She began to crawl along the side of the grass-covered hill. Every foot or so she stopped for a moment, tilting her head and again lifting her hand. What was she doing? Did she have a death wish? She was almost out in the open. Lije was about to reach up to yank her back to safety when a smile crossed her face.

"Hey, you," she whispered.

Crawling up to a point beside her, he said, "What is it?"

"Can you feel a cool dry breeze right here?"

He concentrated, but sensed only heat and humidity.

"Give me your hand," she said. After he slipped his hand into hers, she pulled it forward a few feet. "Now do you feel it?"

He felt something, like a faint breeze. "Yes."

"There's a cave here," she whispered. "Find it!"

He looked ahead but saw nothing. He held his hand up, felt the cooler air, and inched forward. Then it was there, just behind some shrubs, a small opening in the ridge. It was about five feet away from where he was lying, almost completely hidden by a berry bush. Judging from the soil and small rocks that were piled beneath the opening, the recent floods had washed away enough of the hillside to expose the hollow spot.

"I see it," he whispered, "but the opening's not very big. It might just be a washout. Doesn't look like there's a cave."

"No," Janie said, "the cave's good sized. I can tell by the smell and the way the air feels. If we get in there, the odds change in our favor."

Lije quickly pushed his way through the brush to the one-foot-wide hole in the side of the ridge. Rolling over onto his back, he hit the soft soil above the opening with his feet. Large chunks of still moist clay began to give way. He scrambled back down to the troop, staying as well hidden as he could.

"I think there's a cave up there. I need a flashlight."

Curtis opened her kit and pulled a small maglight from the case. Lije grabbed it and crawled back up the hill. Sticking his arm and then his head into the opening, he shined the light into the cave. Janie was right; the cave was huge. The only problem: an eight-foot drop to the floor. Without a rope, the only choice would be to crawl in feet first and let go. It wasn't going to be easy on the ankles, but it beat waiting behind the rocks to get shot.

Pulling his head from the cavity, Lije again scrambled back down the incline. "There's a cave just up the side of the ridge. It's big, but there's a drop to the floor of about eight feet, maybe more."

Five more shots, these hitting much farther down on the boulders, interrupted his explanation.

"I'm going back up there and jumping in. I'll yell when the next person should follow. I'll try to catch you. Professor, you bring Janie first. Janie, slide your feet and legs into the hole, then just drop. I'll catch you. Professor, as soon as Janie's clear, you drop too. Kent, you're next. Diana, toss the kit and backpack in before making the leap."

Not waiting for a reply or questions, Lije snaked his way back up the hillside. Sliding his legs through the opening, he turned over onto his stomach and pushed off. The fall seemed to take forever and the hard surface that met him was anything but friendly. Crumpling to his knees, he winced, then, realizing he was relatively unhurt, sprang to his feet. Pulling the light from his pocket, he quickly flashed it to his left and right. The chamber was at least a hundred feet wide and more than forty feet high. The hole he had dug out was about ten feet from the left wall. The cave might have been dark, cold, and foreboding, but at the moment, it seemed like the most wonderful place on earth.

"Now," he said, his voice echoing off the walls as he glanced back toward the sunlight filtering through the opening. He heard a few more muffled shots before Janie's legs blocked out the sunlight. "Okay, push off and let go." Acting on faith alone, the woman dropped. Lije caught her around the waist and lowered her to the ground. The little bit of light from the hole above shined on her smile.

"Move to the right, Janie." After she had taken a few steps, Lije got into position for the professor. Cathcart fell into Lije, knocking both of them to the ground. Thankfully, McGee needed no help with his landing. Curtis tossed her kit in and then dropped into McGee's waiting grasp. Turning, she laid the backpack on the floor of the cave and reached into her pocket for her flashlight. Shining it on the quartet surrounding her, she grinned and asked, "Is everyone all right?"

"Fine," Lije replied. Carthcart and McGee nodded and Janie smiled.

"I'm pretty good too," Curtis noted.

But Lije's flashlight's beam revealed something else. "You're bleeding."

"Yep, he got me just before I got to the cave. It's clean. We can treat it with stuff in the kit."

Picking up the kit, Cathcart walked toward her. Shining a light on the wound, he shook his head. "You're lucky. Just grazed your arm." He pulled sterile wipes and bandages from the box.

"Professor, just wrap some gauze around it for now. We need to move away from the entrance. They are going to come after us. Our best bet is to find a hiding place."

Not waiting for the others, Lije had already begun to explore their temporary home, shining his light down to an area that must have been an inner wall. From where he stood, it looked as though they were in a side chamber. A much larger cavern appeared to angle to the right and run almost parallel to the river. Grabbing Janie's hand, he led the way toward the larger room. After reaching the base of the wall, he turned left into what could be the main cave under the ridge.

He shined his light both ways. It looked like they were in a long, high tunnel. And in the middle of the cavern, stretching as far as he could see both ways, was a set of rails. They walked along the shining ribbon of track and saw the rear of an antique wooden caboose. His light caught several more cars beyond it.

Coming up beside him, Dr. Cathcart's eyes followed the beam. "It's Ole 74."

DR. CATHCART AND LIJE WERE ALL BUT PARALYZED by the reality caught in the flashlight beam. Ole 74 was here. In the cave. That's why the tracks had been laid. It was all about the train. Suddenly they forgot the men with guns; they forgot everything. There was no fear, no pain, no fatigue. Everything took a back seat as they stared at the answer to a mystery more than a century old. It called out to them, demanded their attention, begged them to come closer, pleaded with them to drop everything and study the train closely, to step forward and uncover the secrets it had hidden for so long.

Curtis merely glanced at the missing relic. If she was interested, she didn't show it. "Okay, we have killers on our tails," she announced. "Now, Lije, you keep your eye on that opening we crawled through. If you see anyone trying to come in, let me know. I've got enough rounds left to discourage them."

After taking another look at Ole 74, Lije gave his maglight to McGee, who shined it onto Curtis's arm. After gently cleaning the wound with alcohol, Cathcart wrapped it with gauze and applied an elastic bandage.

Satisfied, he said, "Diana, how's it feel?"

"It's not bad, but I think I'll try to stay away from getting shot in the future."

"Probably a good idea."

When Curtis tested her arm, she winced a bit, but she still seemed in pretty good shape. "We're safe for the moment, but there are at least two ill-humored folks out there right now who'd love to play target practice with all of us. Keep an eye on that entrance. See anything, Lije?"

"Nothing yet." Her orders proved his earlier assessment. She was tough. Winged or not, she felt well enough to think she was in charge. And for the moment, she was.

From out of the darkness, Janie spoke. "They're up there."

McGee shined his light over to her. She was leaning up against a wall, her head cocked toward the opening. "Are you sure?"

"Yes," she replied, "they're just above the entrance. I can't make out their words, but I can faintly hear their voices. Or at least I could until a few minutes ago."

Curtis grimly studied the place where sunlight filtered into the cavern. "Does anyone else hear anything?"

No one spoke. Curtis cut her light, rested her arm on a boulder, and fixed her gun barrel on the small, lighted hole. Lije killed his light.

For the next forty minutes, four sets of eyes and one pair of very sharp ears remained glued to the only ray of sunshine to be found in this mysterious subterranean world. In silence they waited. When would the men make their move? The waiting was maddening. As the clock ticked, they felt more trapped than safe.

As they waited, Lije realized he was praying. It hadn't been a decision. It was almost a reflex. A small grin etched his upper lip. He had seen Kaitlyn react this way every time she had been confronted with a monumental challenge or when she had been presented with a moment of joy. Often she didn't know she was praying. For her it was like breathing. And now he was doing it. Even though she was gone, he still felt her influence. A part of her was with him. Maybe a part of her had always been there. Too bad he had to fall into a cavern to figure that out.

"They're up there again," Janie whispered, bringing Lije back to the reality of their danger.

"Can you hear anything else?" Curtis whispered.

The cave was bathed in an eerie hush as Janie tried to pick up sounds no one else could hear. "I think one of them just asked about a light."

As the blind woman's keen ears stayed focused, the other four continued to stare at the bright tiny circle. For what felt like hours, silence ruled, then suddenly Janie became excited. "We better move back, now, fast!"

Janie reached out and found Lije's hand. He grabbed McGee's elbow. The chain was almost complete when he reached out for Curtis, but she balked.

"Someone has to keep an eye on the entrance. Besides, they can't see us, much less get to us, until they get in the cave. We have that advantage, and there's no use giving it up."

"Trust me," Janie pleaded, "we have to move and move now!"

Curtis grumbled something about the blind leading the blind.

"Where is Dr. Cathcart?" Lije asked.

"I've got him," Janie said.

"I'm right here, Lije," Cathcart said.

Janie said, "Trust me, and follow me." As she held onto his hand, the woman confidently pushed forward into the darkness. They were all blind in this cave, but to Janie, that was nothing new. There was nothing tentative about her movements. She led them behind the thick rock wall where the entrance was no longer visible.

"Don't turn the lights on," Curtis ordered. "If they do come in, I don't want them to have a target."

"They aren't coming down here," Janie assured her.

A huge ear-piercing explosion shook the very chamber where they were hiding. As they huddled in the darkness, they heard a low rumble as rocks and huge clods of dirt rolled down the hill above them. A thick layer of dust seeped into their lair. It felt like an earthquake, but this was not a product of nature's power. This was man-made.

In the pitch blackness, they leaned against the cool stone wall, each sensing the thin line that separates life and death. For Janie, McGee, and Cathcart, this was a new experience, but for Lije, it was beginning to feel like a part of his routine.

An eerie silence ushered in the illusion of peace.

Curtis turned on her flashlight. The beam revealed that the large tunnel-like chamber was dusty, but secure. Taking a few steps to her left, she shined the light back toward the entrance. There was no longer any light. The hole had been filled in when a good portion of the hill had fallen in on itself.

"They blasted the entrance," Curtis said.

McGee grabbed Lije's light and aimed it in the same direction. "We won't be leaving the same way we came in."

From beside him, Janie calmly chimed in, "Caves are interesting places. In many cases, when an earthquake or some other cataclysmic event closes off one entrance, it opens another. Do you all remember that when we came into this chamber it was deathly silent? Now that has changed. I hear water. So whatever they did to trap us brought something new into this world. As my house father used to say, when one door closes, another opens."

Water? No one moved. What sound? What had she heard that they had not?

"I hear it," Cathcart said. "It's not the river. It's more a tinkling sound, like raindrops on puddles."

"Something like that," Janie replied, "but there's more water than that involved here. I'd guess more like a small spring or maybe an underground creek."

Turning and flashing her beam around the chamber, Curtis asked, "Can you tell where it is?"

Janie concentrated for a moment. "I think so." Pointing with her left hand, she said, "It seems to be down the chamber a ways, to the left."

"That would take us by the train," Dr. Cathcart said.

67

"JUST KEEP WALKING, PROFESSOR," CURTIS WARNED AS
they made their way past the train and down the long corridor.

"Fascinating," Dr. Cathcart said as the flashlights lit up the
sides of the antique wooden cars. "Lije, look at them. They're all
in such remarkable condition. It's like this train could be fired up
and taken for a run today!"

Lije was walking just a few steps ahead of Cathcart. Like the
professor, he desperately wanted to stop and explore each and every
corner of the relic parked on his left. Yet this was a life-or-death
situation, not a school field trip. This cave was rapidly becoming a
tomb. And he didn't want to die. The train could wait.

To Lije's side, her arm wrapped around his, walked Janie Davies. "Stop," she said. The shuffling feet came to a halt and four
sets of eyes turned her way. She stood there, still, her head tilted
to the right. She listened intently for a few moments. "It's kind of
muffled, but the water is somewhere to our right."

Curtis turned and shined her light against the wall. Her beam
revealed a number of small rocks and a boulder the size of one
that had served as their fort a short time before. Walking over to
get a better look, she shined her flashlight into an area between
the large hunk of sandstone and the interior wall. There, caught
in the beam, was an opening, not more than a yard high. The way
the rocks sat around it, it looked as if the entrance had just been

uncovered. Janie had been right, a new door had opened. Curtis squeezed through the hole and disappeared.

McGee took Lije's flashlight and wandered ahead. The other three waited in the dark. The darkness was more than a little unnerving for Lije and Dr. Cathcart as the void engulfed them. A minute went by, then another, finally it was five.

"Is she trapped or lost?" Cathcart asked.

"No, I hear her walking around," Janie replied.

Amazing! All Lije could hear was McGee stumbling around in the big chamber.

"She's coming out now."

If he could have seen the professor's face, Lije was sure Cathcart would have looked as confounded as he felt. How had she heard that?

McGee's light bounced into view.

Curtis appeared and flashed a quick smile. "We're not going to die of thirst. On the other side of that wall, there's a small spring. The bad news is that the room is no more than a couple of hundred square feet and, except for where the water disappears into the far wall, there is no exit. The good news is that we have a source of water. And the better news is that there might be something we haven't found in this chamber yet."

"Don't think so," McGee announced. Caught in Curtis's beam, McGee's face looked as bleak as his voice sounded. "While you were exploring, I did a quick survey of my own. I just walked to the front of the train. The locomotive's cowcatcher ends at a rock wall. It's resting up against it. The wall is solid. No obvious breaks, not even as you look up toward the ceiling. This chamber's huge, but it evidently leads nowhere."

A hush fell over the party as the news sank in. With no way to remove the tons of debris now covering the entrance, there appeared to be no light at the end of any of the tunnels.

Turning around, Lije found himself standing beside the baggage car, about in the middle of the train. After studying the wooden-sided boxcar, he walked over to the steps leading up to the platform. Bathed in the beam from Curtis's flashlight, he jumped up on the car and twisted the doorknob. The door was unlocked, and he took a step inside.

Backing out on the platform, he waved toward the party. "Diana, give me your light. It's time we did a bit of exploring." As she jogged over to the train, Lije glanced back at the professor. "What kind of things would have been on a car like this?"

"Dry goods, farm supplies, tools, maybe clothing or even wallpaper. It varied from run to run. Think of it as a UPS truck from another century."

Lije grabbed the light. "So, if I get your drift, maybe there'll be something in here that might make our stay more pleasant or give us a way to tunnel our way out. Dr. Cathcart, would you like to join me?"

"I'd love to," he answered. He scrambled up the steps and followed Lije through the door and into an area crowded with a variety of crates and boxes. The space was filled with supplies.

"Look at that, professor—candles. And over there we have a box of lanterns."

"Lije, here's a barrel of whale oil and another marked kerosene."

"Would it still be good?"

"The barrel is sealed. The cave has been dry for years. Doubt if there's been any water in here until the wall broke a few minutes ago and exposed the spring. Now if we can find matches ..."

"Diana," Lije called toward the door, "do you have a lighter in your kit?"

"Sure. I have several."

"Well, go get one. We've now got a way to better light up our world."

Soon a dozen lanterns were sitting along the right side of the old train. Three more were illuminating the baggage car. In the more widely spread light, Lije made a quick inventory of every-thing in the old boxcar.

The contents of the car would be great for a costume party but weren't much good in a rescue. Lots of clothes and shoes and paper, but no digging tools, TNT, or gunpowder. Nothing to use that would allow them to blow their way out of this hole.

"Not much help here," Cathcart said. "Maybe in one of the other cars we'll find something more useful. As for me, I'm just happy to have some light. And judging from the number of lamps and candles and those three barrels of oil we found, we can light up our world for a long time."

Cathcart and Lije dropped down out of the boxcar, and they all walked back toward the caboose. After they'd walked past another boxcar and reached the rear of the car in front of the caboose, Cathcart stopped and just stared at it. "This is the private car that belonged to Godfrey Payens," he said. "Who knows what we'll find in there."

"Only one way to find out," Lije said. "Janie, you want me to lead the way?"

"No," she replied, "I think I'll just sit down and rest here and wait for you to give me the blow by blow."

Curtis looked over at McGee. "Save the flashlight battery. Each one of us can grab a lantern. Professor, this has long been your quest. You lead the way."

Cathcart mounted the steps at the rear of the car and put his hand on the doorknob and slowly turned it. The old wooden door groaned as it swung open. Holding his antique light in front of him, he stepped into a simpler time, no doubt expecting a dynamic look into a preserved exhibit of finery from the gilded age.

Instead, he entered a horror show.

LIJE STEPPED INTO THE PRIVATE RAILROAD CAR,
following right behind the professor.

Sitting at a wooden table were five men. It would have appeared that they were engaged in a meal or a discussion if not for the gruesome disfigurement of their faces. It reminded Lije of a display in a haunted house he had visited when he was ten. His fear then had been tempered because he knew the scene was fake. This was real.

Each mummified man's hands were bound behind him, tying him to the chair. Pushing past Lije, Curtis set her lantern on the table and took a quick look at the bodies. Glancing back toward McGee, who had just entered the car, she said, "Get my kit." McGee nodded, hurrying out the door and returning quickly with the case. Curtis pulled out a pair of gloves—probably out of habit—slipped them on, and began examining the closest body.

"Amazingly well preserved," she noted as she studied the skin. "The dry conditions in the cave mummified them. Now if, a century ago, that wall had been opened, allowing the spring water and its humidity in this chamber, these men would look much different. Professor, do you know who they are?"

Cathcart cleared his throat. "I can make a good guess. The one nearest me has to be the engineer or brakeman. The man you are examining is the conductor. The clothes give him away. The one on my left may be the fireman. The man to your right again is either the engineer or the brakeman—their clothes are similar enough to make it difficult to guess without proper identification. And the final man in the nice suit at the end of the table would have to be the Canadian who owned this car and the next."

Curtis moved over one chair to her right. Reaching into the top pocket of the man's bib overalls, she pulled on a gold chain, lifting out a watch. Turning it over she held the back toward the lantern's light. "James Forbes, Engineer."

"Can you tell how they died, or has it been too long?" McGee asked.

Lije looked over at McGee. If the scene shocked him, he didn't show it. He appeared interested, but not horrified. As a defense attorney who had once worked with the attorney general's office, he'd probably seen much worse than this.

"They were each shot," Curtis explained. "The action was deliberate and straightforward. One bullet entered the back of each of their skulls. This is an execution scene."

Curtis was now on her hands and knees at the base of the table. She'd evidently found something else.

"If you'll look toward the floor, you'll see that all five men's trouser legs and shoes are covered with dried mud. They wouldn't have gotten that way in the cave. Wonder why that happened?" She studied the anomaly for a few more moments and posed another question. "Professor, do you know if there was anyone else on this train?"

"The postman should have been on board."

"Well," Curtis said, "at this point he'd probably be our chief suspect. If he masterminded this operation, he was probably gone before the entrance was covered. And if he was thirty when it happened and lived another fifty years, he would have died before anyone here was born. When we find our way out, I don't think I'll need to put out a warrant for him."

Dead or not didn't matter to Lije. He was curious about where that long-forgotten trail would lead. Could the man have done all this and gotten off scot-free? And why? And would his actions have haunted him all the way to the grave?

Lije turned his attention to the forward section of the old coach, shining his lantern as he moved past the dead men. He noted carefully crafted wood furniture, fancy brass light fixtures, and ornate wall coverings. He placed his lamp on an ancient rolltop desk, eased down into a creaky swivel chair, and slid the desktop open. In the tiny cubicles so common to rolltops was everything from unopened bottles of ink to penny postage stamps and even letters. A Memphis newspaper was open to the right of the work surface. The paper had a front-page editoral questioning if moving pictures, such as the one shown at the National Federation of Women's Clubs convention, would ever generate any real financial returns. Another story gave a round-by-round description of the sixty-one round heavyweight title bout between Jim Corbett and Peter Jackson that ended in a draw. Kingman won the Kentucky Derby, but the paper was picking Foxford in the upcoming Belmont Stakes.

Lost in the past, reading ancient news as if it had just happened, Lije all but forgot about the cave and the bodies resting in anything but peaceful slumber just a few feet away. He was about to turn to page two to catch up on Memphis news when something even more interesting caught his eye. Underneath where the paper had been was some kind of journal.

Opening the green leather cover, Lije encountered an unfamiliar name — Andrew Farnsworth. "December 24, 1890. The last of it came out of the well today. While the others continue to search on the far side of the island, I was able finally to decrypt the stone tablet and realize the pit was naught but a ruse. The clues I was given led to a dry well and just a few feet below the bottom, I found a king's ransom. But the cache contained only gold, silver, and jewelry. The sacred relics were not there. Did the Knights never have them? Was this just a legend? I guess I will never know.

"January 1, 1891. After much prayer I have decided to use the treasure in the American West. Though the land is rich, many who have sought to uncover its wealth have found little but pain and misery. Many areas are immersed in poverty. I am going to secure a private railcar and make my way to the area. My only fear is that the one man who knows of my find, my brother Jacob, will follow me. He constantly dreams of wealth and his greed probably puts my life in jeopardy. I have given him a great deal already, but I fear it will not be enough to fully satisfy his own desires. Thus from this day forward I will no longer be Andrew Farnsworth. Henceforth I will be known as Godfrey Payens."

Lije skimmed through several more pages, noting the days and times until he finally came to the final entry of June 5, 1891. "I believe I spotted my brother in Memphis. A railroad official informed me a man had been inquiring about my private cars. I did not see him when I left the city, and I may be safe, but I wonder. As I made these connections and finalized the contracts more than a month ago, I fear he might know the route I am now taking. Tonight, as I read the Scripture and as I said my prayers, I felt real fear for the first time in months. My fear is not for my life—that is in God's hands—but I hate to think that the treasure, given by believers centuries ago, will be used for the pursuit of worldly pleasures. It was probably not Jacob, and still my faith is weak."

Incredible! Maybe it wasn't the postman but someone much closer to Payens, or Farnsworth. Lije closed the journal and walked back to the rear end of the car. He handed the book to Cathcart. "Professor, this'll answer many of your questions about what happened here and what this wild ride was all about. I'm going to move forward to the next car."

"I didn't see a door to Payens' private boxcar on the side where we found the spring," Cathcart said. "So I suggest we grab our lanterns and exit toward the other wall of the cave."

"Well, not really much we can do here," Curtis noted. "We're a few years too late. Kent, why don't you get Janie. I want her on the same side of the train as we are."

McGee left by way of the steps at the rear of the car, and the three others moved forward to the steps at the front. Lije stepped down from the private car. He was followed by Curtis. Neither had to hold their lanterns very high to see that they'd been beaten to the prize.

Curtis shook her head. "Someone has blown this place wide open. The door's gone and the boards on each side of it are badly splintered."

"They sure made a mess getting in," Cathcart said as he joined her.

"Actually," Curtis said as she examined the evidence, "the mess came from the inside blowing out."

Lije took a second look at the boxcar. Well, so much for the treasure. He turned his light back toward the far wall. While the flickering illumination from the oil lamp had been adequate inside the coach, with the thirty-foot ceiling, rising to more than seventy feet in some spots, as well as the wide expanse of open space between the boxcar and the wall, the lantern now did little but create exaggerated shadows. Still, as poor as the flickering light was, it was enough to see the body count had just risen by three. It appeared these deaths had been just as violent as those in the car.

"Diana, look behind you," Lije said.

Curtis turned and moved toward the mummified remains. The victims were lying in a triangular pattern about twenty feet from the train, each about ten feet apart. Pieces of wood, evidently from the boxcar, littered the cave floor around them. Two men were on their backs; the other was face down. Curtis stooped to examine the man closest to the rear of the car. She then moved on to the next man. Finally she leaned over the last body. Now, seen for the first time in the flickering light created by Curtis's lantern, about twenty feet in front of the dead men, was a large wagon with what appeared to be a team of dead horses or mules lying in front of it.

Moving over to the wagon, Curtis studied the mummified beasts. She finally returned to the damaged boxcar.

Lije and Cathcart looked at her expectantly, and she didn't disappoint them.

"It looks as if the Canadian who owned this car had it booby-trapped. If someone opened it incorrectly, a blast sent a lot of nails and other pieces of sharpened metal flying directly into the faces of those trying to board. It's my guess these three would-be robbers and probable murderers were blown back to where they now rest by the force of the explosion. I think the concussion alone would have killed them, but if not, the metal that pierced their bodies made sure they died."

"This is like visiting a haunted house," Cathcart said.

Curtis glanced back toward the flash point of the explosion. "Now, before boarding the car, I think we'd better see if there are any other surprises. While I realize you both are itching to know if the original cargo, whatever that was, remains in place, let me examine the car first. This place might end up being our grave, but I don't want to die as they did. In case there is more gunpowder, I'll leave the lantern behind and use the flashlight."

Lije watched enviously as Curtis eased onto the wooden railroad car. Using her flashlight, she cautiously viewed her surroundings, then disappeared behind the wall of the boxcar. Except for occasional flashes of light from her maglight, they saw nothing.

Lije shuffled back and forth about twenty feet from the track. Along with the others, he was holding his breath, praying that an explosion would not take another life. Finally Curtis appeared in the splintered opening where the door had once hung.

"It appears nothing was taken," she said. "There are four large crates. There are no markings on the sides. And that's it."

Lije glanced at the ring on his right pinky and approached the train. He now was certain the ring was part of the treasure buried by remnants of the Knights Templar and was, or had been, on this train. Would he now see the rest of the treasure?

Curtis reached down and helped him into the boxcar. Then they both helped Cathcart up. The trio walked over to look at the four crates that had remained hidden for more than a hundred years.

Taking a pry tool from her case, Curtis carefully worked on the lid on the wooden crate closest to them. After making sure there were no surprises, she lifted the lid. Inside was a huge stash of gold and silver coins, rings, large ornamental crosses, and a host of relics from the Middle Ages. The trio tried to comprehend what was spread out before them. Gauging the value of what rested in the crate was impossible.

"Let's open the others," Cathcart begged.

Curtis moved over to the next crate and stuck the pry bar under the top. Using the leverage, she pushed down and the lid moved upward. Moving the bar, she repeated the effort. With her third effort, the lid finally came off.

They were stunned. The crate was empty.

She quickly moved to the next one. Putting her hand on the side of the box, she gave it a shove. It scooted across the floor. "This one is empty too. It's much too light to have anything in it."

"As is this one," Lije said as he pushed the final crate.

"What happened to the rest of the treasure?" Cathcart asked.

Like Cathcart, Lije was mystified. What had happened?

"We may never know," said Curtis. "And we still have another mystery that we haven't solved."

"What's that?" Lije asked.

"The postman," Cathcart said. "We haven't seen his body."

Curtis jumped from the boxcar and, after retrieving her lantern from the ground, signaled for her informal team to follow her forward past the baggage car. Jumping up on the steps that led up to the mail car, she gave the knob a twist. The door didn't give. Running to the other end of the wooden car, Curtis tried the far door. It was also locked.

Holding her lantern up to the wooden entry, Curtis pointed

out a lot of small holes. "He wouldn't come out voluntarily. They sprayed this car with lead."

"That was the nature of the mailmen of the day," Cathcart explained. "Many of them would fight to the death to protect the property of the United States Postal Department."

Curtis dipped into her case and retrieved another set of tools. "This man may have done just that."

Going to work on the lock with her picks, she unlocked the door in short order. While the others waited, she walked into the long-sealed car. In a few moments, she appeared back on the landing. "He died at his post. His dog died with him. So he couldn't have planned all this."

"I've got a good idea who did," Lije said. "In the journal I found in the desk of the private car, the Canadian, whose real name was actually Andrew Farnsworth, wrote about discovering a huge cache of treasure that had been buried by the remnants of the Knights Templar on an island somewhere. And he wrote that his brother had been following his train and traced him to Memphis. I'm guessing he planned the heist."

"Then the flood," Cathcart said, "was just a lucky coincidence?"

"I would guess so," Lije replied. "It worked in favor of whoever planned the heist. Had to be more than one person in on it. That must have been some planning to build the track into the cave. They didn't have much time."

Cathcart jumped in as if he were conducting a school lecture. "The track was laid across the old bridge to this cave. There must have been an opening where the ridge is now. The old switch was probably still in place then, so it was little problem to lay the track in the days before they hijacked Ole 74. That's why they didn't use as many spikes. They were in a hurry."

Curtis said, "It looks to me like initially the plan went well. They forced the engineer to drive the train into the cave, then they rounded up the five we met in the first car and had them cover the exposed track with dirt. That's why their pants and shoes were muddy. After blowing the bridge, which is probably why we found no TNT or gunpowder on the train, they brought the men back into the cave, put them on the private car, and bound and shot them. Then they grabbed the treasure. They pulled the team and wagon up to the boxcar and forced the lock. When they started to swing open the door, the explosion ended their dreams of untold wealth."

Cathcart added, "And I think I can shed light on the final bit of irony in this case. The heavy rains that caused that flooding in June of 1891 created landslides all over this part of the Ozarks. Those rains probably loosened a great deal of the clay and rock on the hills above the cave. Driving the locomotive into this area put even more strain on the saturated hillside. Then the explosion caused by opening the boxcar door created a landslide. Thus the cave disappeared."

"And that would explain my early deed search," Lije said, "that stated there were three caves when the newer one listed only two."

For reasons he couldn't comprehend, Lije suddenly felt a sense of great loss. Six innocent men had died for nothing. Three others had paid for their greed. As he contemplated their lives, he wondered if it was too late to say a prayer for each of them. He was about to search for some type of meaningful words when Curtis broke his trance.

"You know, Lije, everything here legally belongs to you. It's on your property. As I recall the laws concerning such finds, after the state and the feds get their cut, it's yours."

"That's ironic," he answered. "It's probably not going to do me any more good than it did the men in this cave."

As the three each thought about the real possibility that it might be a long time before their own bodies would be found, a voice called out to them from the darkness.

69

"I'VE FOUND SOMETHING," JANIE CRIED.

Grabbing a lantern, Lije worked his way quickly down toward the engine at the end of the cavern's main chamber. When he finally came to the wall, he saw no signs of life.

"Janie, where are you?"

"Up here," came her calm reply.

"Where's McGee?"

"Over here, Lije. She told me to stay put, so I did."

Now joined by the other three, Lije lifted his light above his head and saw Janie standing on top of Ole 74. She had worked her way to the front of the engine and was holding her right hand toward the wall. A whimsical smile framed her face. She was almost glowing and seemed lost in an experience that Lije could not understand. "What is it, Janie?"

"One of you needs to come up here."

Curtis leaned over and whispered, "She trusts you."

Lije passed his lantern to Curtis and stepped onto the cowcatcher. Finding handholds where he could, he stepped up on the platform over the huge iron wheels and then grabbed onto the smokestack. Pulling upward, he climbed to a point where he was directly behind Janie.

Leaning back, she said, "It's easier if you start in the cab."

"Now you tell me." His voice was as unsteady as his position on Ole 74.

"Put your feet outside of mine. That'll balance you. Once you feel as if you're secure, reach toward the cave wall. It slopes back toward us at this point, so it's really just inches in front of the train."

Following her instructions, he moved into position, yet he was having a difficult time gripping the locomotive's curved surface even with his tennis shoes. He slipped twice before discovering a position where he was comfortable enough to let go of the smokestack behind him.

Janie giggled. "You need yoga. It would improve your balance."

As he reached toward the wall, he said, "I suppose you go to classes?"

"Actually, I'm a teacher at our church. I know eighty-year-olds who have better balance than you do."

"When we get out of this mess, you can sign me up."

His chest pressed into Janie's back as he found the wall. Having his hands now locked into place brought him a greater sense of security.

"Okay," Janie said, "do you see my right hand?"

"Yes."

"Put your hand on top of mine. That's good. Now you leave yours in place while I move mine away from the wall. Tell me what you feel."

At first Lije felt nothing, just the smooth rock surface. Yet as he allowed his hand to relax, he noted a crack in the rock beneath his palm. Following that fissure with his index finger, he discovered it was about three inches long and maybe a quarter-inch wide.

"Did you find it?"

"The crack?"

"Yes. Can you sense the difference in the way the air feels coming through the opening?"

He desperately tried to sense something he simply could not discern with his hands. "No, Janie, I can't feel anything other than the crack. I don't feel any air at all."

"That's not surprising," she assured him. "You don't have to depend upon your sense of touch like I do. Replace your hand with your cheek. Lay your face against the wall where the crack is."

He leaned forward, his face now touching hers. Turning his head to the side, he pressed it against the wall. Then he felt a warm breeze. Pushing back, he steadied himself. "I feel it. But what does it mean?"

"Does anyone have the time?"

McGee brought his watch up to the lantern. "It's about four."

"That was about what I figured," Janie answered. "How difficult will it be to extinguish all the lights?"

Curtis glanced back down the tracks. There were at least a half dozen lanterns down there, plus the four they had brought with them to the front of the train. "It wouldn't be that hard. Might take me a few minutes."

"Would you all mind doing it while Lije and I stay up here?"

"No problem."

What did she have in mind? What was Janie trying to show them?

Curtis extinguished the lanterns behind them, placing the front of the cave in darkness. When she returned, the trio blew out the four lamps that were still burning. "They're all out."

"Welcome to my world," Janie announced. "Okay, it might take your eyes a while to adjust to the darkness, so just relax and get used to the new environment. Believe me, even when you think there is no light at all, you're seeing a great deal more than I do."

The dark, which a few hours before had seemed so frightening, now brought a soothing, almost healing spirit. Even from his precarious perch, Lije felt somewhat safe in the blanket of blackness. As the moments crept by, all of his senses became accustomed to the new world around him. He suddenly noted fresh dynamics and elements in this strange subterranean prison. The spring, which earlier he couldn't hear, now happily bubbled in the background. Frogs that probably lived in that water and were as blind as Janie were chirping. How had he missed them before? He could also now hear the breathing of each member of his group. For the first time he noticed that Cathcart's breaths created a slight rasp and McGee's breathing seemed to project a faint whistling.

The smells that filled his head were different too. The oil from the lanterns, the dampness from the water, and even the faint essence of the aftershave he had put on that morning were things he had failed to notice before. Clinging to these new sensations caused him to wonder just how keenly developed Janie's senses were. How many things did she note each moment of her life that he missed? He was so overwhelmed by that thought he almost failed to hear Janie's whisper.

"Do you remember where you felt the crack?"

Shaken back to reality, he said, "Yes, I put my hand back on it."

"Move it and tell me what you see."

Lije eased his palm from the wall. What greeted him was a thin ray of light. As he focused on the barely discernible bright spot in the darkness, she asked, "Do you see it?"

"It's daylight from the outside world."

"Look to your left and right. You'll see more."

Slowly moving his eyes from side to side, he saw what a few minutes ago had not been there. He marveled at the transformation. "There are scores of little cracks of light. Do you see them down there?"

"Yes," Curtis replied, "I do."

"So do I," the other two chimed in.

"Okay, you all can relight the lanterns," Janie said. "And Lije, you and I can get back on the ground. I think you'll feel far more secure down there."

By the time he and Janie had joined their comrades, the lamps were again illuminating the walls and a new sense of hope rained down on the group. Each now believed there just might be a way out. Their home world was not that far away.

As McGee and Cathcart climbed onto the cowcatcher, tapping on the wall in an effort to estimate its thickness, Lije looked into Janie's face. In the soft yellow light, her features were almost angelic. A few hours ago, he felt that he'd been placed on the river at just the right moment to save her. Now it seemed more likely that she was the guardian angel sent to save them.

"Pretty amazing," he whispered.

"What is?" she asked.

"It took a blind person to see the light at the end of the tunnel."

A look of bemusement crossed her face. "Nothing amazing about it at all. It happens all the time. Of course, seeing freedom and actually finding a path to it are two different things entirely."

70

JANIE WAS SORTING THROUGH STUFF IN THE OLD train's caboose, looking for anything that might help them break through the cave's thin back wall, when McGee joined her.

"Nobody knows we're in this cave ... except the men shooting at us," McGee said.

"Are you giving up?" Janie asked.

"No, but I'm at a loss right now. If you knew my friends, they would tell you I'm the guy with all the ideas. Do you know how frustrating it is not to have one? You'd think in the age of cell phones and wireless internet I could rig a way to get a message to the outside world. I'm kind of a techno geek, but here I'm about as helpless as the men who died at that table in the railroad car. I'm out of my element."

"We all are," Janie said. "Though I might have a bit more of an advantage here than any of you. Still, it's hard to order a pizza and have it delivered in a cave. And wouldn't a thin-crust Canadian bacon and sausage hit the spot right now?"

She was hoping her remarks would elicit a laugh or at least a snicker, but they didn't. Instead, McGee seemed to grow even more serious.

"Did y'all find anything useful on the other cars?" she asked.

"You'd think there would have been some kind of large tools somewhere on this train," McGee said, "but there are none. Not even a sledgehammer. I mean, what's an antique train without a six-pound hammer?"

"If the professor's theory is right," Janie said, "they used the shovels and picks to bury the rails. When they finished burying the rails, they either left them on the bank or tossed them in the water. We'll find a way to break through that wall. I'm sure of it." She wanted him to believe it too, but he wasn't ready to believe in miracles, at least not yet.

"It's going to be awfully hard to break through a thick stone wall with one pry bar and a few pipe wrenches," McGee said. "Plus, while we're pretty strong right now, a few days of hard labor without food and our output will match that of a group of preschoolers."

Janie just listened. Sometimes it's better to listen to heartache than try to soothe it. If enough hurt is allowed to ooze out, a lot of times the pain departs with it. So rather than speak, she sat by, waiting for McGee to continue.

"Do you have regrets?" McGee asked.

"I guess a few. I'd be crazy not to admit that I'd like to see, though no one could do anything about that. And now that I think about it, I probably would have been much better off if I hadn't signed up for the canoe trip. I don't really like the water that much anyway." She was disappointed when again she heard no laughter. Was she losing her touch or was her timing off?

Or maybe it was because they were all about to die.

"What do you do?" McGee asked.

Janie laughed. That question came from out of the blue. "I work in a law office."

"Really?"

Why did that surprise him? Surely by now he had figured out she had brains and skills. After all, she had saved his life when she'd led them behind the wall and away from the explosion.

"Yes, and I'm pretty good at answering the phone, taking notes, and even typing letters. And don't ask about typos. I have a printer that prints out a Braille version and a regular version. I can proof my own copy. I'm also on the team that evaluates potential jurors. It seems I sense things others don't notice."

"I didn't mean that the way it sounded," McGee said. "I'm aware of how much we owe you."

The silence that followed his apology indicated he couldn't come up with anything else to say. That had to be a first. The Kent McGee she'd heard of—and everyone in law had heard of him—was legendary for never being at a loss for words. No one ever caught him off guard. He rarely lost a case and had even appeared before the U.S. Supreme Court several times. He was one of the stars of the state and was known for his dynamic and eloquent summations. Yet the confidence, the energy, and even the spirit she'd actually heard as a spectator on two occasions in the courtroom were not in evidence now. He was like a lost and scared little puppy.

"Janie, I've spent my life living to be in the spotlight. I thrive there. I share it with no one. Guess what? Now I find myself about as far removed from a light as I can be. And in the blackness of this cave, I don't like what I can see. Now that sounds kind of funny."

And she thought *she* was blind. Yeah, she understood seeing herself in the dark better than anyone. It's hard to hide flaws when all the lights are out. It's almost impossible to hide your insecurities when you have no control over your world. Your confidence sinks to nothing.

For a couple of years after she'd gone completely blind, she had wanted to die. She hated herself and her world. She had no hope. The future had seemed like a prison. Then she learned to dig deeper. She discovered talents she didn't know she had and found new abilities.

But that wasn't what saved her. Learning to like herself saved her. She discovered she was pretty cool. The world needed to know that. So in different ways, she made that known every chance she got. She also learned she had to quit feeling sorry for herself.

That was something McGee hadn't figured out yet. But when she finally had figured it out, she really started living and loving every minute of her life.

"I'm all alone," he confessed.

As if she needed to hear a confessional. Being blind didn't make her a priest. Still, she didn't stop him from unburdening his soul. As if lawyers really had souls. That was a crack she kept to herself.

"I've had a string of relationships, but no wife. My parents are dead. I have no siblings, and I've never had a child. Probably will never have children. I've got more money than I need. I've been on the cover of *Time*. Heck, I was once even a judge at the Miss USA contest. But what does all that add up to right now? Nothing. Absolutely nothing."

"Hey, there are a lot of folks who owe their freedom to you."

"True," he admitted, "and a lot of them were guilty. But right now, that doesn't seem like much to hang my hat on. Can't you see me before God, explaining, 'I know the guy killed his wife, but I found a loophole'? That'll go over real well."

"Well, we've all done a few things we aren't proud of."

"A few things doesn't begin to cover mine. The only man who would mourn my passing will die with me."

"At least you have someone who cares about you now."

There had been a time when she had no one too. She lost her sight before her teens. Her father died when she was twelve, her mother when she was fifteen. She'd spent three years in foster care, then an orphanage, and finally shot out of the system at eighteen. She'd had to find her own way in the world. If she'd died during that time, no one would have mourned for her either. But she changed that. She had tons of friends now.

Someone bounded up the steps of the caboose. "Hey, we've been looking for you two," Lije said from the doorway.

She could feel his energy, his excitement.

"Dr. Cathcart's got an idea."

"WHAT WE HAVE HERE IS A BALDWIN-BUILT 4-4-0 locomotive. It was the common model used in the late 1800s in the United States. Note that it has four drive wheels, two on each side—they are the big ones behind me—along with two more guide wheels on each side at the front of the locomotive. The design used on this model has the flared stack, which I have always felt made them the most beautiful engines on the rails. Note our locomotive was painted green, red, yellow, and black. This proves the unit was seen as more than just a piece of equipment. It was deeply treasured by the men who worked on it and by the crew who ran it.

"For its time, this was a very powerful locomotive. It had to be in order to climb through the Ozark hills while pulling heavy loads. And the great news is that my initial examination leads me to believe it was fully serviced not long before it took its final run.

"Now, here's the interesting part. I had an opportunity just three summers ago to work as part of a team that restored a twin to this machine. That locomotive had been out of commission for years, sitting outside in a damp climate, but our team got it working. It's currently hauling passengers through the woods of New Hampshire."

Janie found his story fascinating. It brought back memories of a time when her father took her to a train museum. But she sensed the woman standing to her right was not as moved as she was.

Confirming Janie's intuition, Curtis said, "I'm sure this is fascinating to you, but we need to get out of here."

Undaunted, Cathcart continued his lecture. "I know what you want and what we need. What I'm trying to tell you is that the dry climate in this cave has left this locomotive in excellent condition."

"And?"

"Do you remember a story of a large 1930s vintage plane that ferried some men up to Greenland during World War II?"

"No."

Janie knew the story well, but decided not to mess up the professor's rhythm. Besides, she liked to hear him speak. His voice had all the warmth of a hearth in the wintertime.

"Let me refresh your memory. The plane was abandoned when the men closed the small support base. I think it was a B-29. It sat there on the cold ground in Greenland for decades, exposed to the region's cruel elements. It was finally spotted by someone flying over the area. A crew flew up there a few weeks later, drained and replaced the oil and fuel, greased the motor, put on new tires, and in a matter of days had the plane running. After they built a temporary runway, they flew it back to the States."

Janie spoke up. "You're saying this thing can run?"

"I think so. We have what we need. The materials for lubrication are here. We have a tender filled with very dry wood, and the spring offers us a source of water."

Curtis still didn't get it. "I don't see us taking any long trips. We're in a cave, with rock walls."

"The wall right in front of the engine is not very thick, but even with proper tools, which we don't have, it would take us a long time to make any kind of hole in it. Without tools, we're not able to do anything except dream of how close we are to freedom.

I know you're aware of that. That's obvious by the look you're sporting right now."

Janie could feel Curtis's glare, so she figured the look must really be scorching to those in the lantern light.

Undaunted, Cathcart continued. "If I can get this locomotive running again, I'll back it up as far as possible, then unhook the engine, stoke up to maximum pressure, and put it in forward. We'll build up as much speed as possible over the two to three hundred yards of empty track it'll travel to this wall, and I think the tons of force exerted by the collision will move a lot of rock. My guess is the opening will be large enough for us to escape."

"You can make it run?" Curtis asked.

"With some help. Just carrying water from the spring to fill up the boiler is going to take a long time. And getting this thing lubed will take a lot of effort. But this old gal's in surprisingly good shape. I don't think anything is stuck, and the general maintenance tools are in the cab, so I can examine most of the potential problem areas before we try to bring her back to life."

"How long will it take?"

"Are you the mechanical sort?"

"My dad was a mechanic," Curtis said. "I worked in his shop when I was in high school. And since this thing contains a lot of pipe, I can throw in the fact that I used to go on service calls with my grandfather, who was a plumber."

"Even better than I could have hoped for," Cathcart replied. "Now, I guess that makes the rest of you the bucket team."

"I'm good with water," Lije announced.

Janie added, "I'm not big, but I'm strong for my size. And a few hours ago I became very familiar with water."

"I'm in," McGee mumbled. "Better than sitting on my rear waiting for the Grim Reaper to club me over the head."

"We've gone pretty much this whole day without eating," Curtis said. "We have some food, peanut butter and crackers. And if anyone gets tired, it's all right to come back to the train and take a nap. There are a couple of bunks in the caboose. I put the backpack with the food in there."

All through the meal, Cathcart provided a lesson in 1880s technology. Except for a few questions from Curtis, no one spoke. After they finished eating, Curtis and Cathcart went to start the mechanical work. The others tried to figure out how to get water to the train.

Lije suggested pouring the whiskey out of the two barrels they'd found and use the barrels to carry water.

"Even if we did," McGee said, "I'm not sure how much good it would do. We couldn't lift a full barrel. But the booze is also a food source, so we have to find something to empty it into. Since we can only carry one barrel at a time, let's leave the second one intact."

Janie grinned. "I take it you drink."

"Actually, Miss Davies, it wouldn't be for me. If we somehow manage to get out, I could use that aged brew to extract some large favors from a few judges I know. So, if possible, I'd like to save it for a bargaining chip."

"That brings a whole new meaning to the bar association," she replied. So he was planning on getting out of here. She wouldn't have guessed that an hour ago.

McGee could read a jury like a book. Janie was even better at reading folks in one-on-one situations. She'd been around these four long enough to see who they really were. Lije and Cathcart were optimists; they had faith Ole 74 would be able to push through the wall. That's just the way the professor was. It was natural for him. And the fact that Lije, who just recently lost his best friend (it was all over the news; it didn't take long for her to put two and two together), still had such hope was something she found remarkable. It spoke volumes on what his wife's life must have stood for.

Curtis acted tough, but she was as scared as anyone. Maybe more so. She was like McGee; she seemed to have spent her life avoiding people and was now scared no one would miss her when she was gone. She now worried that her career had caused her to miss the stuff that made life meaningful. She also seemed loaded up with guilt, so even though she didn't want to be, she was a skeptic. Still, she pretended to believe. Why the charade? Why was she trying to fool herself and the rest of them?

Because she yearned for a second chance. Right now, they all did.

"I have an idea that might save time," Janie said. "There are two buckets in the caboose that we can use for dipping in the spring. The opening in the chamber to the spring is too small for the whiskey barrels, but the buckets should be the right size. The wagon's in pretty good shape, so I think we can roll it over to the cave's side wall, bring the water out a bucket at a time, and dump it into the two whiskey barrels. Then we can push the wagon across to the locomotive."

Lije and McGee were speechless.

After delivering a few loads of water to the train, they took a break. Janie found herself sitting next to McGee while Lije went to check up on Curtis and the professor.

"So you haven't given up yet," she said. She could feel McGee looking at her, surprised by her question.

"I wouldn't call it giving up. I'm not a quitter. I just evaluate every element. I know the problems we're facing and I know the odds of getting a train that has not run for twelve decades to function. Those odds are simply too long to figure. So naturally I'm not optimistic."

"I understand what you're saying, but your concept is deeply flawed."

"How?"

"You only have faith in what you can see. I learned a long time ago it's the things I can't see that have the most effect on my life."

They sat in silence.

IT HAD BEEN FORTY-SIX HOURS SINCE DR. CATHCART
had convinced Curtis to participate in the effort to resurrect a locomotive that hadn't run for one hundred and twenty years. With
hardly any rest and very little nourishment, Cathcart and Curtis
had crawled over, under, and around almost every part of the ancient Baldwin-built engine. They had freed stuck pistons, lubri-
cated ancient fittings, and checked even the smallest couplings.
It was a difficult job requiring as much plumbing as mechanical
expertise. The task was made even more challenging by having
to illuminate their work area with inconsistent lantern light and
candles.

Lije, Janie, and McGee had finished hauling the water. Bucket
by bucket, they had splashed water into the boiler. After complet-
ing that task, the sore and exhausted trio were left to their own devices. McGee and Janie spent the first of those hours sleeping. Lije
tried to rest, but after a couple of futile attempts, he pulled himself
from the bed he had fashioned with clothes and blankets found
in the boxcar. Then, as if drawn by a magnetic force, he found
himself in Andrew Farnsworth's private car. Sitting at the rolltop
desk, with five lifeless bodies to witness his moves, he opened each
drawer, examining everything he touched with the same rever-
ence as a monk would employ while handling a scroll found at the
Dead Sea.

For most of the night, he read letters, notes, expense records, and inventories. It took several minutes just to scan the itemized treasure list. How much was missing? Which items had been in the empty crates? What had happened to them? Had there been another man who somehow escaped death?

This backward leap in time, with all the questions that came with it, offered a chance to immerse himself in not just another age but another identity. As he read Farnsworth's writings, he essentially became the man. The more he pieced together from the mysterious man's life, the more he saw through his eyes.

In a darkened world where time stood still, in a place where there were no sunrises or sunsets, the movement of the clock meant nothing. A minute and an hour were twins; so when the groan of the car's steps signaled a visitor had come calling, he had no clue as to the hour or how long he had been lost in time. Lije glanced over his shoulder and saw Janie slowly working her way through the car.

"Janie, you have a new dress."

She smiled. "I got tired of the old clothes, used the spring water to clean up, and went through some of the stuff in the boxcar until I found a number about my size. I passed on the wool socks though. By the way, what color is my new frock?"

"Ah ... I'm not really very good at this. It's kind of dark red and a medium blue, a checked pattern would be the best way I could describe it. The belt is blue."

"So, you're saying it's colorful."

"I can honestly say there's no doubt you're making a fashion statement."

Her hands pressed down the front of the vintage cloth as she tilted her head to the left and looked toward the point where she had heard Lije's voice. "The crate this dress was in was so well sealed, the material feels almost like it's new. I may have to take you back down there in a little while to find a matching bonnet."

A bonnet! Who knew a blind person could or would care so

much about appearances? It surprised him. But why shouldn't she care? In the lantern light she almost glowed. Maybe it was the blonde hair or those blue eyes. There was simply something different about her. Was it coming from the inside or the outside, from the heart or from the skin? He couldn't tell.

"They have men's clothes too," she added. "Some flannel things, some wool suits. I even came across a couple of vests and a lot of boots. And the fact I'm mentioning this is more than a suggestion. I think the two words that best fit what I'm smelling are stale socks."

He marveled at her honest charm. She was nothing if not direct and sincere. Kaitlyn would have liked her, not just a little but a lot.

Feeling beside her until her hands latched onto the arm of a chair, Janie took a step to her left and eased down on the leather cushion before turning her face back toward him. "I always wanted to go to Graceland."

"What?"

"I said, I always wanted to go to Graceland."

"I know what you said, Janie, but I don't understand."

"Just always wanted to see where Elvis lived. That's all."

She said the word *see*. How could she see Graceland?

"Oh, I get it. You're wondering why a blind person would want to go sightseeing."

She was right, but he wasn't going to admit it. "Ah, no. I was just wondering why you, ah … wanted to …"

"See it. It's just two words. You can say them. I'm not going to break if you say 'see.'"

He took a deep breath. "Okay, why do you want to see Graceland?"

She seemed suddenly pleased. "Like anyone else who goes there, I like his music. That makes me want to know more about him as a man."

Made sense.

"I do see," she said. "Just a bit differently than you do."

"There are many things you see and do better than me."

She grinned. "You said 'see' pretty easy that time. I'm sure you'll figure out that I'm pretty tough."

"I learned that when you clubbed me in the water." It had been just days ago, but it seemed like a lifetime. No, it seemed like a different lifetime. A much different lifetime. "What made you think about Graceland?"

She grinned. "A part of it was considering my 'things I have to do before I die' list. The other was remembering Elvis's hits. One of the first was 'Mystery Train.'"

73

"SO WAS OUR MYSTERY MAN WORTH THE STUDY?" Janie asked. "I figured you must be going through that old rolltop desk."

Lije nodded, then, realizing she couldn't see that motion, leaned back in the squeaky wooden desk chair and tried to explain what he had learned. "Yes. He was from another time. He was a well-educated man, even spent time at Oxford. He was married once, but his wife died in her twenties of a sudden illness. I found some notes in his Bible indicating he spent the next decade looking for comfort in a bottle. His life changed one night when he was rolled by a group of orphaned street youths in London. Rather than get angry, it seems he felt sorry for the kids. That experience led to his giving up drinking and beginning to teach in one of the city's early Sunday school programs. This led to his undertaking some pretty extensive Bible study. A few scribbled entries, coupled with three letters I read, told me that his life really changed when he began to understand the message found in Matthew 25:35–40."

"Ah." Janie smiled. "Whatever you do unto the least of these, you do it unto me."

He was not surprised Janie knew that Scripture passage. He was convinced that nothing the woman did or knew could surprise him.

"Yes. That changed his focus. But there was something else that drove his life. It's all in his journal. Farnsworth had learned about the legend surrounding the undiscovered wealth of the Knights Templar. He devoted at least a year to studying this group, which propelled him on a quest to find the treasure. A decade later, after traipsing all over Europe and northern Africa, he finally translated a code and discovered where the treasure was hidden.

"Then this is that treasure," Janie said.

"It is. There's one entry where he reveals how shocked he was to learn that after traveling thousands upon thousands of miles all over the globe, he discovered that his goal was just a few miles from his boyhood home. His goal all along was to give away anything he found."

"That's what he was doing with this train."

"He was. I believe he had given away some of the treasure during the journey that led him to this spot. There are notes in his text that hint at, but do not entirely explain, his complete plans. He has written a little about the Chinese, as if he knew of slums and people with great needs in San Francisco's Chinatown. He also has several short entries on locations of Indian reservations. He also lists towns where former slaves lived. There are names of orphanages, a school for the blind.

"Anyway, this trek doesn't appear to be a random journey. I think he was going to specific spots where he could help people, turn his dreams into reality. And my sense is that he wanted to make sure that no one knew he was behind the gifts."

Janie smiled as she gently rocked in her seat. "What makes you think he gave the stuff away and it wasn't stolen?"

"I came across an item in his inventory that I once saw in a museum in Memphis. Another description sounds like something I once saw in Chicago."

"He sounds like a pretty wonderful guy. I'd like him. In one way or another he might have even touched me, or maybe you, with something he did."

"No doubt, which makes it all seem like a much greater loss

because he was not able to fulfill his mission. He might well have rewritten the history of many places in the Old West if he could have given away the rest of the stuff to finance his special causes."

Rising from her seat, Janie moved slowly toward the car's forward exit. She opened the door and was halfway onto the platform when she stopped and turned back toward Lije.

"You know, he might well have fulfilled his part of the mission. Maybe he was meant to get only this far. If this really is now your treasure and the train that brought him to this place becomes your vehicle to freedom, then perhaps you're the one meant to finish the job. Maybe Lije Evans, using the means found in a modern world, will meet the needs of those Farnsworth saw in his vision."

"Do you believe that?"

"It doesn't matter if I do; it only matters if you believe it."

She stepped out of the car, closing the door behind her. Lije closed the old Bible and peered through a window into the void. Did he believe?

He laid his head down on the desk. He felt peace, the first peace he had known since that night on Farraday Road. In seconds, he drifted off. It would be hours before he awakened.

AFTER HIS LONG NAP, LIJE JOINED MCGEE IN THE caboose and the two friends talked of everything from college sports to canoeing down Spring River. They laughed. They were serious. But the one topic they ignored was the locomotive. And though the subject was never on their tongues, it was always central in their minds.

It was midafternoon and everyone was tired. Tired not just from their efforts but tired of the darkness, tired of the prison that held their bodies and their spirits, and tired of wondering if they could beat the odds. And long odds they were, the longest any of them had ever known.

Lije was worried about more than just the fate of Ole 74. It seemed that the time in the cavern had worn on McGee much more than on any of the others. He looked ten years older than he had just a week ago. He was also starting to have problems following conversations. In the past hour, he had asked the same question three times. Finally, aware of his mental stumbles, he quit talking and just stared out into the blackness. Without a word to Lije, he got up and stretched his arms and rubbed his neck. He walked out onto the back platform.

For a while Lije allowed him his solitude. Then, needing to stretch his legs, he got up and joined him. "Sorry I got you into this."

"No reason to apologize," McGee replied. "I welcomed the chance to get out of the office and away from the Jameson case for a few hours. It's just a *few* more hours than I had figured it would be."

"We could consider these billable hours," Lije said. He looked at McGee, who seemed as if he hadn't heard a word.

"It's strange," McGee said, "I'm starting to get used to the dark. It used to scare me, make me uneasy, but now I almost find it comforting. There's a peace in this dark world that I never found in the other one. I'm beginning to think this wouldn't be a bad place to die."

They stood there in silence.

"By the way, Lije, I found out what Janie does for a living. Did I tell you?"

"What's that?"

"She works at a law office in Little Rock. She answers the phone, takes dictation, uses the word processor for correspondence, that sort of thing. Works with firms in picking juries. She may be a lot smarter than both of us put together."

"Doesn't surprise me."

"If we get out of here ..." He didn't finish the thought. Perhaps he couldn't.

From out of the darkness, Janie chimed in, "When I update my resume, I'll list both of you as references."

The men both looked in the direction of her voice. In the shadows they could barely see Janie's small form. Lije grabbed a lantern from the caboose and held it toward her. "You changed clothes again?"

"Yep, new dress. I got grease on the other one. I've spent the last couple of hours under that huge metal puzzle. It seems that I'm better at working in situations where you can't see to start a nut than Diana or the professor. Can you imagine that? By the way, what color is this one?"

"Green, with yellow flowers," McGee said.

"Not my best color, at least that's what I've been told. Personally, I think I look about the same in everything."

Wanting to laugh, but unsure if he should, Lije smiled, and McGee shuffled his feet uneasily.

Janie shook her head. "No one in this group has a good sense of humor. Oh well, probably not time for joking anyway. I was sent back to tell you the engine's ready. The professor would like y'all to come forward."

Walking much more confidently than the men holding their lanterns and squinting to find the path, Janie led the way back to the locomotive. Lije was surprised when she took a quick step to her right to miss tripping over a trunk that had been pulled out of the baggage car. He was shocked when she suddenly stopped.

Holding up her right hand, she whispered, "Don't move."

Lije had enough faith in her powers to freeze. McGee either didn't hear her warning or didn't think she was serious. After all, she had proven herself a jokester. He waved her off and quickly moved beyond where she stood.

"No!" she screamed. Jumping to her right, she slammed into the big man, knocking him down onto the cave floor.

"What are you doing?" he yelled.

She didn't answer. Disoriented by the fall, she moved to her right on her knees. It was the wrong choice.

Lije's lantern light caught a movement on the cave floor. A snake, a big one. A cottonmouth. It stopped, raised its head, and struck. Its fangs found their mark, jabbing into Janie's new dress.

Lije stepped forward and kicked the snake. It flew into the air, whirling like a propeller, and hit the side of the boxcar. McGee, enraged, raced toward the slithering menace. Crazed by anger, he jammed his foot down on its head. He continued stomping and cursing until he had all but pounded the creature into the stone.

Lije moved over to Janie. "Where did it get you?"

"I don't know. I heard it strike, but I didn't feel anything."

"Stay here, I need to get my lantern." He was back almost

before the words had left his mouth. Inspecting her dress, he found where the snake had torn into it. About six inches above the bottom hem. Lifting the material, he ran his hand along her ankles, then her calves. Where is the bite? Every second counted. He had to find the bite mark, had to get the poison out before it went too deep into her system.

"What's the verdict?" she asked.

"I can't find where it bit you."

"I wasn't taking about that; I was asking about my legs. Do they meet your approval?"

"Not funny, Janie. We need to treat the bite." He was close to panic. "Help me out. Where is it?"

"I told you. I didn't feel it, so it must have just gotten my dress."

"Not you?"

"No. If it had, I'd be screaming my head off. Now can I get up?"

Grabbing her hand, he helped her to her feet. Thank God she was all right.

"I'm sorry," McGee said. "I should've listened. How bad is it?"

"Well," Lije said, "after a few stitches, the dress will be fine. The critter missed Janie altogether."

McGee picked Janie up and twirled her like a rag doll, almost squeezing the life out of her.

"Great," she whispered, "escaped a cottonmouth only to be snagged by a python."

"Oh, sorry." He dropped her to the ground, but didn't drop his grin. "Don't worry about the snake. He's visiting his ancestors. Now tell me, how did you know it was here?"

"The smell."

"Snakes smell?" Lije asked.

"Of course, and it's hardly pleasant."

"WHAT'S GOING ON BACK THERE?" CURTIS YELLED. "Everything okay?"

"Yeah," Lije hollered back, "we're fine." He smiled at Janie and then at McGee. "Shall we join our friends?"

"Let me and my nose lead the way," Janie announced, not waiting for any protest. And there was none.

The trio made their way to the engine, where Cathcart was standing, wiping his hands on a rag. "Kent, Lije, Ole 74's as ready as she's going to be. I'm sure you can smell and see the smoke. Curtis has already started the fire in the box. In an hour or so, when the water boils and the pressure starts shooting up, we can see if she'll work.

"We're going to get a lot of smoke and steam in here, so your breathing's going to suffer. You might want to move to the smaller spring chamber or to the part of the cave where we first came in."

The old iron horse continued to moan, groan, pant, and pop, each sound louder than the last. All eyes were glued to the old machine, almost as if by staring at the locomotive they could will it back to life.

"Anything you need us to do?" McGee asked.

"Not right now," Cathcart replied. As Curtis added more wood, the professor checked the gauges. "The pressure's good and the wood's burning hotter than I figured. Faster too. Of course, it's had a long time to dry out. I think we'll be ready in another twenty minutes. Diana, why don't you let me stoke the fire for a while?"

Lije climbed up in the cab. "Let me feed the fire, Dr. Cathcart. You take a few minutes to rest."

After tossing a few pieces of wood into the flames, Lije asked what he knew no one else dared to bring up. "Is it going to work?"

Cathcart spoke in a hushed tone, serious, nothing like the jolly banter he had shown a few minutes before. "I think the train'll move, but do I believe it will knock out that wall? I have my doubts." Leaning down, his words barely audible, he said, "I removed the safety valve. I'm going to build up more pressure than is recommended. I'm hoping that'll give me more speed, but it might also lead to the boiler's exploding on impact. Therefore I want to make sure everyone is well away from this engine when it hits the wall."

"What'll happen to you if this sucker blows?"

"I'll die with my hand on the throttle, scalded to death by the steam."

"No," Lije said, "you can't."

Cathcart smiled. "Don't worry. Can you think of a better way for a railroad nut like me to go out?"

There had to be a better way—like old age. Lije just couldn't lose another person close to him. And all of these folks were now close to him.

"Lije, there is one thing that really worries me," Cathcart said. "What if this old gal does explode? That could cause the whole cave structure to give way. Then we all die, crushed by tons of rock."

Lije looked around at the cave and shrugged. "Well, that's probably much better than starving to death in the dark."

"What are you guys talking about?" Curtis asked as she climbed back into the cab.

"How nice it will be to order pizza again." Lije jumped back down to the ground, patted Ole 74, and walked over to where Janie was standing. McGee quit pacing and joined them. In silence they waited, their eyes and ears tuned in to the sounds of a mechanical monster fighting to be brought back to life.

"Stand clear!" Cathcart shouted from the cab.

The locomotive belched a huge blast of smoke. Steam burst from around the wheels. The engine's driver arms jerked into action and the big wheels moved a half rotation backward, then another half rotation. But the train did not move. The wheels only spun on the tracks. The professor adjusted the controls and leaned his head out the window of the cab. Through the haze of smoke and steam, he watched the iron wheels struggle.

"He's not going to be able to move it," McGee shouted over the noise.

Not taking his eyes from the engine, Lije yelled back, "It'll move. Just let the professor get up some power. The wheels'll get some traction." His voice indicated hope, but his tone reflected a sense of apprehension. His words were more an effort to convince himself than McGee.

Come on, you mechanical marvel. You've got one more run in you.

At first the iron horse fought the track to a stalemate. Then, a few inches at a time, Ole 74 began to jerk backward. The trio on the ground cheered as the engine picked up steam, backing slowly away from the wall.

Curtis grabbed a lantern and jumped from the cab's ladder. She jogged beside the train as if she were racing it. When she reached the end of the tracks, she waved the light from side to side as a marker for the now smiling engineer.

Slowing the engine, Cathcart continued to ease the cars backward over two hundred more yards of track toward the far wall. Finally, when Curtis held the lantern motionless, he hit the brakes, stopping the train just as the caboose nudged against the rock and dirt wall.

"Let's do it!" McGee yelled, running up to the cab. Holding Janie's hand, Lije followed a few steps behind. He also wanted to cheer, but decided to save it for the moment the train crashed through the rock.

Grabbing his tools and an oilcan, Cathcart backed down the ladder to the ground. He uncoupled the locomotive from the other cars. Curtis made her way back to Ole 74 and started adding more logs to the fire.

"Fill it up!" Cathcart cried from the ground. "Give her everything she'll hold!"

As his fireman followed instructions, the engineer walked over to Lije, Janie, and McGee. "I want you to light all the lamps and place them along the sides of the track. They don't have to be close to the rails, they just need to be there as markers to show me clearly where I'm going. They'll also help me gauge my speed. You can leave the three that are burning down by the far wall where they are.

"A word of warning, and you need to take this seriously. I know you want to watch, but you need to find a safe place in the cave that offers some cover. I'd suggest behind the wall and in the chamber where we first entered. If the boiler explodes upon impact, it could send sharp, hot metal flying all over the place.

"Even if nothing like that happens, give it a few minutes before you rush down. I'll yell when I think it's safe."

In the background, Curtis hollered, "She's ready! The pressure needle's in the red!"

"Be right there!" Cathcart said.

McGee grabbed Lije's arm to get his attention. "Lije, grab the lanterns from the cars and bring them down here. I'll run the three from the boxcar down toward the far end. Let's get these lined up! Let's do it!"

McGee's orders brought a smile to Lije's lips. Janie leaned over and said, "I think he's starting to believe."

"I think we all are."

As they raced to position the antique lanterns, Lije had a memory of their college days, racing each other to the girls' dorm. They were just as excited now as they were back then.

Cathcart checked and rechecked Ole 74's mechanics, and Curtis kept stoking the fire.

Only Janie was still, satisfied to take in the ancient steam machine's almost musical cadence.

Lije dashed back to the cab and climbed up. "The way's lit. Good luck, sir."

"Say a prayer," Cathcart said with a grin. He glanced over his shoulder. "Diana, here's where you get off. This run will be solo. No fireman or brakeman needed. Let this old man enjoy this ride by himself."

Curtis hugged him and planted a quick kiss on his cheek.

"Now that makes a bachelor's day!"

Lije and Curtis hurried down the ladder of the cab and joined McGee and Janie. Pointing to a spot on the other side of the train, Curtis took out her flashlight and led the way up and over the boxcar's platform to the cave's smaller front chamber room. Lije guided Janie to the safety point. McGee brought up the rear.

The quartet stood where they could witness Cathcart setting the old iron horse into motion. The locomative groaned as the wheels fought for traction. This time, nothing could hold it in place. Steam and smoke billowing, Ole 74 started forward, slowly, too slowly, and then it began to pick up speed. From a walk, to a jog, to a run, Ole 74 was alive and racing.

The noise of the wheels and the engine was now deafening, but no one covered their ears. The soot and smoke burned their eyes, but still they didn't move. They remained anchored to the rock floor, three sets of eyes and one pair of very sharp ears monitoring each and every revolution of the wheels.

Closer and closer it approached the wall, faster and faster it raced. When it was about a hundred feet from the wall, Lije glanced at Curtis, looking for a signal to move to cover. There was none. She seemed intent on peering through the smoke until iron met rock. McGee also had his eyes glued to the spectacle. Janie had cocked her head to one side, intent on following the action in her own way.

Lije, his eyes stinging and watering from the smoke, turned back to Ole 74. In the dim light, the end of its sprint was nothing more than a blur.

THE COLLISION UNLEASHED A BOMBLIKE CONCUSSION, shaking the walls and the decoupled train cars. Dust poured down from the ceiling. Chunks of rock fell, sounding like huge bowling pins bouncing against one another.

Then came the flash of light.

"Get down!" Curtis screamed, dragging McGee to the floor.

Lije pulled Janie to the ground just as an explosion, followed by a blinding yellow flame, set the cave afire. The old cave shook as if it had been hit by an earthquake. Eyes closed, his head pushing into the rock floor, Lije listened to the clang of what had to be pieces of Ole 74 hurtling throughout the chamber and ricocheting off the walls and ceiling. The heavy rain of iron continued. Huge boulders rolled away from the walls. Two of the lanterns overturned, spreading oil in tongues of fire along the floor. A section of track lifted off the cave floor and buckled.

Then it was over. After a final few volleys of metal against stone, the only sound was the faraway hiss of steam.

Lije stood up and pulled Janie from the floor. Thick smoke filled the cave. He couldn't see the point of impact, so he had no idea if Cathcart's bold plan had worked. He was sure of one thing from the destruction he'd just witnessed: the professor had given his life in a final attempt to open the door to freedom.

"Is everyone all right?" Curtis asked, rolling slowly to her feet.

McGee coughed a few times. "I'm fine. Do you know if it punched out the wall?"

"Don't know," Lije replied. "Do you think it's safe to walk down there?"

Not bothering to respond, Curtis headed for the chamber. She reached into her pocket for the flashlight and walked into the smoke-filled nightmare that stretched out before them. Several pockets of flames flickered in the distance.

"Come on, Janie," Lije said. "Be careful where you step. The floor is littered with pieces of metal and rock."

The smoke was now so thick none of them could see much. It was almost like being blind.

Almost, but not quite.

McGee found the tracks, grabbed a lantern, and handed his flashlight to Lije. "Let's go, buddy!"

They picked their way through the chamber. Smoke filled their lungs and clouded their vision. With only the flashlight and the lantern, they picked their way as much by feel as by sight. With each step, stumbling over the littered terrain, they tried to penetrate the smoke to see if Ole 74 had broken through. They each had one prayer, one goal, one hope.

Unwittingly, the four got separated in the smoke. Foot by foot, Lije and Janie moved toward the wall, using the track as their guide. They stumbled several times, but never fell. The smoke, like a thick London fog, gave up nothing.

Lije began to panic. If they didn't get out soon, the smoke would kill them. Where was the wall? Where was Ole 74? Had Cathcart's death ride failed?

78

JANIE WAS THE FIRST TO REALIZE WHAT THE PROFESSOR
had done. "There's a hole in the wall!"

Lije still could not see a thing. "Janie, how do you know?"

She coughed for a few seconds. "The smoke's not as thick and
there's a new smell in the cave. I can hear the river over the hiss
of the steam."

"Are you sure?"

"There's fresh air now mixing with the smoke. I'd guess the
hole's big enough to crawl through."

"Don't rush!" he warned, all the while fighting the urge to race
forward. "The closer we get to the wall, the larger the hunks of
debris we're going to run into. There could be a hole in the floor.
Watch your step."

"I'll do my best. Stepping's easy, it's the watching that's always
been a bit hard for me."

"Sorry."

Janie laughed. "Just trying to lighten the mood."

As they navigated through the litter in their path, Lije became
aware of what Janie already knew. The smoke was clearing. The
smoke was half as thick as it had been. A lantern was on the floor,
still lit. He picked it up and held the flame aloft. There, just a few
feet away, was the crumpled remains of Ole 74. The cab was still
recognizable, but what now sat in front of the cab was a pile of

scrap metal. When the locomotive's boiler blew, it destroyed most of the engine. To one side sat the mangled smokestack and one of the locomotive's huge drive wheels.

"Where is the professor?" Janie asked.

Lije dropped her arm and headed toward the cab. "Stay here. I'll climb up and see."

"Watch out for hot metal," she warned.

Moving to the bent ladder, Lije tapped the metal rungs with his right hand. They were warm, not hot. Lifting himself to the platform with his dominant hand, he held the lamp aloft with his left. He peered through the dissipating smoke into the cab.

"Is he up there?" Janie yelled.

"No." Lije looked ahead of the cab and saw no trace of Cathcart.

Choking now as much from emotion as from the smoke, Lije set his focus toward freedom. His quest for the truth had now taken another life. How many more would die for whatever was on Swope's Ridge? Or for the treasure?

He jumped down from the cab. He couldn't think about that now. There would be time later.

The cave floor was piled with wreckage. Lije and Janie skirted the most tangled mounds and moved cautiously forward toward the wall, slipping on jagged pieces of metal and rock, catching their balance, and again inching forward.

"Light!" Lije yelled. Sunshine pierced the smoke about a dozen feet ahead.

From the other side of the locomotive, Curtis cried, "It's the size of a garage door! It worked!"

"We'll be there in a second," Lije called out. "Save some fresh air for us."

He found the wall. The light was now much brighter and about four feet above them. He turned Janie to face the wall and, with both hands on her waist, he lifted her toward the light and freedom. She reached forward, felt the jagged edge where the wall had been pierced, and grabbed on and pulled herself up. She was finally able to scramble through the opening. He climbed up and crawled through. Outside was a green meadow overlooking the river. McGee and Curtis, exhausted, were leaning against a large section of what, just a few minutes before, had been the cave wall.

Five had gone in. Four had come out.

Lije remembered what the professor had said. The choice he had made ... for all of them. He stretched his arms above his head and took in a deep breath of fresh air — the first any of them had breathed in days. He wiped the soot from his eyes with his shirt and realized an almost forgotten sense of hunger. He said, "I could go for a steak."

"That's not on the menu." The voice was flat, cold, and unfamiliar.

Spinning to his left, Lije found himself looking into the face of a man he'd never met but knew very well. The man was holding a gun.

"YOU'RE SMITH'S FRIEND." LIJE SAID IT AS MUCH to alert Janie as to acknowledge he knew the identity of the man standing a dozen feet in front of him.

The stranger smiled. "We thought you were dead. This time I'll make sure you are."

"I remember you now," Lije said. "I can see you just as clearly as if we were back on Farraday Road. Except you weren't holding a gun then. Thought I was dead then too, didn't you? And where's your buddy?"

The big man grinned. "Oh, he's around."

"Help!" A man's cry came from a stand of trees to the left of them. Surprised and confused, the gunman jerked his head in that direction.

A shot rang out and the gunman dropped, hit in the shoulder.

Lije spun around and saw Curtis with her ABI weapon out. She'd kept it on her the whole time. Then she started running toward the trees and the cry for help.

From the ground, the wounded man fired a single round. Curtis fell. But her courageous sprint had given Lije just enough time to take two long strides forward and launch himself into the air.

Swinging back, still on the ground, the big man managed to squeeze off another round, but it was well wide of its mark. Lije landed on the man and knocked the weapon away. Arms locked around each other, legs and knees seeking a weak spot, they rolled through the grass and down the slope of the riverbank.

Like two evenly matched wrestlers fighting for a hold, for a few moments neither man could gain an advantage. Finally able to pull his right hand free, Lije rammed a short jab into the thug's flabby gut. He managed three more quick blows to the bleeding shoulder before the two rolled to a stop on the edge of the riverbank.

Lije was on top. He held his knuckles against the man's wound and shook and punched him, finally venting the fury toward Kaitlyn's killers that he had held back for so long. "What do you want with this place? What is worth so many people dying? Who are you?"

The man lay still. Lije didn't know if he'd given up or was just waiting for a chance to break free. The man winced and started to struggle, but Lije held him in place, increasing the pressure on his shoulder. Blood oozed through Lije's fist.

"It's just a job," the man said. "Whatever the boss says, I do."

"What's so important here?"

"I dunno ... some World War II secret."

So it wasn't the treasure on the train. "What's your take? What do you get out of this?"

"I get to retire." He looked defiantly at Lije.

"And your boss?"

"He gets to control the world."

Lije couldn't believe what he had just heard. And in that split second of hesitation, the man threw his head forward, bashing Lije's nose, and, still holding him, rolled off the ledge, sending both of them into the cold water of Spring River.

LIJE BOBBED UP IN A DEEP POOL ABOUT TWENTY feet above the rapids. Treading water, he spun in a circle until the head of the other man surfaced a few yards downstream. The big man gasped, taking in more water than air, and disappeared under the surface. Lije scanned the river, trying to see where the thug would next emerge. Finally the fleshy and frantic face appeared in an area just above the river's main channel, where the current was the strongest. For a few seconds the man's entire body was visible as he stretched out, searching frantically for something to grab on to. Then a whirlpool snagged him, pulled him back under, and spit him out into the rapids.

Exhausted, Lije swam to dry land. He pulled himself up on the bank and stood up. McGee was standing on the bank, his eyes fixed on the rapids where the gunman had disappeared. Janie was a few feet behind him, picking her way down the slope. Lije saw Curtis farther up the hill. She was holding her shoulder and striding through the grass toward the river. And twenty feet behind her, limping toward the bank at an even brisker pace than Curtis, was the biggest surprise of all—Dr. Cathcart, clothes torn, face bruised and bloody, but alive.

All were safe. All had made it out alive. He couldn't believe it. No one else had died for Swope's Ridge. Not today.

Lije turned back toward the river. He scanned the white water, looking for a body, but saw nothing. He figured the locomotive had broken through the cave wall upstream from where he had discovered the rail. Probably three hundred yards or more. He could see the old post oak tree on the other side of the river. He made a second pass. Still nothing. The man had disappeared. With a sinking feeling, Lije jogged toward McGee, who had moved farther downstream, still searching. "Where did he go?"

"I don't know!" his friend hollered over the roaring water. "I lost him when he went through those first rapids."

Lije stood on the bank, not willing to give up. He knew that if the man didn't panic and simply rode it out, he might have made it through the rapids. Still, as big as he was and no better swimmer than he appeared to be ... Lije should have spotted him. But he saw no sign of the man. Not a hand holding onto a branch, an arm wrapped around a tree limb. Nothing.

Lije had had him. And still the man had slipped through his fingers. And nothing was solved. "Come on, McGee, he's gone."

The two walked back to the group, where Cathcart was the center of attention.

"Professor, I'm sure glad to see you," Lije said. "I thought you had been killed in the blast. What happened?"

"I was so sure that Ole 74 was going to go through that rock that I locked the throttle down and jumped about fifty feet from the wall. I have some pieces of metal in my back and legs and more bruises than I can count, but nothing seems broken. And what a ride it was! That old engine went out in style!"

Lije grinned. "It sure did."

"When the locomotive blew, I thought I might be too close. But I waited, hunkered down, and after things calmed down a bit, I crawled outside before you all had a chance to make it out of the cave. When I emerged I saw the two men coming down from the ridge. I slipped into the woods before they saw me and worked my way over to the one that was hiding in the trees. I clubbed him on the back of the head with a rock."

"Where is he now?"

"He's gone. I took his weapon and ran down to tend to Diana. When I went back, he was gone."

Lije sat down on the bank and looked out at the river. Dog tired — where did that phrase come from? But that's what he was. Dog tired. Bruised. Beaten. He had been through all of this and not nabbed the man he knew was responsible for Kaitlyn's death. That failure trumped everything else that had happened. He had let her down again.

Lije stood, observed the group that had been through so much together, and then, as a final reminder of the last few days, looked out at the rapids that had carried away a killer and brought them Janie. His eyes fixed on a single spot. He walked toward the water to get a better view.

"What is it, Lije?" McGee said.

"I don't know." Lije pointed at the rapids. "That branch there. On the other side. There. Right there. See? Look at it when the water settles a bit. It'll happen."

"What's going on?" Cathcart asked. "I don't see anything."

Lije glanced back toward the professor, then looked back at the rapids. "There. See it? The guy's arm. It got hung up on that tree branch when he went down the river's main water chute. The pool held him under and that branch kept him from escaping. We never saw him because he never broke free."

Curtis put a hand on Lije's shoulder. "That's a pretty strong measure of justice," she said. "Swift justice. Don't you think?"

"Maybe in your mind, but it doesn't bring the innocent ones back from the dead. Not at this moment, not tomorrow, not ever."

Lije bent down to pick up a stone and looked up toward the German's old house.

There stood a man watching them. He looked right at Lije. Then the man turned and walked away from the edge and disappeared.

He'd been there all along.

IT HAD BEEN THREE MONTHS SINCE KAITLYN'S DEATH.
The case had gone cold, and so had Smith's trail. The media circus had moved and left Salem the sleepy little town it had always been. Curtis was back at Hillman's side. Lije hadn't talked to her in weeks. McGee had used what he had learned to get Heather released and cleared. But Lije hadn't seen her since that day he visited her in jail. She had left Salem. In all the time she had been gone, she hadn't called. Lije's log home on the Shell Hill, once the happiest place in the Ozarks when Kaitlyn was alive, felt cold and gloomy.

Lije had returned to Swope's Ridge. It was as if the spirit of Micah Dean had invaded his own. He couldn't ever leave the place for long. The lure was simply too great. The answer to the mystery was there somewhere and he had to find it or die trying. Beyond that one goal, what else was there in life?

On this Saturday in late September, he was working his way through the mountains of stuff the German had stored in his fortresslike home. It was a monumental task that ate up time like a hungry hog consuming fresh corn. He had been spending every spare moment for weeks searching, yet during all that time had found nothing. Complicating the search was not knowing what he was looking for. Too often he rated the search as an exercise in futility. Still he kept at it, always led by the belief that one more day or one more hour would pay off.

Janie Davies had joined him on the latest trip out. She had cleared a spot at the kitchen table and was munching on one of the famous hot-link sausage sandwiches from Sonny Burnes' Barbeque Stand. Lije looked up, noting her obvious joy as she savored each bite of the spiced meat. Realizing he had quit thumbing through the yellowed pages of another book, she asked, "Still nothing in the books?"

"No," he admitted, "only a few scraps of paper and some dog-eared pages."

If Smith and his partner couldn't find it, and if Curtis and the ABI turned up nothing in their exhaustive searches, then odds were pretty much against an amateur stumbling onto whatever it was. But still, just being here, checking things one more time, then boxing them up, was therapeutic. Plus, if he was ever going to get any good out of this place, the cleanup needed to be done.

"I know you've been back and forth on this," Janie said, "but now you're telling me you're going to keep the house?"

Lije shook his head. "I wish you could see the look on my face right now."

"I'll take that as a no."

"Remind me again why I hired you away from that firm in Little Rock."

She grinned. "Probably because I'm cute. At least that's what I've been told."

What would he have done if she had not come into his life? She had forced him back into his law practice. She'd made him focus on his work. And she had encouraged him to be honest with his grief. Then, when he felt he couldn't pull himself out of the dark depression created by that loss, she had made him laugh.

"So what *are* you doing with it?" she asked.

"With what?"

"This house. Can't you follow even the simplest conversation?"

"Yours are never simple," he said, laughing. "And on this house, I'm going to sell off the antique stuff. Then, after storing anything that could be a clue, I'm going to tear it down. I'm building a stone and log cabin that fits in with the land. This place is much too dark. This spot needs a home that is filled with light."

"Maybe for you, but ..." she grinned, not feeling the need to finish her thought.

He was used to her humor now. And she was funny, maybe not as funny as she thought she was, but funny.

It was time to go through another book, page by page.

He was halfway finished with that goal when Janie announced, "A car's coming up the lane."

"Probably Don Ried. He's an antique dealer in Hardy. I asked him to come up and help me figure if there is anything of value here."

An engine cut off, two doors slammed, and a few seconds later a voice called out from the front door. "Lije, you in there?"

He knew that voice, and it wasn't Don Ried.

82

HOW HE HAD MISSED THE PERSON WHO OWNED THAT voice! Bouncing up, he rushed across the room and flung open the dark wooden door. He greeted his visitor with a hug so strong it almost pushed the air out of her body. "Heather, how are you?"

Patting his back while trying to catch her breath, Heather choked out, "Fine and I'm glad to see you too."

Though he didn't want to, Lije released her and stepped back. He took a long look and smiled. "You look great."

"Thanks."

Then he realized Heather wasn't alone. He looked, unsmiling, at her companion. Diana Curtis, also unsmiling, held his look.

She had gone back to the ABI. She had returned to Hillman in spite of what she knew. He wanted nothing to do with her. He didn't want her in the house.

"How did you know I was here?" he asked Heather.

"Well, you weren't at the office or at home, so Diana figured this would be the next place you might hang out on a Saturday."

Curtis knew him well. He'd give her that much.

Lije stepped back from the entryway and held an arm out to direct Heather into the living room. "Forgive my manners. Come in, come in. I'm thrilled to see you. Move some books and find a seat."

Perhaps it was the dust, but Heather opted to stand. Though she hadn't been asked to sit down, Curtis moved to the far side of the room and took a seat on the arm of the couch.

"Did you find out anything about your brother?" Lije asked.

"He is alive. We got him back home." Heather smiled. "They found him doing work in a small Iraqi hospital. He has a great deal of psychological damage. It will take some real professional help to put him back together. I've been trying, but there's nothing more I can do to help him. Time will tell if he comes back to be the person he used to be."

"What are your plans?"

"I really needed to be back up here. This is home now. And if you'll have me ... I want to work for you again."

"I'd love the help. ... Sure. We've got a heavy caseload right now."

"Super!" Heather said. "So what're you doing?"

Lije glanced up. "You've probably read about the train and its cargo. We're fighting to keep as much of the train treasure as we can. It's working its way through the courts. Battling the government's a big job, and I'll be more than glad to have you do your part."

"That's a relief," she said. "How about you? Are you all right?"

"I am. I've set up a charity foundation. Most of the money from the treasure will go to the foundation. I know both Kaitlyn and Andrew Farnsworth would approve. It seems a fitting testimony to them."

Heather nodded. "What about the old train? What's going to happen to it?"

"Well, the locomotive's nothing more than scrap iron, but train aficionado Dr. Robert Cathcart, who was with us, is overseeing the removal of the cars. They're filming every step of the process for a TV special. We've cut a pretty easy trail from the house to the river and the cave's now wired with lights. Maybe later in the day we can go down and see the progress they've made."

"I'd like that," she said. "I've read so much about it. I'm sorry I wasn't here."

She looked over at Diana, as if it was now her turn. And when she didn't say anything, Heather said, "Diana told me the guy who killed Kaitlyn is still on the loose."

"Well, I haven't caught him," Lije admitted, then added, "and something tells me it won't be a top priority at the ABI."

"That's why I'm here," Curtis said. "For me, the ABI is history. I couldn't work with Barton knowing what he did. I didn't go back to forgive him. I went back to find a way to bring him down."

"Did you," Lije said, not as a question but as a challenge to what was the truth. He was wary of what might be next.

"I've got an insurance policy of sorts," Curtis replied. "You remember Bear's computer, the one he left in the bowling alley and got tossed from the car during our wreck?"

"Sure."

"It was pretty banged up, and Bear just let it sit while working on a new one. Then I needed something off the hard drive. And lo and behold, I discovered he had backed up the whole DVD of Dean's murder onto his old laptop before we saw the video. I now have several copies."

"Why not take it to the police? Clear Jennings' name at least."

"I'm working on that. Hillman's wreck story still holds. I can't prove he staged the accident. But Barton knows I have the DVD. Better yet, he knows I'll now be watching his every move. I'm going to bring him down. It might take some time, but I'm going to do it."

Curtis reached into her purse. "And this is for you, Lije. Hillman was in possession of a letter that was supposed to be delivered to you. I lifted some files before I left the ABI and this was in one of them."

Lije took the envelope from her. The address was handwritten, no return address. He studied it, then set it down on a table. He'd open it later. He was afraid of what might be in the letter.

He wasn't willing to open a door on the past. Not now. He hesitated, then he picked it up, tore open the envelope, and quickly skimmed the one-page note.

Amazing. This was word from the other side.

"WHO'S THE LETTER FROM?" CURTIS ASKED.

Lije read and reread the two paragraphs. "Jonathon Jennings."

Except for the distant sounds of the river, the room was quiet.

Jennings had written the letter the day before his execution. It was carefully written, no words wasted. He thanked Lije for meeting with him and offering to help. And asked Lije to help out a pen pal of his, a man on death row in Texas who claimed his innocence.

You didn't have time to save me, Jennings wrote, *but maybe you can save him.*

Lije looked up at Heather and Curtis.

"Diana, help me. We're changing the direction of the law firm a little bit — moving toward criminal defense. Death row inmates. And I also need help tracking down Robert Smith. I can't pay much right now. I'm not personally getting a dime of the treasure."

Curtis paused and stared out the window for some time. Finally she turned to face Lije, a light in her eyes he hadn't seen before. "Long as I can eat, I'll be fine," she replied.

"Does this mean I'm getting a pay cut?" called out Janie from the kitchen.

Heather whirled around. Apparently she hadn't even seen Janie yet.

"Oh, Heather, this is our new legal assistant, Janie Davies," Lije said.

Janie waved from the kitchen. "I've heard a lot about you, Heather. Hey, Diana."

Heather smiled, "Nice to meet you." She watched Janie as she picked her plate up from the table, slowly turned, and worked her way to the counter, using her left hand to find the sink.

Heather turned back toward Lije and, as if playing a game of charades, used her arm to silently pose a visual question.

Before he could answer, Janie cracked, "Please tell me she didn't just do the wave-the-hand-in-front-of-the-eyes thing. That's so old!"

Heather yanked her arm down to her side and froze, embarrassed.

Janie laughed. "Don't worry, everyone does it. Yes, I'm blind, but I still think you'll find that on occasion I can offer a few special things to the team. By the way, don't make fun of me if I wear clashing colors at times."

"I promise I won't," Heather said. Then she moved closer to Lije. "Can I ask you a question?"

"Sure."

"It's just something I keep thinking about. I don't know why. Just curious." She paused. "Did Kaitlyn say anything before she died? I mean, any last words?"

He looked down at his hands. "She urged me to get up and make it to the ridge at the top of the hill. She said ..."

No! Kaitlyn wasn't urging him to get to the top of the hill that night on Farraday Road. She was apologizing. For the attack. She had been warned by Mrs. Dean. She didn't believe her. She realized the attack was all about this place. She thought it was her fault! He looked at Heather. "She said, 'The Ridge.' I think she ..." He let the words trail off.

Lije leaned back and closed his eyes. How could the property he now owned have been the cause of his Kaitlyn's death? He replayed everything he had learned about the Ridge—Swope's Ridge, the curse, the warning. Why was he now so caught up in solving this mystery, in finding the unknown? Had Kaitlyn been warning him that night? Was she warning him now?

Janie had joined them in the living room and was sitting on the floor, her bare feet shoved beneath the old divan. She wiggled her toes, as if stroking the underside of a pet. Then she bent over, stuck her hand underneath the divan, and ripped the lining loose. She pulled out an oversized book. "What's this?"

Easing down beside her, Lije took the book from her. One look at the cover gave away its origin. It wasn't from Germany.

"It's a high school yearbook. It's from Ash Flat, 1936. That's south of here." He opened the cover. "Belongs to 'JoJo' ... at least that's who all the autographs are signed to."

Curtis moved to look over his shoulder. "This is the only book in the house from here locally, right?"

"Only one I've found."

"Why would it be in the German's home?" Janie asked. "And hidden up underneath the divan?"

"Don't know," Lije said. He thumbed through a few pages. "Here's a photo of JoJo. Wow!"

"What?" Janie demanded.

This was far too much to believe. He knew who this woman was—or had been.

"Lije?" Heather said. "You look like you just saw a ghost."

"Her name was Josephine Worle. I never heard her called JoJo, but she was my grandmother's sister. She disappeared sometime after World War II. I remember my mother telling me about it. She was a kid when it happened. Josephine was about thirty and didn't show up to work one day at the Palace Drug Store in Mammoth Spring. They searched for her for a long time, but never found her. She disappeared without a trace."

Curtis took the book and scanned the pages. "From the awards and write-ups, looks like she was popular and very active. She was in just about everything."

"That matches what I was always told," Lije said, "but that

doesn't answer why her annual is in here. Nobody was ever allowed in this house. At least, that's what I was told."

"Lije," Curtis cut in, "look at this photo of the senior class in front of the school. Look at that bus in the background. See the school name and the bus number? Isn't that the bus that's sitting over in the weeds beside this house?"

He studied the photo. Since it was mostly hidden by small post oaks and cedar trees, he had only glanced at the old vehicle a couple of times as he'd walked by. But even a casual look at the grill gave away its bloodlines. It was a 1930s vintage Ford, and even though the paint was faded almost into the primer, the outline of an eagle was still barely visible on its side. In the middle of the bird was a number. What was it? Oh yeah, three, just like in the yearbook photo.

"Yeah, I think so," he said. "It could be the same bus." But how was JoJo tied to this house? How far back did this thing go in his family?

"Have you searched the bus?" Curtis asked. "Has anybody searched the bus?"

"No," he replied, looking up. "Let's go."

Curtis was the first out the door. A shot rang out and she dove back into the house.

"Are you hurt?" Lije asked.

"No," Curtis replied. "She opened the door a crack and waited. Nothing. She opened it farther, waited, then looked out. A car engine started and they heard the sound of tires on gravel. Glancing over her shoulder, Lije caught a glimpse of a white SUV driving away on the narrow logging road at the top of the ridge. It disappeared in a cloud of dust.

Curtis closed the door and looked at three frightened faces. "We'd better find out what is so important in this place pretty soon or we'll all be dead."

to be continued ...